Revenge Runs Deep

By

Pat Young

First published in 2019 by Learig Publishing,
Icona Point, London.

Cover Design by Michael Andrew Kelly
https://michaelandrewkelly.weebly.com

Print ISBN: 978-1-9160680-0-1

Also by Pat Young,
Winner of the Scottish Association of Writers' Constable Stag
Trophy
and Imprint Writing Award

Till The Dust Settles

I Know Where You Live

One Perfect Witness

Praise For Pat Young

'An accomplished plot, plenty of twists and turns and excellent characterisation made this book a real page turner'.
Kate Maloney - Bibliophile Book Club

'Till The Dust Settles is an intriguing read and one I actually flew through in one sitting.'
Joanne Robertson - My Chestnut Reading Tree

'Loved it from start to finish.' **Jo – Goodreads Reviewer**

'This is a you gotta read book, a brilliant debut. Really excited about this lady's writing. Superb!'
Susan Hampson - Books From Dust Till Dawn

'Till The Dust Settles is an intense powerful and heart-wrenching read about love, loss and ultimate devastation.'
Kaisha Holloway - The Writing Garnet

'What a clever book, I couldn't put it down.'
Cariad - Goodreads Reviewer

'It was suspenseful, thrilling, addictive, captivating, and left me guessing the whole way through.' **Dash Fan Book Reviews**

'… it has the author's excellent attention to detail and great writing style and I loved the lot.'
Donna Maguire - Donnas Book Club

This book is dedicated to all the fine teachers I've known in my life, among them my darling friend, June Gilliland, now lost to us all.

For Hugo Brierley, my darling grandson,
who lights up our lives.

August 2018

Their bodies were easy to spot. Skinny limbs tangled and snagged like pale sticks in a dark, underwater forest of weeds. Impossible to tell the drowning pal from the daft hero that tried to save him. One of their mothers was sucking on a cigarette at the side of the loch, desperate to find someone to blame, her heartache masquerading as anger. Danny hadn't wasted time on false comfort. There was no chance of a happy ending.

Freeing one boy from the clutches of his friend, Danny cradled him and kicked for the surface. The mother screamed, and stumbled into the water to meet him. She grabbed her boy, hugging his lifeless body to her breast, wailing like the world would end. Danny took the weight of mother and son, struggling to keep his footing as he dragged them to the shore.

He pushed back his mask and took in the scene. At the water's edge three pale-faced youths shivered in their underwear. 'Can somebody no save him?' asked one, his voice breaking as he looked from the police to the paramedics and back to Danny.

Danny shook his head. 'Too late for that, son. Sorry.'

'Did ye find Liam?'

'Aye, we found him. He'll be out in a minute. Put your clothes on, pal, eh? You could be here a while.'

'Is Liam okay? He only went in to save Jamesy.'

Danny knew he should be feeling a lot more sadness but this wasn't the first time the team had been called out on a hot day to a drowning caused by drink. Something in the Scottish mentality equated warm weather with the need to get bevvied. Probably the same gene that made Scots sacrifice their skimmed-milk skins to the sun god. March, May or August, a wee blink of sun and it was 'taps aff'. If you passed out after a few cans and woke up with second degree burns, so what? Your mates got a great laugh and you were a legend. If you drowned yourself trying to rescue your mate you were a hero. In a few hours this place would be covered in cheap bouquets and football strips and these clowns would be 'lost angels' on Facebook. RIP Liam and Jamesy.

Danny waded back into the loch, his mind on the tragic waste of two young lives. He found his mate gently retrieving the second body from the grasping weeds. A shaft of sunlight lit up Liam's face. He was just a kid. Pasty skin dotted with acne, hair dyed a blotchy blonde by an amateur hairdresser, probably himself. His faded boxers were worn into holes, their designer waistband a dirty grey. Didn't seem to matter how long Danny did this job, it didn't get any easier. Every loss of a young life still ripped his heart out.

With Liam accounted for, Danny flashed his torch in a quick scan of the underwater vista. The beam disappeared into the distance, only just picking out the ledge where the water depth plummeted from feet to fathoms. Danny saw the shape of something big resting on the edge. It had to be a car. Maybe he'd dive down for a closer look, or maybe he'd pretend he'd never seen it and head home to his barbecue. If there was somebody inside they'd been fish-food for months. It was much more likely to be empty, a motor stolen in town then dumped by some thieving arsehole covering his tracks.

Danny turned for the shore. Tonight's priority was these boys.

And a beer.

*

'And now, at the top of the hour, it's Julie-Ann with the news and weather.'

Sheila preferred to be in the car by the time the eight o'clock news came on, otherwise she got snagged in the rush hour traffic. She hoisted her bag onto her shoulder and reached for the radio's off switch.

'Police divers investigating the tragic drowning of two youths at Loch Etrin reservoir yesterday have discovered a four by four vehicle submerged in deep water. There appears to have been only one person in the vehicle but police say they are not in a position to reveal an identity at this time.'

Sheila froze, wishing for a replay button so she could listen again. Loch Etrin? A four by four? It had to be. She dropped her bag on the work surface and dug for her phone, then for her purse where she kept a number on a tiny slip of paper.

It rang, meaning Marty hadn't changed her phone. It continued to ring.

Sheila didn't dare leave a voicemail. 'Come on, come on,' she muttered, glancing at the clock. Not that the traffic mattered any more.

The ringing stopped. 'Hi, who is this, please?'

'Marty, it's Sheila. They've found a car in Loch Etrin.'

'You're joking.'

Sheila knew not to respond to that statement. It was often a first response to shocking news.

'Sheila, please tell me you're joking.'

'As if I'd joke about this. I just heard it on Clydesound. A four by four with one person inside.'

Sheila heard barking in the distance, as if the dog was outside. She waited, the line quiet for so long she began to wonder if Marty had gone to let him in.

'Marty, are you still there?'

'Yes.'

'Say something.'

'What is there to say?'

'Do you think it's Joe?'

No response. Just the dog, still barking.

'Marty, it must be Joe.'

'Listen, Sheila. I'm hanging up now. Don't try to contact me again, please. We agreed it's too dangerous.'

'But Marty ...'

'I'll be changing my number, Sheila, so you can't call me.

Might even buy a new phone. I should have done that months ago.'

'But you and I need to talk about this.'

'No, you're wrong. And don't even think about talking to anyone else. Ever. Not unless you want us both in prison.'

***

CHAPTER 1

August 2017 (One year earlier)

She was making dinner, a glass of gin and tonic icy in her hand, when the call came.

Marty switched to speakerphone and laid her mobile on the work-surface. She didn't want his voice near her face.

'Marty, I need a word.'

A word? At this time on a Friday night?

Nerves made her sarcastic, or maybe it was the gin.

'Good evening, Mr Smeaton,' she said. 'To what do I owe the pleasure?'

'I take no pleasure in this, I assure you.'

Something in his tone set alarm bells jangling. Marty touched her forehead with fingers that were damp and cold from her glass.

'Marty, what I'm about to say is very, very serious.'

Nightmare scenarios flashed across her vision. Bus crashes, fires, overdoses, stabbings. All the horrors that haunted a head-teacher. 'Oh God, has something happened?' Her drink slipped from her fingers and shattered on the ceramic hob.

David appeared in the doorway. Looked at the broken glass, then at her. She knew he was thinking of their only son, far from home. She shook her head, it's not Mark.

'You could say that,' said Smeaton, 'but no major incident, if that's what you're thinking.'

'No kids hurt?' She blew out hard, felt the adrenaline ebb away. 'That's all I care about.'

Her heart beat several times before he answered.

'Only one, as far as I know.'

1

'Oh, no. What's happened?'

He ignored her question. 'But others may come forward. They usually do.'

The man wasn't making sense. She wondered if he'd been at the bottle. 'Others may come forward? What are you talking about?'

'May I suggest you moderate your tone, Marty? I also suggest you do not underestimate the gravity of your situation.'

'Sorry, you've lost me. The gravity of my situation?'

More heart beats passed. Their rhythm getting faster.

He cleared his voice as if he were about to make a speech. 'As of today you are formally suspended from your post as head-teacher of Moorcroft Academy. You may not enter the premises under any circumstances.'

'What?' She laughed at him. 'Not enter the premises? Don't be daft. Moorcroft Academy is my school. I run the place.'

'Not any more, you don't.'

'Since when?'

'Since this afternoon. When you inappropriately touched a pupil in your office.'

'I touched a pupil? What pupil? The only pupil in my office today was Lee-Anne McCarthy.' As she said the name, a wave of nausea made her move to the sink and lean over it.

David came and stood beside her, one hand cupping her elbow. She pushed him away. She didn't want him listening to this.

Smeaton, it seemed, could barely keep the excitement out of his voice as he read from Logiemuir Council's official document on child protection.

'Can I just stop you there?' said Marty, her dry mouth struggling to form words. 'I know that document inside out and it has absolutely no relevance to me.' Marty tried to ignore the black fungus of fear growing in her stomach. This was a stitch-up and she knew who was behind it. 'This is the McCarthys, isn't it?'

Without revealing names her boss confirmed her suspicions. She staggered to the chair David pulled out for her and stammered and stuttered an explanation into the phone.

'Lee-Anne McCarthy is a trouble-maker whose mother does whatever the girl wants.'

'Marty, I don't want to hear. It's not appropriate at this juncture. You'll get your chance to explain later. To the police.'

'What? Wait a minute! You can't involve the police. This is crap. You know I would never harm a pupil. Every single person who has ever met me knows I couldn't hurt a child.'

'As I say, you'll have an opportunity to give your statement to the police.'

'What happened to "innocent until proven guilty"? You won't even listen to my side of the story. The true version of events.'

'Someone from my office will clear your desk. We'll send in a senior colleague from headquarters to run the school until further notice.'

'You can't do this to me, Mr Smeaton,' said Marty, struggling to keep her voice steady. She wouldn't give him the satisfaction of making her cry. 'I've been set up by a girl who didn't get her own way. And a parent who promised to make me pay.'

'Perhaps if you had reported the incident to me, I could have pre-empted this?'

'There was no incident. Nothing to report,' she shouted, 'because nothing happened. You know that, Smeaton. You could protect me here. Dismiss this complaint as the nonsense it is.'

'Sorry, Marty,' he said, sounding anything but. 'You know the protocol. I shouldn't even be talking to you, really. I just felt it would be a kindness to break this news to you personally.'

Even in the thrall of shock Marty could tell Smeaton was enjoying himself.

***

CHAPTER 2

Three months later
November 2017

Marty looked around the café, keen to avoid anyone she knew, then took a seat near the window, where she could see without being seen. The very sight of the council buildings was enough to make her squeamish. She put down her cappuccino, all desire for it gone.

She had been building up to this day for weeks. She had to do something before she went mad, playing and replaying, on a loop in her head, the events that ruined her career. It was like an annoying TV advert breaking into her thoughts every quarter of an hour. Day and night.

Marty had known her professional reputation would never recover from her suspension. She veered wildly between anger, at the injustice of it all, and fear she might be charged, if the girl's story became more credible than the truth. Every mention in the media of MeToo made her stomach curdle. Her darkest hour came when the story hit the local newspaper and was picked up by the nationals.

There had been no case to answer, of course. No child abuse. Just a teenage girl angry at Marty and determined to get her own back in the most spectacular way she could imagine. And a mother, too stupid and gullible to realise she was being manipulated.

The girl or her mother, probably both, lost their nerve when the police became involved. The fabricated allegations were withdrawn, Marty was re-instated and everyone was expected to carry on as normal.

There was no hint of an apology from Smeaton. 'As you were,' was all she got, in an e-mail.

She'd phoned HQ, got Carole to put her through to his desk without saying who was on the line.

The moment he picked up, she'd let fly. '"As you were?" What's that supposed to mean?'

'It means what it says. I expect you back at your desk in the morning.'

'As if nothing ever happened?'

'You claim nothing did happen.'

Marty had refused to back down. 'What about an apology?'

Smeaton had sighed, as if he hadn't the time or the patience. 'As a senior officer of this council, my priority was fulfilling my duty of care to the child concerned. As per standard procedure, you were relieved of your duties pending investigation. That investigation having been concluded, you are now formally re-instated and invited to return to work.'

'And what about my reputation? I heard two women talking about me over the tomatoes in Sainsbury's last week. How do you think that felt?'

He'd had the nerve to laugh. 'Oh, for goodness sake, Marty. Yummy Mummies gossiping in the posh supermarket? Where's the harm in that? Act your age.'

She had gone back to work, but it couldn't ever be 'as you were'. Her self-confidence, her vision, her energy were gone. When the heads of department disagreed with a new policy she wanted to introduce, she'd burst into tears and fled the meeting. That was the day she knew it was over. Hoping to make a stand, she'd threatened Smeaton with her resignation, which he'd accepted before she could change her mind. She'd been seething with rage and regret ever since, dying to fight back in some way.

Marty checked her watch. Twenty past five. The stream of departing workforce had dwindled to a trickle. It should be safe to go in now. She got to her feet, put on her coat and pulled the collar up round her face.

The first thing she noticed was a new reception desk which straddled the foyer and effectively blocked access to the building. A bored-looking young man sat behind a glass panel, checking his smartphone. He looked up as Marty approached and said, 'Welcome to Logiemuir Council. How may I help you?' In his local accent the phrase sounded alien and artificial.

'I'm here to see Mr Smeaton.'

'Is Mr Smeaton expecting you?'

She had to get past this guy so she smiled and tried to sound relaxed. 'No, it's just an informal visit. Mr Smeaton and I go back a long way. He's happy for me to drop in anytime.'

'So, you don't have an appointment?'

'Not as such.' She hadn't expected to face an inquisition and her courage was seeping away like charge from a battery. Then she had an idea. 'Tell you what. Why don't you give Wee Carole a ring and check with her? She'll vouch for me.' Marty smiled again.

He pressed a few buttons on a phone, looking like he'd rather be elsewhere, then replaced the handset. He shook his head and Marty's heart sank.

'Carole's not at her desk; it's nearly half-five. Listen, I'm not supposed to do this, so please don't tell anybody.' He lowered his voice. 'If you step up to the barrier, I'll buzz you through. Just this once, okay?'

She was in.

It felt weird to be back. The place smelt exactly the same, a corporate mix of photocopying and cleaning products that reminded her of the last time she had set foot in HQ. Marty shuddered at the memory. Today she was determined to do what she ought to have done months ago. Never mind the Union, the lawyer, the mousy little woman from Human Resources. Marty should have taken matters into her own hands at the time. Maybe she'd be feeling better by now. Having had her wee bit of revenge, maybe she'd have moved on with her life.

Inhaling an enormous breath, she followed a shiny new sign marked Libraries, Leisure, Education and Culture. Smeaton's empire was growing. Bracing herself for the drama to come, she strode towards the inner sanctum. Carole's desk was empty, maybe a good thing. No one to talk her out of it.

Marty hesitated outside the door that said 'T. Smeaton. Director'. What if he was in a meeting? She couldn't just burst in and make a fool of herself. Besides, she didn't want witnesses. Maybe she should wait till he came out.

A pressing need to pee gave her the chance to avoid a decision. She'd have a think about this in the Ladies.

The first cubicle was engaged. As Marty stepped into the second she heard someone crying. Full-on, heart-broken weeping. Marty felt sorry for whoever it was, but wasn't sure what she could do under the circumstances. She wasn't even supposed to be in the building.

She was drying her hands on a paper towel when the crying stopped and the cubicle door opened. Smeaton's secretary peeped out, her tear-damaged face registering shock that she wasn't alone.

'Oh, Marty, it's you.' Carole's face crumpled like a child's. Marty took her hand, led her over to a chair beside the wash basins and handed her a tissue. 'Sit down,' she said gently. 'Can you tell me what's wrong?'

This suggestion set Carole off on another bout of sobbing. Each time she opened her mouth, it distorted into a perfect square. Carole poked the tissue into the corner of her eyes 'See that man? I could swing for him.'

Marty shook her head. Her former boss was still at it.

Marty waited till Carole became a little calmer then whispered, 'If you think it would help to talk, I'm a good listener. I can't promise I'll have any answers, but you know what they say about a problem shared.'

Seeing Carole's worried glance at the door, Marty rose and took a hazard warning sign from the corner. She placed it outside in the corridor.

'There now, no one will bother us for a while. Unless the cleaner comes along and wonders why the toilets are closed for cleaning.'

Carole managed to give her a feeble smile, but when she took a deep breath, it caught on a sob. 'It's Mr Smeaton. I hate him.'

'Join the club. But hey, I always thought you could handle him. I used to wonder what your secret was.'

'Most of the time I don't let him get to me, but he's a horrible man.' Wiping her eyes, she said, 'I used to love my job.'

'What did Smeaton do to get you in this state?'

Carole gave her nose a loud blow. 'You know John and I have been trying for a baby? For ten years?'

'Mmm, I did hear you'd had a few miscarriages, Carole, and I was awful sorry for you. I admire the way you always seemed to bounce back.'

'That's because I had no choice. Mr Smeaton phoned me up and told me if I didn't get back to my desk soon, he'd be looking for another secretary. "It's not as if you're ill." That's what he said.'

'That's shocking. He's not allowed to say that kind of thing.'

Carole looked at her with a grim smile. 'Try telling him that. You know what he's like. Oh Marty, I wish I could quit. All I want is a baby and then I'd give up this crappy job and be a full-time mum.'

'I'm sure that will happen soon,' said Marty, patting Carole's back, aware of how mundane and patronising her words sounded.

Carole didn't seem to notice. 'It's not that simple. We've used up the three cycles of IVF we're allowed on the NHS. We've also had one private cycle that cost us five thousand pounds. Every year that passes makes it less likely we'll ever have a child.'

'You're young, Carole. You must have time on your side?'

'Not according to the statistics. But we do have one last cha…' The word was lost as Carole's voice rose in a tragic howl.

Marty gave her a hug, as she'd had to do with many a female employee in her time. 'One last chance, did you say?'

Carole nodded and sniffed. 'We were told we might be suitable candidates for a new fertility program that's being tested in the States.'

'And,'

'And we've been accepted.'

'Congratulations, that's great news.'

When Carole didn't respond, Marty asked, 'Isn't it?'

'It would be, if we could go.'

'Is it too expensive?'

'No, the program's free to us, because it's still in the trial stages. And I've been saving for the air fare.'

'What's the problem, then?'

'Smeaton won't let me go. Says he's not sanctioning a jaunt to Florida. Says that's what holidays are for and I should have thought about it before I used up all my annual leave.'

'That's unforgiveable. Can't you go over his head?'

'No. I need his permission to apply for special leave and he won't grant it. Told me the last thing he needs is a pregnant secretary throwing up in the toilets all day long, or running off to ante-natal appointments right, left and centre.'

Marty didn't know what to say. All she could come up with was, 'He's a despicable man, but Carole, no boss should reduce you to this state. It's atrocious. You have to do something about it.'

'What can I do? Look what happened to you.' As if she had just realised, Carole said, 'What are you doing here, Marty? Did they give you your job back?'

Marty laughed, 'It doesn't quite work that way, Carole. No, I came to punch Smeaton in his smug, pompous face.'

Carole giggled. Sensing it was a good time to leave, Marty helped Carole to her feet and edged her towards the door. 'Come on, let's get you out of here.'

Carole glanced in the mirror. 'Look at the state of me.' She ran her hands through her hair and pulled a sad face. 'Now I have to go home and explain to John why we can't go to

America. He'll be gutted. I swear to God, Marty, I could kill that man.'

***

CHAPTER 3

In a distant corridor a cleaner was singing at the top of her lungs, accompanied by the whine of a vacuum. Marty stood outside Smeaton's office, her hand trembling as she reached for the handle.

Suddenly the door opened and she and Smeaton came face to face. He gasped and stepped back. When he'd regained his composure, he held out his hand. Programmed by some code of behaviour, she took it. Her skin crawled at the touch of his small, delicate fingers that barely made contact with her own. She withdrew her hand and, without thinking, wiped it on her hip.

'What can I do for you, Marty?'

'I want to talk to you.'

'Oh? Well, I'm sure that would be nice, but, much though I'd love to catch up with you, I don't have the time.'

'It won't take long,' said Marty. Do it. Do it now, while you've got the element of surprise.

To her disgust, Smeaton put his hand on the small of her back, as if he were escorting her into dinner.

'Take your hand off me.'

The smile slid like slime from his face. He made a show of removing his hand from her back. All joviality gone from his voice, he said, 'Very well. May I assume you are in the building without authorisation?'

Marty ignored the question. She could feel her fingernails pressing into the palm of her hand. Surely she could do this one thing. How hard could it be? Men did it all the time, didn't they? Smeaton was a bantam-weight at best and barely matched her in height. One good thump would knock him over. It would be a pathetic little scrap of revenge but better

11

than nothing.

'I take it, from your silence, that I've guessed correctly. Therefore, I invite you to leave.' He indicated the exit and waited for her to go.

'Aren't you even a tiny bit curious to know why I'm here?'

He sniffed, his nostrils flaring. 'To be honest, I'd almost forgotten you existed. You'll have to enlighten me.'

Marty knew this was one of his power-play tactics, she'd seen it before. But still, she suddenly questioned herself. What had she hoped to achieve, barging in like this? She'd imagined the scene countless times. Take him by surprise, on his own, tell him what she thought of him, hit him one good, hard whack and walk away.

She'd reasoned that he wouldn't try to have her charged, not after his last attempt at involving the police in her life. His word against hers and all that. And if she was charged, it would be with a minor offence, like breach of the peace. Worth a court appearance and a fine to strike a blow for herself, literally, and all the others Smeaton had damaged.

The vacuum cleaner droned on in the background. It was now or never. She raised her fist and took aim. Fast as a snake, Smeaton lunged towards her, grabbing her forearm. He squeezed it hard, his skinny fingers and sharp nails pushing into her flesh.

'I think you'd better go, Marty,' he said, his face level with hers, 'before you do something you might regret.'

Marty held his gaze, staring into his small dark eyes. Reptilian eyes, mean with malice, she thought as she wrenched her arm from his grip.

He patted down his jacket as if he'd been soiled by touching her. 'I'm not a vindictive man,' he said, 'and so I may, under the circumstances, be prepared to forget this little contretemps.'

Marty stared him down, refusing to give him the upper hand.

'Or,' he whispered, his face so close Marty could feel his breath on her cheek, 'You might have a visit from the police this evening.'

***

CHAPTER 4

Joe checked his watch. Quarter to ten. He'd been told to be here at ten thirty prompt. Typical of the man to make him wait. When the buzzer sounded, Joe looked at Carole, who nodded and whispered, 'Good luck.'

Joe wondered what Carole knew that he didn't, but had no time to ask. The heavy wooden door behind him swung open and a familiar voice boomed, 'Joe! Come in, come in.'

As he stepped over the threshold, Joe held out his hand but Thomas Smeaton had already turned his back and was walking towards his desk. 'I think you know Councillor Cooper, Chair of the Education Committee?'

'And Vice-Chair of Finance,' added the woman, patting her hair with the flat of her hand. Her perfectly coiffed head looked as out of place on her huge body as a cherry on a dumpling.

Joe knew her from a previous meeting. She had sat there like an oversized troll, contributing nothing but a vague sense of threat. She was not on Joe's side and his heart sank at the very sight of her. With a stiff smile on his lips, he inclined his head towards her, acknowledging her presence, if not her power.

'Right then, Joe. What is it you wanted to see me about?'

'I sent you a paper, laying out the points I wanted to discuss. Did you have a chance to read it?'

Smeaton gestured to the expanse of empty desk that lay like a desert between them. 'Don't seem to have it to hand. Remind us what it was about. Briefly, if you will.'

This too was typical of Smeaton. He knew exactly what the meeting was about.

'I was hoping you'd had a chance to re-consider.'

Smeaton and the councillor exchanged a look that said, 'Not this again.'

Joe pushed on, keen to get his argument in before one of them could say anything. 'I understand we're in a recession and I know the council has to make cuts, but,'

'But you'd like us to make them elsewhere, correct?'

'I feel I can put up a very good case for keeping the bothy open.'

'Didn't we hear all this last time, Tom?' said Cooper. Although she was leaning close to Smeaton's ear, she made no attempt to lower her voice.

'We did, Councillor, but perhaps Joe has new information he wishes to share with us. Joe?'

Joe rubbed at his chin, felt the afternoon stubble on his face and said, 'Not really, but,'

'In that case, I'm not sure I understand why you requested this meeting, Joe. We're all very busy people. At least, those of us who run the service are.'

Joe ignored the implied insult and said, 'I know we have fewer kids involved in Outdoor Education than we used to, but,'

'There you are,' interrupted Smeaton with a smug look at his companion. 'You've put your finger right on it. I remember when we had hundreds of kids involved. How many instructors had we when Matt Harvey was in charge? Six, was it? Or seven?'

Joe nodded, 'Seven.'

'And now it's just you, Joe, and a handful of boys.'

'No girls?' asked Cooper.

'No, Councillor. No girls. Just Joe and a bunch of boys, all on their own up at a secluded bothy in the hills.'

Joe felt his ears go hot, knew they would be burning bright as beacons. He fought to keep his temper under control. Losing it would play right into their hands.

'The boys who use the service are from the Bankside estate. Getting them out on the hills, away from that drug-infested, gang-run environment, shows them alternative choices. Some of my boys are heading for the armed forces and they'll do well there. I know they will, because they're good lads. They just don't have a chance, living where they do.'

Smeaton reached across the huge desk, holding the flat of his hand out towards Joe's face. 'Let me stop you there, Joe, before you have us both in tears.'

Cooper sniggered like a besotted teenager, the sound incongruous with her large, matronly appearance.

'No. Sorry. I can't stop,' said Joe. 'Kids in Bankside have nothing. No chances, no choices. With Outdoor Education we can save a few. Maybe not all of them, but some. You must have read about the great work Glasgow City Council are doing with their anti-violence initiative?'

'Glasgow City has a lot more money in their coffers than our wee council in Logiemuir,' said Cooper, obviously needled by the comparison.

'I get that, Councillor, but can you think of anything more worth the money than saving young lives?'

Smeaton shook his head, a look of pity on his face, 'Oh Joe, you're so naïve. Do you really think Logiemuir Council can afford to keep you and a bunch of neds running about in a minibus, canoeing here, hill-walking there? Grow up, man.'

'But it's important,' insisted Joe, hating himself for sounding so pathetic.

'Joe,' said Cooper with feigned patience, 'you need to realise we are living in a time of austerity. Cuts have to be made somewhere. People are screaming for road repairs, care for the elderly, support for the disabled. My goodness, we've had to shut a day-care centre. You can imagine how that went down.' She turned to Smeaton. He responded with a sympathetic smile then spoke to Joe, all warmth gone.

'Our decision stands, Joe. We cannot afford luxuries like the bothy. It will close at the end of the financial year and will not reopen. It will be your responsibility to clear the premises and to that end you may continue to run the minibus.'

He turned and smiled at the woman by his side. 'Well,

Councillor, coffee time?'

Joe knew he had been dismissed, but was not prepared to give up. He stood, towering over the two at the desk. 'You can't do this. What am I supposed to tell the boys?'

'Tell them what you like. You're the one with the great relationship, after all.' His attention on the councillor, he said, 'Oh, Joe, there is one more thing …' He paused, making Joe stand and wait. 'On your way out? Could you tell Carole to bring us two coffees?'

***

CHAPTER 5

Marty had lain awake all night, waiting for the police to come to the door. She'd considered confessing to David that she'd gone to see Smeaton, but had decided against it. He would be appalled that she'd pulled such a stunt.

Morning, when it finally came, brought no relief and as she'd stood in the shower, she felt stunned by her own stupidity. Why on earth had she given him yet another opportunity to humiliate her, another chance to demonstrate his power over her? Why couldn't she just walk away from this nightmare, put it all behind her? David kept encouraging her to get on with her new life.

And here she was, doing her best. Doing her bit. Helping out at the local charity shop. Unfortunately, this wonderful new life was getting right up her nose, literally. She took a step away from the table, her face averted, as if that could protect her from the stench of decay. Holding the bin bag at arm's length she tipped out its contents. A jumble of meagre possessions lay exposed, painting a bleak picture of an old man's life. A tangle of single socks, a well-sucked pipe still reeking of tobacco, a small, leather bound bible whose pages had been thumbed till their corners eroded. A pair of shirts, their pattern faded and a bundle of squalid underwear. Marty extricated a string vest, so stained it would pass muster as desert camouflage. It dangled from the pincered fingertips of her rubber gloves, an unlikely last straw for her camel's back.

Felicity Matthews looked up from the computer as Marty stepped into the little office.

'Good morning, Marty. Everything okay?'

'What do you think?' Marty dropped the vest, pleased to see

it land right under Felicity's nose.

The woman removed her glasses and positioned them in her blonde-streaked hair. Her glossy lips pouted into a perfect moue of distaste as she picked up the vest with the tip of a pencil and dropped both into the waste paper basket.

'This isn't the job for me,' said Marty.

'Oh, I'm so sorry to hear that. Most of us find it rewarding. Sorting the donations can be a bit, how shall I put it, unsavoury at times, but actually, I think it's quite exciting, knowing I might turn up a gem. I'll never forget the day I opened a bag of Chanel suits. What a thrill.'

'I'm afraid, from what I've seen, I'm more likely to be traumatised than thrilled. See that string vest? It smells like its owner died wearing it.

Felicity tutted. 'Oh really, Marty, don't exaggerate.'

'When I volunteered, I imagined myself helping folk, not picking over the belongings of dead people. It's as if someone clears their house, bags their possessions and drops them off here instead of the dump.'

'I agree it might seem like that. Occasionally. But I think you'll find most of our donations come from benefactors who change their wardrobe every season. As many of us do.' Felicity looked her up and down.

It was time to leave. 'It seems I'm not cut out to be a volunteer. Sorry.'

'Oh, don't apologise, Marty. Not everyone has what it takes to do this work. And you have rather been through the mill lately.' With a patronising smile, she added, 'Fortunately, some of us don't mind getting our hands dirty in the service of others.'

Marty could not resist a pointed look at Felicity's perfectly manicured fingers before she left, slamming the door for effect. She knew the whole episode would be repeated to the local ladies who lunch, but she didn't care. It would give them a new tasty morsel to add to the gossip about her.

Marty undid the lock that tethered her bike to a streetlamp, grateful to have escaped into the cool, fresh air. As she climbed on she wondered what David would have to say about this, her latest in a line of failures.

She couldn't bear to face traffic, fumes and impatient drivers in this mood. She'd be likely to commit road rage if someone cut her up at the traffic lights. Although it was the long way round, the path by the canal might calm her down. By the time she reached home she might be ready to laugh at the ridiculous Felicity. Marty had already offended similar acquaintances when they'd invited her to join the 'girls' for lunch or to 'pop round' for coffee. She couldn't remember the exact words of her refusal, but it was caustic enough to ensure she hadn't been invited to any other daytime events. Word had gone round like measles in a playgroup.

Of course, her real friends had been loyal and sympathetic throughout the whole Lee-Anne affair, but, like David, they failed to understand the devastating effect it had on her psyche. Every morning she woke to the chilling realisation that the loss of her job had left her with no reason to get out of bed. Without work her life lacked purpose. No amount of coffee mornings or ladies' lunches could ever fill that gap. She wasn't interested in idle chat or gossip, had always been too busy to bother about fashion trends, and couldn't give a stuff about so-called celebrities. She had nothing in common with people like Felicity and would rather her days remain empty than spend time with them.

When she had to swerve to avoid a broken bottle, Marty swore and skidded to a halt, expecting at least one puncture. She waited, ready to throw the whole bike in the canal, but no, both tyres seemed to be intact.

Marty sagged under a burden of worry about the future and anger about the past. As heavy as an overloaded rucksack, it was wearing her down, chafing her shoulders, lowering her head. All day long she raged through inner dialogues that solved nothing.

She would recall conversations she'd had with Smeaton in the past and wish she'd played them differently, imagining the things she could have said. Should have said.

Like the day he said, 'Maybe we made a mistake appointing you. Not sure it's a job for a woman. Men and boys feel more secure with a man at the helm, you know.'

Or the Friday afternoon meeting when he dropped the bombshell, 'Everyone says you're the most difficult head-teacher they deal with.'

Everyone says. Classic bullying talk. She knew that. She'd heard kids at it often enough.

How she wished now she had stood up to him. Why didn't she challenge his claim? 'Who says that?' she could have said. 'Name me one person who says I'm difficult,' she should have said.

But she didn't. Because he was her boss. And there was only so often you could contradict your boss. Especially when he was known to be ruthlessly vindictive when crossed.

On the few occasions she had dared to stand up for herself, he'd been merciless. 'Marty, Marty, Marty,' he'd sneered one memorable time. Shaking his head in that patronising way he had. Like she was some kind of disappointing child. 'You've got a lot of growing up to do before you make a decent head-teacher.'

Well, she was all grown up now. And she was just about at the end of her tether.

Boy, she wished she could find a way to get revenge. She'd love to teach Smeaton a lesson he'd never forget.

***

CHAPTER 6

The boys were huddled in the back of the mini-bus, sheltering from the chill wind blowing off the loch. This might have to be their last canoeing session. It was getting colder every week. Even with the proper gear, these boys were too malnourished to withstand the elements. Except for Slug, a sloth-like giant of a boy, they were mostly skinny, puny-looking kids.

'Come on, lads,' shouted Joe. 'Any chance of you giving me a hand to get these canoes loaded before it gets dark?'

Daron Dykes, the undisputed leader of the group, barked out a command. 'Right, boys. Big Joe needs us to move the canoes.'

'It's pure freezin, Dykesy. Can we no just wait in the van?'

'Get yer arse out here, TJ. If the Big Man wants a hand, he'll get it, right?'

Slug didn't budge but TJ, Liam, Smithy and Dangermoose jumped from the minibus and started to manhandle the canoes onto the trailer.

Dykesy, at five foot one, was an unlikely alpha male, but rumour had it he was a hard wee bastard, afraid of nobody. Joe wondered if that was the secret of success, to let no one ever smell your fear. Maybe that's where he was going wrong.

'Thanks, lads,' he said, when the canoes were safely transferred from the trailer and into the storeroom at the bothy. 'Great teamwork.'

'Nae worries, Big Man,' said Dykesy.

Slug's voice came from the van, 'Can we go, Sur? Ah'm pure starvin. Ah could eat a scabby dug.'

'Hey, that's likely what yer mammy's made for yer dinner, Sluggo. Scabby dug wi chips.'

'The Slugster would eat it.'

'Aye, if it had enough gravy. Why no? I like a hot dog.'

The boys hooted and Joe couldn't help joining in. He loved their banter. Didn't mind the way they called him Big Joe or the Big Man. He'd worked with teenagers long enough to know it was a mark of respect, not the opposite. In any case, he'd never get the best out of these lads if he insisted on being addressed as Mr Docherty or Sir. That stuff was for the classroom teacher, not for the likes of him and these rough boys. When he took troubled kids up on the hills or out on the loch, Joe needed to be one of the lads. Their trust in him was vital. And now he was going to have to let them down.

As he pulled into Bankside and slowed down outside a row of boarded up shops, the back door swung open.

'Wait! Hang on a minute, lads.'

The boys spilled out before he could pull on the handbrake. Joe wished they wouldn't do that.

'I've got something to tell you.'

Slug was last out. He turned back and shouted, 'Too late, Sur. They're away.'

Joe rubbed his cheek. What difference would it make, telling them now?

'Do ye want me to pass on a message?'

'Thanks, Slug, but it'll keep. Take care now.'

'See ye next week, Mr Docherty. Are we goin canoein again?'

'Don't know yet, pal. It's maybe getting a bit cold for it, eh?'

'Nae worries, we can always go hill-walkin, eh? See ye, Sur.'

Shaking his head, Joe watched as Slug lumbered after his mates, who were running up the middle of the road, ignoring car horns and giving the finger to swerving motorists. They didn't give a damn for authority, and who could blame them?

***

CHAPTER 7

Long before Marty made it through the gate, Chance had announced her arrival. She bent to stroke his unruly quiff. 'Good boy. Did you miss me?' The dog danced around her, delirious to have her home.

As she leaned her bike against the wall, she could hear David calling from one of the borders. He was cutting back shrubs that had become troublesome and hard to control. A bit like herself.

'You're back early. Find any hidden treasures today?'

'Oh sure. If you'd call grotty string vests hidden treasure.'

David laughed, right on cue. Marty often wished she could be more like him. He was possibly the most good-natured man in the universe. He had gone through his whole working life without falling out with anyone.

Making an effort to be pleasant, she said, 'Cup of tea?'

'Yes, please. I could do with a break. Put the kettle on and I'll be right in.'

When David appeared in the kitchen, she had two mugs on the table, each with a teabag floating in hot water, and a packet of digestives, three of which Chance had already scoffed. Ever optimistic, the dog was lying under the table, one eye open for stray crumbs.

'What?' said David, 'No freshly baked scones or feather-light sponge cake straight from the oven?'

'Domestic goddess, I ain't, David. You knew that when you married me.'

'And yet I live in hope.' He took a digestive and dipped it in his tea.

Marty bit her bottom lip, dreading the next bit of the conversation, but keen to get it over with. 'Don't you want to know why I'm home so early?'

'I assumed your organisational skills had the place running like clockwork.'

'Thanks for the compliment, but wrong.' She broke off a piece of biscuit and dropped it for Chance, who snaffled the morsel before it had time to hit the floor. David didn't like her feeding scraps to the dog but she could see he was going to let it pass this time.

'Okay,' he said, reaching for another biscuit, 'why are you home early?'

Marty took a sip of tea. 'I jacked it in. Fortunately, without beating the Botox out of Felicity's face. God, that woman's patronising.'

David scowled. 'I hope you weren't unpleasant to her. Remember I play golf with her husband.'

'No, I was very dignified, considering how much I wanted to strangle her with a rancid vest.'

David's smile looked strained. 'Never mind,' he said, 'You've got your art class and your yoga.'

Marty raised her eyes to the ceiling and inhaled loudly.

If David heard he hid it well. Still smiling, he said, 'And you'll find another volunteering job, I'm sure. One that uses your talents properly.'

Her tutting made sure he noticed her impatience this time.

'It's okay. There's no rush. Why don't you just enjoy being a lady of leisure for a while?'

Marty had already tried to explain to her husband how she felt, the last time only a few nights ago. 'David, it's the injustice of it all that's making me livid. It's not right, what Smeaton did to me. He knew I never laid a finger on that girl, but he threw me to the dogs. I'm sure he's delighted to be rid of me, because I refused to be one of his yes men.' She searched for the right words to explain why she was so miserable all the time. 'I've been robbed of my identity, my persona, my role in society.'

'Is that what you miss, the power?'

She clapped her hands. 'Yes!' She leaned towards him and

touched his cheek. 'That's it, David, the power. Thank God, you do understand. I had the power to change lives, to make sure vulnerable young people got the best opportunities a school can give them. I had the power to make their world a better place.'

David nodded. 'And it was prestigious, wasn't it, to be known as the Head of Moorcroft Academy? I used to rather enjoy telling the chaps at golf that my wife was rector.'

Marty leaned her elbows on the table and dropped her head into her hands. Through clenched her teeth she groaned, 'You really don't get it, do you, David?'

'Get what, honey?'

'It was never about the prestige. I've never cared about that stuff. It was about doing a useful job where I could make a real difference for youngsters. I don't want to waste my time going to art classes or yoga, or out to lunch with a crowd of 'girls'.' She could hear her voice rising, knew she was starting to shout. Chance hauled himself to his feet and slunk off to his basket. 'I don't want to escort people round the hospital or make tea for oldies or help out at the playgroup.' She stood up, glaring at her husband. 'All I want to do is what I'm good at,' she screamed. 'I want my school back.' She grabbed her mug and hurled it at the sink, showering the kitchen in a spray of broken china and tea.

David sat staring at her, eyes wide. Finally, he let out a long, low whistle. 'Marty, this anger of yours is getting out of control. You need to do something.'

'You know what? That's the first sensible thing you've said since this whole fiasco started.'

She grabbed her jacket and snatched the dog lead from its hook by the back door. Chance rose from his bed.

'Come on, boy,' she muttered. 'Let's go.'

***

CHAPTER 8

It had always been Joe's Friday night routine to wander down for a pint while Sally prepared dinner. Until she became too ill to eat, they had always tried to have a special meal on a Friday. Even when she became too unwell to cook, she had kept the routine going, sending Joe to the pub while she set the table for a carry-out curry or supermarket dine-in deal.

There was no Sally and no special meal these days, but Joe defiantly stuck to his end of week ritual, as if to flip two fingers to fate.

The pub door swung open as Joe reached for the handle. In a waft of warm air and beer fumes a group of regulars filed out, greeting Joe as they passed.

'Hiya, Joe. How you doin?'

'I'm ok, yeah.'

'Sorry, mate, got to rush. Wife will have the dinner ready. You know how it is.'

Joe stood to attention and gave them a jaunty salute, a clown hiding his tears in silliness.

The young Polish guy was on the bar.

'Evening, Bolek.'

'Hello, Joe. The usual?'

'Yep. A pint of your finest Diet Coke when you're ready, barman, if you please.'

'Coming right up.'

Joe felt a sudden draught as the door opened and Sean blustered in, shaking his jacket and muttering about feckin rain. He slapped Joe on the back, 'How are you getting on? Are ya well?'

'Not bad,' said Joe and pointed to the taps on the bar. 'The

Black Stuff?'

'Yup, if ever a man needed a drink. After the day I've had?' Sean watched the young barman carefully pour his Guinness and put it on the bar to settle.

'Today was not so good a day for you then, sir?'

'Bolek, tell me this and tell me no more - have ye ever had to hold yersel back from hittin yer boss a kick up the arse?'

'Sorry? I do not understand.'

'I nearly assaulted my boss today.'

'Ah, Sean, that is not good.'

'Ye're damn right, Bolek, it's not good, but the little fecker deserves it, doesn't he, Joe?'

Sean took a long, slow drink, eyes closed. Finally he put his half-empty glass back on the bar with a contented sigh and Bolek disappeared to serve another customer.

Joe took his drink and gestured with it to a table. 'Want to tell me all about it?' His own news could wait.

'Indeed I do.'

They sat down and Sean drank deeply then wiped the froth from his lip. 'Sure, I could drink this stuff off a sore foot.' He burped, apologised, then said, 'Ye'll never believe what that wee gobshite Smeaton said to me today, Joe.'

'Try me.'

'He's getting worse, so he is.'

'What is it they say about absolute power?'

'They say it corrupts absolutely, and it's true. Didn't he call me into his office this morning to tell me that all the funding is going to be cut from under us? There's to be no budget at all for musical education.'

'But what about your choirs?'

Sean shook his head. 'Everything's been slashed. The music instructors that go into schools to work with individual pupils? Finished. Sure, he's only after telling me all contracts will be terminated at the end of the year.'

'What, folk out of a job, just like that?' Joe hadn't considered that he too might be facing redundancy.

'Luckily, a lot of them have private pupils in the west end, or they play church organs and the like, but yes, they're out of a job. As you say, just like that.'

'He can't get away with it, Sean.'

'Sure he can. Says we can't afford luxuries like music tuition in these times of austerity. "Budget streamlining" Smeaton called it. Budget streamlining my arse.'

'Did you not stand your ground?'

'Joe. What do you take me for? Of course I stood my ground.' Sean drained his glass then banged it on the table. 'Christ, I need another drink. You haven't heard the worst of it yet. At least he had the decency to tell me to my face about that decision. Wait till you hear this. I got home to find a letter from Make Music.'

'Oh no,' said Joe, guessing what was coming. 'Not the kiddies' orchestra.'

Sean took a pristine white handkerchief from his pocket and made heavy work of unfolding it before he blew his nose and wiped his eyes. 'Yes, Joe,' he said on a sigh, 'the kiddies' orchestra. The bastard has slashed the budget on that too and without matched funding from the council, Make Music can't continue to provide instruments.'

'So the Bankside Blast can't go on?'

Sean shook his head, like a man bereft.

'Know how you're feeling, mate,' said Joe. 'I had another meeting today, with him and Cooper. He hardly gave me a chance to speak. The man's a lunatic. How he ever got to have that much power I will never know.'

'Because he's so far in with the councillors, especially that horrible woman, Cooper. I tell you, it's too much for me, so it is. I haven't the stomach to fight them anymore.'

'Sean, you have to fight them. You can't let Smeaton get away with this. Not after all the great work you've done with these kids. God, it makes me so angry.' Joe made a fist and punched it into his other palm. 'Come on, man, we could fight him together. Get other folk involved.'

'Na, it's not worth the hassle. We'd never win anyway. You know what he's like.' Sean coaxed the last few dregs of stout from the bottom of his glass. 'No, Joe, I've decided. It's time for me to retire, so it is. I've had all I can take of that man. Sure, it's making me sick, the worry of it.'

As he wandered back to his empty flat, fish supper in hand, Joe made up his mind. He wasn't going to take this lying down. There had to be something he could do. He transferred the hot supper to his other hand. It smelt amazing, proper old-school fish and chips wrapped, against all health and safety guidelines, in newspaper.

Newspapers.

The very thing.

***

CHAPTER 9

'Finally,' said Sheila, when her friend picked up at last. 'Good morning. Listen, I know panto's not your thing.'

Sheila paused, waiting for Liz to shout something daft like, 'Oh yes, it is!', but there was no response.

'Hey, you okay?'

'I feel grim, Sheila.'

'Oh no, what's up? Flu?'

'I wish,' muttered Liz.

'It's Saturday morning and you wish you'd caught the flu? Jeeso, things are grim. Was your meeting with Smeaton really that bad?'

When Liz didn't respond, Sheila chattered on. 'Why weren't you at the Head-teachers' Meeting yesterday afternoon, assuming you don't actually have flu?'

'Would you believe me if I said I was in the Happy Harvester drinking myself into oblivion?'

Sheila blurted a laugh then stopped. 'So, where were you?'

'I told you.'

'Liz, are you feeling alright?'

'Never better.'

'Sure?'

'Okay, I feel hellish. There, does that give you the picture?'

'Liz! I don't think I've ever heard you swear.'

Liz said nothing.

'Listen, I was calling to see if you fancy helping out with this community panto I'm doing at Bankside. I could use your organisational skills, plus you can be a right bossy bitch when you need to and my God, some of those kids need a firm hand.' Again, Sheila expected a laugh and got nothing.

31

'No, don't think so.'

'Fine, scrap that, how about just going out for lunch and a catch-up? I'll fill you in on what happened at the meeting. Pity you missed it. Smeaton wasn't there. John Hunt chaired it and what a different atmosphere.'

Liz made no comment.

'Hey, I've just thought of something. Smeaton misses the meeting. You miss the meeting. Are you sure it wasn't a secret assignation with him that took you to the Happy Harvester?'

That joke would normally have had Liz choking with indignation. She'd have spluttered and come straight back with something like, 'Not in a million years. Not if we were the only two humans on the planet and the future of mankind hung in the balance.' Today she couldn't seem to muster so much as a snigger.

Sheila could hear the big grandfather clock in Liz's hall ticking away the seconds. It had been Liz's mother's prized possession.

'Liz, what's happened? Talk to me.'

'He's going to send in the inspectors.'

'What? Can he do that?'

'I knew an inspection was on the cards at some stage. It's inevitable, I know that, but it was the cruel way he told me.'

'What did he say?'

'Oh, a few things about my total incompetence. Complaints from the community, unhappy staff and so on.'

'Liz, that's crap. You're one of the most super-efficient, professional people I know. You're fantastic at your job.'

'Obviously not. Unhappy staff?'

'Bollocks! He's making that up. Your teachers worship the ground you walk on. Everyone does. That wee janitor of yours would empty the furnace and dance on his own hot coals, if you asked him.'

Liz didn't acknowledge the compliment.

'Mr Smeaton's not making it up about complaining parents though, is he? You've seen the stuff on Facebook.'

'A bunch of nutters stirred up by that maniac who claims

you're victimising his kid? The same kid who kicked you in the groin last week? They're well known, that family. The kids are practically feral.'

'Yes, but it's all there on Facebook. All that stuff the father's saying about me. And those pictures of me. He's been hanging about the school gates again, by the way, taking his photos.'

'You need to get the police involved, Liz.'

'Oh, for God's sake. Don't mention the police.'

'What?'

'Never mind. Mr Smeaton told me he would have to direct the inspectors towards social media when they came to evaluate my relationships with parents. You know his favourite expression.'

'Yeah, yeah, 'no smoke without fire'. Liz, this is outrageous. You have to get a lawyer involved, the sooner, the better, and the Union. Morons like that guy can go online and post appalling lies, get their illiterate friends to join in and we're supposed to just take it. You're not the only head-teacher being persecuted on Facebook. We were talking about it at the meeting yesterday. You need to log it all. Keep a diary.'

'I just don't think I can take any more, Sheila. The assaults, the Facebook smear campaign and that weirdo standing there whenever I look out my office window. I don't know if I can cope with an inspection on top of all that. Especially if Mr Smeaton's going to poison the inspectors against me before they start. I mean what have I ever done to make him hate me so much?'

'You've done nothing, Liz. Don't you go blaming yourself for any of this.'

'Do you know what else he said to me?' Liz started to sob. 'Everyone in HQ agrees I'm the coldest person they deal with. That's not true. Is it, Sheila? I'm not cold, am I?'

'Liz, you're the kindest, warmest person I have ever known. I've heard you called a gem, a treasure, a sweetie, all sorts of beautiful compliments from all sorts of people. The kids adore you. They'll probably stop the inspectors in the corridor and tell them how much they love you. Think of Shevonne.'

Shevonne was a likeable wee rogue whom Liz loved as much as any of her pupils, but a thorn in her side too. She was a tiny girl with a distrustful little face under scraped-back baby hair. On her very first day at school, aged five, Shevonne had picked up her pink back-pack, after only an hour, and got to her feet. 'Right,' she'd said, 'that'll do me. Ah'm away.' Her attitude to education had altered little since then. She just didn't see the point of it, but still Liz persevered, seeing promise in the wee lass.

'Liz, are you crying?'

No answer.

'Has something else happened? Something you're not telling me?'

Liz sniffed loudly, then apologised and said, 'I drove straight through a red light on the way to my meeting with Mr Smeaton.'

Liz never failed to refer to him as 'Mr' Smeaton although the man deserved no such respect.

'I'd hardly slept, you see, even with two painkillers and a sleeping pill. It serves me right. I'm trying not to look at Facebook, but I was tempted before I went to bed and then I lay awake all night fretting about it.'

'Were you in a collision, Liz?'

'No. I stalled, right in the middle of the junction, causing mayhem. Horns were blaring, drivers were swearing, shouting at me to move but I sat there, nauseous from adrenaline. And do you know what I thought?'

Sheila waited, knowing her friend would answer her own question.

'I thought a car crash wouldn't be such a bad thing. If I got lucky I'd die outright, and if not, at least I'd have an excuse for not showing up at the meeting with Mr Smeaton.'

Sheila couldn't speak; she had no idea what to say.
'I wasn't concentrating because I was too busy trying to work out why I'd been called in at such short notice.'

'That's a regular stunt of his.' Sheila knew Liz had often

asked for an agenda in advance of these meetings. Smeaton met the requests with derision.

'Also I had one of my migraines.'

'You drove with a migraine? Oh, Liz, you shouldn't have done that. Why didn't you take something for it and stay in bed?'

'I took two Ibuprofen, but they don't really help.'

Sheila often worried about the amount of painkillers Liz took. Once when she'd been visiting Liz, she'd opened the bathroom cabinet looking for a paracetamol. It was like a small pharmacy, stockpiled with drugs prescribed for Liz's dying mother.

'Why didn't you cancel the meeting?'

'Oh, come on, Sheila. Anyway, I needed to find out what he could possibly want. I mean, I'm doing my job to the best of my ability. Our old boss was more than happy with the way I ran the school, wasn't he?'

'Of course he was.'

'But no matter how hard I work these days, how many policy documents and mission statements I produce, no matter how I try to please everyone, this man constantly finds fault. The school buses are causing pollution. Or parents are parking on the zigzags. I couldn't understand how he even knows about some of the stuff that goes on. Turns out he looks at Facebook. I should have known. Forewarned is forearmed, Sheila, and I went in there as unarmed as a cow in a slaughterhouse.'

'Oh Liz, I feel so sorry for you. Listen, you had a near miss in busy traffic. That's not the worst thing you can do, is it?'

Liz heaved a sigh enormous enough for Sheila to hear.

'No, there's something much, much worse. And I did it.'

'Did you kill Smeaton?' Sheila immediately regretted her flippancy. 'Sorry, Liz, that was stupid. Come on, tell me what happened and it won't seem as bad.'

'I can't.'

'Yes, you can.'

'Sheila, you're the one person left in the world who makes

35

me feel loved and valued. I can't risk losing your respect.'

'Listen, Liz, I think you should go and wash your face. I'll come round and hear whatever's on your mind.'

'No, don't come. Please. I don't feel like seeing anybody.'

'Excuse me. I'm not anybody. I'm your best friend and it's my job to cheer you up. Cancel the face-washing. I've seen you looking rough before. I'll bring some lunch and a nice chilled bottle of Pinot Grigio.'

'No, Sheila, please. I'm really not feeling up to it. Come tomorrow. Not today.'

'Well,' Sheila dragged out the word, giving Liz time to change her mind. No response. 'Okay, then. If you're sure.'

'I'm sure.' Liz sounded relieved.

'I'll come straight from church, okay?'

Sheila listened to the dead line for a moment before hanging up.

***

CHAPTER 10

'What are you planning to do today, Darling?'

Marty didn't bother looking up from the toast she was spreading. 'Thought maybe I'd jet down to London. Lunch in Harrods. Spot of shopping.'

The silence that followed made Marty wonder if she'd overdone the sarcasm. 'Sorry David. That was unnecessary. Short answer is, I have no idea what I'm going to do with my day. That's the trouble.' She offered a corner of toast to Chance who had appeared at her side. 'Sit,' she commanded and when he obliged she gave him his reward. He licked the butter from his moustache and looked hopefully at her. She caught David's disapproving look and, with an apologetic smile at the dog, said, 'No more. Lie down.'

'You could take that fat lump of a dog for a good, long walk. Look at the size of him.'

Despite her ill-humour, Marty had to laugh. At the sound of the W-word Chance had stood to attention, his skinny frame quivering in anticipation. He was a typical, if somewhat hairy, lurcher, thin as a racing snake, every rib visible under his shaggy, grey coat.

'I've seen more fat on a chip,' said Marty, 'I wish I had his metabolism. That's one of the awful things about this retirement lark. I'm getting fat.' She heard David sigh although she was sure he did his best to disguise it as a cough at the last minute.

'Don't be silly, you're about as fat as Chance.'

'There's a compliment in there somewhere, if I dig deep enough.'

'You know what I mean, you're gorgeous. As slim as the day I first set eyes on you.'

Pat Young

'Okay, enough flattery. Go play golf. I'll see you later.'

When David had gone, she cleared the breakfast dishes, switched on the dishwasher, put a load of washing in the machine and wondered what she could do next to fill the morning. 'I bet my grandmothers never had too much time on their hands, eh, Chance?' The dog's ears perked up at the mention of his name. He walked over to the peg where his lead always hung and stood looking up at it. The hint was too strong to resist. 'Okay, you win. Let's go down the canal for an hour and see some of your pals. It's either that or daytime telly, for God's sake. And I'm not that desperate. Yet.'

She always let Chance off the lead when they reached the path that ran alongside the canal. He loved to race up and down the bank and weave in and out of the bushes that grew there, in some crazy canine game of hide and seek. He would disappear and reappear on the path ahead, or sometimes double back and come charging up from behind. At the bend in the canal she spotted him prancing around a man lying on the path. Every so often Chance would lick at his face then dart away. The dog had obviously mistaken an accident for some sort of game. She broke into a run, calling 'Chance, come here!'

'Bloody dog!' shouted the man, swiping at Chance, who was clearly enjoying the sport. She called again and this time the dog heard and came to heel. She rubbed his ears and tried to assess the situation. 'Are you okay?'

The man rolled over and pushed himself up onto his knees, 'No, I'm not. Thanks to your stupid dog.'

'Oh God. What did he do? Trip you up?'

'Aye, he did, but then he seemed to think it was a great laugh and started jumping about, trying to lick my face.'

'I'm so sorry. He's an idiot. Can I help you?'

When she leaned down and offered her hand, he looked up, saying, 'I'm okay.' He rose to his feet. 'Wait a minute, don't I know you?'

'We're down here a lot. Maybe you've seen us before?'

'Chance, eh?'

38

The dog cocked its head to one side.

'Yes, called Chance because we rescued him from the dog home and gave him a second chance. Best thing we ever did. He's a great dog, just a bit daft.'

As he listened, the man was rubbing his shoulder. Marty hoped he hadn't broken anything. The last thing she needed right now was someone suing her for damages.

'Are you okay?' she asked again.

He nodded. 'Yeah, fine. Are you sure we haven't met before?'

Marty wondered if this was some kind of weird chat-up line, but decided it was better than being told she would be hearing from his lawyer. She smiled and said, 'Do you say that to all the girls whose dogs trip you up?'

'Are you Winker Watson's wee sister?'

Marty burst out laughing. 'Winker? It's a long time since I heard him called that.'

'I do know you. Wait, let me get your name.' He stroked his hand across his jaw then said, 'Margaret or Martha, something like that, wasn't it?'

'Close. It was Martine then, but nobody's called me that since I went to university, including Winker.'

'Didn't you use to have ginger hair?'

'Unfortunately, yes.' Marty flicked her hair back off her face. 'Toned down now, thank God.'

'Wee Martine McLean.' He shook his head, as if he couldn't believe it. 'So what did you change your name to?'

'Shortened it to Marty, nothing very glamorous, I'm afraid.'

He dusted dirt from the path off his hands and extended the right one towards her, 'Joe Docherty.'

'You're joking. Joseph Docherty? My God, I had such a crush on you when I was fourteen, you wouldn't believe it. Joseph Docherty. Now there's a blast from the past. Incredible.'

'Where's big Winker these days? What's he up to?'

'Jim went to Australia about thirty years ago, got a great job in computers and never came back. We've been out a few times to visit. They have a wonderful life. City apartment, beach house. A bit different from this, eh?' Marty pointed to the half-submerged shopping trolley rusting at the canal edge.

'Aye, I guess so. And what about you, Marty? Did you go in for computers too?'

'No, I was in education, for my sins.'

'Was? You one of the lucky ones who got out early?'

Marty felt her mood shift and tried not to sound snappy. 'I got out early, but I would never call myself one of the lucky ones.'

He rubbed at his shoulder and winced.

'I'm so sorry. That stupid dog. I hope nothing's broken. You should go to A and E and have it checked.'

'No need, I promise you, it's fine. I've seen enough sporting injuries in my time to know when something needs medical intervention.'

'Are you a doctor?'

'I wish. No, just a humble PE teacher.'

'No need to be humble. I've worked with a lot of PE teachers and some of them have the best relationships with kids I've ever seen.'

'You sound as if you know what you're talking about.'

'I should do. I was head-teacher of a big comprehensive.'

'Which one?'

'Moorcroft.'

'Wait a minute. Are you Marty Dunlop? I heard you'd walked away.'

'That's one way of putting it, I suppose.' Marty kicked the ground like a teenager, embarrassed to look at him. She dreaded what he'd say next.

'You were the talk of the steamie.' He laughed. 'My granny used to say that, when she'd heard a good bit of gossip.'

Marty tried to smile. She knew the expression but never thought she'd be its subject.

'Yeah, I bet I was. Did the staffroom gossips have a field day? Like knitters round the guillotine.'

Joe looked like she'd lost him. He shrugged. 'Don't have a

staffroom, me. Don't miss it either, I have to say.'

'So who were you talking to?'

'Big Sean. I see him for a pint on a Friday night. He was almost in tears when he told me you'd packed it in. His exact words were, "A fine, talented woman, so she is. Now there's another gifted head-teacher gone. What a feckin waste." I'm pretty sure that's how he put it.'

Marty smiled at his Irish accent, and the thought of Big Sean sticking up for her.

'Aha,' said Joe Docherty, with a twinkle in his eyes that made her feel fourteen again. 'That made you smile. Almost. Why so glum? You've escaped.'

'Glum is mild for how I feel most of the time, and, for the record, I didn't want to "escape", as you put it. Anyway, you're a PE teacher?' Time to steer the conversation away from her. Nobody wants to listen to someone else's woes.

'My background's in PE but I work in Outdoor Education now. With disadvantaged kids, mostly up at the bothy by Loch Etrin.'

'Oh, I know it. We used to send kids up there to do their Duke of Edinburgh award. That was when Matt Harvey was in charge.'

'Yeah, I worked with Matt when I first joined the service. Great guy. Sadly, there's only me left now. And a different kind of kid from the ones you used to send. My lads have all been excluded, permanently. I'm their Last Chance Saloon. Next stop, the jail.'

'Bankside Bairns?'

'Yeah, mostly. They're good lads, Marty. It's just ... living there ...'

'I know.' And she did.

'Without blowing my own trumpet, I'm saving these boys. From drugs, serious crime, you name it. Or at least, I'm trying.'

Marty could sense the man's passion. It was coming off him in waves.

'But my boss, in his wisdom, has decided to shut the bothy.'

'Thomas Smeaton?'

'The very same. I take it you know him?'

'Do I know him? That bastard's the reason I no longer run Moorcroft Academy.'

'Don't hold back.'

'Sorry, perhaps he's a friend of yours.'

Joe snorted. 'Aye right. Want to tell me what happened?'

'It's a long story. Just let's say Smeaton had better hope he never meets me in a dark alley.'

As if her anger was too much for him, like a fire that gets too hot to be near, Joe stepped away. 'Sorry, but I need to keep moving before this shoulder stiffens up altogether. It's been great seeing you again. Tell Winker his old pal said hi, next time you speak to him, will you?'

'I certainly will. And sorry again about that daft dog of mine.'

'Don't give it another thought. These are tough old bones. I'll be fine.'

'Bye then,' she said, regretting her ill-humour. She would have to watch that.

She was walking away, keeping Chance close when she heard her name and turned to see Joe jogging after her.

'Can I give you this card with my contact details? Sorry it's so grotty. Been in my pocket for years. Sally always insisted I keep one on me, in case of emergency. If you can manage to read it, will you pass on my e-mail to Winker? Maybe ask him to get in touch sometime?'

***

42

CHAPTER 11

Marty sipped a gin and tonic while she put the finishing touches to dinner and then, as she lit two candles, she called David to the table. She had been short with him several times this week and was determined to make an effort tonight. She had even put on a bit of make-up, not that David would ever notice.

'This looks lovely,' he said, spotting the candles but not the lipstick. 'What kind of wine would you like?'

'There's a white chilling in the fridge. I'll have some of that, thanks.'

'Righty-oh.'

God, she wished he would stop saying that. If it wasn't 'righty-oh' it was 'okay dokey'. When had these little catchphrases of her husband's stopped being endearing? When did they start to get on her nerves?

'How was your day, Darling?'

She looked up, a sarcastic answer on her tongue, but his smile reassured her he was joking. She remembered her plan to be nice to him. 'Mark rang earlier. He's got a new girlfriend. She sounds nice.'

'Will we get to meet this one, do you think?'

'Who knows? He'll be home at Christmas. I can't wait.'

'You miss him, don't you, Love?'

Marty bit hard on her lip and nodded.

David filled her glass and gave her an awkward, sideways hug. 'Did you get a chance to check out that art class I mentioned?'

Marty reminded herself she was supposed to be making an effort tonight and tried to make her voice sound light and carefree. 'I'm afraid our idiot of a dog put the kibosh on that.'

Chance appeared in the doorway of the utility room, a hopeful look on his face. He had been banished to his bed while they ate.

'Yes, I'm talking about you. Now, go to bed.' The dog obeyed, but not before he gave her a baleful stare fit to melt the hardest of hearts. She and David looked at each other and laughed. 'You did say "dog" and he thinks that's his middle name. What did he do?'

'He tripped up a jogger. A serious runner actually.'

'Oh dear, and was she hurt?'

'It was a guy, and fortunately he wasn't badly hurt although it looked for a little while as if he might have damaged his shoulder. But the thing is, he was sprawled on the path, writhing in pain, when I came along, with Chance licking his face.'

A clicking of claws on the laminate made them both look towards the door. Sure enough. There he was. In unison, they both said, 'Bed!' and the dog slunk off, managing to look offended.

'The stupid beast was lucky he didn't get kicked into the canal,' said David.

'Had the man been able to stand, I think he'd have been very tempted. Once we got him on to his feet he seemed okay but he'll be a bit bruised in the morning.' This was the point where Marty knew she ought to mention that the jogger had recognised her from thirty years ago. And what he'd told her about Smeaton.

'So what did you do all day, Darling?'

'I take it you mean, what did I do all day, apart from cleaning your house, washing your clothes, fetching the weekend's food and cooking you this delicious meal?' At least he had the good grace to look sheepish. 'I sat with my feet up, what do you think I did?'

'Sorry, sorry.' He leaned across the table and took her hand. 'All I want is for you to be happy, Marty.'

'How can I be happy when I've been robbed of a job I adored? I've been put out to pasture long before my sell-by date.'

'A few mixed metaphors in there.'

Marty gave him a warning look over the rim of her glass and took a mouthful of wine so enormous it choked her.

David was out of his chair in an instant, saying, 'Careful!' and slapping her on the back.

'I'm okay. Sit down,' she spluttered, reaching for her water glass.

'Okay dokey. It's just, I don't understand why you're so miserable.'

Why wouldn't he leave it? Marty closed her eyes and hoped he would read her body language and take a hint.

'Half the teachers in the country would bite your hand off if you offered them a chance to retire early on full pension.'

'Yes, but I'm not one of them. I lived for my job, for that school, for those kids and those teachers. I was making a difference to lots of lives and then I was flung on the scrap-heap. And you want me to be happy solving shitty Sudokus or painting pathetic watercolours?'

David's look reminded her how he felt about her swearing. 'You really need to move on, Marty. It was your choice to resign and I know sometimes you regret that, but all this pent-up anger can't be good for you.'

'What do you suggest I do about it, David? Since you seem to be such an expert.'

David, to his credit, ignored her sarcasm. 'Well, I've got a suggestion. You know how they say laughter is the best medicine?'

'Who says?'

David smiled briefly and ploughed on. 'I was telling the chaps at golf that you're at a bit of a loose end.'

'A bit of a loose end?'

'You remember Peter Blenheim, don't you? No? Well, his wife is a social worker over at Bankside, you know, that rough housing estate with all the terrible drug problems?'

'I know where Bankside is, thanks, David.'

'Anyway, his wife says they're looking for volunteers to put on a community pantomime. It's called Itchybella. Like Cinderella, get it?' He chuckled. 'That would be right up your street. Tell you what, I'll ask him to get his wife to pass on the organiser's number.'

As if he'd found the solution she'd been searching for all this time, David drained his wine and pushed his chair back. The scraping noise set her teeth on edge. Slapping his hands on his thighs, he declared, 'Righty-oh. Shall we take a coffee through to the lounge? There's a good documentary about Alaska at half-nine.'

She lifted her wine glass from the table and stood. 'Tempting though that sounds, David, I'll pass. I've had enough of this day. I'm going to bed.'

In the doorway she stopped. 'By the way,' she said, 'I'm planning to do something about my pent-up anger. But it won't be taking part in any bloody panto.'

***

CHAPTER 12

Half-way to Bankside Joe had to switch on the minibus headlights. The rain wasn't so much falling as hanging in the air. You couldn't see it or touch it, but it would have you soaked in no time. The sky was a solid grey that showed no promise of brightening. Some days, dawn and dusk looked the same and it hardly got light in between. Joe tried to remember what sunshine looked like and how it felt to be warm. He hated winter days like this. As if on cue Radio Two played the Boomtown Rats and Joe found himself singing along. When he reached the line about shooting the whole day down he felt for the first time that he understood the sentiments behind the song.

The boys were waiting in the vandalised bus shelter by the community centre. The sight of them huddling there made Joe glad he'd called the newspaper. People deserved to know what was going on. These boys were good lads at heart. Okay, so they'd been expelled from mainstream school, but school wasn't for everybody. The only thing that could motivate them to get up in the morning was the bothy and Smeaton was determined to take that away. The young reporter Joe had spoken to seemed keen to run the story. Investigative journalism was her 'thing', she said. Joe had smiled at her enthusiasm as he fed her all the details.

Slug was first to notice the minibus but last to make a move. He raised his hand to wave to Joe and then, as if that signal had used up all his energy, seemed disinclined to leave the bus shelter.

The other boys piled into the van while Dykesy held the door. 'M'oan Slug,' he said, 'you comin?'

'Naw.'

'How no?'

'Jist no feelin like it.' He walked away in the direction of the shopping precinct.

'Slug's no comin this mornin, Big Man.'

'What's wrong? He's usually dead keen on the bothy.'

'He had a bad pie last night. Or half a dozen,' said Liam, chuckling.

'Shut it, Liam. Somethin's happened to his big brother.'

'Aw sorry, Dykesy. Ah never heard.'

'His unit got ambushed on night patrol. One guy got killed. Nae news about Slug's brother yet, but ah think he's badly hurt.'

'Aw man, that's fuckin terrible. Sorry for swearing, Mr Docherty.'

'No, you're right, it is terrible. Poor guy, and poor old Slug.'

'Ye'll never get me in nae army,' said Dangermoose.

'They'd never take you anyway, Danger, ye're far too wee. You up for it, Liam?'

'Soon as ah'm old enough, ah'm off. So's TJ. Have ye no seen the adverts on the telly, ye can get a great life in the army.'

'Ye can get yer baws shot off as well, man,' said Dykesy.

'No if ye're careful. Anyway, TJ and me are plannin to look out for each other. But ah'm tellin ye, ah'm leavin Bankside.'

'Did you ever get ambushed when you were in the army, Sur?'

Joe pretended he hadn't heard the question. 'Where is TJ this morning? He's never late.'

'He cannae come. He's got nothin to put on his feet. His ma's boyfriend sold his new trainers to get money for drugs.'

Joe shook his head. This was a first, an all-time low. A boy being forced to miss a session because he had no shoes to his name?

'Give him a phone, please, Dykesy? Tell him we'll go and pick him up. My wellies should be in the back there. He can wear them till he picks up his hiking boots at the bothy.'

TJ's street was one of rougher addresses in the town. Many of the houses were vacant, their windows protected by metal shutters. The sparse open space between blocks was littered with everything from supermarket trolleys to burnt-out cars. It reminded Joe of news footage he'd seen of cities under siege. He imagined there must be folk here who were scared to leave their houses. A few windows had blinds or pretty curtains and some gardens showed that the occupiers had pride in their homes. Not everyone here was a drug addict or dealer, but they were the ones that got the place a bad name.

'There's TJ, Sur. Aw no, whit's he got on his feet?'

'It looks like his granda's slippers.' The boys burst out laughing and poor TJ barely had time to get in the van before they started winding him up.

'Thanks for comin fur me, Sur,' said TJ, ignoring them.

'No bother, TJ. Glad you could make it.'

The banter and the hilarity carried on for much of the journey although Jimbo somehow managed to sleep through the racket. Probably been out all night and sleeping off the effects of drink. Or something worse.

Before long they left the main road and took the minor one that led up towards the ruined castle. When that road ran out, they turned on to a track that wound its way up over the hill to the deep loch that served as a reservoir.

Perched on the hillside above the water sat the Logiemuir Outdoor Education Centre, commonly known as The Bothy. Every time he saw it Joe thought how perfect it was for purpose; it was close to town but gave easy and fast access to the hills, yet it was far enough off the beaten track to be safe from vandalism.

'Sur? What was this place before? Somebody's house?'

'Don't be daft, Dykesy. Who'd stay up here? There's no even a chippy.'

'Ah would.'

'Aye, it's pure peaceful. Nae fights nor nothin.'

Joe smiled, proud to think these town kids loved the place almost as much as he did.

'You're bang on, Dykesy. It used to be a shepherd's cottage, then the council bought it and set it up as an outdoors centre. They built that extension on the back to accommodate equipment.'

'So thieving wee basturts like us couldnae steal it, eh, Sur?'

The boys were out of the van before the wheels stopped turning, even Jimbo. Joe stood rubbing his sore shoulder and watched them scampering like puppies, grabbing each other and rolling about on the damp grass. He stood still, breathing in the peaty air and envying the boys their energy. As if to welcome them, the sun broke through, turning the loch to molten silver. Clouds swept in, a dark curtain that killed the light and threatened rain.

For the moment, at least, it was dry. After years of working outdoors in West of Scotland weather, Joe had learned to be thankful for small mercies.

'Right lads, let's get the gear on. We've no time to waste if we're to get a decent walk done before it starts to get dark.' They gathered at his side, jostling for position as he unlocked the door to the extension, the scent of their body sprays overwhelming. Say what you would about these boys, they liked to smell good. They went through the door like a rugby scrum and raced for their boots and waterproofs.

Their enthusiasm made Joe happy and sad at the same time. He thought about the newspaper reporter and hoped she would do a good job. Deep in his inside pocket his phone vibrated against his ribs. Signal must be good this morning. He checked the screen and swore under his breath.

'Hi Joe, It's Carole at headquarters. Mr Smeaton would like a word with you.'

This was a new development. Smeaton never contacted him directly. He usually demanded people report to his office.

'Joe, are you there?'

'I'm at the bothy, Carole. The signal's iffy.'

'Can I put him through?'

'Any idea what it's about?'

'Not really. Can you hear me, Joe?'

He played for time. 'You're coming and going.'

'Don't tell him I told you this, okay?'

'I won't. You know me.'

'Well,' Carole hesitated and Joe's heart sank. 'He just took a call.'

Her voice faded. The line? Or was she whispering?

'Sorry?' said Joe.

'I said someone phoned him, from The Record, and he went through the roof.'

'And?'

'And then he asked me to get you on your mobile.'

Joe felt a lurch deep down in his gut. Should he take the call now or wait until he had time to gather his thoughts? Was that just postponing the inevitable?

'I'll call him back.'

'He won't like it.'

'I know he won't, Carole, but I can't take his call right now.'

'Okay, Joe, but on your head be it.'

'Tell him we got cut off, will you? Just say the line was bad.'

When she didn't answer, he checked the bars.

No signal. No lie.

***

CHAPTER 13

When Sheila woke on Monday morning, it was to a second day in a freezing cold house with no hot water. As she stood shivering in the bathroom, she abandoned her plan to have a shower. From the warmth of the duvet she'd promised herself that, no matter how icy the water, she'd take a quick five minutes under the spray and wash her hair. Five seconds had been enough to change her mind.

She'd stayed in all day yesterday waiting for Wright Plumbers. Always Wright on time, claimed their advert. Sheila cursed them. Why not be honest with people and say they were too busy? Or too lazy-arsed to come out on a Sunday.

A quick lick with a flannel and a 'Paisley shower' it would have to be. She kept her finger on the button of her body spray until she was choking on the chemicals.

Then she looked in the mirror. 'Jeeso, you're like a punk on a bad hair day,' she said to her reflection. Under no circumstances could she appear in public looking such a mess.

She needed to get a plumber today. One day was an inconvenience. Any more would be insanitary.

Then she'd call Liz and find out why she hadn't answered her phone yesterday. Sheila felt a pang of guilt and hoped her friend had at least listened to her voicemail.

Magic Matt claimed to be the Number One Plumber in the Number Two business. He was the first one to answer and he was available that afternoon. Sheila didn't normally like workmen in the house when she was at work, but beggars, choosers and all that.

She was pulling into the school carpark when she realised she'd forgotten to phone Liz. The day was even crazier than usual and it was lunchtime before Sheila had a spare moment to think about Liz again. She went to her office and dialled Cavenhead Primary's number.

'Sorry, Miss Scott,' said Liz's secretary. 'I'm afraid Miss Douglas wasn't in school today. We haven't heard from her.'

'Oh dear, that's not like Liz, but I'm not all that surprised. When I spoke to her at the weekend she thought maybe she was coming down with flu.'

'Poor thing. Will you please tell her we're all asking for her and hoping she gets well soon?'

'I'll do that, Linda. Thanks.'

'Miss Scott? Can you let me know if she's going to be off for a while? We'll have a whip round and send her some nice flowers.'

So much for the 'cold' head-teacher with the 'unhappy staff'. Sheila dialled Liz's number, sighing when it went straight to voicemail again.

The next thing Sheila knew, it was three-thirty and everyone, including her secretary, was heading home.

'Before I go, Miss Scott. Someone called earlier offering to help with the panto. 'Recently retired from education' was how she described herself. She sounds very nice so I asked for her number and said you'd call her back. Is that okay?'

'Okay? It's fabulous, I'll call her right now, thanks, Marion.'

The phone was answered immediately.

'Hi, I'm Marty Dunlop. You don't really know me but I've worked with your friend Liz on her Across the Divide project and though you may not remember, I've seen you at Head-teachers' meetings in the past.'

'Marty? Of course I remember you. You were at Moorcroft Academy. I was shocked to hear you'd resigned.'

'Yes, biggest mistake I ever made in my life. That's why I'm calling, in a way, although it's mostly to please my husband, I must say.'

Marty explained that she was frustrated by early retirement and getting on her husband's nerves. 'I need to find something to do that challenges me. Before I go mad.'

Sheila laughed. 'You've come to the right place, Madam. A

panto in Bankside - this could be the challenge of our lives.'

Sheila made arrangements to meet Marty then rung off and dialled Liz's home number followed by her mobile. The first rang out unanswered and the second went straight to voicemail. Again. Sheila must have left at least ten voicemails since yesterday, the first from outside Liz's door on her way home from church. She'd stood ringing the bell and banging on the door before she'd given up and gone home, trying Liz's number every hour or so but never getting an answer.

'Hello, It's Florence Nightingale again, calling to let you know I'll be there soon to make you a special cocktail - a Citrus Sparkle - Lucozade and Lemsip.' Sheila smiled at her own joke then added, 'Just going home to change first. There's a vomiting bug going round, probably what you've got, and I'm afraid a tiny boy in Primary One mistook my skirt for the toilet pan. Occupational hazard, I guess. Right, see you asap.'

The first thing Sheila did when she got home was touch the hall radiator. It was warm. Thanking God, she opened the bathroom door and turned on the hot tap. It ran cold for long enough to worry her and then gradually heated up. She gave her hands a quick wash and dried them on the towel on the rail. She'd have to call Matt the plumber and thank him for working his magic.

She looked with longing at her bathtub, perched there on its claw feet, waiting for her to succumb to temptation. She could fill it to the brim, throw in a bath bomb and settle deep into the bubbles. Her day had been hectic and a soak would revitalise her, but she couldn't relax until she had checked on Liz. A quick shower, a real one this time, would have to do.

When she reached Liz's gate, the house looked the same as yesterday, windows dark in the failing light of the dying day. There was still no sign of Liz's car. Nothing about the situation felt right. Sheila ran to the front door and rang the bell, then banged on the glass with her fist. When there was no response, she opened the letter box and bawled, 'Liz. Open the door.' Aware she sounded slightly hysterical she told herself to calm

Pat Young

down and think.

She went round to the back door and tried the handle. On tiptoe, she put her face to the glass of the kitchen window, but it was too dark inside to see anything. A sudden noise made her start. Her heart raced as something touched her leg - Jaffa. He wound himself round and round her ankles. She laughed at how easily she had been spooked and said, 'Hey, Jaffa,' more to hear a human voice than to communicate with the cat. She wasn't keen on cats and this one was a particularly aloof member of the species. 'Where's Liz got to, eh, Puss?' She stretched out a hand to stroke him, but the cat slunk back in through its personal door, the flap dropping into place with a slap.

Sheila straightened up and walked to the wall at the bottom of the garden. It was spooky, this place, with its high hedge and thick bushes. Liz's parents had liked to keep themselves to themselves.

She looked at the upstairs window, hoping to see a light in the study. Maybe Liz was working, too engrossed to answer the phone or hear the doorbell. The windows showed only the reflection of a fast-setting sun. The days were short and this garden was getting too gloomy for comfort. Stepping over a pile of clay pots that had been emptied, cleaned and ready for spring bulbs, Sheila took the shortest route to the back door.

On a sudden whim, she flung herself at it, bashing her shoulder against the wood. They made it look so easy in the movies. In reality it hurt like billy-oh. She rubbed at her shoulder and wondered if she'd done any lasting damage. This was stupid. She was never going to break down a door by herself.

She remembered Liz's habit of leaving her key in the lock. If Sheila could break the glass she could reach in and turn the key. It was worth a try. She pulled the sleeve of her jacket down over her hand and grabbed the fleece in her fingers, trying to make a pad to protect her fist. Without stopping to think too much, she pulled her arm back and punched the glass as hard as she could. The pane remained intact but she

55

suspected her knuckles might be broken. Cradling her aching fingers in the crook of her sore arm, she looked around for something hard she could throw. She ran to the pile of clay pots at the foot of the garden. She grabbed the first one she could lift, took it to the back door, raised it high and hurled it at the glass panel. In the silence of the enclosed garden the shattering glass sounded like an explosion. The cat shot out the flap in an orange streak and disappeared into the twilight. With great care Sheila inserted her hand through the jagged edges.

'Hey! What the devil do you think you're doing?'

**

CHAPTER 14

'Try a few sips, dear. It'll help.'

Sheila looked at the concerned face peering into hers. She took the steaming cup and raised it to her lips. The first sip burned the tip of her tongue.

'Mind now, it's hot. And there's a drop of brandy in it.'

The aftertaste was strong and sweet. Despite the pain of her scorched tongue she could taste the brandy and was glad of it. She tried a grateful smile, but was trying hard to maintain a stiff upper lip. She sensed that another kind word from Liz's neighbour might be enough to set her off.

A young woman constable, who introduced herself as Norma, was sitting on the couch next to her, notebook at the ready.

'Do you think you could answer a few questions, Miss Scott?'

Sheila shook her head, the tiniest movement from side to side. Not because she was unwilling to help, but because she couldn't bring herself to accept any of this.

'Take your time,' said Norma, in such a gentle voice that Sheila wanted to weep. She had to pull herself together. She drained her tea, enjoying the syrupy sugar that had pooled in the bottom of the cup, then cleared her throat and said, 'It's okay, I'm fine.'

'When last did you see Miss Douglas?'

'I last,' Sheila's voice caught on the finality of the word. Norma handed her a tissue. 'Sorry, can we start again, please?'

Norma nodded and touched the back of Sheila's hand. The sympathy in the gesture caused another delay while Sheila mopped her eyes and blew her nose.

'I spoke to her on Saturday morning, but Tuesday would be

the last time I saw her, I suppose. We watched Coronation Street together, she's a great Corrie fan.' Sheila noticed the sad smile on the woman's face and said, 'Should I be saying was?'

Norma gave a slight tilt of her head. 'We don't know for sure.'

It might not be official yet, but Sheila knew her best friend was dead. Her whole body felt as numb as her burnt tongue. The nerve endings were still there, still functioning, but shocked and damaged.

'How would you say Miss Douglas was when you last spoke to her?'

'Sorry?'

'Did Miss Douglas seem upset, worried about anything, different from her usual self?'

Sheila recalled the conversation she'd had with Liz on Saturday morning. The answers were yes, yes and yes. As she watched her story being transcribed into a police notebook, she told Norma that Liz was very worried about a forthcoming inspection of her school.

'Who wouldn't be?'

'Exactly. It's stressful for everyone but the head-teacher always carries the burden of responsibility. Liz was very conscientious and took any criticism to heart. She was often upset about things her boss said to her. I was always telling her to try to forget about school at the weekend, take a complete break.'

'So you phoned on Saturday?'

'That's right. I was planning to come over but Liz said she was feeling rotten and insisted I wasn't to come.' It seemed to Sheila that millennia had passed since the last time she spoke to Liz. 'I agreed to wait and see her on Sunday, yesterday, that is. But she didn't answer the door, or the phone.'

'What time was that?'

'I don't know exactly. Middle of the day. I came round after church.'

Sheila's numbness was beginning to wear off, thawing like frozen fingers on a winter's day.

'And what did you do?'

'I rang the doorbell and knocked on the door. Then I looked in the windows and shouted through the letterbox. Something didn't feel right. Then I noticed her car was missing and I wondered if she'd gone away. But that didn't make sense either. She'd have told me if she was planning to go somewhere. Or she'd have asked me to go with her.'

'Did you think of calling the police?'

'No, I didn't. I just had a quick look round the back and then I went home.' Sheila remembered feeling a bit peeved with her friend, but she didn't want to sound childish. Embarrassment made her snippy.

'Are you saying I should have done something sooner?'

'No. I'm just trying to get a sequence of events. When you came back tonight, you decided to break in. Is that right?'

'Yes.'

'Why was that?'

'Because I knew she hadn't been in to work and Liz would never take a buckshee day off. Never. I thought she must be too ill to get out of bed and answer the door.'

'Did you feel suspicious?'

'I felt worried.'

Before she could add that she was also feeling guilty, Sheila heard heavy, slow footsteps on the stairs. Surely they needed to move faster than that to save a life. Sheila ran into the hall.

'Sorry, dear. We did everything we could.' The paramedics walked on.

'Wait, do you think I could have saved her life? If I'd broken in earlier?'

'We can't say, sorry.'

Sheila watched as they carried her friend out to the ambulance. She couldn't bear to contemplate their destination. Norma touched her arm and said, in a very gentle voice, 'I'll let you have a moment.'

Sheila flapped a hand fan-like in front of her face, as if she could waft away the grief. She tried to speak, failed and buried her face in her hands.

Norma said, 'That's been a great help, thank you. We'll be in touch. Will you manage to make it home or is there someone you can call to pick you up?'

'I'll be fine. Anyway, I need my car for work in the morning. If I can face it.'

'I'm sure your boss will understand if you need a few days off. You've had a real shock.'

'It's obvious you've never met my boss. He's the man to blame for this.' She gestured vaguely around Liz's living room.

Norma looked at her, puzzled. 'Sorry? What did you say?'

'Nothing. Never mind. I've no idea why I said that.'

'Well, if you're sure you've nothing more to add, that'll be all for now, thanks, Miss Scott, except to say how very sorry I am for the loss of Miss Douglas.'

Sheila smiled, acknowledging the young woman's kindness. With one last regretful look round the room where she'd spent so many happy hours with Liz, she turned to leave.

At the front door, she heard Norma's voice. 'Miss Scott?'

The young policewoman was holding out an envelope. 'I almost forgot. This was found beside your friend's bed. It's addressed to you.'

'Hold on a sec, PC Wallace. I'll take that, if you don't mind.'

Norma blushed. Whoever this guy was, he was her superior officer. 'Sorry, sir. Miss Scott, this is DCS McCallum.'

The man was offering his hand. As Sheila shook it, he said, 'Miss Scott, I'm very sorry about your friend.' He looked at the envelope in his left hand. She could see her name on it, written in Liz's trademark fountain pen. 'I'm afraid we'll have to hang on to this. The Procurator will want a wee look at it.'

'But it's meant for me. That's Liz's handwriting. She always uses,' Sheila stopped for a moment, pressed her lips together and opened her eyes wide, blinking to prevent tears. Her voice was shaky when she spoke again, 'She always used a fountain pen for her personal correspondence. I'd like to have it please.'

The detective's reply was gentle but firm, 'I'm sorry, Miss Scott. We need to follow procedure. I shall make certain the envelope is returned to you in due course, but we can't give it to you at this moment in time.'

Sheila's sadness turned to indignation. In her best teachery voice she said, 'Excuse me, Norma was about to hand me that envelope and had you not arrived, I would be opening it now, as Liz clearly intended.'

'Well, yes. PC Wallace and I will need to have a wee chat about that.' The young policewoman looked at her feet. McCallum gave Sheila an apologetic smile, but his tone made it clear he would be keeping the envelope.

'We don't know what's in it, of course, but Liz owed me thirty pounds for a concert ticket. She always put notes in an envelope and wrote my name on the front. Can I check the contents, then leave it with you?' As Sheila spoke she realised how awful she must appear to these strangers, as if her only concern was getting her hands on the money her dead friend owed her.

The policeman smiled. 'You don't give up easily, do you?'

Sheila smiled in return, hoping to get her own way, but it was clear this man wouldn't give an inch and she was certainly not about to beg. 'Very well, DC McCallum.'

'It's DCS McCallum, Miss Scott.' He held out a business card. 'Maybe you'd like to take this, in case you want to get in touch. From what the constable at the gate told me, we have no reason to suspect anything untoward happened to your friend, Miss Douglas, but we won't know until we find out a wee bit more. And in the meantime, I'm sure you'd want us to be doing everything we can, in the correct manner?

Sheila noticed he had been diplomatic enough to avoid the word post-mortem.

***

CHAPTER 15

When Sheila woke she looked at the little clock on her bedside table and realised she'd slept through the alarm. Then she remembered the reason. She'd been awake till five am. She tried to get up but Liz's loss was a heavy weight, pinning her down. She had no idea how she could carry on without her friend. She and Liz had been so close for so long, they were more like sisters than best pals. They had a getaway booked for Christmas and an Easter trip to the States planned. She'd have to cancel both. And arrange a funeral. And see to all of Liz's belongings. Including Jaffa. She wondered if the cat had returned home yet or if she had traumatised him into running away. A sudden mental image of Jaffa squashed flat on the bypass jolted her into a sitting position and she swung her legs over the side of the bed. She couldn't lie around in bed all day; she would go mad.

At the risk of being as patient as Medusa with PMT, she'd have to go into work. School was such a busy place it would take her mind off things for a little while. If she stayed here she'd be haunted by the guilt and regrets that had kept her awake all night. Not to mention the spectre of a dead cat.

With her attaché case in one hand and a pile of mid-term reports in the crook of her elbow, she finally managed to open the door. She was turning to lock it, trying very hard not to drop everything when someone appeared at her shoulder.

'Good morning.'

Sheila shrieked and burst into tears. The postman handed her a pile of mail and joked, 'Sorry, was it something I said?'

'No, no, it's me. I'm all wound up this morning.'

While she stood and watched, the poor man gathered up

the reports she'd dropped, chasing a couple that took off across the lawn. She thanked the postie for his help and went back into the house. She shut the door behind her and stood leaning against it. Dropping papers, case and letters to the floor, Sheila let the tears run freely down her cheeks. How could she possibly have believed she could get through a day in school? As if they couldn't bear her weight any longer, her knees buckled and her back slid down the door until she was sitting, legs splayed like a broken doll.

When Sheila woke for the second time that day, she was completely disorientated. Why was she lying on top of her bed, fully clothed? The sun was pouring in the window on to her face and she lay for a few seconds, enjoying the warmth on her cheek. Then it hit her, like a fist slamming into her chest.

Liz was dead.

Lovely, kind, gentle Liz, who had started to enjoy life to the full, freed, at last, from the restraints of elderly parents. She and Liz had talked about taking early retirement and going on a world cruise. Now it had all turned to dust. Her own future loomed bleak and lonely without her best friend.

She sat up and caught sight of herself in the dressing-table mirror. She looked ghastly. Her greying hair stuck out in spikes on one side of her head and was flattened to her skull on the other. Her blotchy, tear-stained face was streaked with the remains of the make-up she had applied this morning in an effort to hide her lack of sleep. She resembled a zombie. On the outside she looked alive but inside she was dead.

A shower soothed, at least superficially, and she hoped some food might help a little with the sick, empty feeling in her stomach. On the way to the kitchen she came across the papers scattered round the front door and her briefcase lying, discarded, in the middle of the hall. She was collecting the report sheets, stacking them into some semblance of tidiness, when she noticed the bundle of mail. She squirmed as she recalled her encounter with the postman that morning. There was the usual collection of junk, a brochure for a cruise line and appeal letters from three charities. The last item was a white envelope and when Sheila turned it over Liz's handwriting stared up at her. She clutched it to her chest, then, dumping the other papers on the hall table, she went into the kitchen and laid the envelope on the work surface. She put the kettle on and stuck a bagel in the toaster, knowing she was putting off the moment when she had to open Liz's letter.

The kettle shrieked at her till she pushed it off the heat. The bagel leapt from the toaster and lay where it fell. She took a knife from the drawer, lifted the letter and sat down at the table. Suddenly impatient, she discarded the knife, and ripped the envelope across the top, revealing a sharply folded sheet of paper.

Dearest Sheila,

Here's a line I never thought I'd find myself writing - If you are reading this, I am dead. Unless I've managed to mess that up too. My suicide, I mean. Yes, dear Sheila, I've taken the coward's way out, but perhaps you know that already? I left a letter for you, a suicide note, I suppose, beside my bed, assuming you'd be the one to find me. After I had written it, I realised I hadn't thought things through properly. There was no guarantee you'd be the one to read that letter, hence this one you're now reading.

You see, I haven't been planning my demise. In fact, suicide only occurred to me as an option when I woke up on Saturday morning. When I woke to the realisation that I had turned into an awful person. A head-teacher who deserts her post and spends the afternoon drinking. If I'd been in the army I'd have been executed for that trick. I deserve to be executed for what I did next. You probably know by now, but just in case you don't; I got behind the wheel of a car, a lethal weapon, and I drove home, so blind drunk I have no memory of the journey. Except for one part of it. Please don't hate me when I tell you that it gets worse, much worse. I was stopped by the police and breathalysed. Eventually, when I had sobered up a bit, they let me go home, but there's no doubt I'll be convicted of drunk driving. Oh God, Sheila, I'm so ashamed. What if I had taken some innocent person's life? A child's life? I can't face the world knowing what I've done. Not on top of everything else.

Blinded by tears, Sheila stopped reading. A huge teardrop landed on the paper, blotting the ink as it ran down the page. She rose and fetched a tissue, dried her face and read on.

What a rush it was to get everything sorted out before you appeared at the door. I'm sure you did your best to get in, to see I was okay, so you must promise me that you won't punish yourself. There was nothing you could do to stop me. My mind was made up, you see, but I was too big a coward to tell you face-to-face.

It's no secret that life has been getting me down lately. I still miss Mother terribly. Then that dreadful man at the gate, that awful stuff he was putting on Facebook, getting other parents to join in his smear campaign against me. And the physical assault, so violent, so unexpected, so undeserved. That shook me to my very heart. And all the time a feeling that I was getting no support from my employers, the people who have a duty of care to protect me in my workplace.

But the final straw? That last meeting with Mr Smeaton, the terrible things he said, telling me there was no smoke without fire, saying I was incompetent at my job and that children were suffering because of me. Said he had a moral obligation to make sure the inspectors got to the bottom of things. Moral? Interesting choice of word, under the circumstances. Going to the pub and getting drunk seemed the best option at the time - something I've never done in my life; but I'd have done anything to mute that man's voice in my head.

I have to go now, dearest Sheila, or I shall run out of time. If you appear at the door with that smile of yours, you might cheer me up enough to keep on going for another wee while, just like you've done since Mother died. This time it's different. I don't want to keep going. I can't bear the thought of people finding out what happened yesterday. Just imagine, the Facebookers will have a field day. I can't cope with the humiliation of this plus an inspection of my school. I know I will be found lacking. That's if I don't get the sack first, which is the very least I deserve.

I can't go on, Sheila. Sorry. I'm too afraid of Thomas Smeaton and what he will do when he finds out.

***

65

CHAPTER 16

Marty could not think of a single good reason to get out of bed until a bark from downstairs asked if she was awake. She looked at the alarm. She'd been daydreaming for an hour. Chance was right, she should have been up ages ago, but some days it took a real effort to rise and face the empty hours that stretched ahead of her.

The dog was waiting for her at the bottom of the stairs, his head moving from side to side with the force of his tail-wagging.

'Morning, Chance. Want your breakfast?'

The dog gave a woof of reply. Marty was convinced he understood everything she said, but David was scathing about her theory. As if to prove her right and David wrong, Chance padded through to the utility room and stood looking at his empty bowl. David would have said this was a Pavlovian response, but she preferred to believe in Chance's intelligence. She obliged him by reaching up to the shelf and tipping the box until his bowl was full of kibble. Polite as always, he waited, eyes fixed on her face, till she gave him permission to eat. 'Go ahead,' she said and went to make herself some toast.

By the time she sat down he was under the table, still hoping for scraps, despite his full belly. She looked him in the eye and said, 'No chance, Chance.' Giving up, he brought his two front paws together and laid his chin on them.

Toast in one hand, she shook the newspaper flat with the other and laid it on the table. She ran her fingers across the page to smooth it, ignoring banner headlines about recession and austerity. They might have to tighten their belts a bit now she had lost her salary. She smiled at the memory of an elderly aunt who used to say, 'To hell with poverty, boil the canary!'

She had just taken a defiant munch of her butter-laden toast when she noticed the article in the right hand column.

Primary head-teacher lies dead for days. Mr Thomas Smeaton, on behalf of Logiemuir Council, was quoted as saying that Miss Elizabeth Douglas was a 'much-loved and highly respected head-teacher who will be sorely missed by pupils and colleagues.'

Marty felt the greasy half-chewed dough stick somewhere between her mouth and her stomach, not sure if it was going down or coming back up.

Liz Douglas? Dead? She was the sweetest, kindest woman you'd ever meet.

Sheila Scott would be devastated.

Marty fetched her phone from the charger and scrolled through recent calls till she found David's number. He answered with his usual, 'Hello, Darling. I was just talking about you, telling Peter you've volunteered to help with that panto after all.'

'Have you seen the paper?'

'No, why?'

'I have to talk to you.'

'Calm down.'

'Don't tell me to calm down.'

She caught the sound of embarrassed laughter in the background.

'Marty, can you tell me what's happened?'

'He's done it again.'

'Who?'

'Chrissake, David. You know who. Smeaton.'

Marty was sure she heard a sigh and a muffled remark followed by male voices, laughing.

As if he was playing to an audience, David said, 'Okay, what's he done now?'

Marty chose to ignore his dismissive tone. You'd think she was phoning to tell him about some cute thing a toddler had said. Not the latest atrocity performed by a madman.

'You know Liz Douglas? The primary head who's doing all that wonderful anti-sectarian work with kids?'

'Not really.'

'David, you do!'

'Anyway, what about her? Marty, I'm about to sink a winning putt here. Can't this wait till I get home?'

'I thought you'd want to know. If you hadn't seen it in the paper yet.'

'Seen what, sweetheart?'

She imagined his mates rolling their eyes. She thought she heard one mutter, 'Come on, Dunlop.'

'She was found dead in her house.'

'What?'

'Overdose apparently. This is Smeaton to blame. I'd heard he was giving her a hard time but this is beyond the pale.'

David laughed. He actually laughed. She shook her head in disbelief, afraid of his next words.

'Darling, I know you think he's the devil incarnate. But I hardly think the man's to blame for this woman's suicide.'

Her voice icy, she said, 'This isn't suicide. It's murder.'

***

CHAPTER 17

'I'd like to speak to DCS McCallum, please. My name's Sheila Scott.' Sheila wasn't sure if it was okay to phone but the man had encouraged her to get in touch if she wanted.

'Hello, Miss Scott? How have you been?'

'Awful.'

'I'm not surprised. It's a dreadful situation. How can I help you?'

'I wanted to let you know I got a letter from Liz.'

'Well, that's most unusual.'

'She was an unusual woman. Very special.' Sheila's voice broke. With her lips pressed closed, she tried to collect herself.

'I'm sure she was. Is there some way I can help you?'

This man must be very busy solving crimes and yet he was making her feel like he had all the time in the world to listen to her. Sheila told herself to get on with it. 'Liz was a very organized person and she anticipated that I might not get to read the letter beside her bed.' She stopped then checked, 'It was a letter in the envelope, wasn't it? A suicide note?'

'Yes, it was.'

'I knew it wasn't money, I just wanted to read Liz's letter.'

'I'd worked that out and I understand.'

'Anyway, I'm calling to tell you I don't need to see it anymore. Liz sent me one in the post. I imagine they're very similar.'

'I see what you mean about organized.'

Sheila smiled. 'Yes. Is it okay if I ask you a few questions?'

'I should tell you that I'm not officially involved in your friend's case. In fact, I just happened to be passing last night. I was on my way home when I saw the blue light and came in to see if I could help.'

'Oh. Does that mean you can't answer my questions?'

'Go ahead and ask me, Miss Scott, and if I can give you answers, I will.'

Sheila took a deep breath. 'Liz didn't hit a pedestrian on Friday, did she?'

'That's a strange question.'

Sheila said nothing, waiting for him to fill the gap.

'I can tell you that there were no serious road traffic incidents in the area on Friday.'

'Thank goodness.'

'Yes, quite.'

Something in his tone suggested he knew Liz had been breathalysed.

'She wasn't a drinker, you know. We used to laugh at how tiddly she got on a lager shandy or a glass of Pinot Grigio.'

McCallum's silence told Sheila that he was not about to comment.

'Will she still be charged with drunk driving?'

'I don't think that will be necessary under the circumstances.'

'No, I suppose you're right. Stupid question. How did the papers know it was suicide?'

'Not from us, I can assure you, Miss Scott. Reporters hear of a lonely death and spice it up a bit, suggesting there might be something more to it.'

'Okay. One last thing; I know you must be a very busy man.'

'Go ahead. What would you like to ask me?'

'The letter I got made it clear who was to blame for Liz's committing suicide. If I give you the name of that person, will you arrest him for causing the death of Liz Douglas?'

***

CHAPTER 18

Despite its minimalist décor and the bank of computers and printers along one wall, Pearson and Goodwin's front office smelt as it had done since she was a small child. Sheila remembered coming in here with her granny to hand in some document or other. For many years P & G had been her parents' solicitors and now, she supposed, they were hers.

'Miss Pearson will see you now, if you'd like to go through, Miss Scott. The last door on the left.'

At the end of the corridor a figure was waiting, silhouetted against the large Georgian window. 'Hello, Miss Scott. Please come in.'

She was ushered into the office by an improbably young woman who offered her hand, introducing herself as Pamela Pearson. She waited until Sheila was seated and then sat down behind an antique mahogany desk. The vast director's chair seemed to swallow her up, giving Sheila a strong impression she was involved in some child's game of let's play lawyers.

'How can I help you?' asked the young woman, a warm, welcoming smile on her face.

'Are you Mr Pearson's daughter?'

'Yes and it depends what Mr Pearson you mean. Strictly speaking I'm the fourth in a long line of Pearson solicitors. But I'm the first female.'

Sheila was reminded of a saying of her father's, 'You'll never get a short answer from a lawyer or a politician.' He had trusted neither.

'And I'm fully qualified.' She gestured with a slender, pink-nailed hand towards the row of framed diplomas on the wall behind her, then put her hands on the desk. 'This was my great-grandfather's.' She gently polished the dark wood with the flat of one hand. 'I like to believe it imparts wisdom.'

Sheila found she was smiling. By being casual and friendly, this clever young woman had put Sheila at her ease. She felt confident she would be given good advice.

'I would like to pursue a legal complaint about bullying in the workplace.'

'First of all I need to make you aware that I'm not a specialist in employment law. However, I can certainly give you some advice on how one proceeds in a case of workplace harassment.'

Sheila said, 'Good,' and took a small notebook out of her handbag. She read from the list she had made up in the sleepless hours of the early morning. Pamela Pearson stopped her before she was anywhere near the end of Smeaton's list of cruelties.

'Without hearing too much more I can tell you that it looks to me as if you have a good case to make. May I check some details with you? Have you spoken to anyone about this, for example, HR, your Union rep or someone from your professional body?'

Sheila shook her head.

'Not to worry,' said the young lawyer. 'Have you kept a diary of these incidents? I know you have a list there in your notebook, but do you have them logged somewhere with dates?'

'No.' She had asked Liz this same question about the stalker at the gate. Liz had said she was too busy running the school and her diary was full enough without noting down that kind of stuff.

'Have you kept letters or e-mails that relate to any of these issues?'

Sheila didn't know the answer to that one, but it sounded more promising. 'That's a good suggestion. I'll look into that right away.' She made a note in her little book.

'Have you seen your doctor? I don't mean to pry or be indelicate, but have you been offered prescription drugs like anti-depressants or tablets to help you sleep?'

She knew the answer to this was a definite no. Liz had refused to discuss the possibility of confiding in her GP.

Pamela had been making notes on a big yellow pad. She put her pen down and leaned forward, her fingers steepled. Were they taught that stuff or had Pamela copied the technique from her dad? Maybe it was genetic, a family trait, like red hair.

'Miss Scott, have you told this man, or woman, to stop? Or have you made a complaint to his or her line manager?'

'He's the big boss, the top dog. Not a person you'd tell to stop. If you could see this individual in action, with his bulging eyes and crimson face, his words caustic enough to take the varnish off this desk, you would understand why everyone's terrified of him.'

'I see.' Pamela sat back in her seat and gave Sheila a long look, as if she were considering her next words. 'I think the best advice I can give you is to go through the steps I've mentioned, logging incidents, contacting organisations that can support you etcetera.'

'Thanks. You've been very helpful. I feel I should be honest with you. I'm here on behalf of a friend. Sorry I didn't say that to begin with.'

Pamela smiled, 'Don't worry. You would be surprised how many clients make their initial enquiries on behalf of someone else. Why don't you ask your friend to follow the guidelines on the ACAS website and,'

Sheila interrupted her. 'It's a bit late for that, I'm afraid.'

'No, not really.'

'Yes, really. You see, my friend took her own life at the weekend. I've got a letter from her. Read it.'

'I'm sure it's personal.'

'Read it, please.'

The young solicitor took Liz's letter and read it. As she folded it closed she said, 'I'm very sorry.'

'Is it any good to us?'

Pamela shook her head sadly.

Sheila stood on the pavement for a minute to give herself time to think. It was clear she needed to get her hands on some hard evidence. Without that, no lawyer or policeman would give her the time of day. If she were going to bring Smeaton down, she would have to find some proof he had bullied Liz to her death. She had to get into Liz's filing systems. Next stop, Cavenhead Primary.

Sheila swiped her own ID badge to let her in through the main door to the school, but as the door swung open a buzzer sounded and Mr McAdam, the Janitor, appeared.

When he saw her, the man removed his cap and said, 'Miss Scott, I am so sorry for your loss. Well it's our loss too. I can hardly believe it.' He looked every day of his sixty-odd years and sounded genuinely heart-broken. She watched in sympathy as he removed a pristine white handkerchief from his trouser pocket and blew his nose. 'I've put in my resignation. Time for me to retire. Miss Douglas was the only thing that kept me here. I had such admiration for the sterling job she's been doing all these years.'

'She thought the world of you. You know that, don't you?'

'Aye, I do. She told me regularly. That's a good boss for you.'

'Will I see you at Liz's funeral?'

'I wouldn't miss it for the world. That's one of the reasons I'm finishing at the end of the week, to be sure I can go. Did you hear Mr Smeaton at HQ is refusing to let us close the school as a mark of respect? The teachers are drawing lots to see who can go to the funeral. I never heard anything so disgusting in my life.' The man walked off shaking his head.

When Sheila opened the door to the school office, Liz's secretary, Linda, was checking her face in a small mirror. She popped it into a drawer, saying, 'Hello, Miss Scott. I don't know why I'm bothering. I know my face is a mess. The mascara got cried off hours ago. How are you?'

'In shock, I think, Linda. It hasn't quite sunk in.'

'I know what you mean. Every time I hear footsteps, I expect her to walk in the door. Did you hear the latest about our request for a special closure on the day of the funeral? He's said no. Can you believe that?'

'Did he give a reason?'

'Apparently, parents would object. Lost teaching time and all that.'

'What a load of rubbish.'

Sheila heaved a great sigh. She pointed towards the door to Liz's office. 'D'you mind if I go in? There's a couple of personal items I'd like to save.'

'Go ahead. The door's unlocked. I found it like that when I came in this morning.'

A vase of withering roses stood on the window sill, dirty-green water showing through the crystal. They would be the last flowers Liz ever bought to brighten her office. Sheila picked up a photo frame from the desk. The snap had been taken last summer when pupils from their two schools had made a joint trip to a theme park. It had been a great success, part of an on-going project to bring two diverse communities together. 'The Bridge' had been Liz's brainchild and one she was convinced was the way forward if Scotland wanted to get rid of the scourge of sectarianism. 'Start them young,' had been her mantra. 'We've got to get to them before the bigots do.'

Sheila stuck the photo in her bag and added a few little nick-nacks that had no monetary but great sentimental value. Then, deciding she had wasted enough time, she opened the top drawer of Liz's desk looking for the key-ring she always kept there. It was missing. Maybe Liz had taken it home, but that was unlikely. She always left it in school so her staff would have access to her filing system, if ever she were taken ill.

Sheila looked at the row of grey cabinets against the far wall. On impulse, she tried a drawer on the first cabinet. It opened and slid out towards her. The next filing cabinet was unlocked too, as were its companions. Sheila checked the alphabetical labels on the drawers and opened one marked C - D. She flipped through the files and selected one marked correspondence. It was empty. She tried L and found a folder marked Letters from HQ - it was also empty. Sheila didn't take very long to work out that someone had been in Liz's office removing anything that could be used as evidence in an enquiry. She wondered if she were being paranoid, so she did a check by looking under P for policies. That drawer was full. Same with H for Health and Safety and M for Mission Statement.

She went back to Liz's desk and looked for her big diary. It was nowhere to be seen. A memo block showed a spotless white face to the world and a shorthand notebook sat open at a blank page. Sheila picked it up and examined the wire binding. Tiny strands of paper were trapped in its spirals. She knew that this was a pet hate of Liz's. Whenever she tore a page out of a ring bound pad, she fished out the little wavy bits of paper that got left behind, snagged in the wire. Sheila had often teased her about the possibility of OCD, but Liz had laughed at her. 'The world's gone mad. Because I'm tidy you want to stick a label on me. I'm not compulsive, just neat. I tear the wee bits out because I hate them scattered all over my desk like confetti.'

Sheila opened the door to the outer office. When the secretary looked up, Sheila asked, 'Has the depute head been in to fetch stuff from Liz's room? Or anyone else?'

Linda looked a bit vacant, as if the question were a strange one to ask. Her dark curls trembled as she slowly shook her head from side to side.

***

CHAPTER 19

'David, did I tell you I was talking to someone the other day who is in exactly the same boat as me?' She took a sip of wine.

'What boat's that, Marty?'

'The immense container shipful of people who have been screwed by Thomas Smeaton, Director of Education, Libraries, Leisure and Culture.'

'Is that his job title?' David laughed. 'No wonder the man upsets people from time to time.'

'Upsets people? He doesn't upset people, he ruins lives. Or takes them.'

David laughed. 'That's a tad melodramatic, don't you think?'

She could tell he'd had a pint or two. Otherwise he'd be choosing his words with more care. Before she could trust herself to answer, she bit down hard on her lip. 'No, I don't think it's melodramatic. I think it's precisely what he did to my life. Ruined it. And what about poor Liz Douglas? He took her life. As surely as if he'd aimed a gun and pulled the trigger. Now her friend Sheila's life is wrecked too. She's in mourning.'

'Would you mourn if something happened to me?'

He'd had more than a couple of pints if he was getting maudlin.

'Don't change the subject. We were talking about Smeaton.'

'Wish we could change the subject,' David muttered, clearly hoping she'd not hear.

'What did you say?' That snappy edge was back in her voice. She couldn't seem to help it.

'I said, you must agree he's got a big job title.'

'That's part of the trouble.'

'What is?'

'The fact he's taken over so many departments.'

'Come on, Marty, be fair. No-one could want that many diverse areas of responsibility.'

'Don't you go feeling sorry for him.'

'I can't help having some sympathy for him. How can he please all the people all the time in a job like that? Trust me, I know what I'm talking about.'

'David, you don't know diddly about this man. He steals people's jobs. Takes over their areas of responsibility and forces them out.'

'Corporate re-structuring, isn't that what they call it? It's all down to funding.'

'That's what he calls it. Other folk call it gathering power, building an empire.'

'Why on earth would he do that?'

Marty could feel her patience running out, like sand in an egg-timer. She tried to hang on to the last few grains. 'Because he's a control freak, that's why. He gets off on being able to wreck other people's lives, I'm telling you.'

'Don't be silly, Marty.'

That was it. The final tiny grain of sand was lost and her temper with it. She stood up, kicked her chair back, slapped her hands on the table and leaned forward.

David recoiled, a look of surprise on his face.

'Don't you EVER tell me I'm being silly when we're discussing that man. What does he know about running a school? Damn all! He's not even a teacher.' She was screaming now. Chance stood cowering in the doorway, clearly anxious. She hated to upset her dog, but there was nothing she could do about it. She could smell the chicken burning in the oven, but she was beyond caring. 'He's a nobody. Do you know where he started? Guess his area of expertise.'

David shrugged.

'Go on, guess.'

'I've no idea, Marty. Why don't you just tell me?'

His long suffering sigh incensed Marty even further.

'Leisure!' she screeched. 'He used to count the fucking deckchairs on Saltcoats fucking beach. That's where he started out, responsible for the amusements at Largs, ice cream vans on Millport. And now he's deciding who gets to run schools, and whether disadvantaged kids get to go canoeing instead of shooting up in some public toilet. Oh no, I forgot. He's the man who decided the public don't need toilets anymore and shut them all. Before he moved to Education and started shutting down bothys and little kids' orchestras.' Her last few words, yelled at the full capacity of her lungs, reverberated in the silence of the kitchen.

Marty stormed to the utility room, grabbed her jacket and said, 'Come on, Chance. Let's get out of here.' She allowed the dog to slide through the gap then slammed the door.

Despite the dark and the damp, Marty felt calmer when she came in from walking her dog; but not calm enough to face David. She made herself a cup of tea and took it through to the computer. She checked her bank balance, read a review of some books and browsed winter fashion, knowing it was all displacement activity. What she wanted to do was contact Joe Docherty. She opened her e-mail account then took her hands off the keyboard, twisting her wedding ring round her finger.

She opened a new message and typed in the address from the little card Joe had given her that first day by the canal.

'*Dear Joe*' she typed, feeling like she was edging out onto a frozen lake. She backspaced and started again. '*Hi Joe*,' Better. '*A quick line to let you know I passed on your contact details to Winker. I expect you'll hear from him.*'

Okay. That was the easy bit done. She spun her ring while she thought about what to type next, if anything, then took another step on to the ice.

'*Enjoyed seeing you.*' Nope. Backspace. Try again. '*Good to see you the other day. Maybe bump into you again. Or* Chance will.' Good, that was the tone she was looking for, chatty and friendly. She sat back in her chair. Her heart was thumping, a little too fast. She touched her face. It was warm, as if she were blushing.

'*Kind regards,*' Too formal. '*Love, Marty.*' Absolutely not. She settled for '*Bye,*' added an M and read the message from the top.

As an afterthought, she typed, '*PS I meant every word I said about Smeaton.*'

She stared at the screen for a moment then deleted the lot. There was no point faffing about, leaving things to chance. Or Chance. If she wanted something to happen, she needed to make it happen.

She moved the cursor to the top of the message and typed.

Hi,

Good to see you. I think there's a reason we met again after all those years.

Someone needs to put a stop to this man before he damages anyone else. There are plenty of folk out there who have good reason to be mad at him but I suspect very few would be willing to do anything about it.

I'm prepared to try. If you'd like to meet and discuss this, reply asap. If you'd rather not get involved, I shall understand. The only thing I ask is that you don't discuss this email with anyone, please.

M

She added her mobile phone number and hit send. It was done.

***

CHAPTER 20

Joe rubbed his hand across his face. His mouth was dry and for the first time in months, he wanted a drink. Try as he might, he couldn't get Smeaton's voice out of his head.

Joe wished he'd never returned the call.

Smeaton had sounded apoplectic on the phone; he was outraged that Joe had gone to the papers with his story of radical cuts to services and widespread bullying of staff. Joe, apparently, was very lucky Smeaton had 'a powerful friend' at the newspaper who had killed the story at birth.

'I could have your job for this, you know. How dare you betray this council? Talk about biting the hand that feeds you? Just what, exactly, did you hope to accomplish?'

Joe cringed to think how pathetic his reply must have sounded, 'I was hoping public pressure might make you change your mind about shutting the bothy.'

'The bothy is shutting, Joe. End of story. The decision has been made and ratified by the council. Get over it. You're already hanging on to your job by the skin of your teeth. Try pulling another stunt like this and you'll be out. Do I make myself clear?'

He had repeated the question and waited until Joe, through gritted teeth, had muttered yes.

Then Smeaton went in for the kill.

'Oh Joe, please take this in the supportive spirit in which it's offered. I was thinking, with your track record, the last thing you need is any kind of investigation into your conduct, if you get my drift.'

Rage had made it almost impossible for him to speak, but Joe had managed to say, 'No. I don't get your drift.'

'Well, we wouldn't want anyone asking why you're so keen

to keep the bothy open, would we? For you and your boys.' Joe had heard him chuckling before the line went dead.

Joe took a glass from the cupboard beside the window and held it under the cold tap. He could resist the urge; he wouldn't let that man drive him to drink again. After Sal died, Joe had stepped right to the edge of that particular abyss, stood with his toes sticking out over the lip. He remembered what a scary place that had been. He'd vowed never to go back there.

The kettle clicked off, reminding him he'd come through to the kitchen to fill his hot water bottle. He found the bed too big and too cold without Sally. The cold he could do something about, at least. He used the last of the boiling water to make himself a cup of malted drink. When he went to put the teaspoon in the dishwasher, he caught sight of his pyjama-clad reflection in the dark window, 'Is this what it's come to?' he asked. 'Water bottles and hot drinks at bedtime? Jesus Christ, kill me now.'

As he passed the study, the spectral glow of the computer screen beckoned him. He hadn't shut it down for the night, something Sally had always nagged him about.

There were three messages in his e-mail inbox. One claimed to be a great deal on Viagra, while the other offered to enhance his manhood by at least eight inches. Joe deleted them both, grinning. The third was from Marty and had been sent only ten minutes earlier. Joe read it twice and wondered if she had been boozing.

He remembered his hot drink, cooling by the minute, and shut down the computer. As the room dimmed to darkness he looked down at the shadowy lane that ran behind his house and thought of Marty's words about meeting Smeaton in a similar place.

'He'd better hope he never meets me in a dark alley. If someone put a dagger in my hand, I swear to God, I'd kill him and walk away.'

Joe shivered, and drew the curtains across the window, shutting out the night and thoughts of killing.

***

CHAPTER 21

Sheila was waiting for her outside their favourite coffee shop. Huddled under an umbrella like a little old lady.

'Hey,' Marty said brightly, 'You should have waited inside. How are you feeling?'

Sheila gave her a tight-lipped smile.

'That bad, huh?'

Sheila nodded, fighting back tears.

'Come on, pal, let's get you a coffee. And maybe a slice of cake to cheer you up.'

'I wish it was that easy, Marty.'

Marty leaned over and patted her arm. 'I'm so sorry for you, Sheila. It must be awful, grieving for your best friend.'

Sheila nodded, unable to speak until she'd blown her nose and wiped her eyes. 'It's not just the grief that's getting me down. I'm so angry I could, aargh!' She made two fists and bit down hard on one set of knuckles.

'Easy,' said Marty. 'that looks painful.'

'The anger is bad enough. What I can't handle is the utter helplessness. Smeaton drove Liz to suicide, I know he did, and there's not a damn thing I can do about it.'

'I know that feeling only too well.'

'I told the police, you know. That he was to blame for her death. I asked them to arrest him.'

'I can't see how they could do that. Liz left a suicide note and didn't the post-mortem show she died of an overdose of prescription drugs?'

'Yes, her mother's. I saw them months ago, in her bathroom cabinet. I asked her, jokingly, if she was hoarding them. She said it was such a palaver nowadays, taking them back to the pharmacy, but she'd get round to it, eventually.

What if she was keeping them for a reason, and I did nothing?'

'How could you do anything, if Liz didn't confide in you?'

Sheila's eyes filled. 'I knew Smeaton's harassment was driving her crazy. Why didn't I make her get rid of those pills?'

'Don't be too hard on yourself, sweetheart. You weren't to know Liz would take them.'

Sheila rummaged in her handbag till she found a fresh tissue and touched it to the corner of her eyes. When she had composed herself and taken a sip of coffee, she said, 'I went to see a solicitor too.'

'What did he say?'

'She, not he.'

'Sorry. What did she say?'

She asked if I had evidence; wanted to know if Liz been keeping a log of the bullying.'

'Had she?'

'I've been on to her to do that for ages.'

'And did she?'

'Unfortunately, I've no idea.' Sheila made a helpless gesture and told Marty about the items that had disappeared from her friend's office.

'And you're sure there were only a few things missing? You don't think the whole place could have been cleared, say, ready for an acting head?'

'No. It looks like nothing has been taken but some files. All the personal stuff is there, photos and so on. I picked this up.' Sheila took out the photo she'd taken from Liz's desk.

Marty smiled at the picture of the two friends. 'This is great. You look so happy. Is that Alton Towers in the background?'

'Yes, we took a group of kids from her school and mine, as part of Liz's anti-bigotry project.'

'Good for her,' said Marty, 'we need lots more of that in Scotland.'

'You did some good work at Moorcroft Academy to cut across the sectarian divide, didn't you?'

'We did and it was effective, to a certain extent, but that's what I mean when I say we need more of it. Something good gets started, people get involved and then, just when it's gaining enough momentum to really make an impact, the money's withdrawn. Why does Smeaton just roll over to please the politicians?'

'Marty, listen, I'm convinced it was Smeaton behind the clearing of files from Liz's office.'

'What makes you say that?'

'I think he's terrified it will come out that his bullying drove Liz to suicide. He was getting rid of evidence. If he's destroyed any log of his bullying and lack of support, there's nothing to prove he was harassing her.'

'You've got her suicide note, don't you?'

'The solicitor says it proves nothing. Without evidence to back it up.'

'Oh, that's awful.'

'Marty, the things he said to her last Friday, and the threats he made? Unforgiveable. And my friend, a beautiful person, took the only escape route she could see.' Sheila brushed away a tear. 'He's to blame for her death. I know he is. But there's not a thing I can do. Is there?'

'There might be.'

'Marty, come on. You, of all people should know. He has all the power. Did Smeaton ever apologise to you for getting it wrong?'

'Did he hell! I was expected to pick up where I left off, as if nothing had happened. Resigning seemed like the best way to make my protest about the lack of support I received from my employers and the hell that man put me through. I know now what a stupid move that was, but at the time it felt like a grand gesture.'

'Didn't I hear something about a petition to get you re-instated?'

'Yes, the kids organised that although I believe some members of staff quietly suggested it to the sixth years. As far as I know, every single teacher and pupil in the school signed it, plus the office staff, janitors, dinner ladies, cleaners, you name it. Oh, and several hundred parents.'

'And it had no effect?'

'Quite the opposite. Smeaton hit back and threatened to discipline the teachers who instigated the protest. Nobody at HQ gave a damn. I'd resigned, end of story. Smeaton got rid of a troublemaker, replaced me with a yes man. I played right into his hands.'

'No wonder you're bitter.'

'Bitter? Oh, don't get me started, Sheila. I'm raging. It's like an acid, eating away at me. But I've decided it's time I did something to make Smeaton pay. I want revenge. For me, for Liz, for all the other poor sods he's harmed. And I want you to help me.'

***

CHAPTER 22

Joe's trip had gone well but the memory of blue skies and crisp dry days vanished when the plane touched down in Glasgow. Ribbons of light reflected on the wet tarmac and passengers hugged themselves against the damp air that slapped them like a cold cloth. What a welcome to Scotland.

He hadn't paid much attention to where he'd left his car, thinking it would be simple to find his huge, beat-up, old Land Rover among smaller cars. When he eventually found it, the driver's door was stuck, as usual. He gave up with a sigh and went round to open the passenger door. He threw his bag into the back and clambered over into the driving seat, narrowly avoiding damage to his privates.

Sal had nagged at him for years to get a new car, but he'd refused, claiming the car suited his lifestyle and was part of his image. He slapped the dashboard and said aloud, 'We're a team, you and me. We'll rust into old age together.'

He turned the key in the ignition and the engine roared like a great beast coming to life. A cloud of exhaust hung smoke-like in the cool, night air. He smelt diesel fumes as he reversed and watched the miasma in his rear mirror. He could almost hear Sally's voice, 'Not very environmentally friendly, Joe, for a man who loves Nature.' She'd been right. It wasn't eco, plus the door was always jamming shut, the hand-brake was dodgy and it would be lucky to pass another MOT but Joe loved this old car. It would break his heart to part with it, one of his last links to Sally.

When the traffic thinned out after Livingston, Joe began to relax and think about the contacts he'd made on his trip and how they'd helped him find exactly what he was looking for. Now he had a plan, all he had to do was sell the flat and get his hands on enough money to execute it.

Third letter P, fourth letter M, and Joe was into his digital bank account. He clicked on the screen that allowed him to see recent transactions. Good, he had enough in his current account to set the ball rolling.

A Google search quickly found Western Union and Joe logged in his e-mail address and password. He had been told to pay in US Dollars which had surprised him although he understood why an international currency might be preferred to the local one. He would have thought euros would be the currency of choice, but then, what did he know? He'd been instructed to make a down payment of two thousand dollars. Western Union's website promised him that his money would be transferred immediately and available for collection tomorrow. He typed the amount into the little box and continued through the process till he got to the security section. Choose a question and answer. It all seemed a bit cloak and dagger but the last thing Joe wanted was for someone else to get their hands on the money and his deal to fall through.

He considered possible questions and rejected several. Manager of the Scottish football team? That was no good; the answer changed as often as the players' shirts. Mother's maiden name? Too easy to find out if someone could be bothered to try. Pet's name? He'd never owned a pet in his life, not even a goldfish. Where did Joe meet Sally? Perfect.

On the next page he checked all the details and stopped, overwhelmed by last minute panic. He took his hand off the mouse and rubbed his face, feeling the bristles on his unshaven jaw. He needed to be sure he was doing the right thing. It would be very difficult to get the money back if he changed his mind. Or at least, very difficult without pissing off people he might not want to piss off. What would Sal say, if she were here?

'You know the answer to that, Joe,' her voice seemed to whisper.

He grabbed the mouse and slid it across its mat. The tiny hand on the screen moved towards the yellow button marked 'send money'. It hovered there and hesitated for one heartbeat. Click. In the silence of the flat it sounded like a gunshot.

***

CHAPTER 23

Joe had decided this was the day he must tell the boys. The council had made a decision to shut the bothy. No more outdoor education and not a thing he could do about it. He'd let them down, big time.

He had arranged to pick them up at eleven o' clock, which meant an early rise for most of them. They were at the bus shelter when he pulled up in the van. He did a quick head count. Good, all present and correct. As usual, Slug was last up the step and on to the minibus. 'Any news of your brother, Slug?'

'Aye, he's goin to be aw right, Sur. Jist bad cuts and bruises, ye know? Ma mammy says she wishes he'd lost a leg cos at least that wid get him oot Afghanistan.'

Joe remained silent while the boys discussed the merits and demerits of losing a leg. Joe was shocked by Slug's mother's comment and by the cold-blooded way the boys discussed the loss of a limb. For Joe that fate would be worse than death.

'Everybody bring some lunch?' he asked, in an effort to change the subject.

'Aye, and ma granda gave me the Thermos flask he had when he worked in the pits.'

Joe moved his head to look at the boys in the rear view mirror. TJ and Dykesy were deep in conversation.

Dangermoose piped up, 'Whit is a Thermos flask anyway?' There was a belt of laughter followed by a decent explanation from Dykesy. Clever wee bugger. Should be in school sitting five Highers.

Someone, maybe Smithy, asked in a very proper upper-class voice, 'So, Liam, tell me, what did you put in your Thermos flask?'

'Irn-bru.'

This was greeted with a gale of guffaws.

'Irn-bru?' screeched Smithy, 'Whit? Oot a bottle?'

'Naw, oot a can.'

This time Joe joined in the mirth, amused by the idea of Liam opening a can of juice and pouring it into his prized vintage Thermos.

'Were you "de-can-ting" it, Liam?' asked Dykesy, but there was no answering laughter from the boys. Dykesy's humour and intelligence was often way beyond his mates. He covered up the unfunny joke by asking, 'Whit are we doin the day, Big Man?'

'We'll need to see what the weather's like when we get up there. Does anyone fancy a spot of canoeing?'

'Def-in-ate-ly!'

The weather had settled to a mild, sunny day when they got to the bothy. The loch shimmered silver in the weak, wintery rays. The surface was calm, for once, no wind tearing it to shreds.

'Okay lads, canoeing it is. Let's get organized.' Moving as one, the boys gathered everything they needed, like a well-drilled army unit. Some of them would thrive in the forces. It was the only escape route from Bankside these days, that or the jail.

Out on the reservoir Joe watched the skill with which the boys paddled and manoeuvred, and savoured a pride in their achievements. With their blue boats, red waterproofs and yellow life preservers, they made a colourful picture on the surface of the graphite loch. Against a diluted blue sky dark firs contrasted with the pale golds of last year's grass and the rusts of withered bracken. Joe thought he'd rarely seen a prettier sight and his heart contracted with emotion. How was he going to take all this away from these kids?

With the canoes pulled clear of the water, the lads skimmed stones from the little gravel beach, shouting insults at each other's efforts.

Joe had planned to tell the lads about the bothy closing after they'd eaten their lunch. He wasn't looking forward to it. 'Anybody fancy going up the hill to eat?' he asked. 'It's a great day to be outside.' To his surprise, everyone agreed, even Slug, who was never keen on delaying food.

When they sat down the boys seemed in good humour, their spirits as high as the hill they'd just climbed.

'Hey boys, ah can see America,' said Dangermoose, pointing west, 'an ah can see hooses. D'ye think that's New York?'

TJ stood up and went to his side. He gave the wee guy a good-natured shove and said, 'That's no America, ya dobber. That's Ireland.'

'Naw, it's no,' shouted Liam. 'I was born in Ireland. Tell them, Sur. That's no Ireland, is it?'

'You're right, Liam, it's not Ireland. It's Arran.'

'Is that the place ye go on the boat fae Ardrossan, Sur?' asked Dykesy.

'It is.'

'Could ye no take us? Ma nana went on a trip wan time. She said it wiz, like, pure beautiful.'

'Your nana was right.' Joe took a deep breath and decided now was as good a time as any. 'Lads, there's something I need to tell you.'

'The Big Man's gonnae take us tae Arran,' said Smithy.

'Gonnae shut up and let Big Joe talk?'

Joe could hardly bear to look at them. He thought of the line from a song he loved - I started out with nothing and I still got most of it left. Now he was having to take something from kids who had nothing.

Dykesy prompted him, 'What is it, Big Man? Ye're no leavin, are ye?'

The other boys picked up on it. 'Aw no, don't, Sur.' Then one of the boys started a football chant, and the others joined in. 'One Joe Docherty. There's only One Joe Docherty.'

Joe couldn't help smiling. He shook his head. No, he wasn't leaving. At least not yet. Joe let them sing, enjoying the moment. When they finished, his eyes were filled with tears. He was turning into a right softie since Sally died.

Joe decided these boys would get their trip to Arran. Even if he had to pay every penny himself. They deserved it.

The lump in his throat made it hard to swallow and Joe barely tasted his sandwiches. All he could think about was the news he was due to deliver and the effect it would have. When every scrap of food had gone and the last dregs had been poured from Liam's Thermos, Joe said, 'Listen up, lads. I've got good news and bad news.'

He looked at the expectant faces, some gaunt with poverty, Sluggo's fat and childish, Dykesy's streetwise beyond his years. What shone from every face was the trust they had in him.

'Okay,' he hesitated, 'the good news is … I'm gonna take you lot to Arran for a day. My treat. I'm paying.'

When the cheering died down, Liam asked, 'Sur, whit's the bad news?'

***

CHAPTER 24

David came into the kitchen dangling a bunch of keys from his pinkie, looking as if he'd found the Holy Grail. 'Got them,' he said, stating the dazzlingly obvious. 'Right, I'll be off. I should be back about five.' He stood at her side, like Chance, and waited for her to respond.

'Okay, bye,' she said, staring at the newspaper. When she sensed he hadn't moved, she looked up.

'Kiss?' he suggested.

She offered her cheek and he plopped a wet kiss on it. Something inside her shuddered but she pinned on a smile. 'Bye then.'

Still he didn't go. What was the man waiting for?

'Could you take my dinner suit to the dry cleaners, if you've nothing else to do? I need it for the Gentlemen's Dinner on Friday night, remember?'

'As you so rightly say, I've nothing else to do. Yes, I'll see to it.'

'You meeting Sheila?'

'Might be.'

'Righty-oh. Have a good day.'

Chance came and sat at her feet, then laid his head on her knee. Raising his fluffy eyebrows, he looked straight into her eyes. She leaned over and kissed him on the nose, with considerably more affection than she had managed for her husband.

Joe answered on the third ring.

'Joe, it's Marty. Did you get my email?'

'Oh hi, good morning to you too.'

'Sorry. Good morning. And sorry to ring so early. I wasn't

sure you'd be up.'

'Not only up, but been for my run.'

'Impressive.' Marty relaxed, pleased that there didn't seem to be any tension between them. 'Have you had time to look at the Herald this morning?'

'No, I was about to sit down with a coffee and have a read.'

'Look at page four.'

Marty could hear the sound of pages turning. 'Do you see it?'

'Head-teacher's suicide blamed on inspectors. Is that what you mean?' He read aloud, '*Elizabeth Douglas was found dead at her home three weeks ago. Miss Douglas, who lived alone, was Head-teacher at Cadenhead Primary School, where pupils and teachers have been offered bereavement counselling. One pupil, Shevonne Haggerty, described Miss Douglas as 'a lovely lady, like a granny but more brainy' and Facebook messages echoed her sentiments: 'To the best teechir ever. RIP Mrs Douglas. We will never forget you.' There is speculation in the community that Miss Douglas feared the school was due to undergo a full inspection in the near future but a spokesman for the local authority would not confirm this. The school was last inspected four years ago when inspectors identified the following key strengths: the high quality of leadership provided by the head-teacher, Miss Douglas, and the strong partnerships with parents and the community. A spokesperson for the main teachers' Union said that teachers and head-teachers are under more pressure than at any time in the profession's history. She declined to comment on individual cases.*'

Joe stopped reading and Marty held her breath, waiting to see what he would say next. In the silence she heard him sigh. Then he said one word, 'And?'

'I know about this woman, Joe. She was a force for good. She was building bridges over the sectarian divide that blights this part of the world. She believed we need to start when children are young, before the bigots poison their minds.'

'And?'

Marty swore she could feel her blood pressure rising and her patience dwindling. 'And Smeaton didn't seem to recognise any of the good she was doing. Instead he was constantly hounding her to stop parents parking on the zigzags, make sure the school buses didn't keep their engines running - crap like that. He failed to back her up against ignorant parents who kicked up hell because their out of control kids weren't allowed to behave like thugs in the playground. Sheila told me one man was even running a smear campaign on Facebook. What did Smeaton do to help? Nothing. Just his usual 'No smoke without fire' routine that we've all heard. He threatened her with the inspectors. That was the straw that broke poor Liz's back.'

Joe said nothing.

'Joe, are you there?'

'Yes, I'm listening. Marty, did you phone me up to ask me if I'd seen this article?'

She took another precarious step over the ice. 'I phoned you up to ask if you'll help me stop this man.'

'Stop him how, Marty?'

'I haven't worked that bit out yet, but someone has to do something before he wrecks any more lives. I thought I could count on you.'

'Don't think so, Marty. I really don't need the hassle, to be honest. You'll have to find someone else to join you on your mission.'

***

CHAPTER 25

Joe was thinking he should have stuck to his guns and was wondering if he should leave before Marty got there, when he saw the dog. Chance was prancing on skinny, ballet dancer's legs around the edge of the pond. He stopped beside a group of small children who were feeding the ducks. Close enough to have a nosy at what they were doing, but not close enough to scare them. Joe heard a voice say, 'Doggy, Mummy.'

'Yes, he's a nice doggy, isn't he?'

Chance appeared to take the words as a compliment. As Joe watched, the dog sat and offered a delicate paw in acknowledgement.

Then two things happened at the same time. Marty appeared on the scene and Chance dived into the pond after a piece of bread. Ducks scattered in all directions, honking their outrage. A little girl took fright and started screaming and another mummy grabbed her toddler and clutched him to her chest. When Marty called his name, Chance bounded to her side and shook the water from his coat, spraying everyone within wetting distance.

Marty spotted Joe, probably heard him laughing. Together they found a table at the café and sat down. Chance, now on a lead, skulked under Marty's chair, his eyebrows twitching as he tried to work out what he'd done wrong this time.

'Poor Chance,' Joe said.

'Poor Chance? He'll be the death of me, this dog.'

'Sure you're okay to sit outside? It's cool but quite nice in the sun.'

'Might as well make the most of it, while it lasts. And we won't be overheard out here.'

A young waitress brought their coffee and Marty took a sip,

put the mug down and said, 'Thanks for agreeing to meet me, Joe.'

'Against my better judgment, by the way. I almost did a runner before Chance distracted me.'

With her voice lowered, Marty said, 'Okay, I'm going to cut to the chase. Here's the plan. We abduct him.'

'Abduct, as in kidnap?'

'Yes. Kidnap and frighten the living daylights out of him. Can you think of a better way to take revenge?'

Actually he could, but said nothing.

'It's still vague,' she admitted.

'It's not just vague, Marty, it's crazy,' he said. 'It won't work.'

'Oh, it'll work alright. I'll make it work and once we get the right people to join us, we'll have assembled so much talent, we can't fail.'

Joe tore the top off three little sugar sachets and emptied them into his coffee. 'This is a pretty outrageous thing you're suggesting. How do you plan to get these "right people" on board? What if you approach the wrong person and they go to the police?'

Marty looked around, as if checking for eavesdroppers, but the mid-afternoon buzz was over. 'I've thought about that. And you're right, we can't say to any random punter, "Hey, we've got this great idea. We're not entirely sure it's legal, but hey-ho, are you in anyway?"'

Joe snorted and said, in a low voice, 'Not sure it's legal? I'm damned sure it's il-legal. Very illegal.'

'Yeah, but we don't need to tell folk the whole plan right away, do we? Not until we're sure they are rock-solid dependable.'

'What whole plan? You've not even got half a plan, it seems to me.'

Joe shook his head again. This was the last thing he needed. To get involved in some madcap scheme when he had enough life-changing plans of his own to worry about. He had mapped out the future and there was no place in it for this crazy woman and her scheming, no matter how easy she made it sound. 'Like they say on Dragon's Den, "it's an interesting project, but I'm not investing. I'm out." Sorry, Marty.'

'Please don't say no without taking some time to think about it.'

'Okay, I've thought about it. No.'

'Joe, we can't let him get away with hurting any more people. Not when we have the power to do something.'

'That's just the thing. We don't have any power.' He told her about his attempt to whistle-blow and how badly it had ended.

'Just because that didn't work doesn't mean to say we can't try something else.'

'This is personal for you, Marty.'

'Of course it's personal,' she said, her voice rising indignantly. 'How much more personal can you get than depriving someone of their livelihood, their reason for getting up in the morning, their persona, their role in society, their usefulness. How can it not be fucking personal?'

Joe heard someone tutting and looked round. A white-haired couple at a nearby table glared at Marty, making evident their disapproval of her bad language. He turned back to Marty and raised his eyebrows at her.

'Sorry,' she muttered, her eyes on the coffee dregs she'd been stirring for ten minutes, 'but no wonder. It's enough to make anyone swear.' When she looked up at him, he could see she was disappointed in his lack of enthusiasm for her plan. 'Will you at least give it some thought?' she said. 'I need your help.'

'Sorry, Marty. The answer's no. And I don't think you should contact me again.'

***

CHAPTER 26

The boys' reaction to Joe's bad news had been as anticipated. Not the real bad news that the bothy was shutting. He didn't have the heart to drop that bombshell. He'd chickened out of that one.

Instead he told them that outdoor activities were to be limited from now on.

The boys had groaned. When he told them they had to complete five indoor sessions to merit one outdoors, the groans had turned to curses and expletives.

'Nae chance!' said Dykesy. 'Sittin in a classroom? No fuckin way, man.'

So Joe did not expect a good turn out today. The first indoor session.

When nobody had turned up by half past eleven he was about to give up and leave. He was packing up the handouts he'd prepared when he heard voices in the corridor.

Dykesy was dragging TJ by the arm. 'M'oan, TJ.'

Joe sighed. Only two boys, and half an hour late. The project was doomed if this was to be a typical turnout. Smeaton would win an easy victory. There would be no boys to take to the bothy and therefore no reason to keep it open.

Dykesy, as usual, appeared to be spokesman. TJ stood behind, his head hanging as he picked at a scab on his hand.

'Sur, TJ needs tae talk.' Punching the other boy on the arm, he said gently, 'G'oan, TJ, tell the big man whit happened.'

TJ shook his lowered head and said nothing.

'Ye need tae, TJ, and ye'll have tae dae it quick.'

Still TJ said nothing.

'Don't be a dobber, TJ. Sur's your only chance. Ask him.'

'Ask me what?'

'He needs yer help, Sur. Big time. TJ, ah'll wait outside. Aw right, mate?'

'Come on, TJ,' said Joe. He touched the boy's elbow. 'Let's sit down and you can tell me what's troubling you.'

'Ah stabbed a guy.'

Joe hoped he had heard wrong. 'What did you say?'

As if it had taken all his energy to say it once, TJ shook his head, then blurted, 'Last night. Ah stabbed a guy.'

Joe laughed nervously and TJ's head jerked up. The boy's eyes were red-rimmed and bloodshot with crying. This was no joke.

'Ah owed him money. For drugs. Ah'm clean noo but ah still owed the basturt an he wouldnae let it go. Tells me tae meet him last night an when ah turn up without the cash, he pulls a knife on me.'

The boy started to sob, then sniffed loudly and swiped his hand across his face. 'Ah never meant for it tae happen, Sur, ah swear oan ma mammy's grave. Ah wis jist defendin masel an the next thing the knife's in his neck. Ah don't even ken whit happened. Ah swear tae God. It wis that fast.'

'What did you do?'

TJ looked as if Joe had just asked the world's most stupid question.

'Ah legged it. Whit else could ah dae?'

Joe chewed his lip.

'Sur, will ye help me? Please?'

TJ looked about five years old, pleading, but without hope, as if he knew he was asking too much.

'TJ, your fingerprints will be on the knife.'

'Naw, ah hud ma gloves oan. It wis pure baltic last night.'

He held out his hands in their cheap knitted gloves. The left one had a slash and the right a stain that could have been blood or ketchup. Joe's forensic experience was too limited to tell.

'Don't you think you should maybe get rid of the gloves?'

The boy looked down at his hands in horror. 'Aye. Goadsake, man.' He stripped off the gloves and stuffed them in his pocket.

'Give them to me. I'll dispose of them. What about the rest of your clothes?'

'Dykesy got rid. We forgot the gloves.' He shook his head as if he could not believe their stupidity.

Joe said, with genuine sadness, 'I don't see what else I can do to help, TJ. I'm sorry.'

'Ma alibi.'

'What?'

'Ma alibi. Dykesy says you could be ma alibi. You an' him.'

'How, son? How can I be your alibi?'

'Jist say ah wis wi' you last night. Up at the bothy. You, me and TJ.'

Joe thought about it. It was crazy. But it wasn't impossible.

'Did anybody see you last night?'

'Naw, jist ma da an' he wis aff his face oan cheap voddie.'

'Will he remember?'

'Nae chance, he wis passed oot.'

Joe's head was buzzing. This was exactly the kind of situation he'd warned Smeaton about. This was what happened when kids with no hope got involved with drugs. Why couldn't Smeaton see that?

Joe knew he should tell this lad to go to the police, or call them himself.

'Maybe you should own up, TJ.'

The boy looked as desperate as a drowning pup. And about as vulnerable. 'Ah telt Dykesy this wis a mental idea. I said you'd have to go straight tae the cops.'

'I won't TJ, I promise you.' Joe's hand went to his heart. 'But I can't give you an alibi.'

The kid got to his feet and sent Joe a quick, apologetic smile. 'Sorry, Sur. It was stupid tae ask.'

As TJ slouched to the door like a condemned man, Joe battled his conscience.

'Wait!' he called, just before the door swung shut.

The boy turned back, tears rolling down his face. 'What?'

'Tell Dykesy to come in. We need to get our stories straight.'

***

CHAPTER 27

Her number was still in his phone. She answered immediately. As if she'd been waiting.

'Joe?' she said.

'I'd like to hear more about this revenge plan of yours.'

'Are you in?'

'Might be.'

'What made you change your mind?'

'Circumstances you don't need to know about. Suffice it to say, I fear for those boys of mine if that bothy gets taken away from them. Who else is involved?'

'At this stage, only Sheila.'

'Who's Sheila?'

'Someone I can trust who has a very good reason to be on board. Remember Liz Douglas?'

'That woman who committed suicide?'

'Yes. Sheila was her closest friend. She found Liz's body. Can you imagine? Thing is, she hoped something good might come out of the tragedy, that Smeaton would realise how much damage he has caused and back off council staff.'

'And?'

'Well, has he?'

'Not that I can see. He's still hounding me about the bothy. I'm sick of it.'

'You're not the only one he's still bullying, according to Sheila. I'm sure we don't know the half of it.'

'So Sheila's in. Anyone else in mind?'

'There are a few people I know whose lives he has made hell. Remember that lovely guy he appointed to Castledene Academy? Great depute head but no way was he up to the responsibility of running a big secondary school, but Smeaton gave him the job. Everyone said it was a political appointment, a puppet for Smeaton to control and hold up to the rest of us as an example. Six months later, poor guy's ill. He's still off work so I was thinking of him. Another two of my former colleagues are off sick at the moment; they'll have plenty of time on their hands.'

'Hold it, off sick with what?'

'Well Jimmy McCracken had a breakdown, caused by Smeaton's interference in the way he ran his school. And Margaret Boyle has been treated for depression, I understand, due to work-related stress. They're both good people, trustworthy.'

'I know McCracken, he's sound and I'm sure Ms Boyle is too, but I don't think you should involve them, Marty. We need a team that is robust in mind and body.'

'It's not an expedition up the Amazon.'

'Come on, don't play games. If you're going to do this, and if I'm going to get involved, it has to be organized as well as any Amazon expedition. In fact, better, because it needs to be kept secret. Plus, we'll all get the jail if we're caught. Don't forget that.'

'I take your point.'

'Look, Marty, you, me and this Sheila. Why can't we manage it on our own? The fewer folk we have involved the better.'

'Three of us. Is that enough?'

'It's enough to get started and I've got the ideal place for us to have our first meeting. Can you and Sheila be on the road to the castle tonight at six? I'll be in a very ancient Land Rover.'

*

It had been dark for almost two hours when Joe turned off the main road. Days were short at this time of the year.

Up ahead he could see the red tail lights of a car parked in one of the laybys. He slowed as he approached. The driver's door opened and Marty stepped into his headlights, dressed for the hills.

'Hi,' he said. 'Want to jump in the back?'

Another woman joined Marty in the back seat. He didn't recognise her.

'Joe, this is Sheila,' was all Marty said. He could tell she was nervous.

'I know Joe,' said Sheila. 'Don't you help out with transport up at Bankside, bringing kids to the panto rehearsal?'

'Yeah, sometimes, Big Sean talked me into it, but don't let Smeaton know, for God's sake. That's strictly off the record. I pay for the diesel myself, by the way. In case you think I'm ripping off the council or anything.'

'Well, thanks. It's appreciated. Don't suppose I could talk you into being in the chorus?'

'I'll sing to you for the rest of the journey and, trust me, you'll wish you'd never asked that question.' The tense atmosphere evaporated into laughter.

'Bothy's up here a couple of miles,' said Joe. 'Afraid the road gets a bit bumpy after a while.'

'Won't it look suspicious, us being here at this time of night?'

'You wouldn't want to leave your car in that layby too often, but nobody will bat an eyelid at this old girl heading for the bothy.' He thumped the dashboard. 'Very few people live up here and they're used to me coming and going.'

The two women said nothing as the old Landy made its way along the side of the loch. A sliver of moon was just enough to scatter a line of sparkle across the surface. The distant city cast a pale orange glow to the sky that silhouetted the hills on the far side.

'I've never been here before,' said Sheila.

'Then you've never lived.'

'I didn't even know Loch Etrin existed before the Moorcroft kids came to the bothy for Duke of Edinburgh expeditions,' said Marty.

'We're lucky to have it,' said Joe, then corrected himself. 'We were lucky, I should say.'

'It's definitely going to shut?'

'Yip. The great man has decreed.'

'Right, ladies,' said Joe, hauling on the handbrake. 'Jump out, if you can get your doors to open. She's a temperamental old bugger, this one.' He leaned over and gave Marty's door a thump and she got out.

Sheila took a deep breath. 'Smell that air, Marty. It's fresher than any air I ever breathed.'

'That's what the boys always say too. "Disnae smell like this in Bankie, Sur." Pretty special, isn't it?' Joe unlocked the bothy and ushered them inside. He pulled the curtains across the little windows and hit the light switch.

'Electricity,' said Sheila.

'What did you think? Candles? Oil lamps?'

The women laughed.

'I can even make you a coffee, if you like. Though it's powdered milk.'

'I'll pass,' said Marty, taking a notepad and pencil out of her bag. She put them on the table and sat down.

'Sheila?' said Joe, holding up a plastic mug and a jar of instant coffee.

Sheila shook her head and took a seat next to Marty. 'No, thanks.' She cleared her throat. 'I'm quite keen to get started actually. I want to know how I can help. I'm prepared to do anything,' she said, turning towards Joe. 'My best friend committed suicide, perhaps you heard? Liz Douglas?'

'Yes, I heard, it's tragic,' said Joe, 'and I'm very sorry for your loss, Sheila. I believe she was a fine woman.'

'Thanks. Just so you know, I hold Smeaton one hundred per cent responsible for her death.' Sheila's lips trembled as she spoke. She clamped them tight, then made a brave attempt at a smile. 'I don't think he should get away with it.'

Joe saw the anger in her eyes and something else. Something strong that told him she was trustworthy. 'He won't. Don't you worry.'

Marty said, 'I think it would be a good idea to share our

expectations. Shall I start?'

'Go for it.'

'I'm not sure how we go about it, yet, but I want to do something that makes Smeaton pay. Really pay for what he's done. I need revenge. Pure and simple.'

'Well,' said Sheila, 'I can understand, but for me, it's got to be something that makes him realise what a bastard he's been. Pardon my language.'

Marty spluttered with laughter. 'Oh, Sheila, you're priceless. You think that's bad? You should hear what I call him.'

Sheila went on, 'I think I'm so angry because what he's doing to people is criminal, and yet he gets away with it.'

'Some crimes, however evil, go unpunished.'

'Because they're unpunishable, it seems,' said Sheila. 'I've done my best. The law isn't interested.'

'I'm going to be completely honest here,' said Joe.

'I think we have to be.'

'Revenge is what I'm after too. The man's determined to take away the only thing those boys of mine have got going for them. You should have seen the faces on them when I broke the news the bothy was shutting and there was no money to run the bus or pay for outings.'

The others shook their heads in sympathy.

'Would you believe some of them offered to get him beaten up for me? According to Dykesy, one phone call would sort it and our man will wake up in hospital.'

Sheila gasped. 'Were you tempted?'

'I've heard worse suggestions.'

Sheila said, 'Revenge is kind of a powerful word. A bit scary, if I'm honest.'

Marty stared at her. 'What did you have in mind, Sheila?'

'As I say, I'd like to do something that would make him look at himself and the way he treats people. Something that would make him change.'

Joe snorted. 'Change? How do you make someone change who gets off on wrecking other folk's lives? The man has no conscience whatsoever.'

'Doesn't everyone have a conscience?'

'Not Smeaton. He's had a conscience by-pass.'

'Or he was born without one.'

'You might be right,' said Sheila. 'I was called in to HQ yesterday. No warning, just a phone call from Carole to say whatever I had on, I'd to prioritise a meeting with Mr Smeaton.'

'Did you go?' asked Marty.

'What do you think?' Sheila gave her a look. 'And you know what it was about?'

Joe said, 'About him, likely. It usually is.'

'You're not far wrong. It was about my attitude. He doesn't feel we're "on the same page at the moment". When I asked him what he meant by that, he accused me of being rude at the last primary heads' meeting.'

'What?'

'Apparently, I didn't make eye contact with him, I constantly looked at my phone or my iPad. I was making notes, by the way. Eventually he said my behaviour and body language had caused concern.'

'Did you challenge him on it?'

'Yes. He wasn't pleased that I "didn't engage with the discussions". It seems I showed "a complete lack of respect" from start to finish.'

'And there we have it,' said Joe. 'All about him.'

'It was as if he was trying to goad me into a reaction. Tears, anger, I don't know. But I would not give him the satisfaction. So he hit me where it hurt.'

Marty gasped. 'He mentioned Liz?'

Sheila nodded slowly, her eyes filling.

'Bastard,' said Joe.

'Said he'd been concerned about her mental health for some time. Had suggested she take a sabbatical, offered her support from Occupational Health etc. A bunch of lies.'

'Covering his own arse.'

'Of course he was. He mentioned what a pity it would be if my performance were to be compromised because of her death.'

'What does he mean by that?'

'It was a threat. Veiled, but still a threat. And it's absolutely imperative that there should be nothing more about her "unfortunate demise" in the newspapers and certainly nothing that suggested a link with any officer of Logiemuir Council.'

'Himself, in other words? How did you keep your hands off him?'

'By sitting on them. Then he dismissed me.' Sheila snapped her fingers in the air. 'Like that. "You may go," he said, like I was in the presence of royalty.'

'The man's lost the plot.'

'You think? I was shaking with rage when I came out. Wee Carole took her lunchbreak early so she could take me over to The Tea Set to calm down. She knows exactly what he's like. She sees the damage every day.'

'We have to stop him,' said Marty. 'This bullying and harassment has gone too far.'

'It won't bring Liz back,' said Sheila. 'Or undo the damage he's doing to dozens of good people. Half the primary heads are on some kind of anti-depressant, it seems. Or their health has broken down because of stress. These are good, professional people doing a difficult job.'

'I know you don't like the word revenge, Sheila, but that's what they deserve and we're the ones who are going to get it for them,' said Marty. She held her hand in the air, palm out.

'Sheila, are you in?'

Sheila slapped it. 'I'm in.'

'Joe?'

***

110

CHAPTER 28

S heila took the calendar down from its hook in the kitchen and turned the page. A jolly snowman held up a banner wishing her a Merry Christmas. It would be here before she knew it. She noted a dental appointment and counted up the number of days till the end of term. She would be glad to get a break.

In the weeks since Liz's funeral Sheila had been trying to get on with her life. She had treated herself to a new hairstyle and blown her last three months' salary on trendy clothes. School was hectic with the build up to Christmas and all that it entailed, but she was coping.

Itchybella rehearsals in Bankside were going from strength to strength and were the highlight of her life, full of laughter and fun. In between rehearsals, she and Marty were managing dozens of helpers who were making costumes and painting scenery. At these happy times she wondered if she might, eventually, be able to come to terms with her loss.

Then there were her clandestine meetings to look forward to. She and Marty had decided they needed at least one other person on board and Joe had finally agreed. Wee Carole had been approached last week, Sheila taking the chance to speak to her after a meeting at HQ. Carole had looked shocked, then intrigued, then excited. She had tentatively agreed to come to their next meeting in a city centre bar. Sheila hoped she would turn up.

In the bedroom, Sheila smiled at her reflection, admiring her new look. With her greying hair dyed russet brown she looked years younger and the funky short cut definitely made her cheekbones more prominent. Of course, the make-up helped. She'd started wearing it to hide her blotchy face in the days after Liz's death. There was no doubt she'd let herself go over the last few years, a spinster teacher sliding, with Liz, into middle-age.

She gave the wardrobe door a nudge and watched it glide out of the way. At one end of the rail hung her school clothes, a mass of brown, beige and cream. At the other were her off duty clothes, fleeces, denims and pastel-shaded t-shirts. Sheila clattered the hangers along to join the frumpy school clothes on the left and took out one of her new outfits. She'd blown a small fortune in one Saturday afternoon, tempted by a personal shopper in Fraser's and the high-end shops in Buchanan Street. Well, why not?

Glasgow was at its dreariest, despite the glitz and glitter of the Christmas displays in shop windows. There was a drizzle falling, not quite heavy enough to be called rain but wet enough to soak those who ventured out in it. Sheila made a careful run for the door of the pub. It was a long time since she'd worn heels this high.

A loud wolf-whistle, followed by 'Any change, ma'am?' made her look down at the pavement where a young man sat, lotus position, huddled under a wilting sheet of cardboard. An empty Costa cup sat between his crossed legs and a sorrowful pitbull lay at his side. 'Don't worry aboot the dug, ma'am, he'll no touch ye,' he reassured her as she bent to put a donation in his cup. 'You have a nice night now.' He whistled again as she walked away making Sheila wonder if it was stupid to feel flattered.

Opening the pub door she was met with a simultaneous blast of hot air and Christmas music. She scanned the bar and then the booths but she seemed to be first to arrive.

They had chosen a different pub from last time, agreeing it would be better not to risk being seen together too often, especially in the same place.

For a week night, the bar was busy and filling up fast. Maybe something to do with the Karaoke that was due to start later. She bought herself a white wine and a gin for Marty then chose a table in the far corner and sat down to wait for the others.

Carole arrived first, looking very flustered. Before Sheila could attract her attention, Joe came in, pulling down the hood of his waterproof. He greeted Carole at the bar, ordered some drinks and sent her to join Sheila. As he wandered over towards them, a glass in each hand, he smiled at Sheila and said to Carole, 'Diet Coke for you, Madame?'

'Evening, Sheila,' he said, his eyes twinkling. 'No sign of our esteemed leader? You're looking good, by the way.'

'I've just told her she looks twenty years younger dressed like that.'

Sheila was still smiling at their compliments when Marty appeared, apologising for being late. She too commented on Sheila's new look and said, 'Maybe it's time I had a makeover.'

With a quick glance round to make sure no one was listening, Marty said, 'Right, let's get down to business.' Between sips of gin she asked how everyone was feeling. Then, as casually as if she were organising a day out, she revealed the details of her plan.

'Well, what do you think?'

Carole rubbed at her forehead. 'Hang on, Marty. Am I missing something? It sounds like you're planning to kidnap him.'

'I prefer to think of it as an abduction. Less criminal.'

Joe snorted but didn't sound amused. It was always hard to tell what Joe was thinking. He had seemed at ease, enjoying his drink while Marty spoke, nodding every so often, as if he approved of what he was hearing.

Sheila said. 'That's some plan, Marty. Have you thought about how you'll get him to cooperate?'

'Yes,' said Marty, 'We'll have to drug him. I'm thinking Rohypnol.'

'The date-rape drug?'

'Yes, if we can get it.'

'Jeeso, serious stuff.'

'And where are we going to take him?' asked Joe.

'That's where you come in, Joe. Since our visit, I've been

thinking we could use the bothy. You know, that big part at the back where you keep the canoes and everything? You should see this place, Carole, it's ideal, remote yet accessible. Very few folk know it's there and, unfortunately for Joe and his boys, it will soon be vacant.'

Sheila fiddled with her hair. 'This is going to take a lot of organization, not to mention time. I've kind of got my hands full at the minute, what with the panto, and school. Christmas is mental for me.'

'Don't worry about that, Sheila. There's no hurry. I reckon we've got almost four months to get everything in place.'

'Okay then, count me in. After New Year, I'll have more time.'

Joe said, in a very decisive voice, 'Count me in too.' He shrugged. 'I've got nothing to lose. And the bothy is a great idea, Marty.'

Carole seemed to be studying her glass which she was moving in circles on the table. 'I'm flattered you trusted me with your plan, but to be honest, it's all getting a bit heavy for me, kidnapping, sorry, abducting, if that's even a word, and drugs and all. Sorry. I hate to let you all down but I'd no idea.'

'You don't have to apologise, Carole. It would be great to have your help but we'll understand if you don't want to get involved.' Marty put her hand on the young woman's arm and the glass stopped circling.

'I've got too much to lose. My job for a start.' She turned to Sheila. 'You see, John and I are desperate to have a baby and things haven't worked out so far. If we can get enough money together we're going to the States for treatment, but we need to save every penny.'

Sheila leaned over and gave Carole's hand a squeeze.

'Also, there's another reason. Our consultant has advised me to keep my stress levels as low as possible.'

'How will you manage that, working for Smeaton?'

'I'm used to him. Most of the time, it doesn't bother me that he's foul-tempered and impossible to please. But I hate it when he's cruel to lovely folk like Liz Douglas. That's why I'm here.'

Marty said, 'We understand, Carole. Thanks for even considering helping.'

'Oh, don't get me wrong, I'd still like to help, but I can't be directly involved in what you're going to do to him. It would be too stressful. Sorry.' Her face brightened. 'Anyway, I might be pregnant by then.'

Sheila said kindly, 'I hope so, Carole. You'll make a wonderful mum.'

'Look,' said Joe. 'I've got a suggestion. There might be a way for you to be out and still be in.'

'Sorry? I don't get you.'

'We're going to need someone on the inside.'

Marty nodded, 'I hadn't thought of that.'

'What I'm thinking is, you could feed us information about his habits, his diary commitments and so on. What do you think?'

Before Carole could answer, Sheila said, 'There's something else Carole could do to help.' Turning to the young woman beside her, she said, 'I bet you could feed information from us to him.'

'I see where this is going,' said Marty. 'That's inspired. You could be our spy, Carole. Only if you want to, mind.'

'If you think it would help.'

'It will definitely help, and the beauty of it is, he'll never suspect a thing. Can you make a start by finding out his weekly routine?'

'To help us build up a picture of his hobbies, his social life and what have you,' said Joe.

'That won't take long. He has no hobbies and apart from going to church, he has a non-existent social life, as far as I can tell. He seems to live for those two things, the church and his work.'

'He's a Christian and yet he spends his time ruining the lives of good, innocent people?' said Joe. 'How does that work?'

'He goes to Mass, he confesses his sins, his conscience is

115

clear,' said Sheila. 'You know how it works, Joe.'

'Then he's free to start harassing and bullying again. Seems wrong, doesn't it?' said Marty. 'I've been thinking about that a lot.' She gnawed on a fingernail. 'You know what? I'm wondering if his devout Catholicism could also be his Achilles Heel. The missing piece of the puzzle.'

Without warning, the lights went down, the crowd hushed and the Karaoke was kicked off by the oldest Spice Girls Sheila had ever seen. As they belted out 'Wannabe', the noise level in the pub rose. It became clear that there would be no more planning tonight and no one looked surprised when Carole reached for her coat and shouted, 'I've got to go.'

Joe emptied his glass and said loudly, 'Time I was heading off too. Tomorrow's another indoor meeting with the boys. Smeaton's brainchild. Five indoor sessions for every outdoor session. That's what he calls a fair compromise.'

Marty choked on her gin. 'What in heaven's name are you supposed to do with boys like that, if you have to keep them indoors?' asked Marty. 'They can't cope in a classroom. That's the reason they're excluded from school and on your program.'

'If they turn up, I've to lecture them on health and safety. Discuss the various types of equipment we use. Get them to keep a nutrition diary. There's a joke. And you should see the documentation I'm supposed to complete. I've to fill in risk assessment forms for everything. I think he's trying to bury me under paperwork.'

'Do you think the boys will come to these meetings?'

'No, I think it's a clever way for Smeaton to justify shutting us down for good.'

Joe sounded more bitter than Sheila had heard him.

'If the boys don't come to these health and safety lectures, I'm not allowed to take them out on the loch or the hills. And if there are no boys, there's no job for Joe. Simple.'

Marty shook her head. 'You have to admire the man's cunning.'

***

116

CHAPTER 29

Saturday had gone by in a blur, spent at Liz's helping to clear the house. A niece Sheila had never met before was in charge of the whole sad business and Sheila was glad to lend a hand. She'd hoped it might help her heal and move on, but bagging up Liz's clothes to send to the local hospice shop was one of the most depressing tasks she'd ever undertaken. Each cotton top and summer dress reminded her of holidays in the sun. Liz's prized Gore-Tex walking jacket brought back memories of every Munro they'd bagged together. Worst of all, for some reason, was the daft Christmas jumper with the two huge puddings that sat right on Liz's ample breasts. Sheila remembered the first time Liz had worn it, LED cherries flashing like electronic nipples. 'Do you think I could get away with this at the school Christmas party?' she'd asked, in mock innocence, just as Sheila took a mouthful of Prosecco. They'd shed tears of joy that night, once she'd stopped choking.

Now it was Sunday again and it was Sheila's turn to deliver the flowers from St Gerard's. There were a lot this morning, left by yesterday's bridal party.

'We've got enough for at least four bunches, Sheila,' said Father Rafferty. 'Would you like me to help with the deliveries?'

'Not at all, Father, but thanks for offering. It looks like two bunches are going to the same place and one of the others is on my way home, so I'll be passing anyway.'

Sometimes this job took ages and sometimes it was an easy task. It depended on the reason for the flowers being sent. If the recipient was ill, the flowers were often handed in with a note saying, 'Get well wishes from all at St Gerard's', but if there had been a bereavement, Sheila preferred to go in and offer her condolences in person. Sometimes there was no need to stay long and that was the case at the first address on her list.

An elderly man answered the door. Sheila said, 'I've brought you some flowers from St Gerard's and I wanted to say we're all very sorry for your loss.'

The old boy eyed her suspiciously then took the flowers without a word. Before he shut the door, he said, 'She's no great loss to me, hen. I never liked her much.'

Sheila stood on the doorstep for a moment, unsure whether she wanted to laugh or cry. She settled for a smile and a shake of the head. 'Only in Scotland,' she muttered, as she walked down the garden path.

Her next port of call was the big retirement complex by the cemetery. What a place to build a home for the elderly.

As she waited in the front hall for someone to come and let her through the security door, Sheila wondered for the hundredth time why these places all smelt the same. A heady mixture of boiled cabbage and pee.

A kind-looking woman, with a badge that identified her as Doreen, let her in.

'Hello, I've got some flowers from the church for Miss McIvor and,' Sheila checked the name on the second bunch, 'Mrs Scobie.'

'Oh, those look beautiful. Do I smell freesias? They're my favourite, freesias.'

How could someone with such a strong sense of smell bear to work in an old folks' home? She nearly asked but decided the better of it. 'They're lovely, aren't they? We had a wedding in church yesterday and the bride was kind enough to leave the flowers.'

'Oh, that's nice. The ladies will like that story. Do you want to take the flowers through to them, or are you in a hurry?'

'No, I've time to pop in for a wee blether.'

'Oh, that's nice,' Doreen said again, turning to lead the way down the hall. 'I'm sure both ladies are in the lounge. Come on through. You'll make their day.'

The heat in the lounge was overwhelming. No wonder two thirds of the residents seemed to be asleep, their snowy heads hanging at improbable and no doubt, uncomfortable angles. Doreen pointed to the bay window. 'There they are, sitting together as usual.'

Three old women sat in high-backed chairs, engaged in a loud conversation. Sheila sympathized. You'd need to shout to be heard above the huge telly that was blaring canned laughter from the corner. It was surprising anyone could sleep through that racket.

'Mrs Scobie, Miss McIvor, here's a visitor for you. Look at the gorgeous flowers she's brought.' As Doreen started to walk away she turned and laid her hand on the third lady's arm. 'Son not here yet, Ruby?'

The old woman shook her head, frowning.

'Never you mind,' said Doreen. 'There's time enough yet. Oops, Nellie needs the toilet. Hang on Nellie, wait.'

'Wee bastard never turns up,' hissed Ruby, when the carer was out of earshot.

Her two companions tutted. Mrs Scobie shook her head, 'Wash your mouth out, Ruby Smeaton.'

***

CHAPTER 30

Joe hadn't expected the estate agents to respond quite so promptly to his call. Three of them were coming round later, each sounding desperate for the sale, especially when they heard he was keen to offer an early entry date. Apparently the houses in his street were 'prime properties' and he could expect to sell quickly. That was a surprise. It certainly wasn't a 'much sought-after locale' when he and Sally bought the flat all those years ago.

Joe finished tidying the kitchen, took several bags of rubbish down to the bins and fluffed up the cushions in the living room. That would have to do for now. If he didn't get a move on, he'd miss Marty and he wanted to know if her plan was going ahead.

He spied Chance trotting along the canal path, like a dog with somewhere to go. Chance saw him too and came lolloping up to greet him. 'Hiya, boy. Where's Marty?'

Chance trotted off and looked over his shoulder, as if to check that Joe was following. 'God, that is one smart dog. I swear he understands English.'

Marty ruffled the dog's coat. 'Of course he does. He's bilingual. We're the stupid ones who don't understand dog language, not the other way around.'

'I hadn't thought about it like that.'

They both laughed then Joe's face turned serious. 'Have you worked out how we'll snatch Smeaton yet?'

'No, and it's doing my head in. Sometimes I wonder if we should just forget the whole thing.'

'Don't say that. Not without considering every possibility.'

'I've been scrutinising that list Carole gave us, and I'm so glad she's in, by the way. I think the clue has got to be on there. But I can't come up with anything that will work.'

'We'll have to intercept him when he's doing something routine, but the problem is, he doesn't seem to do many things on a routine basis. I think he spends most of his time indoors, plotting evil schemes.'

'And then going to confession to purify his soul?'

'Probably,' said Joe.

'You know, I'd never have guessed he was so devout. It doesn't make him a good person, but it does make him a prime candidate for the type of revenge we have in mind.'

*

Only three boys turned up. That was three more than Joe had expected, to be honest. The last session had been so dry, he'd ended up boring himself.

'Good to see you, lads.' He looked directly at TJ as he spoke. The boy smiled, looking young again, if not quite care-free. The drug-dealer's death had gone reported but unsolved. Joe suspected Police Scotland's finest had more pressing priorities on their to-do list. He also suspected the general public approved of this ranking of crimes, a sort of law-enforcement equivalent of the triage system at A and E. Most serious goes to the top of the list.

The tabloids had said as much when the 'murder' was reported. 'Dealer found dead - big deal'. A national red top went so far as to say what Joe was thinking. 'One less scum-bag on our streets.'

It looked like TJ had got away with his moment of madness. Alibi unnecessary, as it turned out.

'Any more coming today, lads?'

Dykesy looked up from his phone. Slug barely raised his head from the desk.

'Nae idea, Big Man. Smithy's girlfriend's due this week. He's got a lot on his mind.'

'Ach, there's nothing to it,' said Joe. 'Babies are born every second. Smithy won't feel a thing.'

The boys smirked and TJ laughed loudly, as if he was keen to please Joe.

'Thing is, he's no sure the wean's his and he cannae decide if he should go on Jeremy Kyle for a DNA test.'

Joe decided not to comment. 'What about Dangermoose? Where's he?'

'He'll defin-ate-ly no be here. He got lifted on Sunday night.'

Joe couldn't help being curious but had long since learned not to ask questions.

Slug came to life. 'Ah heard he bottled a guy twice his size.'

'Aye, he did, but the arsehole was pure asking for it.'

Joe wondered what you'd have to do to deserve a face slashed with a broken bottle.

Dykesy provided the answer. 'He made a move on Danger's bird, then when the wee man steps in, the basturt asks her why she's brought her wean to the pub.'

Joe laughed, couldn't help it, then remembered himself and his role as mentor. 'Come on now lads,' he said gravely, 'You're not going to tell me a man should get his face slashed for that.'

'Naw, Sur. Danger's used to that kinda talk. He knows he's wee. It's whit the guy said next. Liam heard it and everythin, man.'

Slug seemed keen for details, 'Whit did he say?'

'Danger's girl tells him to fuck off, an the guy's like, 'Ye can keep her, wee man. She's had mair hands up her than Sooty.'

'Fair enough,' said Sluggo. 'Ah would've done the same if some wanker had insulted ma girlfriend.'

Dykesy hooted. 'Whit girlfriend, Slugster?'

Joe decided it was time to start teaching, before he heard any more depressing updates. Looking at TJ, he said, 'Violence rarely solves anything, boys. Please try to remember that.'

He changed his tone, tried to make it upbeat and motivating. 'Right lads, today we're going to talk about nutrition.'

Slug's head went back on to the desk and TJ said, 'New

whit?'

'Nutrition,' said Dykesy, 'the stuff we eat and drink.'

Slug grunted and TJ laughed. 'Whit we drink?' he said, sniggering, 'Trust me, Sur, you don't want tae know.'

When pushed, TJ said that his favourite food was his granny's brownies, and the other two went into hysterics. Joe could only shake his head and wonder. After an hour spent arguing about whether Irn-Bru was made from girders and if Buckfast was a health drink, Joe felt like shooting himself. And he hadn't got to the worst bit.

'Boys, do you think you could do something for me?'

All three replied without hesitation, making Joe feel good for the first time that session.

'No worries, Big Man.'

'Anythin fur you, Sur,' said Slug. 'Are you wantin us to get ye some puff?'

Joe's despair must have shown in his face and maybe a wee bit of impatience too. 'That's ridiculous, lads. You know how I feel about drugs. All drugs.'

'Aw right, Big Man, cool the beans. We're only trying to help. We can get you ab-so-lootly any gear you want, by the way.' Dykesy tapped the side of his nose like a spiv.

It was hard to be cross with them. Joe took a bundle of photocopied sheets out of his bag. 'Could you keep these nutrition diaries for me? Note down everything you eat and drink for a week?'

The boys exchanged looks, then burst out laughing. Dykesy spoke for the three of them. 'No problemo.'

When Joe left the building, he wasn't surprised to see the 'diaries' sticking out of the bin by the front door. At least his lectures about litter had been effective.

***

CHAPTER 31

'Hello, it's Carole from HQ. Can I speak to Miss Scott, please?'

'Speaking. Carole, can you hang on a sec? What is it, Megan?'

Sheila hoped Carole wouldn't mind waiting a few moments. She left the line open so that Carole could listen, knowing the conversations that went on in school offices were often priceless.

'Please may I have my mobile phone back, Miss Scott?'

'Didn't I say you could collect it at home time?'

'Yes, but I need it now. I have to make an urgent phone call.'

'If it's urgent, I can phone your mum for you. Are you not feeling well?'

'I'm fine, thank you. But I have PE later and Mummy packed the wrong shorts. Those ones make me look fat.'

When Sheila had sent the child packing, without her mobile phone, Carole asked, 'What age was that kid?'

'Megan? Nine going on nineteen. A right little princess. You should see the mother.'

'Should we expect a letter of complaint at HQ?'

'Yes, I would think so, and no doubt Mr Smeaton will agree with the parents that we'll have damaged the child's self-esteem by making her do PE in the wrong style of shorts.'

Carole laughed. 'Speaking of style, how did the pupils react to your makeover?'

'Typical kids. Most of them didn't notice. As far as the rest are concerned, it's nothing more exciting than a new haircut and a bit of lippy.'

'Well, I think you look fantastic, but that's not why I called.

Officially, I'm reminding you that your school handbook is due for review. Please send the new version to Mr Smeaton by the tenth of January.'

'Great. Presumably he expects us all to work on them in the Christmas holidays?'

'I couldn't possibly comment,' said Carole, sounding as if she was stifling a giggle.

'And the unofficial reason for this call?'

'While he's out, I thought I'd take the chance to tell you. I've been making some subtle enquiries. You know that question you asked me? You were right. His mother is in Briargrove, the place by the cemetery.

After a hastily prepared evening meal, Sheila surveyed the contents of her wardrobe.

Wondering what Liz would have made of her new style, she fingered one garment then another. Suddenly, on a whim, she grabbed two armfuls and dumped them, hangers and all, on the floor. 'You are going out,' she said, giving a kick to a beige anorak that wouldn't have looked out of place on one of the old ladies in Briargrove.

She stood for a moment, staring at the jacket then picked it up, gave it a dust down with her hand and replaced it in the wardrobe. She retrieved a pleated skirt in a colour that could best be described as dog's diarrhoea and hung it up too. A cream blouse with a bow that tied at the neck was also salvaged before Sheila closed the wardrobe door and got dressed in tight jeans and a white shirt. She added her new, soft leather biker-jacket and gave her reflection a questioning look. Too young for her? Unsuitable for December? Well, so what. She was fed-up with wearing suitable, sensible clothes all the time. The panto cast were in for a surprise.

When she got to St Gerard's Church Hall, Joe was dropping off a bunch of kids in a minibus. He did a three-point turn in the car park and lowered the driver's window as he passed. With a salute he said, 'Hiya, Boss. You're looking good. I'm heading over to the Community Centre now to pick up Margrit and the other ladies. Apparently the costumes are ready for the chorus kids to try on tonight and there are black bags galore. I'll go and get them and then I'll give you a hand here.'

'That's marvellous, Joe. I can't thank you enough.'

'No need, but are you sure it's okay with St Gerard's for us to leave stuff in the hall?'

'Oh yes, Father Rafferty has cleared all that. He knows we're using the Community Centre without official permission.'

The rehearsal was underway when Joe came into the hall, laden with black plastic bags but minus Margrit and her cronies. When he'd dumped the costumes he came and hovered behind Sheila till Jason got to the end of his monologue.

'Can I talk to you, Sheila? It's important.'

Sheila gave him a worried look then turned to the stage where Jason was preparing to sing and said, 'Well done, everybody. Take five.'

She said to Joe, 'What's up?'

Joe handed her a plastic box and said, 'Margrit sent her biscuits as usual, but she and the ladies won't be coming.'

Sheila groaned and said, 'What now? Is there a fortune teller on at the pub or have they all fallen out?'

'No, much worse than that. Bobby the Caretaker has been called in to HQ and disciplined for letting us use the community centre.'

When Sheila swore, Joe said, 'There's worse to come. Bobby was told to look for another job asap as the hall will be shut within the next financial year. The women are taking action because they've had enough of being "shafted" by the council.'

'So what are they doing?'

'They're staging a sit-in. Occupying the hall till further notice.'

'This is all I need. Smeaton will blame me for this when he hears.'

'And it won't be long till that happens. They're expecting The Record to turn up at any minute.'

***

CHAPTER 32

They'd chosen a pub on Byres Road for tonight's meeting. It had been done up in what Marty would have called 'minimalist' style since she'd last been in, which clearly appealed to the student crowd. Marty wondered where students got the money for drink as Joe placed her G&T on the table and sat down.

'Hello there,' Joe said, not to her, but to someone standing behind her left shoulder.

Marty turned. 'Sorry,' she said, 'I didn't see you.'

An elderly lady, stooped over a large handbag, said, 'Excuse me interrupting, dear. Could you help me please?'

Joe rose to his feet.

'If we can,' said Marty.

'Is this the book club?'

'Em,' Marty hesitated, unsure how to reply.

'Do you mind if I join you?'

Without waiting for an answer, the woman sat down on a stool at the end of the table and delved into her huge bag, while Marty mimed helplessness and mouthed, 'What do I do?'

She could see Joe was trying hard not to laugh.

The old woman took out a spectacle case and put on a pair of half-moon glasses over which she peered at Marty. 'What do you read, dear? I hope it's crime.'

Joe leaned forward and said, in his most charming voice, 'Unfortunately, you couldn't have picked a worse night to join us. You see, we're disbanding after tonight.'

'Surely not!' The woman looked so disappointed that Marty found herself feeling sorry for her.

'I hope you find another book club to join and I'm sorry you've had a wasted journey.'

As the elderly woman heaved herself off the stool and onto her thick-stockinged legs, Joe took her elbow to steady her. She rewarded him with a sweet smile.

'Just before I go,' she said, 'do you mind if I ask a wee quick question?'

'Not at all,' said Marty.

'I was just wondering if by any chance you might know my identical twin sister, Sheila Scott?'

'What the …? said Joe.

'Allow me to introduce myself. I'm Violet McNish, a friend of Ruby Smeaton.'

Marty looked Sheila up and down. 'Unbelievable,' she said. 'You look old enough to be my mother. In fact, you look like my mother. But why?'

'I needed to find out if my disguise was convincing.'

'It certainly convinced me,' said Joe.

'Me too,' said Marty, 'but, I have to ask, what are you up to?'

Sheila touched Joe's arm and said in her wee, old lady voice, 'I'll explain everything in a moment, but first, young man, I'll have a small sherry, if you don't mind."

'Violet' stayed in character, chatting away to Marty until Joe came back with her drink. Then she explained about the chance visit she'd made to Briargrove and how she'd come across Ruby Smeaton.

Joe couldn't keep his face straight. 'Sorry, Sheila, I can't take you seriously dressed like that. You even sound like an ancient aunt of mine.'

Marty said, 'Are you sure she's Smeaton's mother, this old lady?

'Definitely. I got Carole to check. There's absolutely no doubt.'

Joe and Marty leaned in close, notepads, pens and drinks forgotten, while Sheila outlined her plan.

'Let me get this straight,' said Joe, suddenly serious, 'you're going to befriend this old woman and use her to get Smeaton.'

'Yes, dear,' said Sheila, in her Violet voice. She patted the back of his hand and said, 'Could you run along, like a nice young man, and buy me another sherry? They're awfully wee glasses in here.'

'You're certainly credible. I'll give you that.'

Marty leaned back in her chair and folded her arms. 'Why should she trust you, this Ruby Smeaton? And more importantly, why the hell would she betray her son?'

'Because I suspect she hates him as much as we do.'

Sheila took a sip of the sherry Joe handed her and said, 'Right guys, tell me if you think this will work.'

When she had finished, Joe blew out a low whistle. 'Have you ever considered a life in crime, Sheila?'

Marty said, 'Sounds pretty watertight to me, except for one thing.'

'What's that?'

'What if his old mother's demented, like so many folk in these care homes? Are you sure you can rely on her to tell you when Smeaton's going to be visiting? Or not to shop us to the man himself?'

'I don't think she's demented.'

'You don't think?' said Joe.

'Well, that's what yours truly, Violet McNish, intends to find out during her regular do-gooder visits to Briargrove House, starting on Sunday. Watch this space.'

'Go for it,' said Marty. 'I think it's brilliant.'

'I'm not convinced,' said Joe. 'On another matter - any news on the Bankside sit-in?'

'Well,' said Sheila's, her voice back to normal and sounding very grave, 'I've been ordered to stay away, or I'll be in breach of my contract as a council employee and could lose my job.'

'Who ordered you?'

Sheila rolled her eyes. 'Take a guess.'

***

CHAPTER 33

Sheila was on her way to the community centre, fresh from a roasting at HQ. Her face was on fire, as if she'd lain too long on a sunbed.

Sheila had expected to have to face Smeaton, of course, with maybe Carole there to take notes. She hadn't been prepared for the Spanish Inquisition. Smeaton had sat centre stage with the head of finance on one side and the torn-faced Councillor Cooper on the other. The sit-in at Bankside had been headline story on the local television news and The Record had run an item. It was made clear to Sheila that the council was embarrassed by being the focus of such media attention. It was also made clear she was being held responsible for creating the problem. It was now her responsibility to make it go away.

'We don't want this to become another Govanhill Baths situation, do we, Sheila?' said Councillor Cooper, her pudding-like features contorting into something resembling a smile. Sheila found her scarier than Smeaton.

The sit-in at Govanhill had lasted for months when Glasgow City Council had tried to close the baths. It had ended in eviction and scuffles with police, all televised. Of course Sheila didn't want that. Nor did she want the responsibility that had been thrust upon her. 'Get it sorted,' Smeaton had said, with more than a hint of menace in his voice. 'You started all this, you put them up to it, now get it stopped.'

'All they want is the chance to use premises that belong to the community.'

'I think you'll find the premises belong to us,' said Cooper. 'That is, to Logiemuir Council.'

Oops. Wee Freudian slip, there, thought Sheila.

'I get that,' she said, nodding and trying hard to sound cooperative. 'But surely you can see that all we want is to stage a show that will bring the community together. The rehearsals have already got people working with folk they would normally fight in the street. It's incredible.'

'Nobody is stopping them using the premises. All they have to do is apply for a let. They need to pay the council to use premises that belong to the council.'

'But that's the point. They don't have the money. And I see it as my duty to facilitate an activity which is such a force for good.'

'May I remind you, Miss Scott, that your duty is, first and foremost, to act as an agent of this council.'

'The same council that pays your wages, don't forget.' Cooper was practically vibrating in her chair, desperate, it seemed, to reprimand. 'You should not, whatever the circumstances, be condoning any activity that contravenes council rules and regulations.'

'Surely improving lives should be our priority.'

'Keeping yourself in a job should be your priority,' said Smeaton. Any more stunts like this and you'll be using your thespian skills to busk in Buchanan Street.' Having delivered his threat, Smeaton sat back in his enormous chair, smug and self-satisfied. Sheila wanted to slap him.

Councillor Cooper had twisted her face into a rigor mortis smile. 'Wait a minute, Tommy. I've just had a thought. We might be missing an opportunity here for the council to be seen in a very favourable light. If we manage this cleverly.'

She swivelled her chair to face the money man, who had remained silent so far. 'John,' she simpered, 'do you think we can afford to give them free use of the hall till they put on their pantomime?'

Sheila held her breath.

The grey-faced man took a calculator from his inside pocket and tapped a few keys. 'It would cost us funds we can ill-afford to lose, but we could manage a few weeks, I suppose.

But it has to be a one-off.'

'That's all we need,' said Sheila, wanting to kiss the accountant.

Cooper made her move. 'Now, Miss Scott, listen very carefully. The council will require tickets for the front rows, complimentary, of course. Plus, a press photo opportunity with some members of the cast, the more disadvantaged-looking the better. Also, you will need to set aside a suitable space for hospitality, so we have somewhere pleasant to spend the interval, with drinks and nibbles. Will you be able to arrange all of that, if we agree to let you continue to use the hall?'

The word 'thank you' got stuck in Sheila's throat, but thinking of Jason, Margrit and the others, she had managed to smile and say, 'Certainly.'

And now she was here to tell them the good news. She pulled on to the pot-holed square of tarmac that served as a car park and looked at the community centre. It was like a scene out of Les Misérables. A dirty duvet cover had been ripped open to make a banner that proclaimed, 'Okupied by Bankies'. Street urchins swarmed around the doors which were guarded by two bears with shaven heads and tattoos. One barred Sheila's path with an arm like a log. 'You fae the council, doll?'

'No, not strictly speaking.' Sheila heard her words echoed by a mocking falsetto voice behind her.

Somebody in the little crowd by the door shouted, 'We shall not be moved, so we'll no. No till yous basturts gie us back our community centre.'

Jason appeared at her side, carrying plastic bags of provisions. 'Goadsake! This is Sheila. Let her in.'

Behind him was Margrit, laden with home baking in see-thru containers. 'You're right on time for your tea, Sheila. Come on in, hen.'

The media seemed to have left, apart from a one-man news team, a boy with a notebook in his hand and a camera round his neck. He looked frozen.

Sheila gestured to him to come over. 'Fancy a cup of tea and an exclusive?'

He nodded as if she'd asked him did he want a corner office at the Wall Street Journal.

'Get your camera ready. It's your lucky night.'

Turning back to Jason she said, 'Could you get everybody out here, please, Jason? I've got some good news to share.'

When she announced they were to have free use of the centre till they had staged their panto, a roar went up that would have done justice to Hampden Park. People grabbed one another and jumped up and down. There were fist-pumps and hugs and Jason, through his tears, gave a passable impersonation of Freddie Mercury singing 'The Show Must Go On.'

Before Sheila could object, the two bears had hoisted her aloft. She clung on for dear life and tried not to scream. When they finally put her down, she called for cast members to come and stand beside her while the photographer/reporter organised the crowd around them.

Then she gave the reporter a statement, being sure to cast the council in the role of the cavalry. She finished by saying, 'Will you please make sure that, whatever else you put in the article, you print, in bold, the date, time and cost of the tickets? This might get us a few more bums on seats on the night, who knows?'

'I guess the venue will be self-explanatory?' said the young reporter with a grin. 'Oh man, am I glad I decided to stick around. To be honest, I was hoping for a riot of some kind, but it's nicer to be able to report good news for a change. Good luck with the panto. Will you keep me a seat at the dress rehearsal and I'll come and do you some photos?'

'With pleasure. Thanks a lot. Want a cup of something hot before you go?'

'No way. I'm going to get this filed, while it's still an exclusive.'

Sheila watched him stick on a crash helmet and jump-mount an ancient scooter. She turned to Jason. 'Right, Il Divo,' she said, 'our paparazzo has gone. You can stop posing now.'

**

CHAPTER 34

Ruby found the afternoons the worst. No wonder folk nodded off. Wheelchairs, parked in a circle like a wagon train. Everybody sleeping or lost in their own wee world. They were the lucky ones, them that were gaga. They didn't have to listen to that telly.

The giant screen blared non-stop rubbish. Nothing but auction rooms, house-hunting, cookery. Imagine. To folk in a place like this?

They'd all been forced to part with everything they held dear. Every single stick of furniture. Left with nothing but a handful of treasured possessions. A few measly ornaments to sit on a shelf in their poky wee bedrooms.

These folk would never shut their own front door again. Never enjoy the privacy of their own home. Forced to eat whatever pap was put in front of them. If they wanted to stay alive.

What about human rights? Criminals up the road in the jail had a better life than her. At least they'd get out some day.

Ruby would never forgive Tommy for putting her in here. Not if she lived to be a hundred. And she hoped to God she didn't. She hoped her release would come long before that. She was ready to meet her maker. She wanted to be reunited with them she'd lost.

Jinty was speaking, but Ruby couldn't hear a thing for that damned television.

'Hang on a minute, Jinty,' she said, heaving herself out of her chair, 'till I turn this thing down.'

Ruby picked up the remote. Telly off.

'There, Lily,' she said to old Mrs Benton, 'that's better, isn't it?' Ruby popped the remote under the old dear's skirt. No one

135

batted an eyelid. That should keep things quiet for a while. At least till toilet time.

She scuttled back to her chair, puffing with the effort. Apart from a few snores, and the carers' voices in the distance, it was quiet.

'Ah, peace,' she sighed. 'Perfect peace.'

'You are awful, Ruby,' said Molly, chuckling. 'You'll get us into trouble.'

'What are they going to do, Molly? Throw us out?' Ruby cackled. 'Now, what were you saying, Jinty?'

'I was asking when last you saw your Tommy? I haven't seen any of my lot for weeks, you know.'

'Now, that's not true, Jinty,' interrupted Molly, in her school-teacher voice. 'You had a whole lot of visitors at the weekend, don't you remember? Your granddaughter brought her new baby. You had photos taken of the four generations.'

'So I did. I remember now. Bonnie wee thing. What was her name again?'

'Cody, like Buffalo Bill, remember?'

'Funny name that for a wee lassie,' said Ruby. 'Remember when folk gave their kiddies decent names?'

'Like mine?' asked Molly, 'Mary Matilda Frances?'

'At least they named you Molly, not Fanny.'

The three old ladies laughed until Jinty said, 'Oh no, I think I've had a wee accident.'

Ruby and Molly looked at each other and laughed till they had to wipe the tears from their cheeks.

'Anyway,' said Ruby, dabbing at her eyes, 'to answer your question. I last saw my son, Thomas Ignatious Terence, now there's a fine name for you, a fortnight ago. And he only stayed ten minutes. Long enough to brag about his work. How he put this one in his place and gave that one a final warning.'

'You were a bit nasty to him, Ruby. I heard you,' said Molly, who never missed a trick.

'Och, no wonder. He's a pompous, pious, wee bully. Always was. Used to pick on his brother Archie something terrible. Biting and scratching like a wild animal. Behind my back, of course. Then he'd give me that butter-wouldn't-melt look and say, "He started it." He was a year younger than Archie, but he always had to be top dog. From the day and hour he came into the house. How I rue that day.'

Jinty asked, 'Does Archie ever come to see you, Ruby?'

'Jinty!' Molly scolded, 'you know Archie doesn't come. Ruby told you.'

'It's alright, Molly. I don't mind telling her again.' She turned to face her friend. 'My Archie, that precious, darling boy, was taken from me. Far, far too soon.'

'Oh, so you won't see him this weekend?'

Molly and Ruby gave each other a sad smile and shook their heads. 'Probably not. But you never know', said Ruby. 'At our age, Jinty, you never know.'

***

CHAPTER 35

Sheila peeled the price tag off the 'floral bouquet' she had picked up from the forecourt of the filling station and rang Briargrove's doorbell. While she waited for someone to come and open the glass security door, she patted her grey wig, keen to reassure herself it wasn't going to slide off half-way through her visit.

A large, overweight woman trudged down the hall towards her. The look on her face did not say welcome. Nor did her mouth when she finally opened the door. 'Yes? What you want?'

'Hello, I've brought some flowers for the residents.'

The woman reached out for them, 'I take.'

Sheila held on to the stems. 'I usually stay for a little visit.'

'You have badge?'

Sheila hadn't thought of that. She laughed a tinkle of surprise at such a suggestion. 'Oh no, dear. I'm from the Church. We don't need to wear a badge to do the Lord's work.'

Sheila gave an imperious wave of her arm, brushing the confused woman aside, and swept through the doorway. 'But I do understand that you will want to take a note of my name for your records. My name is Violet McNish. That's McNish of the Perthshire McNishes, but I was born and brought up in Glasgow. Kelvinside, of course.'

The care assistant closed the door and backed away down the hall. Sheila pursued her, chattering like a budgie. 'Would you like me to spell McNish for you? That's capital m, small c, no space, capital n.' The woman turned her back on Sheila and hurried out of sight.

Sheila peeped into the lounge, trying to ignore the

138

conflicting smells of urine and air freshener. The room was busy but there were only two old biddies sitting in the bay of the window, almost hidden by the high backs of their geriatric chairs. Ruby was one of them.

Sheila reminded herself how important it was to remember her name was Violet.

'Hello, ladies. I'm Violet. I've brought you some flowers from the church.'

Ruby looked at her. 'Were you not here last week?'

'No, no, no. I was away my holidays last week. Up at Crieff, at the Hydro, for the weekend. Oh, it's very posh. Have you ever been?'

'What did she say?' asked Jinty.

'Jinty's lost her hearing aid,' explained Ruby. Without it she's as deaf as a post and twice as daft.'

'Good job she can't hear you then, my dear.'

Ruby took the gentle reprimand and acknowledged it with a toothless grin. She covered her mouth with her hand and muttered through her fingers. 'I forgot to put my teeth in this morning and that Fati's too lazy to get them for me. Did she let you in? You couldn't miss her. An arse big enough for a solar eclipse.'

Sheila tried her hardest not to laugh but couldn't keep her smile under control. This wee woman's son spent half his life issuing lists of politically correct terms, reminding his staff what they could and couldn't say and here she was, utterly outrageous and hilarious.

'What did she say?' asked Jinty.

Ruby leaned towards Sheila and said, 'Ignore her and she'll go to sleep. When her mouth falls open, you can pinch her false teeth for me.'

Sheila was horrified till Ruby burst into a rasping laugh. The old woman's eyes were sparkling with mischief. This visit might turn out to be fun.

'Pull up a chair,' said Ruby. 'I'm delighted to have a visitor. Molly's not feeling well. She's in her bed. She's the only one in here I can talk to. The rest are away with the fairies. Look at them.'

When Sheila looked round she saw the fat woman who had let her in hovering in the doorway, watching. Suddenly Ruby started to sing in a loud, demented voice.

The care assistant came over and said to Sheila, 'Maybe you go now?'

Unsure what to do, Sheila started to rise. Ruby grabbed her arm, shrieking, 'No. No.'

Sheila turned to the carer and used Violet's know-all voice. 'I understand it often soothes patients with dementia to have someone sit with them, and I know you folks are terribly busy. Perhaps I should stay. Would that be a help?' She flashed her best Mother Teresa smile. The woman shrugged and left. When she'd gone, Sheila said, 'What was all that about?'

'I can't stand the sight of that woman. When she's on duty, I pretend to be doo-lally. It works a treat, every time. She's so stupid, that one, she'd ask the price in a pound shop.' Ruby chortled. 'Stay and have a wee blether, please.' she said. 'I'm Ruby Smeaton, by the way. What church did you say you're from?'

Sheila thought it best to avoid answering so she asked, 'Oh, are you a church member yourself?'

That seemed to do the trick. Ruby was off on a rant. Sheila had a feeling the old lady enjoyed a good rant.

'I used to be a good Catholic, but I've no patience with religion these days. It's the root of all evil. Look at history and you'll see that. And the most pious are the worst, if you ask me. Hypocrites, every one of them. Priests listening to other folk confessing impure thoughts and abusing altar boys right, left and centre. If's that's not evil, I don't know what is.'

'I agree, that was shocking. It will take a long time for the Catholic church to recover.'

'It certainly will. I can't stand hypocrisy. I might be a rude old bitch, but at least I'll be rude to your face.'

'Burns got it right with Holy Willie, didn't he?'

To Sheila's delight, Ruby hunched her body into an obsequious parody, clasped her hands in prayer, and started to recite, 'That

I am here afore thy sight, for gifts an' grace. A burning and a shining light to a' this place.'

Clearly there was nothing doo-lally about Ruby Smeaton. The two women laughed.

'You should meet my son. Now, there's a Holy Willie if ever there was one. Never misses mass. And spends his working life making other folk's a misery. Then he comes in here bragging to me. How powerful he is. How many departments he runs. How the councillors love the way he keeps his staff in line.'

'That's a terrible way to speak about your own son, Mrs Smeaton. I'm sure he's not as bad as that.' Sheila was struggling to keep her face straight and longed for a distraction.

As if to oblige, Jinty suddenly took an enormous snoring breath. Her lower jaw dropped as she exhaled, displaying a set of dentures that would have fitted a horse. Ruby nodded towards her friend and gave Sheila a wicked grin. 'Quick, get me her teeth.'

When they'd stopped giggling like schoolgirls, Ruby said, 'I'll tell you two things about my son, Tommy. One - he's every bit as bad as he sounds and Two - he's not my son.'

'Sorry, you've lost me.'

'I had only one son, Archie. He was named after my father. As sweet-natured a boy as ever walked the earth. He had eyes like a summer sky and hair the colour of ripe barley.' The old lady's eyes were misty.

'He sounds like a darling.'

'He was a perfect boy. I was enchanted from the day he was born. Couldn't believe I'd been blessed with such a wee cherub.'

Sheila waited, sensing there was drama to come.

'Then, when Archie was a few months old, my sister told us she was pregnant. Now, in those days it wasn't a case of parading around with your bare belly sticking out. Girls didn't get handed a council flat and a fancy pram. There was a stigma attached to unmarried mothers, especially Catholic girls.'

'What happened?'

'Well you see, our Pearl was the brainy one. A great future ahead of her. So my mother cooked up a plan. Sent her to the nuns till the baby was born. Then Billy and I took him in. And off she went. To the university. Not a care in the world.'

'Did the wee boy know about his real mum?'

'Oh aye. She was supposed to take him when she qualified. Never happened. Then it was "when she's had a chance to get settled in her own place". That never happened either.'

'So he was abandoned twice?'

Ruby bristled. 'I'd hardly say he was abandoned. Billy and I brought him up as our own.'

'But he knew?'

Ruby nodded.

'What happened to your sister?'

'Haven't set eyes on her for forty years. She lives in a luxury retirement village in Arizona. In a condo-min-ium, whatever that is. I get a Christmas card. And a photocopy of a bragging letter.'

'I hate those,' said Sheila, 'especially the ones that don't even add a handwritten line asking "How are you?". I call them the annual trumpet, as in blow your own. The ones I get are usually full of news about little Tamsin's ballet and Benjamin's karate. The family dogs even get a mention.'

'Our Pearl's always crowing about her latest cruise and her golf handicap.'

'Does she ever ask about Tommy?'

Ruby shook her head. 'Not once in his whole life.'

'Oh, that's sad.'

The old lady looked fierce. 'Don't you go feeling sorry for him. Or her. She waltzed off in the arms of a dreamboat. As free as a fart in a park. It was Billy and me, and poor wee Archie, that had the hard time.'

They were distracted by the rattling of cups and saucers. A woman in a plastic trilby and a striped tunic was wheeling a trolley into the lounge. Stirred by some Pavlovian instinct, the sleepers woke one by one and accepted drinks and biscuits with shaky hands.

'Cup of tea, Ruby?' asked the woman, holding one up as a visual aid. Ruby nodded her head in reply.

'Would you like a cup of tea, dear?' the kindly woman asked Sheila.

'Is that okay?'

'Of course, we always offer visitors a cup. It's so nice to see the residents with someone to chat to. Not that Ruby will say much. Will you, Ruby?'

Ruby gave her a blank stare, but Jinty had perked up at the sound of the trolley and said, 'Could I have a large cappuccino with extra froth, please? And two biscuits.'

'Coming right up, Jinty,' said the tea-lady, handing over a cup of milky tea and a handful of biscuits. 'Extra froth, just the way you like it.' Jinty smiled her gratitude and got stuck in. The trolley rattled its way towards the door and along the corridor.

'Now, where was I?'

'You were telling me about you and Billy, bringing up your two boys.'

'Sadly it was me bringing up my two boys by the time Archie was five. Billy had a heart attack at thirty-four, never worked another day and died two years later.'

'How did you manage?'

'No other option. Cleaned houses while my boys were at the school. Managed to make ends meet. Most of the time. Not many luxuries but those boys never went without. I can promise you that.'

Seeing the determined look on Ruby's face, Sheila didn't doubt it. 'But what about your sister? Didn't she help out with money?'

The expression changed to one of disgust. 'Our Pearl? You must be joking. A right selfish madam. She never gave us so much as a Christmas present for Tommy. Never mind Archie.'

'That must have been hard, Ruby. Sorry, do you mind if I call you Ruby?'

'Not one bit. What did you say your name was?'

'It's Sh-Violet.'

'Sh-Violet? That's unusual.'

'Just Violet.'

Sheila hoped she hadn't blown it and was relieved when Ruby said, 'Sorry, Violet. Can't hear a thing for that bloody telly. On all day long. And look, nobody's even watching it.'

Sure enough, most of the old folk seemed to have nodded off again. They were like babies, waking up to feed and then going back to sleep. What an existence.

Ruby picked up her story where she'd left off, without the need for a prompt. 'It wasn't easy. I missed Billy. But Archie was the light of my life. He made it all worthwhile.'

'And Tommy?'

'Tommy was an evil wee boy, Violet. A foul temper and a cruel streak a yard wide. Always hurting Archie when he thought I wasn't looking. Archie was a few months older, but he was a delicate wee thing. He would be ailing even then, I suppose.'

The old lady seemed lost in the past, as if she were considering something that had never occurred to her before. She took a hanky from her sleeve and rolled it into a ball while she spoke. 'Archie and Tommy both took scarlet fever. Tommy first. He gave it to Archie. Tommy got better. I expected Archie to do the same, but he got worse.'

Sheila could see how it still broke this woman's heart to think about her suffering child. She reached for the old lady's hand and patted it gently.

'We couldn't save him. I lost the wee soul. Two days before his ninth birthday.'

Sheila could think of nothing to say. Her own loss was too recent and raw. She could only sit and wait.

Then Jinty pointed out the window and piped up, 'Look, Ruby. Here's your son coming.'

***

144

CHAPTER 36

Sheila didn't know whether to fight or flee, but the full cup of coffee in her hand made it awkward to stand up and leave.

'Oh hell's teeth,' said Ruby, 'what's he doing here? Just when I was having a nice time.'

'Maybe I should scoot,' said Sheila, thinking she might go and hide in the ladies then sneak out. When the doorbell rang and a carer immediately went to answer it, she knew she was trapped.

'Stay where you are. You'll get the chance to meet my beloved son. Oh look, here he is.'

Sheila lowered her head and watched him over the rim of her cup. Smeaton, out of the office, had the air of a prosperous businessman. He was wearing a camel coat that looked like it might be cashmere and he held soft leather gloves in one hand. In the other he carried a folded newspaper which he held out as he walked towards her. Sheila felt her stomach lurch. What if he'd recognised her?

He pushed past as if she was invisible. 'Hello, Mother. I brought you a paper.' He tossed it down on the coffee table by Ruby's chair. 'I know you like to see what's on television.' He made no attempt to embrace her, nor did she offer her cheek for a kiss.

Ruby pointed to the selection of newspapers on the table by the door. 'We get papers in here, you know. We're not entirely cut off from the world.'

Smeaton glanced around, as if he expected someone to pull up a chair and invite him to sit. He screwed up his face and said, 'Pooo, how do you stand the smell in here?'

'What smell?' said Ruby, 'You're a cheeky bugger.'

Smeaton eyed up a stool by the piano and dragged it across. 'Think this is clean enough to sit on?'

Ruby ignored the question and said, 'Tommy, this is my new friend.'

Sheila looked over the rim of her cup and gave him a fleeting smile, hoping Ruby wouldn't remark on her sudden shyness.

'Pleased to meet you, dear,' he said. Even with her eyes downcast, Sheila felt him looking at her. Had he sussed her out already?

'What's your name?'

'Violet,' said Ruby. 'McNish.'

'Let the woman speak for herself, Mother.'

Sheila cringed at his tone. It was all too familiar to her but she was surprised to hear him patronising his own mother.

Sheila was terrified to open her mouth in case her voice gave her away. Deciding desperate measures were appropriate, she took a gulp from her cup and pretended to choke, spluttering coffee all over Smeaton's coat.

He jumped to his feet. 'Watch what you're doing, you stupid old,'

'Tommy,' said Ruby. 'Manners!'

'Manners? Have you any idea what this coat cost?'

'Och, we don't give a hoot about your coat. Stick it in the cleaners. What about poor Violet?'

While Smeaton dab-dabbed with a hankie and continued to rant about his coat being ruined, Violet put down her cup and spluttered and choked her way to the front door where she waited for a carer to let her out.

*

Arrol Gardens looked quite different at night. Both sides of the street were packed with cars, parked nose to tail.

Marty hadn't seen Joe for more than a week. He had been 'away' and although she had asked, he hadn't been forthcoming about his destination.

As she pressed the button beside Joe's name, Sheila came bounding up the street towards her, calling, 'Wait for me.'

They climbed the staircase together. 'I'm surprised to see a For Sale sign. Didn't know Joe was moving.'

As Joe ushered them into the hall, Marty joked, 'We've come to view the flat that's for sale.'

'Sorry, you're too late. I verbally accepted an offer half an hour ago.'

'That's great news.'

'Yeah, I guess it is. I feel a bit stunned.'

Marty touched his arm. 'Joe, I wouldn't like to think Smeaton is robbing you of your home as well as your job.'

'No. This place is a bit big now. Too many memories. It's time I was on the move.' He led them into the lounge, a huge high-ceilinged room with a vast window.

'I hope you charged extra if you're planning to leave those beautiful curtains,' said Marty. 'They must have cost a small fortune.'

'Sally never confessed how much they cost, so I suspect you're right.'

Sheila asked, 'Where are you thinking of going?' but Joe gave a shrug instead of an answer.

When they had sat down Marty said, 'Trip go well, Joe?'

'Yeah, not bad. Got some things seen to, some business attended to.'

'Not much of a suntan,' she joked, hoping it might get him to spill the beans, but he reached for his glass of water, took a drink and said nothing.

Marty asked for updates. Joe reported that he'd been given a date for the closure of the bothy. It was to be de-commissioned no later than the end of February, cleared and cleaned by the end of March and all keys returned to HQ. 'Don't worry' said Joe. 'I've already had a set copied.'

Marty made some notes then turned to Sheila who looked excited. It was clear she was bursting to tell them something.

'I got caught by Smeaton when I was visiting his mother.'

Marty gasped, 'You what?'

147

Joe said, 'Did he see you?'

'I got lucky. Her friend announced that Ruby's son was arriving, so I was forewarned.'

'Shit,' said Marty. 'What did you do? I'd have sprinted to the Ladies and then sneaked out the door.'

'Thought about it, but he was too quick for me.'

'So?'

'So I spat coffee all over his fancy cashmere coat.'

'Aye, sure,' said Joe.

'Oh, it's true. I did. And know what? I enjoyed every minute.'

'What if he recognized you?'

'He didn't. I was disguised as Violet and anyway, he was more interested in his precious coat. That's what I was counting on. Still …' She drew the back of her hand across her brow.

'Yeah, close shave,' said Marty. 'Well done. Fast thinking but a high risk strategy.'

'It was worth it. Now I'm more confident the Violet character will work plus I'm glad I didn't run away. I learned a lot. Sounds like he's always had a cruel streak, even as a child.'

'Why are we not surprised to hear that?' said Joe. 'You can imagine him pulling wings off butterflies, can't you?'

Sheila filled them in on a bit more of Ruby's story and added, 'I am sure she's the key to getting Smeaton.'

'Are you also sure she doesn't have any kind of dementia?'

'Let's say she has selective dementia.'

Joe looked puzzled until Sheila described how Ruby chose to play 'gaga' when it suited her but was otherwise sharp as a tack and twice as spiky. 'What's more interesting is this, she has no time for Tommy.'

'Tommy? Hard to imagine him as a Tommy, isn't it?'

'Not hard to imagine him biting and kicking a smaller brother, though, is it?'

'No, he's a horrible specimen of humanity,' said Marty, 'but surely his own mother loves him? I would love our Mark no matter what he did, without a doubt.'

'That's the sad bit. His own mother, that is, his real mother, handed him over as a new-born and hasn't acknowledged him since.'

'Obviously an excellent judge of character,' said Joe.

'Did she put him up for adoption?'

'No, she let her parents pass him over to her married sister, Ruby, and got on with her life. She's now living it large in Arizona.'

'Aw,' said Marty, feeling for any unwanted, rejected child. 'Maybe that explains a lot about his behaviour. I almost feel sorry for him.'

When Sheila went on to tell them about wee Archie dying of scarlet fever, Marty felt as if she might cry.

'Poor Ruby,' she said, 'losing her husband and her little son.'

'And being left with Smeaton as a consolation prize?' said Joe. 'You're right, Marty. Poor Ruby.'

'How does this help us, Sheila?'

Sheila leaned forward in a conspiratorial pose, 'We know the man has no social life, never goes anywhere unless it's work-related. The only thing he does with anything resembling regularity, apart from church, is visit his mother. I think we have to intercept him on his way to Briargrove.'

Marty and Joe nodded. 'That could work.'

'One other thing,' said Sheila. She bit her bottom lip.

'What?'

'I think we should enlist Ruby.'

***

CHAPTER 37

Marty had only just finished stacking the dishwasher when her phone rang.

'Sheila, what's up? I only saw you two hours ago. You missing Liz to chat to?'

'I'm not calling for a chat, Marty. I don't think I can go through with this.'

'But you were so enthusiastic earlier. Is it because of Joe?'

'No, it's because of the drug.'

'The drug will be fine.'

'How can terrible stuff like that ever be "fine", Marty?'

'We're using it safely.'

'Ok for you to say. I'm the one that's drugging him.'

Marty poured two cups of decaf tea and took one to David.

'Who was on the phone? Oh look, you should sit down and watch this, Darling. It's got baby Polar bears in it.'

'Actually, do you mind if I take my cup through to the study, David? I need to make another phone call.'

'Oh no, you don't.'

'Sorry?' Could he have overheard her conversation with Sheila?

David repeated, this time in a big panto voice, 'Oh no, you don't.'

The penny dropped. 'Ah, very good, David. You got me. Ha ha.'

'What was all that blabbing about anyway? Has Sheila lost the back end of the pantomime horse?'

'Something like that.' Marty smiled, pointing to the TV as she left the room. 'Enjoy.'

Joe took ages to answer. 'What's up?'

'I've just had a call from Sheila. I think she might be pulling out.'

'Why? Wait, is this my fault? She was all fired up earlier. Is she pulling out because I was a bit negative about Ruby?'

'No, it's nothing to do with you. It's the Rohypnol. She's worried about using it. And given that she'll the one to administer it, I can understand that.'

'Did you tell her about all the research I've done? Both the scientific stuff and what the boys have told me?'

'Yes, I tried to reassure her that it will do him no long-term harm.'

'Are you still okay with us using it, Marty?'

'Yeah, but you know how I feel. I'd happily give him strychnine if I thought I'd get away with it.'

Joe laughed. 'Ach, I don't think you should worry too much about Sheila. She's sound. Probably just losing her nerve.'

'Do you think so?'

'I'm sure of it. I mean, she's got as much reason to hate Smeaton as the rest of us.'

'You're right. Maybe she's just got too much on her mind, what with the panto and everything. I haven't forgotten how stressful it can be, running a school. Especially in the run-up to Christmas. And she's still grieving for Liz.'

'Also, I think I might have been a bit dismissive of her suggestion that we involve old Mrs Smeaton.'

'Dismissive? You think?'

'Okay,' said Joe. 'Sorry. I've been thinking it's maybe not such a mad idea after all.'

'I think it's a great idea.'

'Do you trust Sheila's judgement?'

'Absolutely.'

'That's good enough for me. What about you, Marty? Are you okay?'

'Yeah, I'm okay.'

'Still up for it?'

'Hell, yeah.'

'Good. Because I've just been online to order the

Rohypnol.'

'Oh God. It's starting to get real now, isn't it?'

'Yip. Hang in there, kid. Even if it's just the two of us, you and I are going to see this through. One way or another, believe me, Smeaton's going to get what's coming to him.'

Marty felt a shiver run all the way up her back and into her hairline.

***

CHAPTER 38

The curtain closed for the final time.

'Sheila! Sheila! Sheila!'

Marty joined in the chant while she waited for a chance to congratulate her friend. The problem was, everyone wanted to thank Sheila but Jason wouldn't put her down. He had hugged her and lifted her off her feet so many times, poor Sheila must be getting vertigo.

With a melodramatic, 'I promise I'll never ever forget you, Sheila, even when I'm famous,' Jason swept off the stage and went to meet his adoring public.

Sheila and Marty looked at one another and giggled. 'He was brilliant. You have to hand it to the boy.'

'He is talented. I hope he makes it in London and I'll be praying he stays safe down there.'

'I wouldn't worry too much. He's got his head screwed on, that one.' Marty grabbed Sheila in a tight embrace. 'That was an outstanding show, each night better than the one before.'

'Three full houses. Who would have believed it? All that publicity for the sit-in did us a good turn, didn't it?'

'Yeah, pity about the councillors taking the best seats in the house on opening night, without paying a penny.'

'Did you see Smeaton and the Troll? Oops, that sounds like the title for next year's pantomime.'

'How could I miss them, sitting there like smug philanthropists, milking the publicity.' Sheila mimed spitting out something nasty.

'Never mind them. Did any of your pupils come to see the show?'

'Quite a few, surprisingly. The ones whose parents weren't scared to venture into Bankside at night. Some of them treat it like the Gaza Strip.'

'I must admit, I'd have been wary myself a few months ago, but the folk here are great. Real salt of the earth.'

'Are yous ladies talking about me?'

'Yes, Margrit, we are indeed. Come on, give us a hug and thanks a million. I'm going to miss that home-baking of yours.'

'It wis nothin, hen. No compared to the work you've put in. Everybody's sayin Itchybella wis better than the panto at the King's Theatre. You should be proud of yersel.'

'I'm proud of Bankside and special folk like you.'

Margrit blushed. 'Away,' she said as bustled off. 'Cheerio now. There's a big Bacardi and Coke wi' my name on it.'

'I think we've earned a drink too, Marty. Come on, let's go to the pub.'

'Boy, am I ready for this,' said Sheila, raising her pint of shandy.

'It's Champagne you deserve. Wish you'd let me buy a bottle, at least some Prosecco. That was an absolute triumph, Sheila.'

'Yeah, it turned out alright in the end, I suppose.'

'Alright?' said Marty. 'It was spectacular. I had a ball. In fact, I'm sorry it's over.'

'Well, I'm not. I'm shattered.'

'You must be. Never mind, all your hard work paid off. People will talk about this for years.'

'And yet it's not enough to make Smeaton appreciate the sterling work that goes on in these communities. I went to see him today.'

'Did he heap praises on your head for turning Bankside into the West End?'

'Did he hell! Would you believe he didn't mention the pantomime? Didn't even say thanks for the free tickets.'

'He should have presented you with a magnum of Moet for the good publicity you brought the council. His ugly mug and his sidekick's were all over the local paper.'

'Did you hear they're sticking to their plan to kill off the kids' orchestra?'

Marty leaned on the table, her head in her hands. 'Oh, that's outrageous.' She looked up, as if she'd had an idea. 'Why don't you mobilise the residents to protest again? It worked for the panto.'

'Yes, but the panto only cost the use of the hall. The orchestra needs major funding. Big Sean's so gutted, he's giving up, retiring at the summer. He says he hasn't the energy to fight them anymore. There was an appeal, but it was a total farce, as usual. Carole showed me the minutes of their discussion.'

'Carole's been great, hasn't she?'

'She's been invaluable. Filling us in on Smeaton's habits, keeping us up to date on his commitments. I don't know how we'd have managed without her. And that idea she had about telling everyone, when the time comes, that he's gone to a conference? That was inspired.'

'Yes, everything is starting to fall into place.'

'Marty, I'm sorry I threw a bit of a wobbly after the last meeting. I just had too much on my mind.'

'We thought that. Are you okay now?'

Sheila nodded. 'Yes, I think I am. Sorry, but I had a bit of a panic about using Rohypnol on someone, even Smeaton. It's such a disgusting drug and used for such vile purposes. And what if he dies?'

***

CHAPTER 39

January 2018

When they reached the canal side Marty let Chance off the lead and watched as he raced away, a grey streak. 'Any luck with the house-hunting, Joe?' she said. 'I don't mind going with you to have a look.'

'Thanks, Marty, but I'm thinking of building.'

Marty said, 'I'm envious. That's always been my dream. Find the perfect spot and build the perfect house.'

'Why don't you?'

'David says we already have a perfect house in the perfect spot, within walking distance of the golf course.'

'What would be perfect for you, Marty?'

'Somewhere with less rain, for a start,' she said, pulling up the hood on her waterproof.

'Would you ever move abroad?'

'I don't know that I could leave my son. Or this idiot.' She pointed at the dog who had reappeared at her side and was now nosing her pocket for a reward. 'Could you live abroad?'

No mention of her husband. 'Oh yes,' said Joe. 'I certainly could.'

They walked in silence for a bit. Traffic sounds filtered through, diluted by distance.

Suddenly Marty said, 'Isn't it great news that Sheila's committed again?'

'Yeah, she'll be solid now. And she's come up with an inspired idea for disguising the bothy. Remember those thick black drapes from the panto?'

'The ones you used to create the dragon's lair?'

'Yip.'

'Will it work, do you think?'

'Hope so. Sheila and I took some up to the bothy last night. It looked good.'

'Won't it arouse suspicion if you're seen going back and forward?'

'Nah. Folk will expect to see me up there now word's got out that it's closing.'

'Why does Smeaton have to shut a place like that? We used to send Moorcroft pupils up there all the time. Remember Matt Harvey? I trusted him implicitly. He had kids camping out in the wild, canoeing, abseiling. He even got me to try it one day. Abseiling. Can you believe that?'

'I'd believe anything of you, Marty. The shy wee sister that used to blush when I spoke to her seems like a different person.'

'Oh, she is, Joe. You'd better believe it.'

'What happened to her?'

'Life happened to her. Toughened her up.'

'Yes,' said Joe, thinking of Sally, 'life does that to people, doesn't it?'

***

CHAPTER 40

Straight after work, Sheila went to Briargrove. She peeped into the lounge and found Ruby sitting by herself in the bay window. The Christmas tree had been taken down, the decorations had gone and the room looked even more depressing than usual.

'Happy New Year, Ruby.' Sheila stooped to give the old lady a peck on the cheek. 'Cheer up,' she said, in her best Violet voice. 'You've a face like a horse in the huff.'

There was no response, which made Sheila wonder if this was going to be one of Ruby's 'demented' afternoons. She looked around for the carer that Ruby disliked so much then pulled up a chair and took Ruby's liver-spotted hand in hers. It felt frail, the slender fingers knotted with arthritis. In her other hand Ruby clutched a sodden bundle of tissue.

'Ruby, what's happened?'

'Oh, Violet, we lost poor Molly. It's her funeral in the morning.'

Sheila knew Molly was Ruby's last link to sanity. 'The only one in here that talks any sense,' was how Ruby had described her friend. 'Jinty's nice enough, but she comes and goes, if you know what I mean,' she'd said, tapping one finger to the side of her head.

Remembering how much she missed her conversations with Liz, Sheila spoke with genuine empathy when she told Ruby how sorry she was for her loss. She took out a pack of tissues and handed one to Ruby.

'There's a nice fresh paper hanky for you, and I've got plenty more if you need them.'

The old lady gave her nose a mighty blow, loud enough to rouse the nearest sleeper, making them both smile. She gave her eyes a quick wipe, and tucked the hanky up her sleeve.

'What happened to Molly? Or would you rather not talk about it?'

'No, I don't mind talking about it. Not much point being squeamish about death. Not when you get to my age.' She looked around and added, 'Especially when you live in a place like this. God's waiting room, right enough.'

'Molly seemed fine the last time I saw her.'

'As fine as you can be at ninety with a failing heart. But the minute you take to your bed, that's it. Pneumonia gets you. That's what got Molly.'

'What time's her funeral?'

'Doesn't matter, I won't be going anyway. I've already phoned Tommy to ask. Says he can't take time off for every death in this place, or he'd never be at his work.'

'Oh, dear me,' said Sheila, feigning shock and surprise while feeling neither, 'That's a little bit harsh.'

'Harsh? You don't know the half of it, Violet.'

Although another funeral was the last place she wanted to go Sheila did some quick calculations in her head, wondering if she could risk making an offer without checking her diary. Another look at Ruby's sad eyes convinced her. 'I'll take you to Molly's funeral.'

'Oh, I can't ask you to do that, Violet.'

'You're not asking, Ruby. I'm offering. In fact, I'm insisting.'

Ruby started to cry again. 'Thank you so much,' she murmured between sobs.

Sheila unfolded another tissue and handed it over, saying, 'Where's that tea trolley? I could murder a cuppa.' She had to fight the urge to say, 'and I could murder your son.'

Sheila had called her secretary first thing to say she would be out of school this morning, attending the funeral of an elderly aunt. She was waiting for the taxi she'd ordered, checking the mirror to make sure her grey 'Violet' wig was secure, when her secretary rang.

'I'm so glad I caught you. I've had HQ on the phone. Mr Smeaton wants you in his office asap.'

'Please call Carole back for me and ask her to pass on the message to Mr Smeaton that I have promised to attend the funeral of an old lady who is unlikely to have many mourners at her graveside. Ask her to tell him I have no intention of breaking that promise.'

Sheila heard the gasp of disbelief followed by a silence. She knew her secretary was waiting to hear her say she had been joking. She hung up.

Ruby was sitting in the hall waiting for her. She was wearing a black woollen coat and a hat. 'You must be boiling hot, Ruby,' she said, as Doreen let her in.

'I told her she could wait till you arrived to put her coat on, but she wouldn't hear of it. Off you go then, Ruby,' she said, helping the old woman to her feet. 'Give Molly a good send-off for us, will you? There should be a nice big floral tribute from all at Briargrove. Look out for it.'

Doreen turned to Sheila. 'She was such a sweet person, was Molly. A real lady, with immaculate manners. We'll miss her.'

'Right,' said Sheila, taking Ruby's arm. 'Let's go.'

Sheila was hoping nobody would give her a second glance at Molly's funeral. It would be a good test of the Violet disguise.

She needn't have worried. As it turned out, apart from Ruby and herself, the only other mourners appeared to be members of Molly's family. As they enjoyed a 'wee refreshment' after the service, Ruby seemed to relax and started to chat. Maybe the small brandy had loosened her tongue or perhaps it was the freedom to speak without fear of being overheard in the lounge at Briargrove. Whatever the catalyst, Ruby wasn't holding back today.

'See when our Tommy told me he wasn't taking me to my friend's funeral? It was the final nail in the coffin for me.' Realising what she'd said, Ruby grimaced. 'Ooops, that's not the thing to say at a funeral, is it, Violet?'

'Oh, I think Molly would have seen the funny side, don't you?'

Ruby giggled, like a teenage girl trapped inside an old woman's body. Then she got serious. 'Know what he said? He told me he'd better things to do with his time. Now, Violet, I ask you. What kind of a son says that to his old mother? The next funeral could be mine.'

Sheila patted Ruby's hand. She had no answer.

'Well, I've had enough. I'm finished with him. I'm going to instruct Doreen not to let him in the next time he comes.'

While Ruby ranted about Smeaton's failures as a son, Sheila was thinking fast. If Ruby severed all ties, the plan for the abduction would go up in flames.

'It sounds like his job keeps him very busy and he seems to be an important man. Aren't you even a wee bit proud of him, Ruby?'

'He's done well for himself. I'll give him that. But I'd rather he emptied dustbins and was a nice person. I wonder where I went wrong.'

'I expect you did your best, Ruby. I don't think you should blame yourself for your son's shortcomings.'

Ruby leaned close. 'You know what else I often wonder?' She waited, obviously expecting a response from Violet.

She obliged, 'What?'

Ruby lowered her voice to a whisper. 'I often wonder who his father was. Our Pearl would never say. Didn't matter what my mother and father said or did. Pearl never let on.'

'Did she have a boyfriend at the time?'

'Not that we knew of. She always was a dark horse, our Pearl. My father doted on her, so she was spoiled rotten. If I'd been the one expecting a baby with no ring on my finger, he'd have thrown me out. But not our Pearl. She could do no wrong.'

Around them, tables were starting to clear 'We should probably think about leaving now, Ruby. Let's go and say goodbye to Molly's family, shall we?'

By the time they got back in the car, Ruby seemed to have

sobered up, but no matter what Violet said, she was adamant she would have nothing more to do with Tommy.

***

CHAPTER 41

Joe had decided that, instead of another useless indoor education session, he was taking these boys to the bothy. They could help him get the place organized, under the guise of learning about equipment and keeping it maintained. He could argue the merits of the session if Smeaton took him to task over it, although frankly, he didn't give a damn.

This would probably be their last day up there together. Stowed in the back of the van was a monster bag of goodies and a dozen cans of Irn-Bru.

He checked his watch. They were late. He felt as deflated as a burst airbed. He hadn't seen some of the lads since he'd been forced to introduce the 'Indoor Learning Modules'. TJ rarely missed a session and there was usually a core of diehards who attended. Jimbo had dropped out, fulfilling his own prophecy, if the rumours were true. Once, at the top of a hill, he'd told Joe how great it was to come to the bothy. 'See this hill-climbing an canoeing an stuff?' he'd said, 'It's the only thing that keeps me aff the drugs, Sur, ah swear tae God.'

Joe crossed his fingers, expecting nothing but hoping some of the regulars might still appear. He would wait another five minutes then give it up as a bad job.

A burst of profanity echoed along the corridor. 'Whit the fuck are we gonnae tell the Big Man?' muttered Dykesy, as he opened the door.

Joe had learned never to ask. They'd tell him in their own good time. 'Morning, lads. How do you fancy a day at the bothy?'

'Ah thought the bothy was getting shut, Sur?'

'It is, but there's a fair bit of work to be done first. I could use some help up there and I'd rather have you boys than some of these numpties from the council. What do you say? Are you up for it?'

The lads looked at one another. They were hardly dressed for the hills. Dykesy was in a pristine white tracksuit with brand new trainers to match. TJ, as usual, was clad in a thin t-shirt that looked as if it could use a wash. Dangermoose was sporting a designer-label hoody that was either a knock-off from the Barras or the result of a 'five finger discount' at Braehead.

'I've brought a picnic,' said Joe in a coaxing voice that made them laugh.

That was the decider. Slug was already making for the van, saying, 'Don't let me eat any more than three packets o' crisps, Sur. I'm on a diet.'

'That's the best news I've heard all week,' said Joe, thinking the boy's behind did look a bit reduced though it was hard to tell with the out-of-shape tracky bottoms Slug favoured. 'What's the reason for the diet, if you don't mind me asking?'

'Decided to go to the army, same as my big brother. He says it's a great life. Even if you get shot at, it's a better life than here, ye know?'

'Ye can get shot in Bankside, Sluggo. Ye don't have to go to Afghanistan. Wee Malky got shot in the arse on Friday night.'

'Aye, wi an air gun? Some Muppet shooting oot his granny's bedroom windae?'

'We should pure go to New York, Dykesy. See some real gangstas.'

And so it went on, while Joe drove to the bothy. As he slowed down to let a sheep wander across the road in front the van, Joe smiled and braced himself for the obscene jokes he heard every time.

'Haw, Sur, whit dae ye call a sheep wi nae legs?'

This was a new one. There was a pause while they all waited for the answer. When Slug shouted, 'A cloud!' Joe felt relieved.

Before the van had a chance to stop, the boys were tumbling out, raring to go. Joe slid from the driver's seat and stretched his arms and legs, easing the stiffness out of his old limbs. As the boys disappeared into the bothy, all he could hear was the lonely call of a curlew. In the weak winter sun the reservoir lay before him like a scatter of sequins.

Against his better judgement he had been talked into letting the lads use the canoes one last time although, officially, all outward bound activities had stopped. The boys had promised to stay near the bank. They knew how suddenly the floor of Loch Etrin fell away. He'd warned them often enough about the underwater precipice and the unfathomable depths below.

He helped Dangermoose carry his canoe to the water's edge and waited there for the others to catch up.

'Sur,' said TJ, when he arrived, 'Your phone keeps ringing in the van. Sounds like somebody really wants to talk to you.'

'Mibbe it's your boss, eh, Big Man?' said Dykesy.

'Lads, if I go and get my phone, you need to promise me you won't go out on the water till I come back.' He looked from one face to the other. Liam, the least trustworthy in the group, was smirking. 'I mean it, Liam. I'm serious. You know how deep it gets. If you drown in there, your body will never be found. And I mean, never.'

Joe paused to let the severity of his words sink in.

'Nobody goes out onto the water till I come back. Is that clear, boys?'

'Crystal,' said Dykesy and the others nodded in agreement.

Joe left them sitting in a circle on the grass discussing TJ's new 'burd' and went to check his phone.

He was shutting the van door when Dykesy appeared at his side. 'Sur, you need to come,' he screamed, grabbing at Joe's arm. 'Slug's tipped his canoe and Liam's went in after him.'

Joe raced down the short slope and straight into the water. Dangermoose hesitated in the shallows while Liam was in up to his chest, trying to haul Slug from under his upturned canoe.

'Right, lads. On the count of three, I'm going under to push Slug up. You try to roll the canoe. One. Two. Three.' Joe dived and grabbed the dead weight that was Slug. The huge boy did not seem to be struggling. Joe feared the worst. With an almighty heave he shoved Slug towards the surface and felt the momentum shift as the boys rolled the boat. When he came up for air the canoe was sitting on the surface with Slug slumped over unconscious, or worse.

'Push him to the shore,' Joe shouted. 'We have to get him out of the canoe.' Dangermoose was sobbing. Dykesy took one look at him and said, 'Shut it, wee man, and help.'

They hauled the canoe to the tiny beach and grabbed Slug by his life jacket, dragging him on to the sand where he flopped like a beached whale. Joe's training kicked in. 'Phone an ambulance,' he shouted and put his lips to Slug's to administer mouth-to-mouth. Slug spluttered and shouted, 'Naw man, no that.'

Joe sat back on his heels and thanked God. The boys cheered and high-fived each other.

When the adrenalin rush passed, Joe felt sick. Images of what might have been flashed through his mind. His face and Slug's splashed across the front page of tabloids. Accusations of negligence - a field day for Smeaton and his like. Dismissal. Shame and guilt dogging him for the rest of his life.

He deserved to feel guilty and ashamed. He had left excited teenagers unattended and was stupid enough to trust them to stay out of the water. He looked at Slug, surrounded by his mates, apparently none the worse for his adventure. 'You sure you're okay, Slug?' he asked.

When the boy nodded, 'Aye, Sur. No worries,' Joe remembered the ambulance that would be hurtling along the main road, sirens blaring. Fuck, this would all come out now. 'Cancel that ambulance,' he shouted at Dykesy.

'No problemo, Big Man. Didnae make the call.' He held up his phone and shook his head. 'Signal's shite.'

Relief washed over Joe. He looked at the boys, who were soaked to the skin, and noticed they were all shivering. Only Slug seemed fine, basking in the warmth of popularity.

Joe burst into the circle and grabbed Slug by the shoulder of his life jacket. The boy was so heavy he barely moved. Joe lowered his face to Slug's and said quietly, 'What the hell were you playing at?' Then he straightened up and shouted, 'What were you all playing at? You promised me you'd stay out of the water.'

The boys hung their heads, knowing they had narrowly avoided tragedy. He didn't have to spell it out for them. He looked away towards the hills, his eyes filling with tears. Slug struggled to his feet and came towards him. 'Mr Docherty?' Joe did not respond. 'Please, Sur?' Joe looked at the boy's face. 'Sorry. Ah thought it would be a laugh to kid on ah wis drownin, ye know?'

'But why did you keep kidding on?'

'Ah could tell it wis a pure panic and ah wis too scared to admit it wis a wind-up. Ah thought you would kill me. Ah'm a hundred and fifty per cent sorry.'

The other boys had gathered round, listening. Joe knew his reaction in the next few minutes could finish his relationship with these lads. If he got it wrong, all his work with them would be lost and he'd be just one more adult who'd let them down. He had to swallow his pride and accept Slug's apology, then use it as a learning experience. For all of them, the boys and himself.

He looked at their faces, one by one, stopping at Slug. Joe poked his finger into Slug's shoulder. The others took a step back, readying themselves for fight or flight.

'I will tell you this, boy. If you ever pull a stunt like that again …'

Slug looked scared.

Joe grinned. 'I will give you mouth to mouth resuscitation, whether you're breathing or not.' He lunged at Slug, as if he were going to kiss him and the boys hooted and howled with delight. Grabbing Slug in a bear hug, Joe said, 'Thank God you're okay, lad.'

'Nice work, Big Man,' said Dykesy.

'I don't know about you lads, but I'm freezing. Let's get into that bothy and get warm and dry. Then we'll break out the picnic. What do you say?'

'Bring it on,' shouted Dangermoose, 'I'm that hungry I could eat a baby's arse through a dirty nappy.'

From long years of experience Joe knew boys that age never wasted time talking when there was food to be eaten. Especially shared food. He waited until every last scrap had been scoffed, then said, 'Lads, there's two things we need to do. We have to get those canoes back up here and loaded on the trailer so I can take them away. And we need to talk about what happened this morning to see if we can learn anything from it.'

Liam was the first to speak. 'Sur, I have to tell ye, like, I learned more this mornin than, like, all the other canoe trips put together.'

Joe decided he'd misjudged this boy. 'Oh aye?' he said, giving Liam the chance to say more.

'Like, you had a good reason for, like, tellin us to wait. We were, like, pure mental to go in the water without you.'

The others were muttering in agreement, but Liam hadn't finished 'I learned other stuff as well, like.' The boy hesitated.

Joe wasn't sure whether Liam was struggling for the right words or the courage to say them in front of his pals.

'Like, I learned to be, like, brave and that.'

To Joe's surprise, there were no catcalls, no banter.

'And I learned, like, stayin calm and doin somethin to help was better than, like, just watchin or runnin away.'

'I know what you mean, man,' said Dykesy. 'No offence, Danger, but you pure kinda went to pieces.'

Dangermoose looked mortified and cleared his throat before he spoke. 'Aye, well, there's a reason for that.'

Everyone waited for the boy to continue. The only sound in the room was the kettle coming to the boil.

Dangermoose coughed before he spoke. 'Ah thought we'd lost Slug, so ah did. And ah couldnae take it. No after what's happened to Jimbo.'

Joe looked from one face to another, waiting for someone to tell him. So this was what they were talking about earlier.

It was TJ who spoke up. 'Jimbo's in the Vickie. Wi an overdose.'

'Heroin?' asked Joe, thinking it had been only a matter of time till this happened, but TJ's next words shocked him.

'Naw, paracetamol. He tried to top his self.'

'Stupid basturt didnae even manage to get that right,' said Dykesy.

'Aw, c'moan Dykesy. He's in intensive care wi liver failure. Gie the boy a break.'

'What a sad waste,' said Joe. 'Jimbo was a good lad.'

'Aye, before he started messin wi drugs,' said Dykesy in a low, angry voice.

Liam was the one who tried to raise the tone, 'At least we've still got the Slugster, eh, Sluggo?'

Slug raised his hand in salute. 'Sur, ah learned stuff too. Like how some jokes are no funny, especially when they're dangerous, but ah didnae mean any harm, just wanted to make the boys laugh. Cheer them up a wee bit, ye know?'

'Funny ha-ha, Sluggo. Ye nearly drowned, ya big eejit.'

'Ah know that.' Slug dropped his head, creating a ripple of chins. He spoke quietly and everyone strained to listen. It was amazing to see these noisy, boisterous lads sit and discuss their feelings.

'Somebody else could've got drowned tryin to save me, and ah was jist havin a laugh.' Slug paused, and no one spoke. 'There's somethin else ah want to say. Ah realise now how stupid it wis to keep it goin jist cos ah wis too scared to own up to what ah done.'

Joe took a deep breath. If these kids could be honest, then so could he. 'Aye, well, I hesitated calling an ambulance because I was worried my boss might find out I'd left you on your own.'

The boys were quick to leap to his defence. 'But you told us to keep out the water, Sur. We're tae blame for ignorin you.'

'And you did try to get an ambulance,' said Dykesy.

'I took too long to send for it.'

'But, Sur. It's okay,' said Slug, 'Ah didnae need an ambulance anyway.'

'Still, I'm going to take you to casualty and get you

checked.'

'But what will your boss say?'

'D'you know what, boys? I don't give a damn what my boss says. If I hadn't been scared it was him on the phone, I would never have left you.'

Dangermoose asked, 'How can you be scared of anybody, Big Man? Look at the size of ye.'

The boys hooted, but Joe sensed it was a serious question. 'Because my boss is a vicious bully and sometimes, no matter what size you are, a bully can frighten you into doing something you know isn't right.'

'Aye, like that scumbag that was dealin at the school gate. Tried to get me to work for him,' said Dykesy.

'You didn't do it though, did you?' asked Joe, regretting the words the moment he'd said them.

Dykesy looked at him with distaste. 'Sur, ah cannae believe you asked me that. You know how ah feel about drugs.'

'That's what I meant, Dykesy. You proved that the bully doesn't win if you're brave enough to stand up for what you believe in.'

The boy looked at Joe for a long moment, then smiled.

Joe hoped he was forgiven. 'That's the difference between you and me. I haven't stood up for myself. But that's going to change.'

'What are you gonnae dae, Big Man?'

'I'm going to resign.'

Amid a chorus of 'no', one voice said, 'What's resign?'

'He's gonnae tell his boss to stick his job up his arse.'

'Aye, and then I'm going to sort him out.'

***

CHAPTER 42

Marty left Chance under the café table, the end of his lead tied around the leg of a chair. He'd been running wild since they came to the park and appeared to fall asleep the minute he dropped to the floor. Just in case he was faking, she said, 'Stay!' and went to fetch herself a coffee.

She joined the queue and kept one eye on the door, watching for Joe. Her heart skipped a beat when he appeared. Tall and athletic, he stood in the doorway and scanned the room. His clean-shaven face looked sculpted and severe until he saw her and grinned. The woman ahead of her nudged her friend and pointed. Marty smiled to herself when Joe came over and asked her to get him his usual. The merest whiff of aftershave hung in the air. Marty ignored the two women who were now inspecting her quite openly. Enjoying herself, she leaned close to Joe and whispered, 'I'll bring it over. Chance is keeping us a seat.'

'There you go,' she said, putting a tall mug down on the table. 'One latte. Skinny, like yourself.'

'Thanks, Marty. I'll get them next time. Any goodies?'

She removed a cling-filmed muffin from her pocket. 'This do?'

'Perfect. Want half?'

'Just a bite, thanks, I'm putting on weight.'

'Don't be daft, you look absolutely gorgeous.'

Why couldn't David say things like that, make her feel good about herself? 'Maybe I should start jogging. You can be my running guru.'

'I'll take you running, anytime you like. We can get hot and sweaty together.'

Marty raised her eyebrows and Joe flushed. It made him

look vulnerable.

When he had finished the muffin, he said, 'Look, Marty. I've got something I need to tell you.'

Her heart stopped for a second and she told herself to act her age.

'I nearly lost a boy yesterday.'

'What, on the hills?'

'No,' murmured Joe, 'worse than that. In the water.'

'Joe,' she said, touching his arm, 'Is he okay?'

Joe let out a long breath, as if he were still getting over it, and nodded. 'Yeah, he's fine.'

'Thank God.'

'Do you know the worst thing about the whole experience? How scared I was that Smeaton would find out. It almost stopped me getting help. Isn't that pathetic?'

She squeezed his arm. 'It's not pathetic, but I can see how you would feel that way. It's the effect the man has on everyone.'

'He won't have that effect on me anymore. I've tendered my resignation.'

'Oh no, Joe, you love your work.'

'I used to love it, Marty. You're right. I always loved my job, but not any longer.'

'Are you sure that's the right thing to do? It wasn't for me.'

'Yeah, I'm sure. I feel free for the first time in years. There's nothing tying me down and I'm answerable to no-one. I can do exactly what I want. And what I want right now, more than anything in the world, is revenge.'

***

CHAPTER 43

Carole had been invited to the planning meeting at Joe's. The four of them were gathered round his kitchen table, looking serious.

'Okay, Sheila,' said Joe, as if he were impatient to get started. 'Run your idea by me again, please.' He drained his water glass and put it down.

'First you need to know that Ruby's as desperate as we are for him to "learn a lesson".' Sheila's fingers drew quotation marks in the air. 'She's told me that a dozen times.'

'And you really think we should tell her we're planning to teach him a lesson? What's to be gained by involving someone else at this stage? Especially someone we don't know.'

'I'm a good judge of character, Joe, and I've spent a lot of hours with this old lady over the past few weeks.'

Joe wouldn't drop it. 'I'm not sure,' he said, rubbing one hand up and down his cheek, 'I mean, what's the point? What could an old woman like that possibly contribute? And what if she tells somebody? We'll all be screwed.'

'She won't. Look, I know you're still not convinced, Joe, but I am. Ruby's the key to the whole thing. The missing link. The last piece of the puzzle.'

'How?' asked Joe, sounding as if he were running out of patience.

'Well, we still haven't worked out how and where we can get him without endangering ourselves. Ruby's the key. She will get Smeaton to take her out for a drive. She'll also make sure he's on a certain road at a certain time.'

'In other words,' added Marty, 'she'll deliver him into our hands.'

'Exactly,' said Sheila

'And what are we supposed to do with the old dear? Bring her to the bothy too?'

'No,' said Sheila, in a calm, gentle voice. 'I'll also be going on the outing, remember? Dressed as Violet, of course. When you take Smeaton, I'll drive Ruby back, then get rid of his car.'

'That's another thing; you still haven't told us what you plan to do with the car.'

'No, but I will, don't worry,' said Sheila. 'And there's something else Ruby can do for us. She knows exactly what makes him tick. And we were right, his religion is vitally important to him.' Sheila paused. 'Ruby says he's obsessed with getting to heaven.'

Joe laughed so hard, Marty worried he would choke. She ran to his kitchen and filled a water glass. When she came back, Carole was thumping him on the back.

'Here, Joe, take a drink.'

When the spluttering had stopped, Marty said, 'I can see why you'd choke on the idea of a heaven full of Smeatons.'

'God forbid,' said Sheila.

'The man's deluded. The way he treats people, he's going straight to hell. Don't forget I grew up Catholic too.'

'So did I, Joe,' said Sheila, 'and if he dies without mortal sin on his soul and lives his life so as to avoid mortal sin, he will go to heaven.'

'The man sins every day of his life. What about Liz?'

'That's not the point. Bullying is not a mortal sin and I'm not even sure Smeaton knows he's bullying. Anyway, you know how it works. If he sins, but confesses, even a mortal sin, to a priest in the sacrament of confession with true repentance, he should go to heaven.'

'And we know from Ruby that Smeaton is devout and regular in his worship and his confession,' said Marty.

'Yes,' said Carole, 'apparently he assists at Mass and does a lot of work for the church. He boasts about it.'

'Know what?' said Joe, 'if heaven is full of folk like Smeaton, I hope I go to hell.'

Sheila laughed. 'Don't be too rash, Joe. Maybe you should

wait to see how bad hell can be before you write off heaven.'

'Remember, our plan is to make Smeaton believe he's in purgatory, not hell,' said Marty. 'We need to give him some hope of redemption.' Silence followed that statement and Marty allowed the moment to last, to give everyone a chance to think their own thoughts.

'Before we take a vote on making Ruby a full accomplice, and remember she may not want to have anything to do with it, does anyone else have something to say?'

Carole took a deep breath and said 'I'll get right to the point. I'd like us to consider bringing the operation forward.'

'Forward by how much?'

'Several weeks.'

'Can you be more precise than that? Do you have a date in mind?'

'Yes, in about three weeks' time.'

'You're joking,' said Sheila, 'three weeks' time? February instead of April?'

'April was notional, remember,' said Marty. 'Why the change of date, Carole?

'I'm going to the States.'

'Ah, the IVF program? said Sheila. 'That's fabulous, Carole. Best of luck.'

'It's as simple as this,' said Marty. 'If we don't bring it forward, it can't happen. We need Carole on the inside and she'll be gone in a couple of weeks.'

'Give or take,' said Carole, 'we still have to finalise some details but three weeks at the most.'

'Actually,' said Marty, 'I've been thinking that the change of timing might suit us. I've got an idea. Didn't you say something about Ruby's birthday coming up, Sheila?'

'Yes. Saturday, seventeenth of February.'

'That's right. He's got it marked in his diary,' said Carole, 'to remind me to send flowers. He does that every year. I buy the card too and get him to sign it. But at least he goes to see her on her birthday, usually takes her out to lunch.'

Sheila nodded wildly and looked very excited. 'I see what

you're thinking. Tie it into Ruby's birthday outing?'

Marty nodded and Carole clapped her hands. 'Perfect.'

Marty ran through the revised plan one more time and asked for a decision. 'Let's take a vote on making Mrs Smeaton an accomplice.'

Joe still looked unsure, and was last to cast his vote. Finally, he raised his hand and made it unanimous.

'Can we run through the jobs that everyone was delegated and see if we could be ready for February seventeenth? Joe. You ordered the Rohypnol, yes?'

'Yes, and I was tracking the delivery online earlier today. It should be here the day after tomorrow.'

'Good. And the bothy?'

'I'm due to have it cleared by the end of January and I've already started stowing our stuff we'll need in the attic. Under lock and key of course.'

'You okay with a change of date then?'

'Actually, it would solve a problem with the electricity.'

'What do you mean?'

'To be honest, Marty, it's been bothering me how we were going to manage if they cut off the power. I mean, candles are okay for a wee while, but not for what we need to do.'

'I hadn't even thought about electricity,' said Sheila. 'Will we be okay, Joe?'

'We will now.'

'So we'll be fine for lighting, warm water and cooking.' said Marty, scribbling in her notebook.

Marty ticked off items on a spread sheet as each person reported on his or her progress. 'Have you two finalised your design for where we keep our prisoner?'

'Just about, but I'm going to require lots of help to get it set up and make it secure.'

'Count me in,' said Carole, 'I'd like to see inside this bothy place. I function better when I can visualise the setting.'

Marty said, 'Good idea. Let me run through a couple more items on my list and then we'll make arrangements for a visit to check the place out.'

Joe gave her a grim smile. 'And to see how we can turn a wee corner of heaven into Smeaton's hell on earth.'

***

CHAPTER 44

Ruby seemed a bit down.

'You're not your usual self, Ruby. Is it because of who's on duty today?' No response. 'Is that why you're keeping quiet? You like Doreen better, don't you?'

Ruby gave Sheila one of those 'Duh!' looks much favoured by her pupils, but at least she followed it up with a gummy grin. Sheila wondered how many old folk's moods were affected by the personality of the carer who turned up to look after them.

'Are you still mad at your son for not taking you to Molly's funeral?

'That and a thousand other sins he's committed in his lifetime. The funeral was the final straw for me, that's all, Violet.'

'He sounds like a very busy, important man, Ruby. I'm sure he felt terrible about letting you down.'

Ruby looked at her as if she were completely insane. 'That boy has never felt terrible about a thing in his life. He was born without a conscience.'

This might be a productive line of conversation. 'Did you not bring him up as a good Catholic boy?'

'Of course. I may have lost my belief when Billy and Archie were taken from me, but I made sure Tommy was brought up in the faith.'

The old lady's eyes misted over. 'Oh Violet, I wish you could have seen the two wee boys on the day of their first holy communion. They were a picture.' She reached up her sleeve and fished around.

'It must have cost you a fair bit of money to kit them both out in their finery,' said Sheila, offering Ruby a tissue.

'I wouldn't have had it any other way. I had to save every penny I could, but it never bothered me one bit.'

'How on earth did you make ends meet?'

'To tell you the truth, Violet, I didn't eat very much. As long as the weans were well fed, I was satisfied.'

Ruby sniffed, touching the tissue to her nose and eyes. Her voice took on a sharp edge when she said, 'And look how he repays me.' She gestured to the room around her, filled with dozing companions. 'I could be living independently, Violet. I had a good wee cleaner and nice neighbours who kept an eye on me. I'd plenty of folk willing to come in every day, to help me out. He wouldn't hear of it.'

'It must cost a lot more to pay for Briargrove?'

'Our Tommy doesn't mind paying for me. As long as he doesn't have to be bothered with me. Do you know how he justifies putting me in here?'

Sheila shook her head, sure that nothing she was about to hear could surprise her.

'He says it makes sense for me to be in a home. It might be a bit expensive, but since he's cash rich and time poor, it's the best solution for everyone.'

'Everyone except you, Ruby?'

Ruby nodded. 'Can you see why I'm so angry with him, Violet? How I wish, every time I hear him crowing about how high and mighty he is, that someone would take him down a peg or two.

It was now or never. Time for Sheila to take a leap of faith and go for it.

'Ruby,' she said. 'What if I had worked out a wee plan to do precisely that?'

***

CHAPTER 45

Marty had to concentrate, holding the too-full mug of coffee with both hands. She used her foot to push open the door and gave it a gentle kick behind her. She took a sip from the mug and put it down so she could dial Joe's number.

'Hiya, Marty. How's tricks?'

'Sheila rang. Ruby's in.'

'That was quick.'

'She said it was easy. Ruby was feeling a bit down when Violet went in to visit her and looked about thirty years younger when she left. She says the old dear is so up for it.'

'I hope Sheila knows what she's doing.'

'I'm sure she does. I think we should relax. It's going to work.'

Marty looked round, startled by the sound of the door opening. Chance pranced towards her, as delighted to see her as if she'd been gone for a week.

'Oops, Chance seems to think I'm playing hide and seek. Lie down, boy.'

'He's a cool dog. I've been thinking I might get a dog, once I'm settled.'

'Speaking of settled, anything to report?'

'Think I've found the perfect place to build. I'll tell you when I see you.'

'I'm excited. Tell me now.'

Chance got to his feet. She watched him amble to the door and greet his master.

'Marty?'

'David! Don't sneak up on me! How long have you been standing there?'

David seemed surprised at her tone. 'Sorry. I came to offer you a cup of coffee while you're chatting, but I see you've got one.' He turned and walked away.

'Shit,' she whispered into the phone.

'What happened? Was that your husband?'

'Yeah, and I've no idea how long he was standing there.'

'How much do you think he heard?'

'I haven't a clue. Did we say anything incriminating?'

Joe took some time before he answered. 'No, I don't think so. I can't remember word for word, but I don't think you said anything suspicious.'

'Look, I need to get off the phone. Damage limitation and all that.'

'Yeah, go. Maybe see you in the park later?'

'Maybe. Bye.'

David was in the kitchen. She made an effort to smile and said, 'Sorry to be snippy. You made me jump. I didn't hear you come in.'

David kept his back turned. Marty tried to recall her side of the conversation. Had she been flirty with Joe? Had she given away any information about their plans? All that stuff about trusting Sheila. How must that have sounded? 'I'll have that coffee with you now, if you don't mind?'

'Why don't you make your own, Marty? That seems to be the way you prefer to do things these days. On your own.' David plonked a teabag in a cup, stirred violently and banged the spoon several times on the rim. He knew how much she hated that. When he turned and walked past her, Chance gave her a knowing look and followed David out of the kitchen.

***

CHAPTER 46

Joe watched the last of his furniture and belongings being loaded into the back of a removals van. It was time to say goodbye. Time to move on.

He rubbed at his face. A shave and a shower would be a good idea before Marty arrived to help him 'deep-clean' the flat. The purchasers had paid a premium to get a very early move-in date, not knowing how well it suited Joe to get his hands on their money. This time tomorrow, the new folk would be in and he'd be four hundred grand richer.

The doorbell rang.

'Chance not with you?' he asked, as Marty dumped a huge Ikea bag full of cleaning products and took off her coat.

'No, he would have been an idiot. Sliding like Bambi on newly mopped floors.'

Joe smiled at the image. 'Don't you need the dog as a cover for being here?'

'No, David's gone to play golf, as usual. Anyway, I can give a friend a helping hand without having to ask his permission.'

'Oooh, prickly,' he said, with a smile to let her know he was joking.

'Actually, he's being a bit of an arse. I'm worried he overheard us on the phone. I think he might suspect there's something going on.'

'Has he said anything?'

'No, but confrontation's not his style.'

'You're just stressed with organizing everything. Come on. Relax.' Without thinking, he grabbed her in a hug. He was surprised how good it felt to have a woman in his arms again.

With a pang of regret, pain, guilt, maybe all three, he realised how much he missed physical contact with another human being. Enjoying the closeness, he whispered, 'You've been amazing, thanks.'

Did Marty cling on a second too long? It was enough to make the moment awkward. She must have felt it too because she became brusque, thumping him on the arm and walking through to the kitchen. 'You're right. I'm being neurotic.' She surveyed the room, rubbing her hands together. 'We should start in here. If you leave the kitchen and bathroom spotless, your buyers will love you forever. I brought my own rubber gloves and a pair of extra-large for you.'

She handed him a plastic bucket. 'Make yourself useful and fill this, will you?'

'Would you like a coffee? I've kept two old mugs and the kettle.'

'To be honest, Joe, I'd rather have one when we've finished here. Whenever I start a job, I prefer to see it through to the end.'

'Okay, you're right, let's crack on.'

They worked in silence for a while then Joe said, 'So we're ready to roll in two days' time?'

'Indeed we are. I hope we haven't missed anything.'

'If we have, and I doubt it, someone will think of it before tonight's meeting.'

'I keep running it through in my mind. I see Violet and Ruby being picked up by Smeaton at Briargrove, then I start to panic. What if he recognizes Sheila? What if he won't stop at the place we've agreed for the snatch? I'm driving myself mad. I want to get on with it now.'

'I know. I feel the same way. Listen, is that your phone?'

Marty ran for her coat and retrieved her mobile from the pocket. Joe heard her say, 'Oh hi, David.' Something in her voice made him look up, expecting to see her in the doorway. But she didn't come into the lounge. She stayed in the hallway and continued her conversation.

Joe was scouring the sink when she came back into the

room and said, 'I need to go.'

**

CHAPTER 47

When she got home, David was in the kitchen, waiting for her. She found it hard to read his expression. She tried to make her voice light, 'Didn't expect to see you home this early. Golf rained off?'

'I didn't play golf.'

'Okay.' She had no idea what else to say.

'Marty, I'm not very good at this stuff.'

'What stuff?'

'Emotions. Intrigue. Pretence. All that stuff.'

Oh God, he knew. 'David, we should talk.' Marty felt nauseous.

'No time for that. You need to pack your bags.'

'What are you talking about?' Surely he wasn't throwing her out? Bile rose in her throat.

'You're leaving.'

Marty swallowed hard. 'I don't understand.'

'Understand this. You are going to Paris.'

'When?'

'This weekend.'

Her legs gave way and she flopped onto a kitchen chair. Paris? She couldn't go to Paris. And yet, how could she refuse? David was grinning at her, clearly delighted to see her so shocked.

'Gotcha!'

Marty exhaled for a very long moment. 'You certainly did.'

'Paris. City of lovers, isn't that what they call it?'

'Yeah, something like that,' said Marty, distracted by dozens of thoughts clamoring for her attention. 'What made you think of this?'

He took her hands and pulled her off the chair into his

arms. It felt strange and artificial. 'I decided to do something spontaneous for once, to surprise you.'

'You certainly pulled that off.'

'And maybe I've been neglecting you a bit. I'm going to try harder from now on, promise.' He leaned in close and touched her lips with his.

She turned her face and said, 'When will we be back?'

'Sunday night.' He smacked her bottom and pushed her away. 'Now go and get packed. As for dinner tonight? I've got it all organized.'

***

CHAPTER 48

For fear of being overheard in a pub, Sheila had suggested having their final meeting at her place.

'Marty's going to be late. If she can make it at all.'

'Is Marty okay? Is something wrong?'

'She didn't say, Joe. Just that she would be in touch later on and that we should run through the final details. She sent me her spreadsheet, look.'

Carole giggled. 'You are honoured.'

'I know. Right, let's take it from the top. Joe, you'll head up to the bothy on Friday afternoon and make sure everything is ready for Saturday. Marty will drop me round the corner from Briargrove on Saturday morning, complete with picnic. Then she'll meet you, Joe, and you'll drive up to the bothy together. She'll bring all the food. I'll be at Briargrove no later than ten to eleven. That should give me time to brief Ruby before Smeaton arrives to pick us up.'

'You'll be dressed as Violet?' asked Joe.

'Yes.'

'And you'll dump his car then morph into Sheila, right?'

'That's right, I'll have Sheila clothes under my Violet gear. A little extra padding does not look out of place on an elderly lady. Think of Mrs Doubtfire.'

Joe didn't laugh. He looked like a dog with a bone. 'What will you do with Violet's stuff?'

'Thought of that. The shopping centre has a big wheelie bin on each floor. Violet's gear will end up in one of them. Inside a black bag.'

'And the leftover picnic stuff? You can't dump that at the shopping centre, or at least not the special drink you're going to give Smeaton.'

'I'll rinse out his cup and get rid of it and all the other rubbish and leftovers in a bin in one of the laybys. They're always full of discarded food wrappers and drink bottles, even at this time of the year. I noticed the other day. That sound okay, Joe?'

Joe was nodding his head. 'Yes, Sheila, better than okay. Sorry, I don't mean to be picky.'

'I know. You want to make sure we haven't missed anything. I understand. That's good.'

Sheila continued with details of the plan, including the signals that would tell which picnic spot they were in and when she was ready for them to come and collect Smeaton.

'And then it's over to you guys. I'll drop Ruby back at Briargrove, ditch Smeaton's car, do a bit of shopping in town, acting normal, and head home on the bus.'

'Sounds perfect, and you're sure of the dose you need to give him?' asked Carole.

'Yes, I worked it all out after you got Smeaton to reveal his weight. Joe double-checked the dose, and the pills are ready for me to dissolve in his drink.'

'I heard that stuff turns blue if it's used to spike a drink,' said Carole.

'You're right,' said Joe, 'but the stuff I sent for stays clear. We tried some in a few different drinks to make sure. It will work particularly well in Smeaton's favourite.'

'Then, as I said, it's over to you guys.' Sheila looked at Joe.

Carole said, 'How long are you planning on keeping him?'

'As long as it takes,' said Joe.

'A couple of days,' said Sheila. 'Three at the most, we reckon. Right, do we need to run through the plans again, or are we good to go?'

'I think we're good to go. The video camera is in place and the projector so we can watch. The white noise is downloaded and the speakers have been checked. Yip, all sorted.'

Carole raised her hand like a little kid. 'Sorry to sound dim, but what's white noise?'

'It's a kind of whooshing, soothing, water-gushing sound

that masks distracting noises.'

'People use it to soothe babies. My friend's daughter has it going all night long.'

'Have you listened to it, Joe?'

'Yeah. I think it sounds like someone pouring a never-ending bag of rice into a giant bowl. Should keep old Smeaton from hearing any sounds from outside the bothy.'

'What a great idea. You guys have thought of everything.'

'One thing we haven't thought about is alibis,' said Joe.

'I'll be in the States, so that's mine sorted,' said Carole. 'But why would you need an alibi?'

'Just to be on the safe side. You never know. Say something happens and Smeaton claims we kidnapped him.'

Sheila burst out laughing. 'That's ridiculous, Joe. But I'll be sure to watch all the programmes from that weekend on iPlayer so I can say I've been home in front of the TV like a good wee spinster schoolteacher.'

'It's never gonna happen, but still, I like to cover all bases. I'll say I was at the bothy, clearing up and closing down. The lads will vouch for me, if need be. They owe me a favour or two.'

When Sheila's doorbell rang, the three of them said, 'That'll be Marty.'

Chance burst into the room first followed by a very flustered Marty. 'I haven't got long. David thinks I'm walking the dog but I had to grab a taxi.'

Joe stood and put his arm round her shoulders. 'Are you okay?'

'Yes, I'm okay.' She stepped away from him. 'Folks, I'm sorry but I'm going to Paris for the weekend. My husband decided to surprise me.'

'What about our plans, Marty?' Joe touched her arm.

'We'll need to put them on hold. You guys will have to work out how.' Grabbing her dog by the collar, she said, 'Sorry, I have to run. The cab's waiting for me. Let's go, Chance.'

'Wow,' said Sheila, 'I didn't see that one coming. What do

we do now? Call it off?'

Joe groaned like a man who'd set fire to a winning lottery ticket. 'No, we don't call it off. We have to put everything on hold, as she says. Not much else we can do.'

'A week's delay isn't so awful. It's not ideal, when we're all ready for action, but it isn't the end of the world.'

'You're right. What's the worst thing that can happen? Smeaton might have plans for next weekend? Carole will help us get round that, one way or another, won't you, Carole?'

'Is anyone else thinking this is fate? Telling us to stop?' asked Carole. 'Or is it just me?'

'Are you kidding?' said Joe. 'Stop now, after all this planning? All that hard work at the bothy? No way.'

'I agree,' said Sheila, 'we can't let one small setback stop us now. I'm determined to see it through, for Liz's sake. Any idea what's in his diary for next weekend, Carole?'

'Would you believe he's due at a conference?'

'Fuck,' said Joe quietly, rubbing at his face.

'We have to stay cool,' said Sheila, 'and think.'

'I know he's not that keen to go to the conference. It's about leadership and, don't choke when I say this, Smeaton thinks he's an expert on good leadership. He's offended that he wasn't invited to be a keynote speaker. He's been moaning the face off me all week about how he shouldn't have to attend as an ordinary delegate.'

'So,' said Sheila, warming to the challenge of finding a solution, 'You don't think he would be heartbroken if the conference were to be cancelled at short notice?'

'I think he'd be delighted.'

'Okay then, folks, tell me what you think of this. Late next Friday, Carole, you tell Smeaton that you've had a call from the conference organisers. There's a problem at the venue, a burst pipe is always a good one, puts the toilets out of commission. Say he will hear from them with a revised date, apologies etc.'

When the others nodded their approval, she went on, 'Joe, could you call the conference organisers pretending to be Smeaton? Explain that your elderly mother has gone down with flu and you'll need to spend the weekend with her.'

'Great idea,' said Joe.

'Ask if you could have your conference fee refunded, that'll make it sound more genuine. There's no chance but it's the kind of question folk always ask.'

'Good thinking,' said Joe, his voice full of admiration.

'And I'll tip off Ruby. Carole, will you tell Smeaton you've had a call from Briargrove to say Ruby doesn't want visitors this weekend?'

'Why don't I tell him there's been an outbreak of norovirus?'

'What's norovirus?' asked Joe.

'Also known as winter vomiting bug but that doesn't mention the diarrhoea that comes with it.'

'Yuck,' said Joe, 'too much information.'

'Spreads through these places like wildfire. Effectively shuts them down till they get the all clear.'

'Reminds me of an absence note I once got from a mother, telling me that "wee Jimmy had the diarrhoea and it was all through the house". Still makes me smile.'

'Well, I'm not smiling,' said Joe. 'In fact, I think I might vomit myself.'

'Norovirus is an inspired suggestion, Carole. Smeaton will run a hundred miles.'

'Like me,' said Joe.

Sheila felt pleased with their quick thinking and looked at the others. 'So are we sorted? Same plan as before, one week later?'

Carole's brows were knotted in a frown. 'Em, there's just one problem. Wednesday is my last day at work. We leave for the States on Thursday.'

***

CHAPTER 49

Marty was polishing furniture that didn't need polishing when the phone rang. Glad of the interruption, she found her mobile and picked up.

'Can you talk?'

'Yes, David's out.'

'How was Paris?'

'It's a beautiful city.'

'That's not what I meant.'

'Joe, I went to Paris with my husband and we had a lovely time.'

'That's all you're going to say?'

'What else can I say? It was a wonderful surprise and David was great fun to be away with. He spoiled me rotten. Hey, wait a minute, are you jealous?'

'Don't be daft. Let's talk about Smeaton. When I called his office to tell him the conference was cancelled, he answered the phone himself. I nearly peed my pants.'

Marty knew she was meant to laugh, but she was too busy regretting her stupid remark about him being jealous.

'You should have heard the way he spoke to me, and I was pretending to be a complete stranger. A polite, helpful member of the conference centre staff, calling to tell him the conference would have to be postponed. He gave me dog's abuse about short notice and inconvenience and lack of organization. You have no idea. It was unbelievable. I could barely stop myself telling him to F-off. I wanted to slam the phone down.'

'Why didn't you?'

'I was worried he'd call back to complain and find out the conference wasn't cancelled at all.'

'Good move. Are you certain he didn't recognise your voice?'

Joe reassured her in a very credible Eastern European accent.

'Wow, how do you do that?'

'Years of holidaying in Bulgaria and many ill-spent hours chatting to Glasgow bar staff.'

***

CHAPTER 50

Joe threw a book and a giant bar of chocolate onto the back seat of the Land Rover and climbed in behind the wheel. The rest of his stuff was already at the bothy. The women didn't know it, but he'd been living there since he moved out of the flat.

The town was busy with Friday afternoon traffic but once he got out on the open road, he had a clear run into the countryside. He took the turn signposted for the castle and passed the laybys and picnic spots that would provide tomorrow's pickup point. It was down to Sheila and Ruby to choose which one, depending on how many other visitors were around. Joe had to admit that Sheila was right to bring Ruby in as an accomplice. Apparently she was determined she could get Smeaton to agree to a 'wee run up to the castle' and would be cantankerous enough to demand that he park where she chose to enjoy their picnic.

The countryside was bare and yellow, all signs of last summer's green erased by winter. Where bracken met heather, the hillsides were patch-worked in shades of brown. Dry stone walls snaked up impossibly steep slopes. Joe passed the castle, semi-ruined now, and followed the road until it ran out of tar. The Land Rover had no trouble coping with the unpaved track that led round behind the hill to the bothy. It was well-hidden from the main road and far enough from it to feel remote. Joe slowed to a crawl as a ewe and her full-grown lamb cantered off the verge into his path and ambled along at their own speed.

As he approached the bothy, an enervating thrill ran through his body. This had never been part of his own plan but it suited him fine. He parked behind the house and stepped out, his feet sinking into the mossy ground. It was like walking on finest carpet. The honking of geese made him raise his eyes to the sky, and he watched them fly in formation towards the loch. They disappeared into the distance and a silence descended, broken only by the sound of a jet, miles away. Joe breathed in air that smelled of nothing but freshness.

***

CHAPTER 51

Sheila hadn't slept a wink. At five thirty she gave up on sleep, switched on her bedside lamp and reached for her little notebook. She flicked over the pages till she got to the one that said Order of Play. She ran her eye down the list, double-checking the details she had committed to memory over a week ago. She prayed nothing would go wrong today.

Pulling on a fleecy robe, she wandered through to the kitchen to make a cup of coffee, checking her phone. Marty had sent a text at two am asking if she was awake.

At six thirty the phone rang.

'Hi Sheila, did you sleep?'

'Not a wink. You?'

'Far too much on my mind, like wondering if we're all completely mad.'

Sheila poured hot water onto ground coffee and inhaled the rich smell. 'I guess we'll sleep easy this time next week.'

'Yeah. When do you think it will be all over, as a matter of interest?'

'No idea. When Smeaton sees the error of his ways, I suppose,' said Marty.

'And how long do you think that will take?'

'Who knows? No more than a couple of days, I hope. I want this finished so I can move on with my life. He's been ruining it for long enough.'

'Marty, I've been thinking. Once it's done, maybe we should sever all connections between you, me, Carole and Joe.'

'Been thinking that too. For your sake and Carole's. Unless Smeaton can prove we kidnapped him and kept him against his will, he can't do anything to Joe or me, but he could make your lives a misery if he suspected you were involved.'

'Agreed. I'm going to miss you though. You guys have really helped me through a very dark place.'

'The valley of the shadow of death, eh?'

'That's the one. Anyway, thank you.' Sheila could feel tears coming, the last thing she wanted. 'Right,' she said, briskly, 'See you later. About ten. And Marty?'

'Yes?'

'Keep the faith.'

Sheila pulled the belt of her robe tight round her waist and tied a pinny on top. She might as well make a start on the picnic. She banged a little saucepan on to the stove, filled it with water and set two eggs to boil. Ruby's favourite sandwich was egg mayonnaise and Sheila planned to give the old lady a treat. They would need something to do while they waited for the drug to take effect, so Ruby might as well enjoy herself.

By ten fifteen, Marty and Sheila were ready to go. Sheila, dressed as Violet, had added to her disguise a pair of glasses and a touch of make-up. She did not want to risk being recognized by her boss. She and Ruby had agreed Violet ought to say as little as possible in Smeaton's presence and that she would change her voice when she did have to speak.

The picnic was packed and waiting by the front door, including Smeaton's favourite soft-drink. It was vital to the plan that he take the spiked drink and swallow the lot.

They sat at the kitchen table, nursing cups of coffee and willing the hands on the clock to hurry up a bit. Sheila rose to her feet saying, 'Here I go again.' She had already confessed to Marty that fear had been making her run to the toilet constantly for the last few days. 'I hope I can make it through the picnic without having to dash off into the bushes.' Both women laughed at the idea but Sheila was dreading the possibility.

At ten thirty, Marty said, 'Right then, kid. Showtime.'

***

CHAPTER 52

Marty was glad to be taking action at last. This operation seemed to have been so long in the planning. In fact, it was only a few months since she and Joe had met, but it seemed to Marty like she had been waiting years for this day to come.

She hoped Sheila's nerve would hold, especially when she came face to face with Smeaton. Sheila had never had any problems with him. Liz had believed, and Marty agreed, that was because he knew she attended St Gerard's although Sheila said he had never spoken to her at church. They did not attend Mass on the same day, apparently, and Sheila said Smeaton was much more devout than herself. Marty hoped his faith was as strong as they had been led to believe. The whole plan hinged on that.

She glanced across at Sheila, or rather, Violet. She looked every inch the elderly lady, hunched over in the passenger seat, dressed head to toe in beige. Her silver grey wig was mostly hidden under a silk square that had belonged to Liz. Sheila was wearing it for luck. 'I keep reminding myself that this is all for Liz,' Sheila said, as if she had read Marty's mind. 'Each time I find myself wondering what on earth I'm doing, I think about Liz. Then anger floods through me and I feel like one of those turbo-charged cars, ready to race.'

'That's good to know, because we're approaching the starting grid. I think this is close enough, don't you?' She had pulled into a side street and turned to face the way they'd come. She stopped the car and switched off the engine.

'Yes, this is perfect. We don't want you bumping into you-know-who.' Sheila pulled down the sun visor and inspected her disguise in the little mirror. Then she hoisted her huge handbag over her arm, patted her headscarf and turned to Marty. When she spoke, her voice made Marty smile and nod her head in approval, 'I can't thank you enough, my dear. You have been most kind. I wonder, would you do me one last little obligement?'

Marty laughed and said, 'Of course, Violet.'

'Would you mind helping me with my picnic bag? It's an awful awkward lift for a lady of my age.'

Sheila did a very convincing version of an old lady getting out of a car, showing a generous amount of long pink cotton knickers above bare legs and pop socks.

Marty handed her the picnic, whispering, 'Break a leg, Violet,' then patted her on the back and watched her toddle off towards Briargrove.

Marty got back behind the wheel and took a long, deep breath. As she exhaled she said aloud, 'Right, Marty. You've set the ball rolling. There's no turning back now.' She didn't know whether she was excited or scared. Her stomach seemed to choose a mixture of the two. It was full of butterflies, but, for the moment at least, they seemed to be flying in formation.

She reached into her bag and took out her phone. 'Joe?' she said, 'I just dropped Violet off near Briargrove. She looks and sounds exactly like an old woman. Smeaton won't suspect a thing. Shit!'

She dropped the phone and sunk down into her seat, trying to disappear behind the dashboard but keep her eyes high enough to see the road ahead. About two hundred metres away, on the main road, the traffic had stopped. Directly in her line of vision was the profile of a man she would recognise anywhere. It was Smeaton, no doubt about it, but he was here far too early and he wasn't driving his usual car. As she huddled out of sight, Marty became aware of two things simultaneously. One was Joe's voice calling her name from the phone at her feet. The other was the pandemonium in her stomach as the butterflies all flew into one another.

She scrabbled around on the floor till she located the phone and gasped into it, 'Smeaton just drove by. He's too early. He'll be there before Sheila. What will I do?'

No answer. Joe must have given up and rung off.

***

CHAPTER 53

'Time to put your coat on, Ruby,' called Doreen. 'Your son's here.'

That couldn't be right. Ruby checked her wristwatch, in case she had dozed off and lost half an hour. She was feeling well and alert this morning and sure enough, no more than five minutes had gone since she last checked the time. Violet was meant to get here first, but Tommy had turned up early. She had been hoping Violet would run through the plan again. She didn't want to be the one to ruin everything by making a mistake.

In he came, strutting across the lounge in that self-important way of his. He was developing a little pot belly and he carried it before him like a prized possession.

He stood in front of her, slapping his gloves against his leg, impatient as a Gestapo officer in a war movie. It occurred to her that it might make sense to be a bit nicer to him than usual. A lot depended on him, he had to do what she asked over the next few hours.

'I got the flowers you sent for my birthday, thanks.'

'Ah yes, your birthday. Many happy returns. Sorry to hear you were a bit poorly last week. They said no visitors were allowed. How are you today?'

'Fine, thanks.'

'Looking forward to a wee outing?'

'Yes. I am.'

'Get your coat on then and we'll go.'

'We need to wait for Violet.'

'Why would we wait for Violet?'

'Because I told her she could come too.'

He leaned in close and said, 'Listen to me, mother. I don't

201

mind taking you out, but I draw the line at taking any of these …' He stopped and looked around at Ruby's co-residents, as if trying to find an appropriate word to describe them. He settled on, 'old dears. Half of them aren't even awake. It would be a complete waste of time taking them anywhere.'

Ruby said, 'Violet isn't an old dear, she's a good bit younger. She's not even a resident here. And I promised we would take her. You said it was okay last week.'

'I've changed my mind. I've got a new car and I don't want some incontinent old biddy wetting herself on my upholstery.'

Ruby ignored his remark but she heard Jinty make a loud tut of disapproval from two seats along. 'We can't go without Violet. She's bringing the picnic.'

'Oh, Mother,' he said in a long-suffering voice, 'we're not going to celebrate your eighty-fifth birthday with a few soggy sandwiches and some over-stewed tea in a flask.'

'Eighty-third,' said Ruby in a quiet voice, knowing he wasn't listening anyway.

'I'm taking you down the coast to Trump Turnberry for lunch. That's why I'm here early. Thought we'd have an aperitif looking out at Ailsa Craig while we listen to someone tinkling the ivories on the grand piano. Lunch is sixty-five pounds a head, you know.'

Ruby wondered if she was supposed to be impressed. She was about to ask him, when she remembered her plan to keep him sweet. 'Oh, Tommy, that's an awful lot of money for a meal. You don't need to go to all that expense for me.'

His chest inflated like a courting pigeon's. 'Nonsense. I can easily afford it.'

He looked around the room but no one seemed impressed, least of all Jinty who gave another loud tut.

'Come on now. Where's your coat?'

'I want to wait for Violet.'

'Mother,' he hissed, 'I'm not buying lunch for some old woman I've never met before. Besides, she won't have the palate to appreciate luxury food.'

'I don't think I have either. Or the stomach for it.' She

smiled to take the edge off her words though she meant what she said. He gave her a look. She was about to say she'd prefer an egg sandwich when Violet appeared.

'Oh, good,' she said, 'here's Violet now.'

'Hang on, isn't she the one that nearly ruined my good coat?' He shook his head. 'You have to be joking, Mother.'

***

CHAPTER 54

Ruby was impressed. If Violet was shocked to see Tommy there too early, she hid it well. All credit to her. 'Hello, Violet, dear,' said Ruby. 'Have you met my son Tommy? Tommy, this is my friend, Miss McNish.'

'Of course, she's met me, Mother, remember? Hello again, Miss McNish.'

Violet offered Tommy her gloved hand. She smiled, but said nothing. She was sticking to their plan.

Ruby asked, 'Did you bring the picnic, Violet?' When Violet nodded, Ruby said, 'Did you put plenty of mayonnaise on the egg sandwiches?'

'Sorry, Miss McNish,' interrupted Tommy. 'We've had a bit of a last-minute change. I didn't realise you were planning a picnic and I'm afraid I've booked a table for lunch at Trump Turnberry. A table for two.'

Violet's disappointment showed on her face, but she quickly recovered her composure and said, 'Oh, that's nice. Bon appétit.'

'Thanks,' said Tommy, taking his mother's arm to hurry her out of her chair. 'Right, Mother. Let's get going.'

Ruby refused to budge. 'I don't want to go to some posh restaurant. I told you what I wanted for my birthday treat. A wee run in the car and a picnic somewhere with a nice view. I told you. I like the road up to the loch. Me and Billy used to go there, when we were courting. You said you'd take me and now you're going back on your word.' Ruby sniffed and poked her fingers up her sleeve in search of a hanky. Violet looked on in silence, clutching her handbag to her chest.

Ruby continued with her weeping act until Tommy relented.

'Okay,' he said, face like thunder. 'You win, mother. Since it's for your birthday. But I'll need to phone Trump Turnberry and cancel.'

'You'd better go outside with that thing.' Ruby pointed. 'They don't like folk using phones in here. Violet will help me on with my coat and we'll be out in a minute.'

They waited by the window until Tommy appeared in the car park then Violet burst into nervous laughter. 'Good God, Ruby. I thought the game was up, right there,' she whispered.

'Yes, damn you and your pals. I'm missing a sixty-five quid lunch at Turnberry.'

'If this comes off, we'll pay you back. I promise you a very posh lunch, but it won't be at Trump's place. And I won't be dressed like Violet. Okay?'

'Okay. It's a deal. Now remind me of my part in this, just to make sure I've got it right.'

Violet looked round, checking for eavesdroppers.

'Don't fret about them,' said Ruby, 'they're as deaf as that doorpost.'

Jinty appeared to be asleep, but Violet kept her voice very low; she was taking no chances. 'All you need to do is make sure we go into a layby with no other cars in it. Then keep him chatting throughout lunch so he doesn't notice anything strange.'

'I can manage that. And you'll bring me back afterwards?' Ruby was buttoning her coat as she spoke.

'I certainly will. Have you got a hat and gloves?' asked Violet, as if they were going on an ordinary trip. 'It's quite nippy out there.'

'Tommy' was waiting by his car. 'A picnic in February?' he muttered. 'I must be mad.' He opened the passenger door for Ruby. She groaned and complained of aches and pains as he helped her in. Violet, as planned, sat behind the driver's seat. She kept the picnic bag close by her side as Tommy got in, started the engine and roared out on to the main road.

***

CHAPTER 55

Sheila sat as low in her seat as she could, hoping to keep out of Smeaton's line of vision. She studied the back of his seat and concentrated on what she had to do.

'How do you know my mother, Miss McNish?' he asked, catching her off guard. Before she had time to answer, Ruby pitched in and all Violet had to do was murmur agreement here and there. That single question seemed to satisfy, either his curiosity, or his need to show polite interest. After that, to Sheila's relief, he made no further attempt at conversation with her.

He was driving fast and the journey was going by quickly.

'Lovely car,' Violet remarked.

'Thanks, I only got it yesterday. Bit of an impulse buy, really. It's the new Merc. Top of the range. A tad over seventy-five grand, but I decided to treat myself. Because I'm worth it.'

Sheila assumed he was making a reference to the shampoo ad but decided not to laugh in case he was serious. Instead, she repeated, 'Lovely.' Suddenly she realised Joe and Marty would be expecting to see Smeaton's previous car. Already the plan was going awry. She would need to find a way to tell them they were now looking for a Mercedes.

When they reached the junction with the signpost for the castle, Smeaton turned off the main road and slowed down a little. Sheila was grateful. She gave Ruby the coughing signal that meant she could choose any layby from now on, provided it was empty. Smeaton drove straight past the first one before Ruby could react. 'Slow down, would you, Tommy? You're making me feel car sick.'

'The smell of new leather upholstery can be a bit overpowering.'

The next layby had two cars in it and at the third a minibus was loading youngsters in wheelchairs. 'See that?' said Smeaton, pointing. 'That's the ridiculous sort of outing I want stopped. What's the sense in bussing kids like that to a place like this? Waste of public money. Austerity is the name of the game, and everyone's got to play their part.'

Sheila bit her tongue. The man was reprehensible. She gave another cough to remind Ruby they needed to find a parking place soon. 'Why don't we pull in beside them?' the old lady asked.

'And eat our lunch with them all watching us? No chance.'

As they approached the next layby they could see a middle-aged couple at the bin, disposing of the remnants of a picnic. Sheila decided it was worth a try. She coughed and Ruby said, 'What about here?'

Smeaton started to swing into the space then turned the wheel and stayed on the road. 'No way. I'm not taking a brand new car onto rough ground like that. We'll have to find somewhere else.'

Sheila did not know how many laybys bordered the road, but she knew the number wasn't infinite. She was becoming more anxious by the minute.

Just as she was beginning to panic Smeaton found a layby with enough room for two cars and parked across it, taking up most of the space. 'There you go, a nice view for you, and I don't have to get my wheels mucky. Perfect.' He patted his mother on the knee and said, 'Will this do you, madam?'

'I think so. What do you say, Violet? Nice?'

Ruby sounded a little unsure so Sheila said, 'Lovely, thanks.'

'Now, about that picnic. Would you mind going outside with it? I don't want anything getting spilled on my new upholstery.'

'Don't be ridiculous, Tommy. It's February in Scotland. Nobody gets out their car to eat.'

'Mother,' he said, his teeth gritted. 'Remember what happened to my coat.'

'Come on, Violet, ignore him. Let's get these sandwiches

open. I'll have an eggie one. So will our Tommy.'

Smeaton didn't argue. Sheila passed their sandwiches over on two plastic plates with two large thick paper napkins.

'See, Tommy? Fancy serviettes.' said Ruby, 'Violet's thought of everything. I'll bet she's even got your favourite juice. I told her you used to love Ribena. Ever since you were wee.'

'Well, I prefer a nice Merlot these days.' He laughed.

Violet joined in. It was Ruby's birthday after all.

'But Ribena will do nicely, thank you.'

Jeeso, thought Sheila, he actually sounds like a normal, decent human being.

She passed a sturdy red plastic tumbler to Ruby who took a few noisy slurps.

Smeaton steadied her hand. 'Careful, Mother,' he warned.

'By Jings, I was needing that,' said Ruby. 'I was thirsty.'

Sheila carefully handed a bright blue beaker over to Smeaton. 'Ribena?' she said.

'Thanks, Miss McNish. Haven't had this stuff for ages.' He took several swallows. Sheila tried not to watch but found herself holding her breath until he gave a burp, excused himself and said, 'That makes me feel about five years old. Funny how things never taste as good as you remember them though.'

Sheila's stomach clenched. Did he detect something wrong with the juice?

He took another drink and said, 'Delicious, mind you. And more refreshing than Merlot, I'll give you that.'

Sheila laughed at his joke as she passed more sandwiches through the space between the front seats. 'Eat up, Ruby dear,' she said, 'Birthday treat.'

Sheila checked her watch. About twenty minutes to wait. She reached into her handbag and texted 'dark blue Mercedes layby five'. All she had to do now was act normal, try to stay calm and wait.

Ruby kept a conversation going with her son all the time they were eating. Violet was rarely required to contribute.

Smeaton ate with gusto, accepting everything that was passed from the back seat. He drained his beaker of juice and asked for more. He complimented the food, especially the home-baking.

When his mother asked him a question about his work, the answer kept him bragging away for some minutes. Sheila noticed a slight slurring of his words. Had Ruby heard it too? Smeaton continued to crow, boasting about budget cuts he'd made and staff he'd got rid of.

Suddenly he stopped talking. A moment later, he announced, almost incoherently, that he was feeling hot and needed fresh air.

Ruby grabbed him and said, 'Give your old mother a birthday hug, Tommy.' Despite his protests she hugged him to her and within moments his head dropped onto his chest.

'He's unconscious,' said Sheila. 'Thank God for that.'

'Will he remember any of this?' asked Ruby, pushing her son back over to his own side of the car.

'Not if the drug does its stuff. He'll wake up at the bothy without a clue. Won't know where he is or how he got there. Scary, isn't it?'

'Is this the stuff you hear about wee lassies drinking by accident, then they wake up in the morning and they've been raped?'

'That's right, Ruby. Can you imagine anything worse?'

'It's a terrible world we live in, Violet. Times were hard when I was young but they were nicer, more innocent.'

'I think you're probably right, Ruby. You wouldn't believe how easy it was to get this stuff on the internet.'

'That internet has a lot to answer for, if you ask me. Right, what happens next?'

'I just need to make one quick phone call.' Violet made the call and had just started to tell Ruby what would happen next, when Joe's old Land Rover bumped its way up onto the grass alongside.

Joe jumped out and opened Tommy's door. 'Hello Ruby,' he said, 'Thanks for your help.' He leaned in, eased his hands under Smeaton's arms and pulled the man towards him. When Smeaton slumped over, Joe locked his hands in front of Smeaton's chest and heaved his torso clear of the car. 'Get his feet, Marty.'

Marty grabbed Smeaton's ankles and sagged under the weight. 'He's too heavy. I can't lift him.'

Sheila said, 'Wait, I'll help.' She climbed out and took hold of one of Smeaton's legs.

'Mind his good camel coat,' called Ruby.

As the three of them edged away from the car, Marty said, 'He looks lighter than this.'

Before Sheila could agree, Ruby shouted, 'Quick! Somebody's coming.'

'Put him down!' said Joe. 'Now hide!'

The three of them ducked behind the car. Sheila prayed under her breath. She could hear Marty taking deep breaths, as if trying to stay calm.

The sound of a vehicle grew louder as it laboured up the hill beyond the bend.

'Please, please, please,' Sheila whispered. She peeped over the bonnet of the Mercedes in time to see the minibus of wheelchair kids pass. Everyone on board seemed to be looking over at the loch, except one kid who pointed at Sheila before the bus disappeared round the next bend.

'Right, no time to waste,' said Joe. 'Let's get him loaded.'

'With a final heave they settled Smeaton in the back of the Land Rover and Joe threw a blanket over him.

'Watch you don't smother him,' said Ruby.

'Don't you worry,' said Marty. 'We'll look after him. You okay, Miss McNish?'

'Come on, Marty. Get in,' shouted Joe. 'See you later, Sheila. Bye, Ruby.'

The jeep's engine revved, it bounced over the grass and disappeared up the road in a cloud of black smoke.

Sheila quickly cleared up the remains of their picnic, babbling nervously all the while. 'I'm not cut out for a life of crime, Ruby,' she said, opening a bottle of water to rinse the beakers. With their rubbish pushed to the bottom of the bin, she got into the driver's seat.

'Ever driven a posh car like this, Violet?'

'Never, but how much different can it be from my wee old Nissan Micra?'

Half a mile down the road, she laughed out loud and said, 'Ruby, I was wrong. This thing is nothing like a Nissan Micra. It's a dream to drive. Do you think there's a chance your Tommy might forget he ever bought this car?'

'Why?' asked Ruby, 'are you thinking of stealing it?'

'Not stealing, Ruby,' she said in an indignant voice. 'More of a swap. I'd leave him my Micra in exchange.'

'Fair enough.'

A few miles passed in silence. Ruby seemed to be enjoying the rugged hills when suddenly she said, 'Do you think our Tommy will be alright?'

***

CHAPTER 56

'Oh no, what now?' Joe pointed up the track to three figures in matching waterproof gear.

'Is it the police?' asked Marty, panicky.

'No. It's my lads. I borrowed those jackets from the bothy for them to wear to Arran. Forgot to return them, you might say.'

'What the hell are they doing up here?'

'We're going to have to find out. We can't wait here till they disappear but I can't just drive on either.'

'This could screw things up for us. We have to get Smeaton inside long before he wakes up.'

'I'll deal with it. You crouch down in the foot well and I'll cover you with this blanket. We don't want them spotting you.'

He rolled down his window and leaned out. The boys heard the engine and turned to check out the approaching vehicle. When they saw it was Joe, their faces lit up.

'It's the big man. Awright, Big Man?'

'Not bad,' said Joe. He pointed to Slug and said to him, 'I mistook you for TJ walking up the road there. You're looking fantastic.'

Slug beamed from ear to ear. 'I've nearly lost two stone since I started, Sur. Another one and a half to go. If I lose that and keep improving my fitness, the army say they'll take me. TJ's in already. He went to Catterick last week for his training. He says it's minted.'

Joe smiled at the news. The boy had got away. In every sense of the word.

'That's amazing. Good luck to him, and you, Slug. What about you, Dykesy?'

'The army's no for me. I'm for the college. Just heard

yesterday. Got a place down in England, starting in August.'

'Good for you, mate.'

Before Joe could ask him, Dangermoose said, 'I'm still a loser, Sur. Still on the dole, still on the dope. But I'm happy.'

'What about Liam?'

'Aye, he's okay. Daft as ever.'

'And Jimbo? How's he doing?'

'They had to switch off his life support,' said Slug, swiping a hand across his eyes. 'That's why we're here.'

Dykesy removed a carrier bag from inside his jacket and peeled back the plastic to reveal a cardboard tube. 'This is Jimbo's ashes, Sur. We got them off his mammy's mantelpiece.'

'You stole them?'

'His mammy's fine wi it, honest. We're going to scatter him up on the hill where he can see the loch. Want to come, Sur? Ah think Jimbo would like the Big Man at his scattering.'

Joe made up his mind fast. 'Tell you what, boys, I'd love that. I'll even say a few words, if you like, but I've got something I need to drop off at the bothy first. You walk on and I'll catch you in, say, ten minutes?'

Dykesy tucked the carrier bag back inside his jacket. 'Nae probs.'

Joe put the Land Rover into gear and drove off.

'How do you get out of this one?' murmured Marty from beneath the blanket. 'Won't they be suspicious?'

'That's a risk we'll have to take. Jimbo was a good lad.'

'What happened to him, Joe?'

'The usual. A life ruined by drugs became unliveable and the boy decided to put an end to it.'

Joe drove the Land Rover right up to the back of the bothy and, with a lot of grunting from Marty, they heaved Smeaton into the special place they'd created for him. Marty told Joe to go hide the jeep and join his boys, assuring him she would make a start on Smeaton.

Joe left her to it, promising to be back as soon as he could. As he stepped out the door he almost walked into Dykesy.

'Do ye want a hand, Sur? We're no in any hurry.'

Joe pulled the door closed, hoping they hadn't been able to see inside or hear Marty talking. 'No, you're alright, but thanks anyway.'

'Could we get a wee look inside, Sur? Like, for old times?'

Dangermoose said, 'Tell the Big Man the truth, Dykesy. We were planning tae break in.'

'Shut it, Danger.' Dykesy looked Joe in the eye, hesitated then said, 'Aye, aw right. We were, but no to do any damage, just to have a look round.'

Joe's heart was beating too fast to be healthy. He put his hand over it and said, 'Trust me, lads, there's not a thing to see. It's been stripped bare, I'm here to finish off the job. You're far better remembering the place as it was.'

'The Big Man's right,' said Dykesy. 'It was a daft idea. Come on, boys, let's go. It's time to scatter Jimbo.'

As the little funeral party made its way up towards the hills, Joe contemplated the scenario had the boys broken in. Then, while they walked in unaccustomed silence, he turned his mind to an appropriate eulogy for Jimbo.

When Joe came back, Marty let out a long low whistle. 'That could have been tricky.'

'Yeah, imagine if they'd walked in on us.'

'I felt sorry for them, grieving for their pal. And I'm sorry for you too. I sense you liked Jimbo.'

'I did. He's exactly the kind of kid this place might have saved, given a chance.' Joe found it hard to say any more and Marty seemed to sense it was time to move on.

'Right, well, thank god you're here.' She looked around the dark prison they'd created. 'This place was giving me the creeps. Imagine me, getting trapped in here with him. Talk about worst nightmares?'

Joe didn't laugh. Just said, 'Let's get him organized. We don't want him regaining consciousness before we're ready.'

'Imagine if he came to and recognized us.' Marty gave a giggle that betrayed her nerves. 'Are you sure all of this will be erased from his memory, the picnic with Sheila, the drive here?'

'If the drug works as it's supposed to.'

Together they knelt and started to remove Smeaton's clothing. Marty had already taken off his shoes and socks. As they pulled his sweater over his head, Marty said, 'You must be sad about that boy?'

'Sad, Marty? I'm not only sad. I'm mad!' He roared the word and grabbed Smeaton by the throat. 'I want to kill this bastard, with my own hands.'

'No! Let him go, Joe.' Marty grabbed at his fingers, pulled them away from Smeaton's neck. 'That's not the way. We agreed.'

Joe got to his feet and walked away, almost disappearing into the darkness. Marty could hear him crying, in that harsh violent way a man weeps. 'These are good kids, Marty.' He sounded as if his heart was breaking.

'I know they are, Joe, I know. Come on,' she said, gently, 'let's get this done and get out of here.

When Smeaton was down to his underpants, Joe took a step back and said, 'Look, is this last bit really necessary? I don't feel comfortable with the idea of stripping him naked.'

'I don't fancy it much myself,' said Marty, 'but it's important. Think about it. We come into the world naked and we go out of the world naked.'

'It still seems wrong.'

'It would be more wrong to ruin the whole thing because we're too squeamish to take his knickers off. He's not daft. If he wakes up wearing his Y-fronts while everything else has gone, he'll be much harder to convince. We're sticking to the plan, Joe. End of story.'

Relieved of his underwear, Smeaton was left in the centre of the floor in the recovery position. Joe straightened up and looked around. A small stone trough stood to one side. Otherwise, nothing.

'You and Sheila have done a brilliant job, Joe. It's incredible how you've transformed the place.'

'Thanks. I hope it has the effect we want.'

'I'm sure it will. You're certain he won't be able to get out?'

'Absolutely certain. He won't get out until we carry him out. Not unless he digs a tunnel and there's no chance of that. Under this stone is soil, so hard packed it's like concrete. He's here to stay. Come on, let's go and get a cuppa. I'm freezing.'

'Don't forget his clothes,' said Marty. 'If you stick them in the back of the Landy I'll make us a cuppa.'

Joe cradled his mug, trying to get some heat back into his hands after standing out there on the hillside. The boys had been solemn. He'd said a few quick words of tribute then each boy took his turn to shake the canister. They'd stood silent as the remains of their friend swirled in the wind and blew away towards the loch.

Feeling sorry for them, and to make sure they left, Joe had taken them to the main road where they could get the bus or thumb a lift. He was draining his coffee when Marty let out a yelp then clamped her hand over her mouth. With her other hand she pointed to their makeshift screen, a white bedsheet pinned to the wall.

The picture was dark, but clear enough for them to see Smeaton lying motionless.

'What is it?' asked Joe.

'I thought he moved.'

'It's too early.'

Marty whispered in a voice so quiet it was more of a mime, 'You're sure he can't hear us?'

Joe shook his head. 'No. Definitely not. We tested it, didn't we, with Sheila shouting at the top of her voice? There wasn't a sound to be heard. Nothing carries through the thickness of these old walls.'

'And what about sounds from outside? Can he hear those?'

Joe tapped his phone. 'Not over the white noise. I've got it playing quite loud.'

'I still can't believe those boys turned up here.'

'I can,' said Joe. 'If I lived in Bankside, I'd want to escape up here too.'

'You must be touched, Joe, that this is where they wanted to bring their friend.'

Joe couldn't answer.

'Look,' said Marty, pointing again, 'I was right. He is moving.'

'Can you see if his eyes are still closed?'

'I can't see his eyes at all. I wonder if we should have had more light in there, but that would defeat the purpose.'

'It's perfect. We can watch him, but he can see very little.'

'Do you think he's starting to regain consciousness?'

Joe checked the time. 'Doubt it. He might be starting to swim slowly back towards the surface, I suppose, but he's expected to be out for a good six hours.'

***

CHAPTER 57

Thomas Smeaton moved his arm. Tried to find a more comfortable position and failed, but went back to sleep anyway.

When he surfaced again, he lay with his eyes closed, working out why he was so cold. The duvet must have slipped off in the night. He reached for it and touched a hard surface where his mattress should be. Made a mental note to buy a softer bed. Sleep swallowed him. Drowned him in weird, disturbing dreams full of demons.

He opened his eyes, relieved to escape. Rubbed at his eyelids, to clear his vision. His room was murky. It must be early. He reached again for the duvet. Still missing. His pillows had gone too. He closed his eyes again but this time sleep didn't re-claim him and he lay, trying to make sense of things. Trying to remember how much he'd had to drink the night before. Too much, obviously. Nobody woke with a head like this after a night's sobriety.

Where was he? Clearly, not where he should be. In his own bed. Or any bed.

He rolled onto his back and scratched his groin. Froze. Then coiled in on himself, foetus-like. He was naked.

Another naked dream. He knew the routine. Any minute now he'd walk into council chambers and address the elected representatives, stark naked.

If only he had a fiver for every naked dream he'd ever had.

He drifted in and out of sleep. Each time he came to, he checked. Still no bed, no duvet, no clothes.

Finally, he could delude himself no longer. Whatever was happening, it was no dream. He was awake. And naked as the day he was born.

How was that possible? Where could he have lost every stitch of clothing?

He racked his brain for what he'd been wearing yesterday but couldn't remember. He thought of his wardrobe. Imagined opening the door. Ran his mind's eye along the rail. Nothing rang a bell. Until he got to his camel coat. Finest cashmere, cost a fortune. It seemed familiar, but nothing else did. He was trying to picture what he usually wore with his camel coat when it hit him like a kick in the guts.

This was it.

The illness he'd been secretly dreading for years.

He would turn out like his mother, living in a home. Maybe the same one she was in.

Steady on. He was far too young to suddenly lose his marbles. And far too intelligent to not be aware of it happening.

He indulged in a few minutes of self-pity, before reminding himself that a clever man like him should be able to use his brain to work out where he was. Terrifying though dementia might be, he knew it did not come on quite so fast.

Concentrate, Tom. Concentrate. Analyse the situation. Find a solution. It's what you do best.

He pictured himself in the camel coat. Tried to recall the last time he had seen it. He had a strong feeling he had worn it recently. Going to work perhaps? It must be winter. That would explain why he was so cold. Right, it's a winter's day.

Suddenly he saw his mother, also in a winter coat.

***

CHAPTER 58

Sheila had dropped a very animated and excited Ruby back at Briargrove, making her promise not to breathe a word. Ruby had pointed to the carer advancing towards them from the end of the hall and started singing.

Sheila smiled at the old lady and bent to offer a hug.

'Ah, you back now, Ruby,' boomed the carer. 'You have good time, yes?'

In response, Ruby glared at the woman and continued to sing. Sheila watched her friend being led away like a docile child. Before she disappeared into the lounge, Ruby turned and gave Sheila a huge, theatrical wink.

Tempting though it was to take Smeaton's Mercedes for a run along the M8, Sheila stuck to the plan. She drove straight into town to the car park by the shopping centre and kept rising, tyres squeaking on the painted floors, till she reached the uppermost level. She was pleased to note that hers, or rather, Smeaton's would be the only car parked there.

Before she got out, Sheila checked the car carefully, then checked again. It was vitally important she leave no evidence whatsoever. Trying to look relaxed, despite feeling like a coiled spring, she closed the car, locked it and checked it was locked before she walked away. Hoping any CCTV cameras had been dealt with by Dykesy and team, Sheila moved swiftly to the stairwell and stopped on the first landing to catch her breath and steady her nerves. There was no camera to be seen so she quickly took off her old-lady anorak and her leather driving gloves, rolled them it into a tight bundle and hid it under her arm. She snatched off the grey wig and re-tied her head-square, Queen-style, over her hair. She walked through to the lift to make her descent to Level Two where she'd left her wee Micra.

She grabbed a bag of her new, trendy clothes from the boot and hurried off to mingle with shoppers and disappear into Debenhams.

She selected a rather frumpy blouse from a rail of beige garments and took it into a changing room. The girl on duty barely gave her a glance. Ten minutes later Sheila had dressed in her stylish, modern clothes, slapped on some make-up and Violet was gone for ever.

Sheila handed the blouse back, saying, 'No thanks, not my style,' and left the store. She found the nearest café and was reviving herself with a double espresso when her phone rang. She was thrilled to see Marty's name displayed then worried, in case something had gone wrong. 'Everything okay?'

'Everything is fine. You did a great job. We're really proud of you.'

'Oh, thank God.'

'You can stop worrying. It's all going according to plan. He's starting to come round and seems fine.'

'So he's going to be okay?'

'Looks that way.

'Where are you?'

'I'm in Millie's. I needed a caffeine rush and a sugar top-up. I dropped the car off, got changed and am now wearing lipstick in a colour that Miss Violet McNish would consider most unsuitable.'

Marty laughed. 'Wait till I tell you what happened. You'll never believe it. Some of Joe's boys appeared, wanting to visit the bothy.'

'You're kidding me. How did you get round that one?'

'It's a long story and quite sad really. See you very soon.'

'I hope so. Take care.' She paused, then said, 'Marty?'

'Yes?'

'Thanks for doing this. For Liz.'

Sheila hung up, not trusting her voice any longer and looked around the coffee shop, which was quietening down.

No one was paying her any attention. She gave her eyes a quick dab with a paper tissue and gathered her things.

***

CHAPTER 59

S omething to do with his mother.

He could see her.

Dressed up, coat on, ready to go somewhere.

She didn't go out much these days. Unless he took her and he didn't have a lot of time for that sort of thing. Special occasions only. Christmas panto at the King's. In the summer a wee run down to Largs for an ice-cream at Nardini's. Her birthday. That was it, her birthday. He always tried to keep it free in his diary. Got Carole to send her a bouquet, or booky, as his mother insisted on calling it. To annoy him, he thought.

When was her birthday? February, yes.

That would explain the cold. He wrapped his arms around his body, shocked again to feel bare skin. What in God's name was going on here?

'Mother?'

His voice echoed back to him, his only answer in this weird, dark place, apart from a shooshing noise.

'Mother? You there?' Was he slurring his words?

He was picking up his mother. Taking her somewhere. For her birthday treat. It was coming back to him now. Drive down to Trump Turnberry, take the old dear for a slap-up lunch. Give the car a good run down the A77. His memory snagged on the mental picture of his car. Something wrong there.

It was so hard to think. He had a pounding headache. Like a hangover, only worse. And yet he never took a drink if he had the car. He despised drink drivers.

Had he been driving? It was so hard to remember. He was going to have to get his memory checked, before it got any worse. Yes, he'd definitely been in the car, yes. A new one.

That's right. He'd just collected it from the dealership. Always fancied a Mercedes. Finally decided to treat himself. Top of the range.

Was that it? Had someone fancied his flashy new Merc? Had he been car-jacked and dumped?

Come on. Concentrate. Re-wind. Back to the point where he picked up his mother at Briargrove. Not just his mother. Somebody else. A carer? No. They were always in uniform. Another old dear like his mother. That's right. He hadn't wanted to take her but Mother had insisted she come for lunch too.

They didn't make it though, did they? He knows that big drive that sweeps up from the road. The huge hotel, all white and sparkling, looking out over the sea towards Ailsa Craig. Round the back a concierge in a kilt greets you. You hand him your keys and he calls a valet to park your car. None of that was ringing a bell.

If only he could think clearly. Work out where he was. Then he'd know what to do about it.

He moved. Tried to get comfortable. Big ask on a hard surface like this. Not a floor. Bare stone. Like in a cave. No wonder he was freezing.

Why the hell did they have to take his clothes? Camel coat he could understand. Whoever stole the car maybe fancied the coat to go with it. But to take the lot? Leave a man without his underpants? Out of order.

Nothing about this was making sense.

His last memory was of driving off with his mother and some other old biddy in the back seat.

A car accident. They must have been in a smash. He started to examine his body. All limbs intact, and moving. No blood. He was breathing okay. He ran his fingers over his arms and torso. His skin rose in goose bumps at his touch but he couldn't find so much as a scratch. There must be some damage, somewhere. Nobody was ever lucky enough to survive a road crash uninjured. Not even in a Merc.

And yet he appeared to be unscathed. He stopped

checking. He'd worked it out.

Hospital. In a coma. He'd read about this stuff. Patients carried on thinking and processing. Brainwaves proved it, unless they were brain dead of course, which, clearly, he was not. Cogno, ergo sum. If he was thinking, he was alive. And as long as he could keep thinking, no one was going to switch him off.

Okay, naked. Fine. On a bed in ICU somewhere, Ayr, perhaps. Or that private place on the South Side. He hoped it was one of the private hospitals. He was paying a fortune for health insurance. It would be ironic if he'd ended up in that huge new NHS place, lying on a trolley in a corridor, while they searched for a bed.

Wherever he was, they would take good care of him. That weird whishing noise must be some sort of medical machine, life-support maybe, keeping him alive.

He could relax. Give in. Let sleep carry him off.

***

CHAPTER 60

Marty woke with a jolt. Her neck hurt and it took her a moment to realise where she was.

'Hello, sleeping beauty.'

'Sorry, Joe. Didn't get much sleep last night. I think might have nodded off for a minute.'

'Nodded off? I thought you were never going to wake up.'

'Is he okay? He's gained consciousness?'

'Yeah, yeah. He came to earlier. Right on schedule. He's woken and fallen asleep a couple of times.'

'That's normal, right?'

'Apparently.'

'What's he doing now?'

'See for yourself. He's just lying there. Doesn't look very comfortable.'

'Good. He's here to suffer.' She yawned, stretched. 'I could murder another cuppa. Want one?'

'No, thanks. Watch this. He's moving.'

She looked at the white sheet pinned to the far wall. Easy to tear down and throw over the tech equipment if, by the slimmest of chances, someone came to the door.

All she could see was a dark space with a paler, rough outline of a person. It looked more like an ultrasound scan of a baby in the womb than a fully grown man lying on the stone floor of a bothy. She rubbed her eyes and watched as he curled into a foetal position and wrapped his arms around himself.

'He's cold.'

'Yeah.'

'Shouldn't it be hot?'

'Not necessarily.'

'You're sure he won't come to any harm?'

'Are you serious? We get this far and you ask me if I'm sure he won't come to any harm?' He laughed, a bitter, mocking sound, lacking any vestige of humour.

'You know what I mean. We don't want him dying of hypothermia before we get what we want.'

'Trust me. I know about hypothermia.'

'Your army training, you mean?'

'That, and years of bringing kids out onto these hills.' He gestured behind him, as if she could see the hills from here. 'Some of the lads I work with don't have a jacket or a jumper to their name. They turn up, summer and winter, in wee thin tee shirts or cheap tracky tops.'

'I know. My son goes out clubbing in just a shirt sometimes.'

'Poverty's not a style choice, Marty. It's to do with having nobody that gives enough of a shit to buy you a decent jacket when they can spend the Giro on smack. It's to do with kids living in a house where nobody ever says, "Son, it's freezing out there. Put your sweatshirt on."' He poked his finger towards the screen, the gesture violent. 'And that bastard there is determined to take away the only decent thing these kids have got going for them.' He shook his head. 'Christ, I hate him!'

As if he knew he was being talked about, Smeaton raised himself on one arm and looked around. He tilted his head, listening, but they knew he could hear nothing but white noise. He pushed himself into a seated position. His head slumped and then jerked up again as he caught sight of his bare legs. He checked his genitals and brought his knees towards his body to hide them. The sudden movement almost tipped him over and he planted both hands on the floor to steady himself. He looked towards the faint source of light high above his head.

They watched him trying to make sense of his surroundings. He rubbed a hand over his chest. As though the tactile reminder he was naked had made him feel colder, he sat up and folded his arms around himself in a hug.

'Yuk,' she said, covering her eyes. 'My old boss naked.

There's a sight I never wanted to see.'

'Me neither, but you're the one who insisted it had to be done.'

'We come into the world naked …'

'Aye, and we go out, blah-de-blah. Got it.'

From a kneeling position, Smeaton rose slowly to his feet. He staggered a little and leaned forward, hands on knees.

'Do you feel sorry for him?' asked Joe.

'Not one bit,' said Marty. 'I could douse him in petrol and sit here enjoying the blaze.'

'That's harsh.'

'Think so?'

On screen, Smeaton was taking small, tentative steps around his new home. He reached out a very cautious arm like a blind man feeling for a wall. They watched his reaction as the black cloth yielded to his touch. He poked at it again and they saw his hand disappear into the material and reappear. Marty had tried it herself. It was like touching the sides of a floppy tent.

He dropped to his knees and scrabbled on the floor, like a dog digging a hole. Joe had made sure there was no escape route and he soon gave up.

'Has he said anything, Joe?'

'Give him time. When he wakes again and finds he's still here, he might be inclined to take things a bit more seriously.'

'I wonder if we're being too clever here. Maybe we should have gone for the obvious. Heat turned up full, a bit of hellfire special effects and Smeaton would have worked out the damnation part for himself. A whiff of brimstone wafting in and he'd have got the message by now. I'm a bit worried we're being too subtle.'

'Marty, we talked about this. You said you didn't want him to think he's in hell, with no chance of redemption. But, here's a thing. Has it occurred to you that Smeaton might be thinking this is heaven?'

Marty looked at him as if he'd gone mad.

'If he sees himself as a righteous man, it might never cross his mind that he wouldn't automatically go to heaven.'

'Take a look at that screen,' said Marty. 'How could anyone believe they'd died and gone to heaven if they woke up in a place as bleak as the black hole we've dumped him in?'

'See what you mean.'

'Hopefully, if we give him time, the penny will drop. And if it doesn't, remember we have more we can play him than white noise.'

'Yeah, he's a nasty man but he's not a stupid man. He'll work it out for himself eventually.'

Marty said, 'Cup of tea?'

'I know this might sound a bit odd, but I'm starving. Any chance of a fry-up?'

'Joe, it's one am. This isn't an all-night café on the M6. You'll have a buttered roll and be grateful.'

'You certainly know how to spoil a guy. Any chance of a bit of jam?'

Tea and rolls scoffed, they settled down to keep watch. Smeaton seemed to have gone back to sleep. Every so often he would roll over or move a limb, enough to reassure them he was alive.

They were reminiscing about schooldays when Marty stopped Joe mid-sentence. She pointed to the screen. Smeaton had sat up, unnoticed, and was looking straight at the camera.

'He's looking at us,' she whispered.

'He can't be. He doesn't know we're here.'

They moved to the remote that operated the camera and Joe zoomed in on Smeaton's face. The light was muted but clear enough to make out the familiar supercilious expression. It was one they had seen all too often in the past.

'This is giving me the heebie-jeebies,' Marty said, shivering to prove how unnerved she was. 'Even shut in there, he's still got the power to make me feel on edge.'

***

CHAPTER 61

Thomas Smeaton woke to the sound of his guts churning. Then his mouth filled with a warm saliva that instinct told him not to swallow. He must hold it in his mouth as long as he could, or he'd be sick.

A warning gurgle, low in his stomach, made him clench his bum cheeks, knowing it was only a matter of time till he'd lose control of his bowels.

A toilet! He needed a toilet. Or a bedpan.

'Help! Nurse!'

When no nurse came, he scrambled to his feet and looked around. This was no hospital. There was no toilet.

As he stumbled back and forth in the gloom, a spurt of warmth sprayed his legs. The smell of it hit his nostrils with a force that opened his mouth and he dropped to his knees, vomiting.

He was nothing but muscles in spasm. Wave after wave made his stomach heave and his bowels gush. Suddenly - blessed relief! It all stopped. Moments later he was back, miserable as before, knowing it hadn't stopped at all; he'd simply blacked out for a few seconds. He lay amidst his own waste, his stomach still heaving even though nothing was coming up. He retched and gagged, long after his stomach was empty. Willing his mouth to fill with fresh saliva, he spat and spat.

Eventually he crawled away from the mess, wishing desperately to be clean. He wiped the vomit from his lips, smearing it with excrement instead. He tried to find clean skin on his inner arm so he could dab his mouth. He tried his other arm, contorting himself in an effort to rid his face and mouth of defilement. Spitting till there was no saliva left, he waited for moisture to cleanse his teeth and tongue. None came.

On all fours he panted, wretched as a sick dog, until his arms and legs gave way and he collapsed, exhausted.

Lucid thoughts were hard to catch and string together, but this much he knew. He was in no hospital. And no coma. Whatever this was, it was much worse than any car crash he could imagine.

How could he possibly have gone from driving a brand-new car to lunch at Trump Turnberry to lying in darkness surrounded by his own shit and vomit? Something horrendous had happened to him in that blank bit in the middle. If only he could work out what.

Feeling as if he was crawling a marathon, he dragged his poor body as far from the mess as he could. The smell lessened a little and the ground underneath him was undefiled. It would do for now. He lay down and closed his eyes, yearning for the oblivion of sleep.

***

CHAPTER 62

He woke to the sound of water, shushing in waves. The sea must be nearby. Had he crashed off the road and been thrown onto the rocky shore? He moved slightly, felt the smooth stone on his bare skin and remembered his nakedness, his wretchedness.

He listened to the water, longing to submerge himself in it, craving the chance to be clean again.

It was rushing but not in regular waves like the ocean. A river then. He was in some sort of cave, perhaps, by a river. No, the sound was too regular, filling his ears with a low but persistent whooshing that made no sense. None of this made any sense.

If he'd come here under his own steam, he would remember something, surely. And if he was brought here by someone else … Why didn't he think of it before? He'd been kidnapped. They wanted money.

Once he understood what was going on he felt a little better. At least now he knew what he was dealing with. Some small-time criminals who saw the big car and thought they'd extort a few quid from a soft touch.

They were wrong and he was about to show them. Scrambling on to his feet, he made an effort to stand tall and told himself it was important to sound in control. His head spun and he felt faint but he daren't show any sign of weakness. Or they'd think they'd won.

***

CHAPTER 63

Joe said, 'You can stop worrying, Marty. It looks like he's back in the land of the living.'

Together they watched Smeaton stagger a little then, righting himself, plant his feet to keep himself stable. He cleared his throat.

'Listen to me, whoever you are.' His voice was surprisingly calm and clear. 'I don't know what you want from me, but if it's money, you can forget it. I'm not prepared to deal with you. Now, I'd like to go home.'

'Shit,' said Marty, 'he's worked us out. This is not how it was meant to go.'

She looked at Joe for reassurance but his brow was furrowed. 'Let's have a close up,' he said, zooming in on their prisoner.

On screen Smeaton's face was larger than life and twice as intimidating. When he spoke, it was with the confidence of a man who was used to getting his own way. 'You should be aware that I have an elderly mother at home, not in the best of health. I need to go to her.'

Marty blurted, 'Liar.'

'My mother needs medication and will become very distressed if I don't go home. You have to release me.'

Marty whispered to Joe, 'This is not going according to plan. He knows he's been abducted.'

After another pause, Smeaton got to his feet and added, 'She will also call the police if I don't return before dark. They will come looking for me quite soon.'

When his appeal was met with nothing but white noise, his voice became higher and louder. 'Furthermore, if anything should happen to my poor mother, I will hold you responsible.

You will be made to pay.'

'This is the Smeaton we know and love,' said Joe, as they watched his face contort with rage.

He started to scream, this time with his back turned to them. 'Let me out of here.'

Joe zoomed out again, revealing Smeaton's bare bottom. Marty tried not to look.

'See, Marty? He's facing the wrong way now,' said Joe. 'He doesn't know where we are.'

Smeaton turned another ninety degrees and spoke in his normal voice again, as if he had told himself that screaming would get him nowhere. 'Please, leave my clothes where I can find them and let me out. You can keep the car. I won't even report it missing. Surely that's enough for you. Anyway, I don't have any more. I spent it all on the car. Take it, but please, I beg you, let me out of here.'

He waited for a reaction then like a child losing its temper he started to shout, his voice rising to the falsetto they'd both heard many times before, 'I'm an extremely important man. People will be looking for me. You'd better let me out before the police get involved. My absence will not go unnoticed. I have a lot of friends.'

Joe muttered, 'Aye right. Now we know the drug has affected his memory.'

***

CHAPTER 64

It had all made sense to him earlier. He was sure he'd been kidnapped. No idea why. He was a powerful man, but hardly an influential political figure. He was fairly-well off, but far from rich. What would be the point of kidnapping him? He didn't know anyone rich enough to pay ransom money.

What if he'd been abducted and then abandoned when the kidnappers found out there would be no payoff? He could be left to rot in this hole, wherever it was. What if he was left here to die? He listened again for any sound that might help him work out where he'd been taken. Nothing but that shooshy watery sound. It was starting to get on his nerves. Apart from that, everything was completely silent, as if he were deep underground. Hairs rose on the back of his neck. Maybe he was at the foot of a mine shaft. He'd been driving through Ayrshire. It was full of pits and collieries. He might never be found, not even his remains. He had to get out of here, somehow. There must be a way in, and that meant a way out. He stood and walked the perimeter of his prison, touching the black walls that surrounded him. They were soft, not hard like stone or concrete, impossible to climb or dig under. He tried to rip through the barrier that held him, clawing ineffectually at blackness till his nails felt like they were tearing off.

'Help!'

He waited, listening for the multiple echo that would reply if he was in a pit.

'Somebody help me.'

No one answered, not even an echo. No kidnapper with demands. No rescuer coming to his aid. He screamed in frustration and hurled himself at the blackness but it simply flipped him back like a kid on a bouncy castle. He sat down to work out his next step. 'Dear God,' he asked the darkness, 'what's happening to me?'

***

CHAPTER 65

Smeaton lay curled up on the floor. He'd muttered away to himself earlier, too incoherently for them to hear, and now he appeared to be sleeping again.

Joe walked away from the screen and joined Marty at the beat-up, old wooden table that dominated the space. There had always been a dozen or more chairs in this room, but Joe had left only four.

'Joe?' said Marty, twirling her wedding ring. 'You know that call you made earlier? When we were waiting to hear from Sheila? Well, I didn't mean to eavesdrop, but I couldn't help overhearing.'

She left a gap which Joe did not hurry to fill. He was too busy trying to work out what she might have overheard. He decided to play for time. 'And?' he said, forcing his face into a smile.

'You sounded stressed.'

She had no idea how right she was. Stressed didn't begin to cover it.

'Did I?' He ran his hand through his hair, combing it back off his face.

'I thought so.'

Joe dropped his head, allowing a curtain of hair to swing across his face and give it some privacy. He heard her seat move then felt her hands on his shoulders. He needed to say something but was at a loss for words.

'You're right. I'm stressed.'

'I guess you've got a lot on your mind right now. We all have.'

Joe knew he was meant to unburden himself at this point.

'Are you in some kind of bad financial trouble, Joe? Is

someone after you for money?'

Cursing his carelessness, Joe tried to figure out what she might have overheard. He'd thought she was too focussed on her own phone, willing Sheila to call.

'Is that why you had to sell your flat? To clear a massive debt? Has Smeaton ruined you financially as well as everything else?'

Joe shook his head slowly, all the time wondering how much he could tell her. She kept on talking, as if she couldn't stop, now she'd started.

'I'm sorry to ask this.'

Oh hell, what was coming next?

'Did paying for your wife's treatment bankrupt you?'

Joe allowed himself a chuckle. He took her hand, 'No Marty. Sally was looked after, right to the end, by the wonderful NHS, and then the even more wonderful hospice, God bless them. They're the only ones I owe anything to, those gifted doctors and nurses, but that's a debt I'll never be able to repay.'

'It's because you've lost your job, isn't it? You're worried about money and had to sell up.'

'Marty, slow down.' He patted her hand as he spoke. 'I didn't lose my job. I resigned, remember?'

'What happened between you and him, Joe?' She pointed to the screen. 'You've got history with him, don't you? This is about more than Smeaton closing the bothy, isn't it?'

***

CHAPTER 66

Joe excused himself and went to the toilet. When he came back, Marty had made him a cup of tea and Smeaton was lying on his side, back to the camera.

'Look at him. Sleeping like a baby. Seems harmless, doesn't he?'

'Yeah, but we know better, don't we? To our cost. So tell me, Joe, what's the full story?'

'Ach, me and Smeaton go way back. He was Depute Director of Education where I worked before I came to Logiemuir. Everybody could see he was ruthlessly ambitious. He had fingers in many pies and was cultivating friends in high places. I was unfortunate enough to cross him.'

'How?'

Joe shrugged. 'When I started my career, PE teachers had to be seen to be macho. It was a common occurrence for a boy to get a bit of a slap to remind him who was in charge.'

'I remember. When I was at school, the PE teacher used to take the bad boys into the apparatus cupboard and "knock some sense into them". Everyone knew he did it, but nobody ever complained.'

'They didn't in those days.'

'I had a PE guy like that, when I took over as head teacher at Moorcroft. A walking relic. Bane of my life. Fortunately, he was only a few months short of retirement. That sort of thing isn't tolerated nowadays. Rightly so.'

'I agree, but I'm putting you in the picture. Anyway, I joined a PE department where that was not only acceptable, it was an approved form of discipline. I remember being told, "Don't waste your time giving out punishment exercises or detentions. Most boys would rather have a quick kick up the

239

arse and get it over with. A lot less hassle for all concerned."
That was the prevailing attitude.'

'So, what happened?'

'I picked the wrong boy. When I gave him a shove he
shoved me back then swung a punch at my face. This was a big
lad, Marty and, I found out later, a bit of a back-street brawler.
Anyway, he had plenty of witnesses willing to say I had laid
hands on him. I admitted I was at fault and apologised to the
boy and his family. They were okay with it, knew the boy was a
hothead, and the matter was closed. But not for Smeaton. He
got wind of it and wanted to make an example of me.'

'That sounds like the man we know and hate.'

'The school and my Union were right behind me, prepared
to fight him all the way. Smeaton's boss told him to drop it.
Didn't want it in the papers.'

'Joe, this must have been years ago.'

'It was. But remember they only banned corporal
punishment in 1987. I swear to you, I never touched another
pupil, but it went on my record and stayed there. And Smeaton
never forgave me for winning.' Joe took a drink of the sweet,
milky tea and warmed his hands on the mug.

'Is that the reason you moved over to outdoor education?'

'No, not really. I was so disgusted by the whole thing that I
walked away from teaching for a while. Then this outdoor
education post came up and I loved every minute of it. Until
Smeaton got the top job at Logiemuir and came back into my
life.'

'What went wrong?' Marty's voice was gentle, encouraging
him to share his troubles.

'Nothing, at first. Life was great. Until Sally became ill. I
needed to take quite a lot of time off for her chemo sessions
and so forth. Eventually, we discovered it was terminal.'

'Most bosses would understand that, and cut you some
slack.'

'Maybe most bosses would, but I didn't have most bosses. I
had Thomas Smeaton. It was okay at first. There seemed to be
some sympathy for my situation. But that didn't last. Maybe he

worked out who I was, hell, I don't know. Anyway, I could have done with some support when the going got very bad. There was none. I was at the worst point in my life and instead of focussing all my attention on Sally, I was worrying about work. And she was worrying about me. That's the part I can't forget and I'll never forgive him for.'

Joe stopped and took a deep breath, trying to keep his voice from shaking. 'And then, when Sally died, it all got out of hand.'

'What did?'

'Everything. I couldn't face life without her, Marty. I was wrecked. I started drinking.'

'Oh Joe,' said Marty, grabbing his arm, 'please tell me you didn't get some kid hurt because you were drunk.'

Joe shrugged out of her grip and said, 'Of course I didn't. What do you take me for?'

Marty looked stricken. 'Sorry, Joe. I shouldn't have said that.'

'I never drank at work or turned up drunk. Ever.' He emphasized the last word. It was important she thought well of him.

'Go on then,' she said, quietly.

'I didn't turn up for work a few times, if I'd had a skinful the night before. All I wanted to do in those dark days was drink myself into oblivion and stay there as long as possible.'

'Is that why you only ever drink diet cola?'

'Yeah, exactly. I wasn't an alcoholic, but I stepped close enough to the edge to be able to look into the abyss. I never want to go back there.'

Marty touched his arm. 'Were you reported to the General Teaching Council?'

'No. It never got that serious. I cleaned up my act and got back to work, but by this time I had drawn Smeaton's attention and he seemed to make it his business to get rid of me.'

Marty was nodding. 'Now it's starting to make sense,' she said. 'What did he do?'

'He played dirty, of course. When he couldn't get me for

absenteeism, he dredged up what he called the assault case from all those years ago.'

'Did you lose your temper and go for him? Come on, tell me you landed one good punch.' Marty was like a child, bouncing in her seat and demanding the end of the story.

Joe couldn't help laughing.

'Nothing that exciting, sorry. I thought about resigning there and then, but I love those bloody kids. I really believe I can make a difference. You heard them today, two in the army, Dykesy going to college. They believe in themselves now, know they have choices that don't involve drugs.'

'And Smeaton and his council mates are pulling the plug on all that good work. No wonder you're angry.'

'It's more than that, Marty. I decided, against my better judgement, to go and beg the man to keep the bothy open. I humbled myself for the sake of those boys. Smeaton humiliated me, in front of Morag Cooper and he made it clear how much he was enjoying every minute of it.'

'Did you drop it?'

'Nope. I don't give up that easily.' Joe told her about his attempt at whistleblowing to the newspapers, and how it was thwarted.

'His friends in high places?'

'Yeah, but can you imagine how angry he was when he found out?'

'Incandescent, I imagine.'

Joe nodded. He rubbed hard at his face, trying to decide whether he should tell her the rest, not sure he could say the words.

Marty seemed to guess he had more to tell. She touched his hand, stilling its frantic motion. 'What did he say to you?'

Joe couldn't answer. He shook his head.

'You can tell me,' said Marty gently.

'He more or less called me a paedophile. Said he would have me investigated if I didn't back off about the bothy.'

'Oh, that's disgusting. Even for him, that is sinking to unplumbed depths. But I know where he got the idea. He accused me of the same thing. And it worked. He got rid of me.' Marty shook her head, a look of revulsion on her face. 'Don't tell me that's why you've resigned too?'

'Nah, I just need to get away from here, Marty. I've had it with Scotland and the likes of him. I'm going to Bulgaria. Buying land there. Sally's old uncle died a few years ago and left her a lot of money. And, I mean, a lot. We had been planning to sell the flat and go build our dream home outside Sozopol. Sally loved that place. We were going to live happily ever after. Just us, horses and dogs, ducks and hens.' Joe stopped, unable to go on.

Marty seemed to sense that she needed to wait for him to regain his composure. 'Let me guess. That's when Sally got sick?'

Joe attempted to smile, nodding, 'And that was the end of the dream. We woke up to a nightmare. Anyway, I'm financially secure for the rest of my life, provided I don't do anything daft.'

'And you want to sort Smeaton out before you go?'

Joe paused, ran his hand through his hair for a moment then said, 'Marty. I'm like you. I wasn't ready to be thrown on the scrap heap. I love kids and I wanted to keep on working. Smeaton has robbed me of that too. My job gave me a reason to live through the darkest years of my life.'

'I was in a dark place too, believe me.'

'Chance did us both a favour when he tripped me up that day by the canal.'

She gave Joe a beaming smile. 'And now it's poor old Smeaton who's in the dark place and it damn well serves him right.'

***

CHAPTER 67

When he woke up, he remembered almost right away where he was. He opened his eyes to confirm. He had no idea how many days and nights he'd been there and that bothered him. With all the sleeping he'd been doing it could be one, it could be twenty-one. His hip hurt from the hard surface and his arm was numb from using it as a pillow. He rolled over onto his back then remembering he was bare, he covered his privates with his hands.

He'd got used to the cold, almost didn't feel it any more. Same with the hunger. But wasn't that what they said about fasting? After the first few missed meals, you really didn't care for food. Anyway, the smell in here was enough to kill anyone's appetite.

What he did long for was a drink of water. His mouth was desert-dry and tasted foul. Also, he was worried about how long he could go on without water. He must be seriously dehydrated by now, with all that vomiting and diarrhoea.

He did feel weak, when he thought about it though it had to be said, he wasn't using up many calories, lying down all day. He imagined his muscles wasting away till he couldn't use his arms or legs. He pictured the flesh dropping off his bones. His eyesight too would be affected, from living in semi-darkness.

Sleeping and waking to the same bad dream, over and over, reminded him of the film where a man had to keep re-living the same day of his life until he got it right. Maybe that's what was going on here, except that every day was spent in this black hole, as if he had no life to live. How could he get it right if he wasn't ever given the chance to try? It was beyond awful.

He started to cry. When he heard the sound, a mewling wail that echoed in this lonely place, he felt like an abandoned infant, but with less chance of being saved.

Whatever had happened to bring him here, it wasn't a kidnap for ransom. He was being too neglected for that. A dead hostage was a useless hostage.

All he could do was hope for a miracle. Hope someone might happen by and find him, wherever he was, and rescue him from this hell-hole.

'Help?' he pleaded, noticing how puny and pathetic his voice sounded. 'Can someone help me, please?'

There would be no miracle rescue.

It was hopeless, he knew that. Feeling utterly helpless, he gave up.

***

CHAPTER 68

'What's that noise?' said Marty. 'It sounds like a baby crying.'

Joe laughed, 'I'd know nothing about that. Probably feral cats fighting. Or a fox.'

Marty concentrated on the screen. 'It's him. Can you hear it?'

Smeaton was curled up like a new-born, and as they watched, his shoulders shook in time with the pitiful cries coming from the speakers.

Marty watched Joe's face. She believed you could tell a lot about a person from the way they reacted to another's suffering. Joe looked sorry for Smeaton, but when she asked him, he answered harshly, 'Sorry for him? Are you having a laugh? Rotting in there for the rest of his days would be too good an end.'

Marty told herself she would have answered in much the same way. But despite her hatred of the man, she felt an unexpected sympathy for him. She found it harrowing to see any human being in such obvious distress. Her reaction surprised her and she sought to cover it up, lest Joe see it as a sign of weakness. 'Yeah, burning in the flames of hell would be better. For all eternity.'

'Do you believe in that stuff?'

'No, but he does, and that's all that counts here.' Marty was keen to block out the weeping. 'Should we turn up the white noise for a bit? I hate his guts but I can't listen to too much more of this.'

'I agree, it's not easy to listen to. Mind you, if we wanted to make some money, I know a few folk who'd buy the CD.'

Even with the volume turned up, the white noise didn't

drown out Smeaton's wails but it took the edge off and allowed Marty to think of something else.

'David suspects I'm having an affair.' She studied Joe, waiting for a reaction but his eyes never left the screen. 'With you,' she added, in a quiet voice. Joe seemed to be concentrating on Smeaton's prone body. He said nothing.

'He's been reading my e-mails. Knows we meet in the park.'

Joe looked at her, 'Where does he think you are right now?'

'I told him I was going away with some friends.'

'Did he believe you?'

'I don't know.'

'How did you explain the e-mails?'

'I told him the truth. That Chance introduced us and we discovered we'd known each other when we were kids. I missed out the part about the huge teenage crush I had on you, focused more on you being my big brother's friend. Said I'd put you back in touch with Jim. I had already told him I was worried about my weight, thinking I might take up running. I used that as the reason for our meetings in the park.'

'And what about your romantic trip to Paris?'

Marty could feel the blush warming her neck. 'It was very nice.'

'Romantic?'

The blush crept to her face. 'He was trying very hard to please me, spoiling me. Now I know why.'

'Because he suspected you of infidelity?'

'Possibly, although he said it was just to cheer me up, show me he doesn't take me for granted.'

'How could any man take you for granted, Marty? You're amazing.'

'Yeah, well, we've been married a very long time. You know how it is.' Marty cringed as she heard the words come out of her mouth. She wished she could swallow them down again. Looking at Joe she said, 'Sorry, insensitive.'

'I was worried for a moment you might have told him about our plans.'

'Not a chance. He wouldn't begin to comprehend what

we're doing here. David can't understand why I'm not happy to pick up my pension and piss about with art classes and volunteering. Thinks I should be "glad to be out", content to meet other retired ladies for lunch and gossipy chit-chat. Wants me to take up golf. I mean, can you see me in tartan shorts and a sun visor?'

Joe was laughing, 'Oh Marty,' he said, 'You're priceless. No, I cannot see you as a golfer. A mad cross-Saharan runner, yes, but a lady golfer? Never.'

'You see? You hardly know me, and yet you understand why I need to be here, doing this.'

***

CHAPTER 69

Thomas Smeaton could remember no further back than driving his new car. He concluded, therefore, that he'd been in a fatal accident.

His mother wasn't here with him so she'd either survived, or she'd gone to the other place. And rightly so. She was a lapsed Catholic, had lost her belief and rejected the faith. The last time his mother had attended mass was so long ago, there was no way she could have died in a state of grace. Fine. Hell was what she deserved.

It didn't matter what he did for her, she was never grateful. It cost a fortune to keep her in Briargrove, but he had wanted the best for her, never mind that it was eating up his inheritance. Did she ever utter a word of thanks? Too busy complaining and moaning about how he had sold her house from under her. He'd spent ages looking for a nice care home, but it didn't earn him the slightest bit of gratitude.

When he considered the possibility of his mother spending eternity in hell, he felt remarkably little sympathy for her. The rules of the church could not be clearer and his mother had chosen to ignore them. She must have known what lay in store for her. Perhaps she had been hoping to receive the last rites on her death bed. The final forgiveness of sins. She wouldn't be the first, after all. Nor would she be the first to leave it too late.

He, on the other hand, had been safe. One of the last things he clearly remembered was being at vigil mass the night before the accident, so there was no doubt he'd died in a state of grace.

An itch on his belly demanded his attention and as he scratched bare skin he was forced to re-consider his situation.

He was lying naked and thirsty, alone in a dark, almost soundless place. This was hardly the celestial paradise he had always imagined. He raised his eyes heavenward and was disappointed to see nothing more than a vague glow through the darkness.

He lay, staring at the meagre light, trying to discern the face of God in the gloom. If this was heaven, then everything he had ever believed in had led him here. A good and faithful servant of his religion should be able to look upon God's holy countenance. That was his promised reward for a lifetime of never missing mass, always avoiding sin and confessing impure thoughts.

He clambered to his feet and stood, staring at the light, willing it to emit at least a little radiance. Perhaps, if he looked hard enough, it might take on the shape of God's face. When he realised he was seeking the image of Jesus that every saint and sinner recognised, he had to remind himself that no one knew what God looked like. No one knew what heaven looked like either. Nevertheless, he couldn't help thinking of all those religious paintings. He wasn't expecting a welcome party of angels playing trumpets, but what he did expect was light. Blinding light. Radiant light. Glorious light.

How could this bleak, dark place be Paradise?

He felt outraged, cheated. A lifetime of goodness rewarded by this?

Had he got it wrong? Had he somehow committed a mortal sin in the moments before he died?

Did some mistake of his cause the accident that cost him his life? Had he taken some innocent driver or pedestrian with him? Terrifyingly, he simply did not know. But surely neither of those scenarios would make him guilty of a mortal sin? He would never have intentionally killed another human being. And anyway, with mortal sin on his soul he'd be roasting in the fires of hell, tormented by demons, not languishing alone in this cold, dark place.

Realisation struck him like a blow to the back of his knees. This wasn't hell. It couldn't be heaven. That only left one other possibility.

Purgatory.

How could that be? The Holy Father had decreed there was no such place as purgatory. Thomas Smeaton remembered Pope Benedict making his announcement, remembered feeling reassured even though he himself had never been at any risk of ending up there. He'd been so confident of that.

He looked around. There was nothing here but semi-darkness. He tried to recall the words of the Pope. The Holy Father didn't actually say there was no such thing as purgatory. What he said was that purgatory was a process, not a place. Thomas Smeaton looked around, touched the cold, beaten earth of the floor, felt his hunger, his thirst, his nakedness. He listened to the near-silence. This was as good a definition of a non-place as he could imagine. Someone famous once said, 'Eliminate all other factors, and the one which remains must be the truth.'

He tried to remember what he had learned about purgatory when he was young. Back then he had taken it all in, terrified of an eternity in hell for the occasional impure thought or night-time exploration of his own body. As he had grown in understanding and sophistication, he'd relaxed, confident he was a good man, guilty of few sins, and none of them important. When he transgressed in little ways, things like keeping too much change in a shop, he always confessed. That sort of thing wasn't stealing, in his opinion, but he confessed it, to be on the safe side. That way, he kept his conscience clear and his soul unsullied.

And yet here he was, a devout man, in purgatory, deprived of God's presence. He remembered an old hymn about souls in their agony. Yes, that would sum up how he felt right now.

It was time to calm down and think logically. He had never expected to find himself in this position. Nevertheless, because of his faith, he knew he would be assured of eternal salvation. Eventually.

The problem was, if he was imperfectly purified at the moment, he would need to undergo purification, so he could achieve the holiness necessary to enter the joy of heaven.

That bit was straightforward enough. He knew where he was and he knew what he had to do to escape. Become purified. Repent his sins. Okay, first he would have to identify those sins. That was going to be difficult; he couldn't think of any.

***

CHAPTER 70

He could start with an act of contrition.

On his knees, he took in a deep breath and spoke the words he had used at every confession. The difference this time was, there was no priest to listen and act as God's representative. This time, it was God himself who was listening. God alone would decide whether he would be absolved.

'O my God, I am heartily sorry for having offended Thee, and I detest all my sins, because I dread the loss of heaven, and the pains of hell; but most of all because they offend Thee, my God, who are all good and deserving of all my love. I firmly resolve, with the help of Thy grace, to sin no more and avoid the near occasions of sin.'

That last line seemed a bit pointless, given he was dead and not in any position to sin? How was he supposed to know what to pray in purgatory? They don't tell you that.

He waited a moment or two in the hope that one prayer might be enough for a good man like himself. He gazed at the light above his head and willed it to create the radiance he so craved. Nothing happened.

He racked his brains for another suitable prayer. Recalling the lines from Psalm 51, he prayed quietly, 'Have mercy on me, O God, blot out my transgressions. Wash me thoroughly from my iniquity, and cleanse me from my sin.' That sounded more appropriate. He went on, glad he could remember enough to make a meaningful prayer. 'For I know my transgressions, and my sin is ever before me.' He wished he could see his sin before him now, so he could work out why he'd been sent to this dark place.

Concentrate. Unless he prayed with all his heart, he might

as well not bother. What was the next bit? 'Cast me not away from your presence, and take not your Holy Spirit from me.'

Nothing could be more relevant to this situation. He said the line one more time for good measure. When nothing happened, it occurred to him he might have been too quiet. After all, he was unlikely to be the only one in purgatory. He would have to make sure his voice could be heard above all the other souls in agony. His knees were beginning to hurt but he made a real effort to keep his posture appropriate. He raised his voice and said both prayers again, much louder this time.

***

CHAPTER 71

Marty bumped Joe with her elbow, 'Tell me what he's saying.'

Joe watched the praying figure and said, 'I don't know. I guess it's a prayer.'

'No shit, Sherlock,' said Marty, quoting for some reason, a saying of her son's that she deplored. 'Sorry, I can see that, but I want to know what words he's using.'

Joe said, 'Not sure. It's hard to make out, but I think he's making an act of contrition.'

'Which means …?' Marty waited for an explanation.

'It's basically a special prayer that expresses sorrow for sins committed.'

'A bit like Our Father, who art in heaven? Everybody says the same words?'

'Yeah, exactly. Oh my God, I am heartily sorry and so on.'

'When did you learn that?'

'No idea, but it's in there for ever.' Joe tapped his forehead. 'Never underestimate the power of rote learning, eh?'

'I wish he would speak up a bit,' said Marty and as if he had heard her, Smeaton raised his voice. 'Wow,' she said, 'that was creepy.'

'That is an act of contrition he's making, I was right. Listen for yourself and you'll hear him ask for forgiveness.'

Marty did as Joe asked and sure enough she heard Smeaton praying.

She repeated his words, 'and cleanse me from my sin.' Does that mean we have a result?'

'No way,' said Joe. 'He'll need a damn sight more than a few Hail Marys to get him off this time. He's going nowhere until I hear him listing those sins and truly repenting. Then, and only then, will I be prepared to put him out of his misery.'

Marty was a bit surprised by the ferocity of Joe's reply, but she knew he was bitter about Smeaton and now that she understood why, she didn't blame him.

'We didn't go to all this bother for some pathetic prayer he's been reciting since his first communion.'

Marty touched Joe's arm. 'All I meant was, are we getting somewhere? As in, is he praying for forgiveness at last?'

Joe looked into her eyes with an intensity that unsettled her. 'Yes, he is. Sorry, but you know how I feel about the man.'

'I understand,' she said, in a low voice. 'Probably better than anyone.'

'Come on, then,' said Joe, 'Let's watch. We don't want to miss the moment when Smeaton repents being an evil bastard to Joe Docherty and Marty Dunlop, do we?'

***

CHAPTER 72

When there was no change in his circumstances, Thomas Smeaton knew he had to try harder. He wanted to be here for as short a time as possible, so it made sense to make sure he got his repentance right.

He moved into a sitting position and stretched his legs out in front of him, trying to get rid of the stiffness in his joints.

He'd start with his mother and work backwards. Even though she was the last person he'd seen before he died, he found it hard to picture her face. He had heard people describe the same experience when they lost a loved one. Except that Ruby Smeaton was not a loved one in the true sense of the word. For the briefest of moments he felt relief that dying before his mother meant he'd never have to stand up in church and say he was heart-broken at her loss.

Strangely the idea that he was dead didn't trouble him. He felt no regret for things undone and places unseen. He'd never believed in 'bucket lists' and since fatherhood had never appealed to him, he had no regrets on that score either. He was ready to meet his maker, it seemed, if his maker was ready for him.

Back to Ruby. Remembering the fourth commandment, he could only conclude that he hadn't honoured his mother enough. Otherwise he would have had the chance to 'live longer on the earth' as promised. He was puzzled. He'd never shown disrespect towards his mother. He was looking after her in her old age. Plus, he went to visit her, which was more than could be said for some folk. He was taking care of her finances, not squandering her money on wine or women. Maybe he'd failed her by not giving her grandchildren, but then, that wasn't his fault. She did a lot of moaning about his having forced her to move into Briargrove; even accused him of dodgy goings-on with the lawyer, but that was paranoia on her part, stupid old bat.

Woah! His train of thought slammed into the buffers as he disrespected his mother.

Admiration for his faith filled him with warmth. It was very simple and yet so sophisticated. A sin he had not noticed was enough to stop him gazing on the face of God. Oh well, that would be easily rectified.

He rolled over on to his knees and clasped his hands like a child in prayer. He was about to make another act of contrition when inspiration came to him. It might be more effective if he used his own words to repent this sin. 'Oh my God,' he said, then, remembering how much more powerful it sounded in a louder voice, he started again. 'Oh my God,' he intoned, with priest-like authority, 'I am heartily sorry for sinning against you and my mother. I regret the times I have called her a stupid, old bat or a silly cow. Have mercy on me, please God, for, in my defence, I would add that I did not ever say these sinful things to my mother's face.' He stopped, aware he was sounding more like a courtroom lawyer than a penitent sinner. He chose his next words carefully. It was important to get them right. 'I deeply regret my lack of respect for my mother who took me in and brought me up as her own. I am sorry I wasn't nice like Archie when I was a wee boy, so she could have loved me more easily. I regret that I did not take her wishes into consideration when she grew older. I ask your forgiveness and promise you this: if I could go back and say sorry to my mother, I would not hesitate.'

Might it be appropriate to offer up a prayer for her immortal soul? He decided to look after number one. Anyway, if, as he suspected, his mother had gone straight to hell, it would be a waste of a prayer that could be better used for himself. He was the one trying to remit time in purgatory, not his mother. He cast around in his mind for an appropriate ending to this prayer and decided on his favourite line. Looking up towards the miserable vestige of light, he prayed,

'Wash me and I shall be whiter than snow.'

***

CHAPTER 73

Marty was in hysterics. 'Will you listen to him? "Wash me? Whiter than snow?" Can you believe that man?' Her eyes were sparkling with tears and her glee was so infectious, Joe couldn't help joining in.

'He's priceless,' she said. 'Only Smeaton could turn a prayer for forgiveness into a pompous demand. The man's surely beyond redemption?'

Joe laughed. 'That little performance proves my point. He hasn't learned a thing. He's speaking to his creator as if he was ordering a fish supper.'

'I have to agree with you, Joe. There's not much sign of humility or repentance that I can see. I'm hardly an expert on the Roman Catholic faith, but wouldn't you expect someone who is trying to expiate his sins to sound a little more humble and apologetic? Dare I say, repentant?'

'I think he's taking the piss.'

'What?'

'I think he knows he's been set up.'

'Why on earth would he think that?'

'He's not stupid.'

'Far from it.'

'That reaction was so over the top, it had to be for an audience. Don't you think so?'

Marty shrugged and said, 'We've got no way of knowing, have we? All we can do is wait and see what happens next.'

'You're right. We're not going anywhere.' He pointed to the screen, 'And neither is he.'

Joe tried to stifle a yawn but Marty noticed and said, 'Joe, my friend, you look shattered. You should sleep.'

'I'm okay. I got used to going without sleep when Sally was

ill. I'll be fine for a few hours yet.'

Marty rose from her chair and came towards him. She took his hand and he got to his feet. She led him, like a child, through to the dorm and made him lie down on one of the bunks. Joe held on to her hand, unwilling to let her go. 'Marty. Stop me if I am out of line here, but I want you to think about something.'

She sat on the edge of the bed opposite. 'Okay.'

'I'd like you to consider coming away with me.'

'Away?' she repeated, as if it was a word in a foreign language. 'Away where?'

'To Bulgaria.'

'Bulgaria? Where you're building your new house?'

'I'm building a new life, Marty, not just a new house.'

'And you're asking me to go? What, to give you a hand?'

'To give me a hand, yes. I guess I could do with a hand.' He took both her hands in his and said, 'Two would be better.'

'Are you saying what I think you're saying?'

Joe nodded, a smile on his lips.

'You want me to move to Bulgaria with you?'

Joe kept on nodding. 'I want you to share my new life with me.'

'But I have a life, Joe.'

'It's not making you happy, though. Is it?'

Marty looked away. 'You don't know that.'

'Sorry. You're right. I don't.' He let go of her hands. It was clear she didn't know what to say. Joe felt embarrassed. He had shown all his cards and now he regretted his openness.

'Look, Marty. Forget I ever mentioned it. I'm sorry.' He raked his hair with both hands and tucked them behind his head. 'That was way out of line. Sorry.'

'Joe,' she whispered, 'it wasn't out of line. But,' she paused, as if she were trying to find the right words, 'I can't walk away. I have a son, you know. Not to mention a husband. And a dog.'

Joe pushed himself up onto one elbow. 'I can't speak for your son. I've never met him, but your husband doesn't seem to make you happy. You've told me as much. And you can bring the dog.' He tried a laugh but it didn't come out light-hearted.

'David's a good man, Joe. I'd never walk out on him. He doesn't deserve that, after all these years.'

'What's the alternative, Marty? You stay with a man you don't love, because he doesn't deserve to be left? What about you, Marty? What do you deserve?'

'I guess I've never thought about it, to be honest.'

He flopped back on the bed. 'Sorry. I've handled this all wrong. Sorry.'

'Joe,' she said, laying her hand on his cheek, 'please don't keep apologizing. Thank you for asking me. I'm so flattered, I can't tell you. Me, boring old Marty, being asked to go away with a gorgeous man like you. I can't believe it.'

'But you're more flattered than tempted, is that it, Marty?'

'Believe me, I'm tempted. I would've sold my soul to the devil when we were teenagers, for one look from you. And now you're inviting me to share the rest of your life? I must be dreaming.' She pinched her arm for effect, yelping when it hurt.

'You make me laugh. Don't you think we could have a great life, you and me?'

Marty sighed. 'Oh, Joe,' she said. 'You don't know what you're asking.'

'You're right,' he said, brisk again. 'I shouldn't have asked. Forgive me.'

'Nothing to forgive. You're offering me a priceless gift. Thank you so much.'

'But you decline the gift, priceless or not?'

Marty got to her feet. 'Sweet dreams,' she whispered, as she slipped out the door and closed it behind her.

***

CHAPTER 74

Thomas Smeaton lay down again, overcome with a sudden, forlorn weariness. He wasn't sure what he expected to happen after the confession of his sins against his mother, but he'd certainly hoped for something. He was becoming more puzzled and disappointed as time went by. Deprived of all the indicators of time passing, he could only guess how much time had elapsed. Everything around him remained exactly the same. There was no change in the quality of light, no alteration to that shooshing sound that he'd do anything to silence. There was no ticking clock, no snatch of television music, nothing. He had slept and woken several times, but that meant nothing. It could be days, it could be hours. And how was time measured in purgatory? He might have millennia to wait for a response to his prayers. He tried to remember any other way that souls could be released from purgatory. Repentance was the big thing and he had tried that. His soul must be badly stained with sin.

His only way out now would be through the prayers of other people. He thought about offering up a quick prayer to St Gertrude on his own behalf but logic told him he couldn't pray for souls in purgatory once he was there himself.

He'd never liked having to depend on others. In his experience, they generally let him down, one way or another. At work for example, he preferred to 'micro-manage'. He called it 'making sure everything gets done properly' but he knew there were many who considered him a control freak. He hadn't got to his position by being casual about the quality of work done by inferiors. A good manager knew his workers' strengths and weaknesses. His style had been to use the strong and get rid of the weak. 'L'enfer, c'est les autres'. That had always been his motto. Other people can make your life hell. Letting you down, not following your instructions, thinking they know better. It annoyed him no end. He didn't care that he had made few friends in his life. He, Thomas Smeaton, needed no-one. He came into the world alone and look at him now. Alone. Precisely the way he liked it.

The problem was, he couldn't stay here in darkness forever, deprived of the light of God's grace. He needed people praying for him. Who would say a novena to St Catherine on his behalf? Even if his mother were alive, she would be no good to him. She never went to mass. The congregation at his church would pray at least once for his departed soul, and there would be more prayers if his solicitor made sure he had a proper Catholic funeral. He hoped he hadn't been dumped onto the production line at the local crematorium. Thomas regretted never making his wishes clear. A serious oversight, but he'd always thought he would have plenty of time to think about that stuff.

He began to picture his funeral and imagined people praying for him. At first he visualised the church, full as on a feast day; he was an important man after all. But when he tried to pick out individual faces in the crowd he found it hard to identify enough to fill the front rows. Unlike many Catholics he had no large extended family to pray for him. There had only been himself and Ruby. There were no close friends to mourn his passing. Work colleagues might help to fill the pews, a few acquaintances from the council, perhaps, but he had no one he could count on to pray for him.

A tear ran down the side of his face and trickled into his ear.

***

CHAPTER 75

Marty knew most women her age would die for the chance to start a new life in a brand new, custom built house in the sun, away from cold, depressing Scotland and a boring, predictable life. With a fit, handsome man she knew was a good person, not some gigolo she'd met in a bar or on a dating site. David was a good person too, just too familiar and a bit boring although she hadn't always thought that and Paris had been a revelation. David had been so caring and kind. He'd also been good company, entertaining and knowledgeable. What about Mark? What would he have to say if she left his dad and went off with Joe?

Remembering there was one more man in her life at the moment, she raised her head and glanced at the screen. Smeaton was lying down, asleep, not dead, she hoped. She watched anxiously for a few minutes until Smeaton proved he was still alive by rolling onto his back.

Marty checked the time. It was still early. She thought about waking Joe, but nerves stopped her. She would start preparing breakfast. The smell of bacon frying was enough to rouse any man she'd ever known.

She was popping rashers of best Ayrshire in the pan when the outside door opened. Marty screamed as a blast of cold wind blew in, followed by a figure in a huge ski jacket and scarf. 'Shit! How did you get here?'

'Jeeso,' said Sheila, 'that's some welcome.'

'You frightened the life out of me.'

'Sorry, I thought you'd be pleased to see me. And I didn't bring my car, just so you know.'

'I am pleased to see you,' said Marty, giving her friend a hug. 'Good morning.'

Sheila unwound her scarf. 'I couldn't stand it, just waiting at the flat, not knowing what was happening, so I decided to come. Hope that's okay?'

'Of course,' said Marty, wondering if Joe would say the same.

As if summoned by her thoughts Joe appeared. 'Thought I heard voices.' He gave Sheila a welcome hug. 'Good to see you. Great job you did yesterday.'

'How is he?'

Marty pointed to the screen where Smeaton still lay spread-eagled. 'See for yourself.'

Sheila covered her eyes with both hands and said, 'Do I have to?'

Joe and Marty laughed. 'Not a pretty sight,' said Marty, 'but you'll get used to it.'

'Is that bacon I smell?' asked Joe.

Over bacon rolls and hot tea, Sheila told them about Smeaton's plan to take Ruby to Turnberry and how determined Ruby had been to defy him and make their plan work. She also revealed how nerve-wracking she had found the whole abduction.

'You did a fantastic job, you and Ruby. We'll have to send her a big bunch of flowers once this is over.'

Sheila looked horrified. 'Please don't ask Violet to deliver them.'

They sat and chatted like old pals who'd not seen each other for ages. Marty was amazed how comfortable and relaxed they all seemed, considering they were in the process of carrying out a serious crime. One that would see them all going to jail if they got caught.

As if she had picked up on Marty's anxiety, Sheila suddenly asked, 'Are you absolutely sure Smeaton will be okay without food and drink.'

'Yes,' said Joe with conviction. 'He will lose a little weight, of course, but he'll come to no harm in the short time we'll keep him here.'

Marty rose to fill the teapot for the third time. As she

crossed to the kettle something crashed through the window and smashed onto the floor at her feet. Marty screamed and dropped the teapot.

Joe swore and ran to the window. Peeking round the edge of the curtain, he said 'Fuck! It's those idiot boys, back again. Turn up the white noise.'

Joe ran to the bothy door.

Marty said, 'Sheila, you need to get out there and pretend you and Joe are a couple. Embarrass them into going away.'

Sheila opened her shirt a few buttons to reveal an astonishing amount of cleavage spilling from a red bra. She ruffled her spiky hair, took a deep breath and went out the door. From a hiding place by the window, Marty watched her slink up behind Joe and put her arms around him. If Joe was surprised, he hid it well, but the look on the boys' faces was priceless. Joe pulled Sheila round to his side and held her close. The boys started to back away, muttering apologies. Then Joe asked, 'Where's Dykesy?'

'Roon the back, Sur, looking fur a canoe.'

***

CHAPTER 76

Joe rounded the corner in time to see Dykesy poke something sharp into the lock.

'Hey,' Joe called, hoping his voice would be neither audible nor recognizable to the man inside. Dykesy stopped, caught in the act. Then he pocketed his tool and turned slowly. A look of sly cunning changed to a mixture of guilt and relief when he recognized Joe.

'Hello, Sur,' he said, attempting his usual bantering tone.

Joe stepped close to the boy, and made his voice as low and threatening as possible. 'What do you think you're doing?' Shock made him sound angrier than he'd intended.

Dykesy took a step back and raised his hands in a gesture of defence. 'Easy, Big Man,' he said, sounding a lot more relaxed than he looked.

Joe was keen to get away from the door, lest any of their conversation carry in to Smeaton. He put his hand on the boy's elbow to guide him towards the corner but Dykesy shrugged him off, as if resisting arrest. Joe told himself to handle this carefully. 'Come on, lad,' he said, 'let's go and talk about this with the others.' He walked off and was relieved when the boy followed a few steps behind.

As they approached the front door, one of the other two said, 'Hurry up, Dykesy. We're getting a bacon roll.'

Joe demanded, in his best teacher's voice, to be told what they were up to.

It was Dangermoose who spoke. Dykesy had the sense to know when to keep quiet but Joe noticed his slight nod to Danger. Permission to speak on his behalf. 'Sur, we just wanted a last shot at the canoeing.'

'We went through all this the other day,' said Joe, in a voice

268

that implied his patience was wearing thin. 'I told you the place was cleared, didn't I?'

Dangermoose and Slug hung their heads. 'Aye, Sur,' they muttered. Slug added, 'but we wanted to see for ourselves.'

'Great. Okay, now you've seen, so sling your hook.'

The boys looked like kicked puppies. Joe immediately regretted his harsh words. He did not want to squander the goodwill he had built up with these lads. Most of them had been let down by males in their lives and he did not want to become one of those who got angry and rejected them. 'Sorry lads, I didn't mean that.' He turned to include Dykesy in his next words. 'But you can't go around breaking into places. I don't want you to end up in jail. I thought I'd taught you to live by society's rules.'

No one said anything until Sheila stepped out of the bothy with a tray of mugs and a pile of bacon rolls. 'Tuck in, lads,' she said.

Dykesy looked her up and down, then said defiantly, 'Is that what you're doing here, Sur? Living by society's rules?'

Joe felt his face turn red. He hoped Dykesy was referring to Sheila and not to Smeaton. 'Look, lads,' he said, as if the boy had never spoken, 'enjoy your rolls and then head off back to town. It breaks my heart to say it, but there's nothing left for you here. Nothing at all.'

Again Dykesy looked at him with a challenge. 'I don't mean to be cheeky, like, but what are you doing up here?' A heartbeat later he added, 'Sur.'

'Having a wee break before I shut the place for ever.' Joe did not need to fake the sadness in his voice when he said, 'I've been bringing kids like you up here for nearly twenty years. That's longer than you've been alive.'

He smiled and said, 'That adds up to a lot of memories. I'm due to resign and I'm up here to think about the good old days.'

'Before the war and stuff?' asked Slug, attempting to show his understanding.

Sheila laughed. 'We don't go back quite that far,' she said.

Dykesy looked from Joe to Sheila and back again. 'So that's all you're doing up here? Remembering?'

'Reminiscing, Dykesy. That's the word for it. Reminiscing.'

'Aye, right,' muttered the boy, loud enough for Joe to hear. The other two sniggered, suddenly appearing very young and immature.

'Come on, eat these up before they get cold, lads,' said Sheila, offering the tray to Dykesy, who took a roll and a mug and murmured his thanks.

Joe had to admire her ability to stay cool under pressure. She had adopted precisely the right manner to deal with troubled boys like these.

'Do you want one, Joe?' she asked.

'No, thanks. I'll wait for the full Scottish you promised me.' Joe did not miss the look that passed between Dykesy and the other two. If he didn't know the lad had a good heart, he'd be itching to give him a slap.

'Any word from TJ?' Joe asked, keen to re-establish the rapport he'd always enjoyed with his boys. 'How's he getting on?'

'Fine. He likes it. Right bastard of a drill sergeant but he's giving TJ peace so far.'

'TJ's a great lad,' said Joe, filled with relief that the boy was grabbing the second chance he'd been given. 'He'll do well in the army.'

'Aye,' said Dykesy, through a mouthful of roll. 'It's the right place for him.'

'Tell him I'll buy him a pint the first time he's home on leave, eh?'

Dykesy gave him a look. 'Sur, have ye ever seen TJ's "home"?' He wiggled his fingers around the word.

Joe shook his head.

'TJ will never be back here and ah don't blame him. He was lucky to get away.' He raised his eyebrows. 'Thanks to you.'

Joe rubbed at his chin. 'Yeah, well, maybe I could have done more.'

'Ye did plenty, Sur. Thanks.'

'Ah'll be back, the first leave ah get,' said Slug, with a grin on his big, soft face. 'Tae show off ma uniform. Aw, ah cannae wait to go, Sur.'

Joe slapped him on the back. 'Good luck, pal. I'm proud of you.'

Turning to Dykesy, Joe asked, 'You sticking to your plans to go to college?'

'Aye, if I don't get the jail first.'

When Joe realised the boy was joking, he gave him a playful punch on the arm, causing him to spill his tea. 'Careful, Big Man,' said Dykesy.

Joe was cheered by the warmth of their relationship and wondered why it mattered to him that he got on well with these youths. After this was over, he was unlikely to ever see them again. He coughed to remove a strange lump from his throat. 'You make sure you behave yourself from now on. I'll patch up that window, but no more breaking and entering.'

'Aye, aw right, I hear ye.'

'You can be anything you set your mind to, Dykesy. You've a right clever head on those shoulders of yours.'

Dykesy's face turned pink and he covered his embarrassment with a cheeky retort. 'Mair than you could say for wee Danger, eh?'

Dangermoose grinned as if Dykesy had paid him a compliment.

'Sur, there was something we wanted to see you about, by the way.'

'What's that?' He expected to be asked to provide a reference or something but Dykesy shocked him with his next words.

'See the guy that shut this place, is he a wee guy called Thomas Smeaton?'

'What makes you ask that?'

'Sluggo wis lookin on the cooncil website and we think he's the basturt you were talking about. Is he?'

'Why do you want to know?'

'We were thinking we could do him in for ye. Kinda

revenge, like.'

Joe was lost for words. He was touched by their loyalty but shocked by how easily they saw violence as a solution. 'Boys, the last thing I want is for you to get into any more trouble. Have you not been listening to a word I've said, Dykesy?'

'Aye, but we'll no touch him, like. No us, personally. But he sounds like he needs a right kickin. We'll get him done for ye. There's plenty nutters in Bankside that love roughin folk up.'

Dangermoose added, 'Aye, like McCafferty or that bamstick Jarvie. They'll dae it fur nuthin.' He laughed as if beating up members of the public was a sport.

Joe was horrified by the casual way these kids discussed GBH. 'Boys, please don't do that. It might come back to me.'

Dykesy laughed, 'No chance, Sur. How would the polis connect it to you?'

'Please don't, boys. I'm asking you. Don't get yourselves into trouble on my account. It wouldn't be right.'

'Okay, Big Man, take a chill pill. We'll no touch him if that's what you want.' He grinned at his two mates, 'But I cannae promise his car'll no get keyed.'

Joe repeated his request for them to keep out of trouble. It was all he could do. The three boys drained their mugs and put them back on the tray Sheila had left on the doorstep.

'Right then,' said Dykesy, 'are we ready for off, boys?' He pushed back the elastic cuff on his waterproof and checked the time on a watch that had to be either replica or stolen, perhaps both. 'We'll get the half-past bus, if we don't hang about.'

One by one, the boys gave Joe a very grown-up handshake, then Slug, looking shame-faced asked, 'Sur?'

'Sluggo?'

'Sur, do you think it would be okay if ah gave ye a hug? In case ah never see you again?'

'I thought you were buying me a pint on your first leave?'

Slug looked confused.

Joe said quickly, 'I think a hug's a great idea, Slug.' He grabbed the boy, giving him a quick hug and a hefty slap on the back. The others stood back for a moment and then took a step forward into Joe's embrace.

Dykesy muttered, 'Be seein you, Big Man.' Handing over a grubby slip of paper he said, 'There's ma phone number. If ah can ever dae anythin for you.'

Wee Dangermoose said nothing and Joe too found it hard to speak for a moment.

Finally, he managed to say, 'Cheerio, lads. Take care of yourselves, now, will you?'

He stood and watched the three red-anoraked figures walk away. A chapter closing. Before they disappeared, the boys turned and saluted. He was glad he'd stayed outside to see that. He waved till they were out of sight, then, wiping a tear from his eye, he opened the door and stepped into the bothy.

***

CHAPTER 77

Thomas Smeaton was doing his best to draw up a mental list of those he could count on to turn up at his funeral. Having no social life, his thoughts turned to work.

He immediately thought of Carole, she'd be there; he could depend on her for anything. She remembered his mother's birthday, bought the gifts he needed to distribute at Christmas, made his dental appointments and reminded him to keep them. He could always rely on Carole. She was a sweet little thing, always so cheery and willing to please him. Try as he might, the only image of Carole he could conjure was one of her tear-stained face. Having employees in tears was part of the job, as far as Thomas Smeaton was concerned. Any manager naive enough to believe it was possible to please all of the people all of the time was a fool.

However, he couldn't recall seeing Carole in tears very often. In fact, he could only think of that one time, perhaps that's why it had stuck in his memory. She had wanted to go off on a wild goose chase to America to try to conceive a child by some new-fangled scientific process. Why couldn't people accept God's will? If she was meant to be a mother, she'd get pregnant without flying half way across the world to some charlatan of a doctor. He had told her as much the first time she'd asked. He couldn't give in to employees who asked for extra leave and he certainly wasn't prepared to make an exception for a secretary, even one as good as Carole.

He remembered how she had pleaded with him to grant her unpaid leave of absence. He'd said no, obviously. How was he to know she wouldn't be swanning around Disneyworld or lazing on some beach? Anyway, he'd stuck to his guns and she'd defied his wishes and gone. So they'd both got their own way in the end. Except, he'd lost the best secretary he'd ever had and she'd have no job if the baby thing didn't work out. Perhaps, on reflection, he could have been a little bit more understanding. After all, he could have managed for a few days without her.

That tiny seed of doubt in his mind suddenly sprouted into a little shoot of regret. In his imagination, he saw it grow into a small tree, with branches reaching out to right and left. To his surprise, Carole's face appeared, hanging from the lower branch. She looked bereft, tears streaming down her face and running into her mouth which formed, over and over, the word, please.

Thomas Smeaton did not want to dwell on that picture, did not like the feeling he might have made an error of judgement. Could such a simple mistake count as sin? He'd no idea.

He turned his mind to other folk with whom he'd worked closely.

He thought of the committee room at HQ, full of head teachers from the many primary schools for which he was responsible. As he searched for a friendly face, he saw false smiles, averted eyes. Right at the centre of the group, framed by that frizzy hair of hers, shone the fat, frumpy face of Liz Douglas, the woman who'd recently taken her own life.

There had been a lot of strange stuff going on at that school. Parents were clearly unhappy, why else would they go on Facebook to complain about the head teacher? But, as he'd told her that last day in his office, there's rarely smoke without fire. He remembered the look on her face, as if he'd loosened her fingers from the edge of a lifeboat and cast her adrift. Then, when he'd mentioned, quite appropriately, in his opinion, Her Majesty's Inspectors coming in to offer advice, the woman had looked unhinged.

One thing about her, she did work awfully hard. Until this recent Facebook carry-on, he'd never had a single complaint about Cavenhead Primary, and it wasn't in the most affluent, easy part of town. Come to think of it, Liz Douglas had done a good job for many years. Pity it ended the way it did. Suicide.

What in God's name drove her to that?

The strange tree appeared to him again, with Carole's sad little face on one branch and dangling from another, noose around her neck, the bloated face of Liz Douglas. Like baubles on a Christmas tree, faces appeared on branches till each one bore a picture of employees, past and present.

***

CHAPTER 78

When Joe went for a shower, Sheila studied Marty. She appeared calm enough, but there was something going on.

'You okay, Marty?' she asked. Marty was sitting by the screen, eyes fixed on the image of Smeaton.

'Not really. Joe's asked me to go away with him.'

'Go where?'

'He's moving abroad and wants me to join him.'

'I don't understand. Joe knows you're married, doesn't he?'

'Yeah, but he also knows I haven't been happy.'

'Oh,' said Sheila, not sure what else, if anything, she could add.

Marty said nothing for a moment, as if she were considering her next words. 'Sheila,' she said, 'Did you know Joe and I go way back?'

Sheila recalled some throwaway line, ages ago it seemed, about how they had been at school together or something.

'I adored him when I was fourteen, but he didn't seem to notice I was on the same planet. Now I've run into him again and he's asking me to start a new life with him. It feels like I've been hit by a hurricane. I'm all over the place. Look at me.' She held out her hands. They were trembling. Sheila took them in her own and squeezed.

'And how do you feel about him now, Marty? That's what counts, not how you felt when you were fourteen. We all had mad crushes on unsuitable people.'

Marty pounced on the word before Sheila had time to regret its choice. 'Unsuitable? Is that what you think of Joe? He's unsuitable?'

'I didn't say Joe is unsuitable, Marty. I hardly know the

man. I'm a bit surprised things have moved so fast, I suppose, but I imagine Joe feels he has nothing to lose by asking you and it's clear there's chemistry between the two of you.'

Marty looked like an excited teenager. 'Do you think so?'

'Oh yes. I've been suspicious about the two of you for weeks.'

Marty smiled, seeming to take it as a compliment.

'What do you think you'll do?'

Marty said, 'I wish I knew, Sheila, but, to be honest, I have no idea.'

'How do you feel about him?'

Marty glanced away, deep in thought, then instead of answering, she shouted, 'Look, Smeaton's on his knees again.'

'Joe! Come quick! You need to hear this.'

***

CHAPTER 79

Picturing his colleagues and realising he had wronged every one of them, in some way, Thomas Smeaton prayed, 'God, have mercy on me. I believed I was a good man, trying to do a good job, managing people and making them work hard. But I might have overdone it. I am truly sorry I didn't have more compassion for some of my employees.' He stopped to think, trying to decide if it would be better to name them. He remembered he was supposed to be praying for forgiveness. It might be a good idea to use the word 'forgive'.

'Forgive me, Father, for not allowing Carole, my secretary, to go to America. I am truly sorry and if I could tell her that, face to face, I would.' He stopped again, struck by the awareness that he meant every word. Pity it was too late. He'd never have the chance to apologise to Carole or anyone else. 'I'm so sorry, Father,' he said. 'Please forgive me. If Carole wants a baby, then it's not up to me to stand in her way. Why didn't I see that before now?' He fell forward on to his hands, feeling worse than he ever had in his lifetime. Abject, that was the word to describe it, as in abject apology. Whispering now, he recited, 'Holy Mary, Mother of God, pray for us sinners, now and at the hour of our death.'

As the words he had known since boyhood rolled off his tongue, he wondered whose forgiveness he ought to pray for next. Liz Douglas. Suicide. Because of him? He retched a few drops of watery sputum on to the ground. Pushing up on his arms he righted himself and looked up towards the trace of light.

'Lord, forgive me for the way I treated Liz Douglas. When she came to me, looking for support, I sent her away, preferring to make her feel the inadequacies were all hers. They were mine, Father. Mine. I failed as a leader, failed as a human being. God, please forgive me for saying I would send in the inspectors to get to the bottom of things. I could tell she was terrified and I must confess, I took pleasure in seeing her suffer.'

Thomas Smeaton could hardly believe his own ears. All this stuff was pouring out of his mouth in an effortless stream. He didn't have to think about it. Was that good or bad? He was tempted to blame Councillor Cooper for the way he had been treating staff recently. There was no doubt she had been a poisonous influence on him. For some reason, he had wanted to please her, and the council, more than he had wanted to support his staff. He had no idea why, but it had made sense at the time.

He now saw Morag Cooper as an unpleasant, powerful woman who had wooed him so that she could control him. It had been she who insisted all schools follow council directives to the letter, with no room for creative or caring head teachers.

'They're either with us or against us,' she'd said to him one day. 'It's your job, Tom, to make sure they're with us. We have no room for the maverick in this authority.'

'But Councillor Cooper,' he'd said, only to be reminded to call her Morag when they were alone together. 'Morag,' he'd muttered, 'some of these head teachers are doing great things, often in very difficult schools.'

'Unless they are sticking rigidly to council policies,' she'd insisted, 'I want them out. Do you understand me, Tom? Out.'

Maybe he should ask forgiveness for listening to the likes of Morag Cooper, when common sense had told him she was nothing but a power-mad tyrant. It was she who'd suggested making savings on the education budget by cutting this and cutting that. Then, when the people of Bankside had stood up for themselves, she'd been right in there, milking every opportunity for publicity. Some said she was hoping to move from local government to greater things. God help Scotland if independence meant being ruled by the likes of her.

'Father, forgive me for putting my desire to please Morag Cooper before my desire to do the right thing for the teachers and pupils in my care. I wish I hadn't listened to her, Lord, and been taken in by her. She was the one who wanted to cut funding to the poorest areas. I shouldn't have done what she told me. But, forgive me, Lord, I was worried about keeping my job.'

***

CHAPTER 80

'Wow,' whispered Marty. 'Now we're getting somewhere. Did you hear that? He's repented his sins against lovely Liz.' She touched Sheila's arm and gave it a squeeze.

'Yes,' said Sheila, 'but have you noticed how easily he's slipped back into his old ways, blaming Cooper for his behaviour, instead of acknowledging his own guilt? The man makes me sick.'

'Yeah,' agreed Joe, 'there's a touch too much Nazi Germany about this for my liking. He had to do it to please his superiors. It's nothing but jobsworth bullshit.'

'Shh ...' Marty pointed to the screen. 'Listen to him. He seems to have moved on from blaming the Troll. Sounds like he might be taking responsibility for his own decisions.'

'Forgive me for cutting the funding to the children's orchestra. I know it does a lot of good in an area blighted by deprivation. If I could, Father, I would beg Sean to pardon me and would do everything in my power to re-instate the orchestra.'

'Too late,' muttered Sheila sadly, 'that boat has sailed.'

Smeaton quietened and sat back on his heels, as if to give his knees a rest.

'What's he up to now?' Marty asked the others, feeling obliged to whisper.

'I think he's wondering what to say next.'

Smeaton raised himself into his praying position and was off again, voice raised as if he were delivering a prayer in a cathedral.

'He looks transfixed,' said Sheila, 'don't you think?'

'Yeah, he's in the zone,' said Joe. 'I hope it isn't an

282

elaborate act for our benefit.'

'Do you hear him, Joe? He's on about your stuff now, I think.'

As they fell silent, Smeaton voiced his regret for the way he had spoken to Joe, asking forgiveness for suggesting he was a paedophile.

'What?' screamed Sheila, then clasped her hand over her mouth. On screen, Smeaton continued his fervent prayer, undisturbed by her outburst. Sheila said, 'Oh, Joe. The man's beyond disgusting.'

'Docherty was a fool, going to the papers, thinking he could get the better of me, but, I have to admit, Lord, he's been doing good work with those boys of his, keeping them off the drugs. Forgive me for pulling the funding from his projects.'

'Blow me,' said Joe. 'This is a day I never thought I'd see.'

'I should never have shut down his bothy and I promise, if I could go back and live my life over again, I would encourage him in his good work.'

Beside her Joe was clasping a hand to his chest, as if he was having a heart attack.

Marty gave him a thumbs-up. 'You're back in a job. Sorted!'

She shook her head. 'He's unbelievable.'

There was a lull in the confessions while Smeaton muttered a few more lines from what sounded to Marty like conventional prayers. Then, to her astonishment, Marty heard her own name mentioned. It was surreal and she glanced at Joe to see whether he had heard it too.

'Your turn,' he said, eyebrows raised.

'God, forgive me, please, for what I did to Marty Dunlop. She was a thorn in my side, there's no doubt, and a really aggravating woman, but I could have dealt with her better. Councillor Cooper was haranguing me to get rid of difficult people. And Marty Dunlop was definitely difficult. And a maverick if ever I saw one.'

Marty choked with indignation. 'Damn you,' she shouted at the screen. Sheila hugged her, but Joe, she noticed, didn't take his eyes off Smeaton, who was confessing his sins at the top of his voice.

'Forgive me, Father. I realise now how much damage I must have done to the likes of Joan Donaldson and Ken Barty, Mary Henderson, mmm, Willie Morgan, mmm, Marie whatsername.'

'Listen to the sad bastard,' muttered Joe. 'He's listing anyone he's ever offended. Can't remember all their names but hoping to cover enough bases to escape from purgatory.' He turned to Marty, his anger clear to see. 'Does that sound sincere to you?'

'No,' admitted Marty, 'but I've never listened to anyone pray before, let alone a man trying to save his eternal soul.'

'What do you think, Sheila?' he demanded. 'You're Catholic. Does that sound genuine to you, reeling off random names?'

'I've no idea, Joe. I'm way out of my depth here.'

Marty said, 'That's how I feel too. We've no way of telling whether he's sincerely repentant. I suppose the only way we'll ever find out is if he changes his ways after this. We've done all we can.'

'I agree. Maybe we should be thinking about getting out of here,' said Sheila. 'We've achieved our objective, haven't we?'

Marty said, 'I hope so. It feels a bit of a let-down though. I expected to feel exhilarated, vindicated. I'm not sure I'm satisfied.'

They watched and waited, hoping for more, but, having reeled off another list of names, Smeaton appeared to have completed his confession. No more prayers were offered. No-one else was mentioned.

***

CHAPTER 81

Although she'd agreed to have a lie-down, Marty couldn't sleep; she had far too much going on in her head. There was tomorrow to be got through and, sooner or later, she'd have to give Joe an answer.

If David were the only obstacle, Marty thought she might say yes, but there was Mark to consider and he was a different matter. Okay, she hardly saw him these days, since he moved away to university, but that was normal, right? And at least she always had the holidays to look forward to. Maybe he'd want to come to Bulgaria on his holidays? He could bring his pals. It would be like the old days when all the boys used to gather at their house.

But what if Mark took his dad's side? What if she never saw her son again? What if she missed his graduation, his wedding? They'd never rowed in front of Mark, in fact they rarely disagreed at all. Maybe that was the trouble, their relationship was totally lacking in passion. They never fell out so they never had the fun of making up. Life with David had become boring. She'd never noticed before, too engrossed in bringing up Mark and running a school, keeping so many balls in the air she didn't have time to see how unexciting married life had become.

Joe, somehow, exuded danger. Maybe she was being daft but she hadn't felt this exhilarated since she was fourteen. She started to work out how many years that was and gave up. Joe made her feel young again, while David seemed happy for her to settle into middle age and embrace retirement. Every part of her rebelled against that idea. Paris had been nice, but it was hardly electrifying. She wanted excitement, and she wanted it now, while she was young enough to enjoy the thrill of the ride.

Trying not to disturb Sheila who was asleep in the next bunk, Marty climbed out of bed, determined to tell Joe, before she changed her mind, that she would go with him.

The living room was empty. All that could be heard was white noise from the speakers and a soothing whirr from the heater. Joe was nowhere to be seen. On screen, Thomas Smeaton lay curled in a ball, harmless as a sleeping child.

Marty went to the window and parted the curtains. The sky was a star-sprinkled navy, the ground white-frosted. The loch, in the distance, lay silent and slick. Nothing moved, except Joe's silhouette prowling back and forth against the pale moon.

***

CHAPTER 82

When Thomas Smeaton opened his eyes, disappointment hit him like a blow to the stomach. He groaned, not understanding how he could still be here. He rolled on to his back and peered upwards, but there was no sign of God's holy countenance, far less the radiant glory he expected to welcome him into heaven. Surely he had done all he could? He tried to conjure up the faces of the folk he had named in his prayers and saw that tree again, laden with images of those whose lives he must have made a misery. It seemed more had appeared while he'd been dozing. The trouble was, while he vaguely recalled the faces, he couldn't remember all of their names. How was he to pray for forgiveness if he couldn't remember the people he'd sinned against and call them by name? This getting out of purgatory was proving to be a serious challenge. Imagine if he were doomed to spend eternity like this. Thinking he had done enough then waking over and over to the realization he was still full of sin and unlikely to ever be released to the glory of heaven.

Thomas Smeaton felt very aggrieved. God wasn't playing fair. What more was he supposed to do? He had repented and begged for forgiveness. Now surely, it was God's turn to keep his side of the bargain and let him out of here.

In a fit of pique, he clambered to his knees then up onto his feet. This was no time to be meek and mild. Being assertive had got him what he wanted in life. Why should death be any different?

***

CHAPTER 83

'Joe! Sheila! You have to come and hear this.'

Joe hurried in the front door to find Marty practically jumping up and down.

'Don't miss this, Joe. He's complaining that he's done enough and yet God hasn't sent a band of celestial angels to escort him through the pearly gates.'

'Has he actually said that?' asked Sheila, rubbing sleep from her eyes.

'Not in so many words, but that's what he's getting at. He's very annoyed and letting God know it.'

Right on cue, Smeaton shouted, 'God! Are you listening to me?'

Joe couldn't believe his ears. It was a long time since he'd been a practising Catholic, but he knew from years of attending church that this was no way to speak to the Almighty. His boyhood training in faith and worship came back to him and he watched the screen fascinated, expecting a thunderbolt or flash of lightning to appear and strike Smeaton to the ground.

'I've done my bit,' whined Smeaton. 'Why won't you forgive me?'

Sheila stared. 'This is unbelievable,' she said. 'The man obviously believes he can bully his way out of anything, including purgatory.'

'Come on, Sheila,' said Joe, grinning, 'be fair. He's only pulling rank.'

Sheila spluttered with mirth. 'You're right. Putting the Almighty in his place and letting him know Thomas Smeaton's not happy with his arrangements.'

Joe listened to the tirade for a moment or two and then said, 'That's exactly the way he spoke to me the last time I saw him.'

'He's bullying God,' shouted Marty. 'That's what he's doing, he's bullying God.'

On screen Smeaton was building up a head of steam. In a style familiar to all of them, he was strutting up and down, his chest puffed out with self-importance, ridiculous in his nakedness.

'This is comical. It reminds me of a story I used to read to Mark when he was small, about the emperor's new clothes. He walked around naked too, believing he was powerful and to be obeyed at all costs.'

'God,' Smeaton shouted, 'I've had enough of this. Fair enough, a little time in purgatory, to remind me I wasn't always as perfect as I thought, you know, vis-a-vis my mother and a few employees. But may I remind you, Father? It was only a few hours before my death that I made my last confession.'

'Don't you expect him to be struck down at any moment?' whispered Sheila, her voice full of wonderment. 'Turned into a pillar of salt?'

'It's what he deserves,' said Joe. 'What a terrible way to speak to your maker.'

'I agree with you, Joe, and I don't even believe in a maker,' said Marty, who sounded as if she might be in danger of choking. 'The man is incredible.'

'Now do you believe he was being insincere earlier?' said Joe, looking from Marty to Sheila and back.

'I've repented my sins and begged your forgiveness. I don't know what else you expect of me. I'm a good man. I live a clean life, give a lot of money to the church and never pass a collecting tin in the street. I even buy the Big Issue, occasionally. I'm not the kind of person you should be keeping here.'

'Oh, I wish Ruby could see this.'

'Don't worry,' said Joe. 'There's a fresh disc in the camera. It's all being recorded. Every ranting word of it.'

'And I do my best to help that lot up at Bankside, don't I? They neither work nor want, those people, but I funded musical instruments, canoes and all the rest of it, so they could be rescued from their deprivation. They're deprived of damn all. New trainers, new phones, everything. And they've always got money for fags and drink, have you noticed that, God? Whereas I never touch a drop.'

The three friends gazed at each other, speechless, but it seemed Smeaton hadn't finished yet.

'What rescued me from poverty? Hard work, that's what, not poncing about with a saxophone or wandering the hills at the taxpayer's expense. My mother worked her fingers to the bone bringing up Archie and me. You didn't see her down the social security, claiming this allowance and that allowance. She was far too proud for that. They've no pride, these people, that's the trouble. No pride at all.'

'Not something anyone could ever accuse you of, Smeaton,' said Marty.

'Ruby described him as a champagne socialist,' said Sheila. 'He's showing his true colours now. Listen to him.'

'There's only so much someone like me can do, Father. I try my very best to provide for those in need, but the councillors don't always see it my way. All they're interested in is power.'

'I wonder what Morag Cooper and his other councillor pals would make of this?' said Marty.

Smeaton had stopped strutting and was now standing, hands on hips, face upturned. 'Are you listening, God?' he roared. 'Enough is enough. You've made your point. I repent all my sins. Now, it's high time you let me out of here.'

'Do you think he's having some sort of nervous breakdown?' asked Joe.

'Who knows?' said Sheila, 'but I'm not sure this is working out the way we intended.'

Their earlier hysteria evaporated.

'I'm wondering if a man, who believes himself God's equal, can ever be made to see the error of his ways,' said Marty, sounding less confident than Joe had ever heard her.

'Look,' said Sheila, 'I don't want him physically hurt, you

both know that, but I was hoping for an outcome that would be worth all this effort.' She indicated the screen. 'And I'm not sure this is it.'

'You're right,' said Marty. 'We're all taking a big risk being here. We could get a ten-year sentence if we're caught. There has to be more payback than this.'

'I was hoping he'd have an epiphany,' said Sheila, looking from one face to another. 'You know, a Damascene experience. Something that humbled him and changed his life.'

'Obviously we've not put him through enough to make him a better person,' said Joe. 'Simple as that. We'll just have to be patient until he shows true repentance.'

'I'm not sure we have the luxury of that much time.' Marty pointed to the screen where Smeaton was holding his defiant stance, challenging his creator. 'How can anyone look at that and believe the man will ever behave any differently?'

Marty's eyes looked moist. When she spoke all the spark and energy had gone from her voice. 'If our plan hasn't worked, who *is* going to do something about Smeaton?

'Let's just give it a bit more time,' said Joe.

***

CHAPTER 84

The morning air was bitterly cold and hung with a dampness that threatened rain. Because of the low cloud, it was still almost dark, only the sky to the east showing any promise of daylight. Wisps of mist lingered in the dips on the track that led back to town.

Sheila thought of Smeaton, lying all night on that cold floor. She wanted this to be over, before it all went terribly wrong. She had a bad feeling about it.

'It's a dreich morning out there,' she said, as she stepped back into the bothy and closed the door quietly. 'I need a cup of tea.' She shrugged off her ski jacket and hung it up on a peg in the kitchen area. 'Maybe I should make us all a spot of breakfast, while Smeaton's quiet?'

Joe said nothing. The word brooding came into her mind.

'Good idea,' Marty said brightly, as if she were making a real effort to be positive. 'I'll give you a hand.'

Sheila whispered, 'For what it's worth, Marty, I think the right decision would be to let him go tonight.'

'We don't really have much choice. We can't keep him here forever. I just didn't want it to end this way. Such an anti-climax. Joe's obviously upset. Look at him.'

'He'll get over it,' said Sheila though she wasn't at all sure that was true. 'Let's focus on getting Smeaton out of here safely. I'm worried about hypothermia. It's really cold. Much lower temperatures than were forecast.'

'He'll be okay. Joe knows all about that stuff.'

'I hope so. We don't want a corpse on our hands.'

'Don't we?'

Sheila studied her friend, mouth open.

'Joking,' said Marty. 'Did you think I was serious?'

Sheila wasn't sure what to think, so she changed the subject. 'When do you mean to give him the Rohypnol?'

'Around midnight. That should give us time to get into town and drop him off before he starts to come to.'

'Don't you wish we'd done it last night? We'd have been home and dry by now.'

'Maybe. But Joe was always adamant we should wait till tonight. He said Smeaton wouldn't see the error of his ways that quickly.'

'Are we sticking to your original plan for the drop-off?'

Marty nodded as she filled the teapot with boiling water.

'You don't think it's too public?'

'That's the point, isn't it? We want him to be found.'

'You sure it wouldn't be better to drop him off at home?'

'No. We can't risk being seen anywhere near his house.'

'You're the boss.'

'I wouldn't say that.'

'Come on, credit where it's due, Marty. You've masterminded this from the start and it's gone like clockwork.'

'Apart from the unexpected visit from Joe's boys. You sorted that one. You, with your sexy red bra.'

Sheila struck a provocative pose, making them both giggle, like giddy teenagers.

Suddenly the door flew open, revealing a huge man on the threshold.

Sheila screamed, grabbing Marty's arm.

A beanie hat was pulled down over his eyebrows and black eyes glared from under its woollen edge. His jaw was square and covered in dark stubble. He looked rough and dangerous.

'Where is Joe?' he said.

***

CHAPTER 85

Sheila could feel Marty shaking. 'You know this guy, Joe?'

Joe ignored her. He walked over to the man, hand outstretched. 'Stanimir?'

'Da,' he said, with a nod.

Sheila noticed he didn't shake Joe's hand. 'Where are you from?' she asked, hearing how stupid the words sounded.

'Sheila,' said Marty. 'This isn't a cocktail party.'

'Don't ask, Sheila,' said Joe. 'You don't need to know.'

Joe pointed to the chairs. 'Why don't we all take a seat and I'll explain.'

'Explain what? Who is this man?'

'Sit down, and I'll tell you. Come on, Marty.'

Marty lowered herself on to one of the chairs. Sheila sat down next to her and took her hand. Joe looked at the stranger and indicated a chair. 'You too, Stan.'

'Stanimir,' corrected the man, who looked like he didn't enjoy being told what to do.

Joe stared at him and eventually said, 'Please. Take a seat.' The man sat, his huge, bulky anorak puffing up around his neck. Joe remained standing, looking tall, fit and confident. Whatever was going on here, there was no doubt who was the alpha male.

'Are you in some sort of trouble, Joe?' Marty's voice sounded much smaller than usual. 'Do you owe this man money or something?'

Joe shook his head. 'No, Marty, I told you. It's okay. Nothing like that.' He gave her a smile, eyes twinkling. 'Don't worry,' he said gently.

A millisecond later the smile was gone. Joe looked from Marty to Sheila and said, 'Stan here has come to do me a favour. Well, to do all of us a favour, really.'

Sheila had the distinct impression Stan was understanding little of what was being said. His eyes, barely visible, looked dead. Nothing about him suggested he went around doing favours for people.

Joe continued. 'I've arranged for him to complete the job for us.'

Sheila gasped. 'You don't mean?' She spread out her hands, hoping to convey what she couldn't bring herself to say.

'What do you mean, Joe?' said Marty, her voice stronger and more like her usual self.

'I mean what I say, Stan has come, at my request, to finish the job.'

'But we have our own plan for finishing the job. Don't we?' Marty looked at Sheila, as if she suddenly wasn't sure.

The intruder pushed the cuff of his anorak up his arm and consulted a grotesquely large watch on his left wrist. Catching Joe's eye, he tapped the face of the watch then covered it again. Joe did not react in any way.

'I know we had a plan, Marty, but I don't think it's enough.'

'Joe,' said Sheila, 'we agreed weeks ago Marty's plan was a good one. We force Smeaton to examine his relationships with other people, wait for him to show some remorse, then send him back into his life. In the hope he'll be changed by the experience and be a damn sight nicer to folk from now on.'

'And right there is the word that's giving me trouble,' said Joe.

'What word?' Marty sounded keen to understand.

'Hope,' he said. 'We hope he will be changed into a nicer person.'

Marty looked confused. 'That's all we can do, isn't it?'

'No, Marty,' said Joe, 'It's not all we can do. It's not enough to hope he'll stop wrecking lives. We have to make damn sure he does.'

'He thinks he's died and gone to purgatory, Joe. It must seem to him like he's damned for all eternity.' Marty gave a little laugh, as if the whole thing was self-explanatory. 'Of course he's going to mend his ways when he realises he's been given another chance.'

'Marty, I love the trust you have in people. I can see how it made you a perfect person to run a school, but you're talking about this as if it's a fairy tale.'

'It's a Dickensian tale,' said Sheila, 'Mr Scrooge in a Christmas Carol.'

Joe gave her a look that made her feel like a child. 'A Muppet Christmas Carol. It doesn't work like that in real life, Sheila. In my experience an evil bastard's always an evil bastard and Smeaton is up there with the worst of them.'

'Joe, we all agree he's foul,' said Sheila. 'That's why we're here, but surely he'll change his behaviour when he wakes up from this nightmare?'

'And if he doesn't?' Joe let the question hang in the air.

Marty cleared her throat and said, 'What is it you're proposing, Joe?'

'Heavenly Father, I am truly sorry.'

Everyone turned to the screen. The man in the anorak leapt to his feet and pointed at the screen 'Is him, yes?' he asked Joe.

'Shh!' commanded Marty, in charge again. 'Let's listen.'

'Ach, we've heard enough,' said Joe. 'Come on, Stan. Time to get to work.'

The man didn't move and again Sheila wondered how much English he understood. Marty grabbed Joe's arm. 'Joe,' she said, 'listen to Smeaton. He's changed.'

Sure enough, Smeaton sounded like a different man from the ranting lunatic they had witnessed earlier. For the first time, something in his voice made him sound genuinely contrite.

'Father, forgive me, please. For the way I spoke to you and for the sins that brought me here in the first place. I accept that I am here for as long as it takes me to truly repent. Please, Father, find it in your heart to forgive me.'

'This is crap,' said Joe. 'We've heard it all before. He doesn't mean a word of it. Let him go and he'll be back to his old tricks in no time. Is that what you want?'

Marty stood up, face to face with Joe and said, 'Of course

it's not what we want. You know that, Joe. But I think he sounds different. Maybe we just have to give him a bit more time. Please. Let's see this through. We've come this far. At least let's see whether he's learned anything at all.'

Joe looked towards the screen, where Smeaton was kneeling, offering up fervent prayers full of apology. He turned to the foreigner. 'When's your flight, Stan?'

The man looked confused, 'Sorry?' he said.

Joe ran his hand through his hair. 'Jesus,' he muttered, 'they might have sent someone who can speak English.' Looking straight at Stan he asked, slowly and clearly, 'When does your plane leave?' Joe mimicked a plane flying, arms out by his sides.

Stan seemed to get the message, looked again at his watch and said, 'Eighty hours.'

Joe held up eight fingers and said, 'Eight? Eight hours?'

Stan nodded and said, 'Da.'

Marty said, 'Eight hours. That leaves plenty of time to let us see how this pans out, Joe. Please?'

Joe looked reluctant, but sat down and watched the screen with the others. Smeaton's voice continued to ring out, minus the arrogant tone they were all so used to. He sounded like a different man.

After a few minutes, Marty said, 'Excuse me, I have to go to the toilet.' She rose and left the table.

The atmosphere seemed to loosen a little and the stranger took off his beanie hat. Without the hat he looked even scarier, his shaven head showing bumps and scars, some not fully healed. Sheila thought one looked like it might be a lobotomy, but decided not to ask the question. No one seemed in the mood for a joke. As she watched, Stan unzipped his jacket half-way and pushed his hand into an inside pocket, checking for something, his passport perhaps.

When Marty came back she sat down for a few moments and then said, 'Well, I guess the tea's gone cold. Think I'm more in need of a strong coffee now. Anyone else?'

Sheila said, 'Me. I'll come and give you a hand.' Her chair

scraped across the floor. Stan sat upright, his hand disappearing inside his jacket again.

Marty stood, twirling her wedding ring round and round. 'Joe?'

Joe nodded. 'Yeah, we could all use a coffee, I guess.' He mimicked drinking from a cup and asked Stan if he'd like coffee.

'Da,' came the reply, but the icy stare did not waver. Sheila thought she'd never seen such cold eyes on a human being. She was reminded of a shark, and told herself not to be so melodramatic.

'I could make up some rolls,' offered Marty, with a smile to Joe.

'That'd be great.'

'I'll come and give you a hand,' said Sheila, watching them all carefully. Marty seemed to have recovered from her initial shock and appeared calm. Was she in on this plan of Joe's?

***

CHAPTER 86

What did Joe have in mind? It couldn't be what she first thought. Could it?

Marty pushed the idea away. It was repugnant.

Any change to the plans would make things more complicated, she knew that much. And they were already tricky enough.

Up on screen, Smeaton continued to pray. She called through to Joe, making her voice light, 'How does he sound to you, Joe? Don't you think he's much more repentant?'

'I'm not convinced.'

She looked at Sheila, the corners of her mouth turned down in dismay.

'What are we going to do?' whispered Sheila. 'Did you know about this? Tell the truth.'

Marty's raised eyebrows said it all.

In a stage voice that wouldn't have sounded out of place in the panto, Marty announced, 'Right, Sheila, you spread those rolls with butter and I will add a thick layer of this delicious home-made jam.' Glancing towards the table, she said, 'Wait till you taste this, Stan. You won't want to go back to Bulgaria.'

Joe shot her a look. 'Who said anything about Bulgaria?'

'I thought he was one of your pals, over for a visit.'

'He's not my pal,' said Joe. 'He's a business associate.'

'To do with the house?'

'No, Marty. Nothing to do with the house. I think you know why he's here.' Joe gave her a hard stare before looking back at the screen.

Marty and Sheila exchanged looks and Marty shrugged her shoulders. 'Take this coffee to Joe and see if you can find out whether Stan takes sugar and milk. I'll bring his over with the rolls.'

Smeaton had gone silent. She could hear Sheila saying sugar in several different languages. Quite impressive.

Joe said, 'Zakar?' and called through, 'Yeah, sugar for Stan, please.'

Marty put the plate of rolls in the centre of the table and handed Stan his sweet coffee.

'Don't you want to take your coat off?' she asked him. When the man did not react she tugged at his collar to illustrate her meaning. He pushed her away, spilling coffee on the table. Glaring at her, he zipped his jacket up to the neck and took a loud slurp of his drink.

'Sorry,' said Marty. 'Only trying to help. Would you like a roll? Joe, ask your friend if he'd like a roll.'

Joe nudged the guy's arm and gestured towards the plate. The man took a roll and began to eat noisily.

'Has anyone else noticed something about Smeaton's confessions?' Joe raised his mug towards the screen. 'He only mentions certain people.'

'What do you mean?'

'Well, I've been listening almost all the time he's been here, and it seems to me there are a lot of names I haven't heard. That poor guy who had the mental breakdown last year, for example. I saw him last week and he's like a ghost. White hair, grey, haggard face. The man's aged about thirty years.'

'I'm not sure we can expect to hear him mention everyone he has ever upset or insulted, Joe,' said Sheila.

'I'm not talking upsets and insults, Sheila,' said Joe. 'I'm talking about lives wrecked, jobs taken away, men and women robbed of their self-respect. We heard him repent what he did to poor bloody Liz, for all the good it will do her. I can see why you might be quite happy with what we've achieved on that score, Sheila. But I want more and so does Marty.'

Marty's first reaction was to say, 'Do I?' but she said nothing. Instinct told her she would get further if Joe believed she was on his side, so she nodded, wondering what she was agreeing to.

Joe drained his coffee cup and slammed it on the table as if to emphasise his intention. 'Right,' he said, getting to his feet. 'I think we've given him enough time. He looks to me like he's done all the repenting he's about to do. Look at him.'

As if the others weren't there, he spoke to the stranger. 'Ready, Stan?' Joe thumbed towards the door. 'Let's go, mate.'

The man put down his empty mug and pulled his beanie hat back on, rolling it down into a balaclava that covered his face. Only the cold, steely eyes could be seen.

Marty watched, horrified, as he opened his jacket, put his hand inside, and removed a gun. She bit hard on her lip but wasn't fast enough to stop a squeal escaping. Joe turned to her. 'You okay?'

Sheila covered her face as if she couldn't bear to look.

Marty tried to speak and found she couldn't. She shook her head, gave a little cough and tried again. 'Joe, he's got a gun.'

Joe looked at her as if she had gone mad. 'Of course, he's got a gun. What were you expecting? A Samurai sword?'

'Joe, can we talk about this? Please?'

There was a loud click as Stan fixed something on to the barrel of his pistol.

'Is that a silencer?'

'It's called a suppressor these days.'

'Is this man a professional killer?'

'I hope so.'

Sheila stood and grabbed his arm. 'Joe, have you taken leave of your senses?'

Joe shrugged and replied in a chillingly calm voice, 'Not at all. Quite the opposite. I know exactly what I'm doing and so does Marty.'

Sheila spun round to Marty. 'Is that true, Marty? Are you okay with this?'

Marty didn't have a chance to answer. Joe took Stan by the arm. 'Sure, she does. She told me weeks ago she could kill Smeaton and walk away.'

Sheila looked appalled. 'Tell me that isn't true, Marty.'

With every face in the room watching her, Marty was

unsure what to say. Deciding it was best to play dumb, she said, 'I'd no idea this was what you had in mind.'

Joe looked as if he couldn't believe he had heard her correctly.

'I mean, I didn't realise you were hiring a hitman.'

'What did you think all those phone calls were about?'

'Your new house.'

Joe gave a little laugh and shook his head.

'Is there no house in Bulgaria then?'

Joe's voice was gentle and kind. 'Of course, there's a house, Marty. Or at least there will be.'

Stan broke the silence. His voice muffled by the balaclava, he asked, 'We go now?'

'Yes, Stan,' said Joe. 'We go now.'

Sheila took a brave step into their path and spread her arms wide. 'No. I can't let you do this, Joe.' Joe moved her gently, but firmly, to the side. Stan pushed his way past Sheila and followed Joe out the door.

Marty said, 'Let them go. There's nothing we can do.'

'Of course there's something we can do.' Sheila barged past her. 'We have to stop this madness.'

'Sheila, don't!' shouted Marty. But her friend was gone. Marty ran after her and caught up as they reached the corner of the building.

***

CHAPTER 87

'Joe. Don't go in there. You can't let Smeaton see your face.'

'Marty,' said Joe, his voice as patient as if he were explaining something to a child. 'That was Plan A. Now we're working to Plan B. If Smeaton sees my face, that's fine by me. It will be the last thing he ever sees on this earth.'

'Joe, please don't do this.'

'Go back inside, Sheila. Wait in the dorm. I'd rather you two didn't see this. Come on, Stan. Earn your money.'

Stan staggered slightly. Joe caught him. 'Steady up there, pal,' he said. 'You've been sitting too long in a jacket and balaclava.'

Stan reached out his arms in a bizarre hug then slumped to the ground, taking Joe with him. Joe rose to his knees and shook the man's inert shoulders. Stan's head bobbed like a kitten's. Joe ripped off the balaclava. Stan appeared to be unconscious. Joe slapped the man's face, saying over and over, 'Stan, wake up. Stan!'

Looking around, as if for assistance, Joe stood up. 'Marty, help me here.'

She shook her head.

Joe kicked the body at his feet and said desperately, 'Wake up, Stan. Come on.'

'Joe. Stop. Please,' said Marty.

'No, I'm going to see this through, with or without your help. I've been planning it for a long time and I'm not going to give up because some woose of a hitman faints on me.' Heaving and hauling at Stan, Joe pleaded, 'Come on, man. Wake up.'

Marty said, 'He's not going to wake up. Not for hours.'

303

'What do mean, hours? What have you done?'

'Rohypnol,' she said.

'Okay, I guess that leaves me only one option.' Joe lifted the gun from Stan's side and inspected it, checking it was loaded.

'Joe, give me the gun.'

'Shut up, Marty.'

Sheila stretched out and touched his arm. 'Don't do this, Joe. Please, put the gun down.'

'Stay back, Sheila. Unless you're prepared to help me move him out of the way.'

Joe grabbed Stan's jacket and pulled. The weight was too much for him. The big man barely moved. 'Give me a hand here. One of you. Please.'

When neither of them moved, Joe slid down onto his hunkers. 'You've betrayed me, Marty.'

'Joe,' she said softly, 'I didn't betray you. I saved you. This is not the way. If you shoot Smeaton you'll forfeit your own life too, don't you see? You would never get away with it. Hiring someone to kill him is bad enough. But doing it yourself would make you a murderer.'

'Stan and I would have been out of the country before Smeaton's body turned cold.'

'Speaking of body. What on earth did you plan to do with him?' asked Sheila.

Joe pointed in the direction of the hill. 'I thought we'd bury him. He'd never be found up here.'

'You had all of this planned, right down to the last detail.'

'I had, but I didn't know Marty would sabotage it by drugging my hitman.'

'Don't be stupid, Joe,' said Sheila. 'Marty's done you a favour. Now hand over the gun. Or I swear, I'll phone the police.'

When the gun was safely in Sheila's hands, Marty blew out an enormous breath. 'I've done all of us a favour. If Smeaton had been killed we'd all have been implicated because we all brought him here.'

'Of course we would and I've got no intention of going to prison for Smeaton. Thank God for your quick thinking.' Sheila hugged her. 'When did you do it? I never saw a thing.'

'When you were over at the table handing Joe his coffee.'

'Jeeso, that was clever. Risky, but clever.'

'Thanks. I had to try something.' Marty pointed at Stan. 'What are we gonna do with this guy?'

'I think we should bundle him into the back of Joe's Land Rover and dump him near the main road. He found his own way here, he can find his own way back. We don't owe him any favours.'

'What about the gun?'

'That should go in the loch.'

'You're right. I'll go and get a plastic bag.' Sheila went back to the bothy.

'Don't be long,' called Marty. She hunkered down beside Stan and checked his breathing. 'When he comes to he'll have no memory of the last few hours. He might even believe he did the job then lost the gun.'

'Marty, are you sure about this?' said Joe.

'Of course I'm sure. How can you even ask me that?'

'But all those things you said.'

She got to her feet. 'That was just talk, Joe. Stupid, meaningless talk. It made you smile and I liked that, but I don't want him dead. I never wanted him dead.'

Joe looked like she'd ripped out his heart.

'We can talk about this later,' she said, bending down to take the hitman's arm. 'Come on, let's get rid of Stan. He'll need to be dropped much further away than the main road. We don't want any chance of him turning up here later on.'

Joe didn't move. It was as if all his energy had drained away.

'Come on, Joe, we need to get rid of him. Fast. I've no idea how long he'll be out. I didn't have time to measure a dose. Please, get up.'

'What's the point?'

'The point is, we need to get Stan out of here. I'll drive your Land Rover if you like, and take Sheila to help me dump him.

You can stay here and keep an eye on Smeaton. As long as you promise not to kill him.'

Joe looked at her, as if he wasn't sure she was joking. 'Nah, you'll never be able to steer the old lady. She's a beast. And the handbrake's a bugger. I'll go.'

'Thank you.' She hunkered down in front of him and tried to give him a hug. It was very awkward and when Joe did not respond, Marty gave up.

She waved her hand towards the door. 'Shit! You don't think Smeaton's been listening to all this, do you?'

'Nah.' Joe looked like he couldn't care less. 'What about when this is over, Marty?'

She offered him a hand. 'Come on, Joe,' she said, her voice kind and concerned. 'Let's get this sorted, so we can all get out of here.'

Joe took her hand and allowed himself to be hauled to his feet. Once he was standing he put his arms round Marty and hugged her. 'Sorry,' he said.

Marty felt sorry too. Her eyes began to fill up.

'Right,' he said, letting go, 'Let's get Stan the Man out of here before he comes back to life and starts asking awkward questions.'

'Aren't you afraid of what will happen if his bosses realise he wasn't allowed to finish the job?'

'I'll deal with that later. If it looks like getting nasty, I'll pay up. After all, it was me who broke the contract, not Stan.'

'Do you really think we'd have got away with having Smeaton killed?'

'I'm absolutely sure of it.' Indicating the man asleep on the ground, he said, 'This guy comes highly recommended. Makes no mistakes.'

Marty shivered and knew it was nothing to do with the cold wind. This casual talk of killing chilled her to the core.

***

CHAPTER 88

Thomas Smeaton rubbed his bare stomach. It was rumbling like a sleepy volcano, each episode getting louder and more demanding. He was surprised to feel hunger and thirst but supposed suffering was the name of the game here. It wasn't called purgatory for nothing.

Being assertive with God had been a waste of time. Nothing had changed. He was still here, still naked, still unforgiven. Was this to be his fate? Was he trapped here for eternity? Deprived of God's good grace and his divine light. The prospect made him weep.

When he had run out of tears, he forced his weak body onto its knees and started to pray again. This time he'd try to sound more humble.

'Lord, I see it clearly now. All I have ever been interested in was flexing my own muscles, showing off how much power I had. Now I know what it feels like to be totally powerless, Father, I regret with all my heart that I showed no compassion for anyone while I was alive and had the chance. Please, please forgive me.'

***

CHAPTER 89

Marty stood in front of the screen and wished Joe could have been here to witness this. Thomas Smeaton confessing a lack of compassion for his fellow man. She wondered with a tinge of regret whether an earlier repentance from Smeaton might have avoided the need for a hitman, but then she reminded herself that Joe had been organizing Smeaton's assassination for some time. She twisted her ring round her finger and then took it off and looked at it as if she had never seen it before. The narrow gold band represented her ties to David and to Mark. Inscribed on the inside she could see the initials DD to MW and the date of their wedding day all those years ago. What madness had made her think she could walk away from the life she and David shared? Having had a wee taste of danger, safe and boring suddenly seemed quite attractive. She was overcome with a need to go home.

But first they had to get rid of the man on the screen whose voice continued to pray for people he had wronged, many of whom Marty had never even heard of.

***

CHAPTER 90

As Joe drove up the track towards the bothy, he wondered how this day could have gone so badly wrong. He had hoped that by this time, he and Marty would have been on their way to the airport, or at the very least, he would have been headed for Bulgaria with Marty due to follow him.

It was getting dark and as the last light seeped away, the sky was turning purple and the loch looked tar black in the distance. A gap in the curtains of the bothy allowed a knife blade of light to slice through the gloom. Joe cut the engine and let the Land Rover coast up in silence. He and Sheila got out and tried to close the doors without slamming. In the distance some wild bird called to the hills. It was a lonely, eerie sound and Sheila hurried to get inside.

Marty met them at the door. 'What took you so long?' she asked, as they piled in and discarded their coats. I made food ages ago, thinking you'd be back much sooner.'

'Sorry,' said Sheila. 'We didn't expect it to be so hard to find a good drop-off place.'

'Where did you leave him eventually?'

'At the back of that big supermarket you pass as you go into town.'

'How do you know no one saw you?'

'We were very careful, Marty. We dumped him in some bushes right in the furthest corner of the car park.'

'Forget about it,' said Joe, his tone abrupt. He could not be bothered explaining all the details.

Sheila said, 'We reckoned someone would find him or he'd regain consciousness and wander into the store. But he'll remember nothing about how he got there. We know that now, don't we?' She gestured towards the screen. 'Anything to report?'

'I believe he is finally, truly repenting his sins. You should watch it on the tape, Joe. It might give you some closure.'

'Fuck closure,' Joe muttered. 'I'd still rather he was dead.'

'Well, he's not, Joe, and I'm grateful you didn't go ahead with your plan.'

'Amen to that,' murmured Sheila.

'You didn't leave me much choice, did you, taking out my hitman?' With no warning, Joe was overcome with a desire to laugh. This whole thing seemed so bizarre, it was bordering on the surreal. He opened his mouth and an immense wave of laughter came out.

At first the two women looked stunned. Then they joined in and the three of them stood in a circle, laughing and hugging with tears running down their cheeks. Marty was the first to break away, going in search of a tissue. 'This isn't glee, you know, this is hysteria.'

'I think you're right,' spluttered Joe, wiping the tears from his eyes.

'Let's eat and then it will be time to clean up our guest and get him out of here.'

'Yuck, there's a job I'm not looking forward to. Did you remember the baby wipes?'

'Jumbo-sized pack. But listen, have we enough Rohypnol left? I've been worrying about that,' said Sheila.

'Don't worry, I've got the full dose for Smeaton. Joe told me he'd ordered some extra in case of emergency. That's what Stan got.'

'I guess you could call doping an armed killer an emergency,' said Sheila, giving Joe a thump on the arm and starting to laugh again. When she stopped, she looked like a drunk trying to appear sober as she said, 'Right. Enough. Time to get serious.'

On screen, Smeaton continued to pray.

'He's putting in the overtime today,' said Marty. 'He's never stopped since you left. I'm not listening any more, to be honest.'

'His prayers will be answered shortly,' said Joe. 'We'll have him out of there in no time.'

'When do you want to give him the drug?'

'I suggest we get this place organised, once we've finished eating, and then we'll add it to some cold water and put it down the tube into the trough. He'll hear it running in and be too thirsty to resist a drink. When we're sure he's out cold, we'll get him as clean as we can, put him in the car and quickly dismantle everything.'

'You're sure he'll drink it?' asked Marty.

Joe nodded. 'Trust me. He'll be gasping for a drink by now.'

'Won't it destroy his illusion of purgatory if he suddenly gets his thirst quenched?'

'Even if it does, he'll have forgotten about getting the drink by the time he wakes up.'

'Remember, he should have no memory of at least an hour preceding the Rohypnol,' said Sheila. 'Just like a few days ago.' She took out her phone and checked it. 'Which leaves us just about the perfect amount of time.' She handed her phone to Joe and said, 'Instead of the white noise I'd like you to play this soundfile to him, Joe. I want it to be the last thing he hears in there. I need to believe he won't ever forget it.'

Joe took the phone. 'What is it?'

'A tiny segment taken from a video I made of Liz on our last holiday, followed by me with a message for Smeaton.'

'But he'll know your voice.'

Sheila shook her head. 'I used a voice changer app. There are thousands of them, free.'

'Oh yeah, I've heard about those,' said Marty. 'My son uses them sometimes, for pranks.'

Joe said, 'What do you think, Marty? It wasn't part of the plan.'

'Neither was having him shot.' Marty gave him a look he found hard to read. 'I think it's a good idea and if it will help Sheila, then why not? Yes, go ahead. Do it now.'

Joe disconnected his phone and the white noise stopped

abruptly. Smeaton reacted right away, probably relieved to hear nothing. Joe attached Sheila's phone to the speaker cable and looked to her for a signal. She nodded and he pressed play.

The sound of a woman's laughter filled the bothy. Smeaton sat up like a meerkat.

'I love my life!' declared the woman. She laughed again.

'Prosecco had been taken,' said Sheila, laughing too.

'And I fully intend to make the most of it now Mum's gone. I've got a bucket list the length of my arm, starting with a luxury cruise.'

Joe studied Smeaton's body language. Did he recognise Liz's voice? Hard to tell.

As Liz's laughter died away, another voice, ghostly and other-worldly, echoed in the space.

'Turn it up,' whispered Marty.

'Well, Thomas Smeaton,' said the voice. 'Did you recognise her? Liz Douglas?'

On screen they saw Smeaton nod his head, vigorously.

'That was last summer. She loved her life. Did you hear that? Yet her life ended prematurely, only a few months later. Liz reached a point where she felt she couldn't go on, didn't she?'

Smeaton nodded again.

'Whose fault is that, do you think?' The voice left a pause. Then said, 'I asked you a question, Thomas Smeaton. Who is to blame?'

'Me.'

'Who?'

'Me. I am.

'You are to blame. Not only for Liz's death, but for wrecking countless other lives and careers.

Smeaton was nodding like the dog in the insurance ad.

'You're a bully. Thomas Smeaton. A workplace bully, of the very worst kind. But I'm telling you now, it has to stop.'

The word boomed and died away. When the voice spoke again, it was quieter, more threatening. 'You will be given one more chance, Smeaton, which is more than you deserve, but know this. I will be watching you. Every moment of every day and if you wrong another human being ever again, your eternal fate will be so much worse than you could ever imagine. Consider this short spell in purgatory a taster of what awaits you. Remember, I will be watching.'

The voice faded and Joe switched back to white noise.

On screen Smeaton was lying face down.

'Hope the bastard's had a heart attack with the shock. How sweet would that be?'

'No, he's prostrating himself. It's a way of showing total and abject humility.'

'It's all an act,' said Joe.

'Let's hope not,' said Sheila. 'Anyway, playing that makes me feel better, so thanks, guys.'

'You're welcome, Sheila. It was a great idea. The last thing we want is for him to think he's got off with it. And I don't think that will have left him in any doubt.' Marty clapped her hands. 'Right,' she said, 'who's hungry?'

They ate their meal in silence, the two women just picking at their food. When someone banged on the door, the three of them froze, each looking to the others for an explanation.

Joe said, 'I'll go. I bet it's the lads again.'

Sheila tiptoed over and cut the power to the projector. Smeaton disappeared from the screen. Next she killed the volume and the white noise stopped. The room became silent for the first time in days.

Joe didn't think it would be the lads. Might be Stan, back to cause trouble. Joe waited for Sheila to follow Marty into the dorm before he opened the door, then braced himself to face the angry young Bulgarian.

'Good evening, sir. We've had a report of some lights up here at the bothy and been asked to investigate.'

Joe explained who he was and that he was putting in a lot of unpaid overtime to get the bothy emptied by the council deadline. 'There should be nobody here after tomorrow, Officer,' he said, adding, as an afterthought, 'Sorry, do you need to see my ID?'

'That won't be necessary, sir. If you could just make sure you leave the property secure when you go? We don't want vandals getting in and torching the place.'

'That's the last thing I'd want. I'm sad enough to see the old place shutting, never mind getting set on fire.'

'Goodnight then, sir. We'll leave you in peace and get back into town where we're more needed.'

Joe said goodnight and closed the door.

Marty and Sheila sneaked back through but no one breathed until they heard the police car start up and move off down the track.

***

CHAPTER 91

Joe drove into town and parked in a dark, disused loading bay behind a closed-down department store.

'Give me five minutes to find Dykesy and Dangermoose. Just to make sure they know what I'm expecting for my fifty quid.'

Marty kept an eye on the street. Apart from one solitary passing drunk, there was no one to be seen until a taxi cruised into view and dropped off two girls who looked like they should have been tucked up with their teddies. What were kids like that doing out drinking on a week night?

'Ready?' she said, when the taxi had moved off. Sheila's nod was barely visible in the dark Land Rover. Marty pulled up the hood of her sweatshirt and dragged it as far over her face as it would stretch. 'Right, then. Let's get him out and wait for Joe's boys to do their stuff.'

Smeaton groaned as they moved his blanket. Marty felt sick. What if he woke up now? All she wanted was for this to be over. She took one end of the blanket and Sheila the other. 'On my count,' she said, like a casualty doctor in some medical drama.

On three, they heaved. He was lighter than she expected; he must have lost weight in captivity. The two of them managed to lift him out of the car and over to the corner of the semi-derelict building, where they gently laid him down.

Marty crept forward till she had a clear view of the nightclub door and the bored-looking bouncer guarding it. At the sound of voices, he tossed his cigarette butt into the street and turned to stare at the two boys staggering towards him.

'Aw right, mate?' shouted Dykesy. 'How's it goin?'

The bouncer said nothing, but he spread his legs and

crossed his arms, chin raised in challenge.

'Any gorgeous burds in the club the night?' asked Dangermoose. 'I'm dyin fur a shag.'

The bouncer laughed. 'In yer dreams, wee man. Away hame to yer mammy.'

Dangermoose drew himself up to his full five feet. 'Ya cheeky basturt! Ah'm twenty-one.' He turned to Dykesy and demanded, 'Tell him.'

'Aye, right, boys.' The bouncer waggled his thumb in the air. 'Get yersels hunted before ye get hurt.'

Dykesy squared up to the bouncer, who was at least twice his weight. 'Wait a minute, man. You cannae refuse tae let us in.'

The bouncer uncrossed his arms and said, 'Watch me.'

'Naw, you watch me, ya bawbag!' Dykesy aimed a vicious kick at the man's testicles. The bouncer clutched at his groin with both hands, roaring his pain, shock and rage. Dykesy and Dangermoose capered around him, two chimps taunting a gorilla. He grabbed at Dykesy's t-shirt but the boy squirmed out of his grasp and ran, stopping at a safe distance to laugh and jeer.

Dykesy shouted, 'M'oan, wee man! Leg it!' and the two boys sprinted off, the bouncer giving chase.

Once they'd disappeared, Marty said, 'Let's go, Sheila.'

'You sure we're doing the right thing?'

'It's what we agreed. Come on, don't lose your nerve now. Lift him.'

They carted Smeaton towards the door of the club and unrolled him gently from the blanket onto the ground.

'Careful. We don't want a mark on him.' They eased the blanket clear of Smeaton's limp body and Marty bundled it under her arm. She sprinted for the shelter of the parking bay while Sheila headed up the lane to grab a taxi home.

Joe was waiting at the car, with the engine running. 'Let's go,' he said, jumping in. Marty stood and watched, shaking her head. Joe leaned across to open the passenger door. 'Get in, Marty, quick. We need to get going, before anyone spots us.'

316

She handed him the blanket. 'I'm not going, Joe. I'm staying here.'

'I'm not talking about Bulgaria.'

'Neither am I. Go on. Get out of here.'

'Come on, Marty, for God's sake. Jump in. Hurry up.'

'Sorry, I need to stay and see this through to the end, Joe. That was always my plan.'

'So you had your own agenda too, Marty? All along?'

'Maybe, but not as final as yours. No hitman in my plan. Quite the opposite. I want to make sure he regains consciousness.'

'Marty? We could be eating in a beachside restaurant this time tomorrow night without a care in the world. Won't you re-consider coming with me? Please?'

'And who would keep my crazy dog from maiming poor innocent runners? Tell me that.' She smiled at him. 'Go on. Get going, will you?'

'Remember you can always come and find me if you change your mind. On the hill behind Sozopol.'

'Goodbye, Joe.'

'Will you get home alright?'

She waved her hand, shooing him away. 'Yeah, yeah. I've got a plan.'

Joe laughed. 'I bet you have.' He gave her a salute and drove off.

Marty made sure her hood was covering her face, took the can of super lager from her pocket and wandered out into the street.

A little crowd had gathered around Smeaton's body. Keeping to the shadow cast by the wall, she watched. One girl was wailing hysterically, 'He's dead. He's dead.' Another, drunk no doubt, screamed like a banshee.

Smeaton must have heard the commotion. He moved. He was coming to. Marty watched him try to sit up. It was only a matter of time till someone decided to get a phone out and this would be all over Facebook.

'Perfect,' she whispered, 'my job here is done.' With a tug at her hood, she staggered away towards the town centre. No one gave her a second glance. After all, she was just another drunk hoodie with a can of lager.

***

CHAPTER 92

He'd resigned himself to his fate when he heard the banshee wailing. There would be no redemption for him after all. He had done all he could, had truly repented his sins, and named all the people he'd wronged, but it seemed that no one had been listening. He was damned to lie naked in this cold dark place forever. He would never see God's radiance or feel the healing power of his forgiveness.

Then he became aware of people speaking.

'That's gross. Somebody cover him up.'

'No, wait, I want to get it on my phone. YouTube here we come. This could go viral.'

Something soft landed on him, and he coiled into a tight ball underneath it, trying to protect himself.

'No photos, folks,' said a deeper, older voice. 'The poor guy's got issues. Give him a break.'

Strong arms helped him to his feet and wrapped a blanket around him. He staggered but before he could fall, he was caught and steadied. When his legs could support his weight, his saviour led him away into the darkness.

The man helped him into the seat of a car, tucking the blanket securely around him and fastening his seatbelt.

He stayed shrunk down inside his fleecy cocoon, teeth chattering with fear and cold.

As the car accelerated the man said, 'You must have had some night of it to end up in this state.'

His face and voice muffled by the thick material, he tried to speak and found he was sobbing. 'Am I alive?'

'That's a weird thing to say, but aye, you're alive alright.'

'I'm sorry. It's just, I've no idea where I am. I thought maybe I'd died.'

'You're every bit as much alive as I am, mate.'

'Can you tell me where I am, please?'

'Well, when I found you, you were lying naked outside Branigan's. Another five minutes and the cops would have turned up. You're lucky I came along before you got lifted for indecent exposure.'

'I don't know how to thank you.'

'Absolutely no need for thanks.'

'Do you think you could possibly give me a lift home? I think I live out at Monksgate. If you wouldn't mind taking me, I'd be so grateful.'

'No problem, mate.'

'This is the kindest thing anyone's ever done for me.'

'Don't mention it. I'm sure you'd have done the same in my shoes.'

Keeping his face buried in the security of the blanket, he confessed to this stranger that his old self would never have gone out of his way to help another human being. He went on to tell the man that he had just experienced an epiphany and vowed he'd be a changed person from now on.

He shivered under his blanket, from cold, shock or both. 'I know I must sound mad to you, but I really feel I've been to hell and back.'

The man said nothing, but it didn't matter.

'Purgatory, to be precise.' He babbled on, keen to share his experience. 'I thought I might have died in a car smash recently, I'm not sure. On the A77. Did you see anything about it in the papers, or even the TV, by any chance?'

Not waiting for a response, he went on. 'Anyway, for some reason, I ended up in purgatory. I remember praying for forgiveness so my soul could be released into heaven, and when I woke back there and heard all the screaming I was convinced I'd gone to hell instead.'

'I don't really believe in all that stuff myself,' said the man.

'Well I do, and now God has given me a second chance. He's even sent you, a good Samaritan. I intend to make the most of it, believe you me. I plan to change the way I live my life. I've done some terrible things to people, you know. I'm so ashamed. The first thing I am going to do is reward you for rescuing me.'

'You don't have to do that.'

'Oh, but I do. And then, I intend to seek out every person I have ever wronged. I mean to give them a genuine, humble apology and ask them to forgive me.'

'Is that right?'

'Oh, yes.'

'And do you think they will, Mr Smeaton?'

***

CHAPTER 93

Smeaton's head shot out of the blanket like a tortoise startled from its shell. 'Do I know you?' he asked.

'You should.'

'Sorry, I don't recognise you. I can't really see your face and I feel a bit woozy to tell you the truth.'

'Take a look at the scenery. Might give you a clue.'

Smeaton looked out of the window and said, 'I think you must have taken a wrong turning somewhere. My mistake, I thought you knew where we were going.'

'Oh, I know precisely where we're going. In fact, we're almost there.'

'But we're miles from nowhere.'

'Exactly.'

'Sorry. I don't understand.'

'You will in a minute.' Joe slowed down as the bothy came into view and directed the headlights towards it. 'Remember this place?'

'I think it's the bothy Logiemuir runs for outdoor education.'

'Used to run, Mr Smeaton. Until you ordered its closure, remember? Same as you shut down the kiddies' orchestra in Bankside. You threatened their community centre too, didn't you? You're a great man for taking from people who've got nothing.'

'Listen to me, my friend. I don't know who you are, or what we're doing out here, but please understand, I had no choice in these things. I had to make savings. That's my job. Honestly, I really didn't have any choice. But can I tell you this? I regret the way I did it and I intend to make changes when I get back to work.'

Joe cut the engine and the headlights died. Darkness engulfed the car, making it impossible to see Smeaton's face. 'Your changes will come too late for some folk. What about them?'

'I'm sorry, I'm not sure what you're talking about.'

'I'm talking about Liz Douglas. You remember? The head-teacher of Cadenhead Primary, who committed suicide? Being sorry isn't going to be much help to her, is it?'

'That was regrettable. A terrible tragedy.'

'You could say that. Some folk would say she was driven to suicide and you're the man responsible.'

'I'm not sure that's true but I am sorry the woman died.'

'Then there's poor Marty Dunlop. A truly good person, doing a great job, till you blackened her name and robbed her life of any meaning.'

'That was unfortunate, you're right. I regret the way I handled that situation.'

'It's too late for your regrets. They're worth nothing.'

'I've said I'm sorry. And I intend to change my working practice. I don't know what more you'd like me to do.'

'I'd like you to bring my wife back.'

'Your wife? Look, I'm sorry if your wife's left you, but I don't see how I can help. I don't even know you.'

***

CHAPTER 94

Joe reached out and switched on the interior light. Smeaton's face registered recognition and shock at the same time.

'Joe Docherty,' he whispered, his eyes never leaving Joe's face. 'I might have known.'

Joe said nothing. There was nothing for him to say.

'I'm very sorry about what happened to your wife, Joe. But I hardly think you can blame me for her death. It wasn't my fault you couldn't cope.'

Joe waited, sure there was more to come.

'Not my fault either that you turned to drink, was it?'

Joe said, 'I never, ever touched a drop in school or came to work drunk or unfit to teach. You know what I went through with Sally's illness. Back and forth to the Beatson, nursing her at home for as long as I could, then practically living in the Hospice.'

'We gave you some time off, didn't we?'

Joe ignored that; concentrated instead on keeping his temper. 'Then my lovely Sally died.'

'Yes, and I'm sure Carole sent a wreath or something. What more did you expect us to do?'

'You knew I was struggling to come to terms with her loss. Couldn't you have cut me some slack?'

'Cut you some slack?' Smeaton's voice rose to the high, outraged pitch that was familiar to Joe. 'I've been cutting you slack for years. You must know I could easily have sacked you a few months back for whistle-blowing to the papers? But I didn't. You'd have lost your pension, but I cut you some slack, as you say. Then, when you didn't get your own way about your blasted bothy, you resigned and I accepted your resignation. Remember? So don't try to pin the blame on me, just because your life didn't turn out the way you wanted it to.'

Joe had heard enough. 'You haven't changed one bit, Smeaton. I knew it. I should have shot you when I had the chance.' He reached for the keys and turned them in the ignition. The big jeep roared into life and the headlights lit up the stone walls of the bothy.

'What are you talking about? Should have shot me? Don't be ridiculous. Look Joe, why don't you take me home now? There's a good man. Just take me home, I'll sling you a few quid for your trouble, and we'll say no more about this.'

Joe put the Land Rover into gear and the car lurched forward. He pulled hard on the steering wheel and the full beam swung in an arc across the dark landscape. The old car started to move down the hill towards the loch.

'You're going the wrong way, Joe,' said Smeaton, his voice a patronising mix of sympathy and impatience. 'The road's the other direction.'

As they rolled nearer to the water, the headlights picked out the loch, laying a silver pathway across its surface.

'Where in God's name are you going, man?'

Joe stamped on the brakes and the car shuddered to a halt, jolting Smeaton forward. Joe grabbed a bungee cord, flipped it over the back of the seat and joined the two ends in front of Smeaton's blanket-wrapped body.

Smeaton wriggled like an amateur Houdini as he tried to free his trapped arms. 'Are you crazy?'

Joe thought about taping Smeaton's mouth shut, but decided against it. 'Ach, I'll let you breathe,' he murmured, as if he were doing the man a favour.

'Joe, let me go, please.'

'No way. Here's what's gonna happen.' Joe leaned forward and tapped the dashboard affectionately. 'I don't suppose you'd know anything about an old car like this and how it works, so let me tell you. The gearing is so low that, when I put her into first gear, this old girl will start to move, without any need for a foot on the accelerator. Did you know that? No? Then, even if I get out of the car, she will gently coast, with no assistance from me, towards her final resting place. Which, incidentally, will also be yours.' Joe pointed towards the loch. The headlights reflecting off the water cast enough light for him to see the terror in Thomas Smeaton's eyes.

'No, no, no. This isn't right.'

'I agree. She should have a much classier ending than this but drowning's a better one than you deserve.'

'Drowning? You can't do that.'

Joe laughed, low and bitter. 'Just watch.'

'Oh, please God, no.'

'Not sure your God can help you now, Mr Smeaton, but it might be time to start praying in earnest, just in case.'

'Joe, listen. You can't drown me. That's not the type of man you are.'

'You know nothing about the kind of man I am.'

'I know you're a decent man. I know you wanted only the best for the kids in your care. I know you felt responsible for their futures.'

A voice in Joe's head was telling him to get on with it. Drown the bastard and walk away. Don't listen to him. 'Tell me something. If you know I'm such a good guy why did you treat me so badly?'

'Because you were trouble, right from the start. Always causing me to question my decisions.'

'So you did sometimes question your decisions? And yet you insisted on going ahead with the one to shut the bothy?'

'Listen to me, for God's sake, man. I'll open it again, if you let me go. I promise. Come on, Joe. Please, I beg you. Don't do this and I'll owe you. Anything you want, I'll see you get it. Your job back, the bothy re-opened. Anything. You name it.'

Joe looked at Smeaton's face. He didn't believe a word the man said.

'Please, can you take this rope thing off me? At least do that. Give me a chance.'

'Why should I? You've had plenty of chances. I've begged you in the past and now you're begging me. How does it feel?'

'This is different, Joe.'

'How is it different? I was begging for my boys.'

'I'm begging for my life,' said Smeaton, lowering his voice, 'and I think you'll grant it.'

'Why?'

'Because I don't believe you're a killer. You haven't got it in you.'

***

CHAPTER 95

Joe had heard enough. He couldn't bear to listen to another evil, manipulative word. He put his hands over his ears and kicked the door open. He slammed it shut and walked away, trying to block out Smeaton's pathetic whining. He needed space. He needed time to think.

Nothing was going according to plan. Smeaton should have been shot dead and buried in a deep grave amongst the heather by now. Instead the man was still alive and still messing with Joe's head. He wanted so badly to do everyone a favour, exact the ultimate revenge and rid the world of Smeaton. So why not just get on with it?

Behind him, the old car suddenly roared, revving into life. Smeaton had somehow managed to get into the driver's seat. He was going to steal the car. He was going to get away.

Joe ran to the water's edge and stopped. He knew how hard he had to pull on that old steering wheel to turn the car. Sometimes it took all his strength. Smeaton had gone without food and drink for days and he'd been drugged senseless twice. He was no match for this car.

The Land Rover ploughed on through the shallow water, barely deviating from its path. Joe could see Smeaton desperately trying to steer away from the danger. The car refused to cooperate, as if it had a mind of its own.

Joe shouted, 'The handbrake's fucked! Use the brakes.'

Smeaton turned to the driver's door and Joe could see him battling with it. He had no chance. Not unless he knew to kick it in just the right place.

Joe raced into the shallows, compelled to help before it was too late. Maybe he could wrench open the door and haul Smeaton to safety. Joe grabbed the handle and tugged, but the door was too old, too heavy, too jammed and already too deep in the water.

'Open the window!' he shouted, hammering on the glass. Counter-intuitive though it was to let water into a sinking car, Joe knew it was the only way to escape.

Smeaton's face appeared in the window, a horror mask, white with fear and desperation. His hands clawed at the glass and his mouth gaped, terrified.

Joe waded through the water, trying to keep up with the car. 'For Christ's sake, wind down the window. Now!'

The car rolled on, slow as a hearse. Black water crept up its sides as the floor of the loch began to drop away. Joe followed, the instinct to save a life powerful enough to draw him further in than was safe.

Chest-deep, he suddenly stopped, the icy water bringing him, at last, to his senses.

His faithful old Land Rover chugged past him on its last journey, and he banged a farewell fist on the tailgate. The headlights caught the silvery flash of a fish before dimming one final time. In the distance an owl hooted, its voice echoing across the dark landscape. As he waded towards the shore Joe imagined its cry joining Smeaton's screams in a grotesque harmony.

For a few moments Joe stood at the water's edge, examining his conscience. When he found it was clear and clean, he turned his back and walked away.

At the top of the slope Joe paused, shivering, and watched the brief maelstrom as car and passenger sank to the depths. The loch folded watery arms over its dark secret and settled into silence.

THE END

Author's Note and Acknowledgements

Writing a book is the easy part. Getting it ready for publication is much more of a slog. Thanks to my readers who make all the hard work worthwhile - I hope you enjoy this one.

I am grateful, as always, to the many friends who read my earliest efforts. Linda Pryde, Winnie Goodwin, Stef Brierley (nee Young), Margo McAllister and (as always) Farley Weir helped a lot with this one. Thanks to my lovely sister-in-law Caren Young, whose feedback and praise I always value. Remember when you asked me how I got Joe's boys to sound so realistic? 'One of the perks of teaching!' I said.

For information and advice on Roman Catholic doctrine, I owe a debt of gratitude to my very dear friends, Margaret and Gerald Donachie. Thank you, Alex McAllister, for sharing your experience and advice on matters police-related. You're a good pal.

More recently Revenge Runs Deep was read by a new team of beta readers whose feedback was invaluable. Mandy Fullerton, Nicola Prigg, Suzy Kelly, Patsy O' Neill, Julie-Anne Gard and Cherry Thatcher - stand up and take a bow.

Thanks to Susan Barry, aka Susan Sinha, co-owner of the fabulous Celt Irish Pub in Carcassonne, for giving Big Sean his authentic Irish voice and for warmly hosting my book events.

One reader parted with more than the price of a book. At an auction in aid of the wonderful Ayrshire Hospice, Sheila Scott's generous bid won her the right to be named as a character. Hope you like your namesake, Sheila.

Thanks to Sarah Hardy for her invaluable advice and for organising the blog tour.

Thank you to all the bloggers and reviewers who support me, in particular, Sharon Bairden, cover revealer extraordinaire.

Many thanks also to those who've helped me live the dream by inviting me to appear in their libraries or at their amazing events: Bloody Scotland, Tidelines and the Boswell Book Festival.

For countless cups of tea, (allowed to go cold and undrunk when I'm lost in the story) and for endless support and advice, thanks and love to my best friend and soul-mate, Grant.

Finally, to Team Kelly: Michael for amazing cover design and Suzy for formatting and countless other bits of help and advice, thank you so much. I could never have done it without you.

Lightning Source UK Ltd.
Milton Keynes UK
UKHW041106300419
341857UK00001B/75/P